THE
FENWOLD
RIDDLE

BY

DAVE EVARDSON

Cortero Publishing
An Imprint of Fireship Press

The Fenwold Riddle - Copyright © 2012 by David Evardson

ISBN-13: 978-1-61179-216-4 (paperback)
978-1-61179-222-5 (e-book)

BISAC Subject Headings:
FIC009000 / FICTION / Fantasy / General
JUV001000 / JUVENILE FICTION / Action & Adventure / General
JUV059000 / JUVENILE FICTION / Dystopian

Cover design by Christine Horner

Address all correspondence to:
Fireship Press, LLC
P.O. Box 68412
Tucson, AZ 85737
Or visit our website at:
www.FireshipPress.com

1.0

THE
FENWOLD
RIDDLE

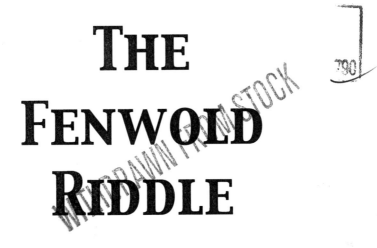

ACKNOWLEDGMENTS

For a writer, it's a long and arduous journey to the end of a novel. Many people have walked alongside me either some or all of the way, offering advice, encouragement, or tea. In particular I would like to thank...

My wife Julie

Moonyeen Cooper

Kristin Gleeson

Jacey Bedford

Jessica Knauss

Yarburgh Writers

I couldn't have made it without them. (The journey, that is. I already knew how to make tea.)

TABLE OF CONTENTS

Chapter One:
When a Good Man Comes   1

Chapter Two:
The Frightened Village   15

Chapter Three:
Baptism of Fire   23

Chapter Four:
A Call to Arms   35

Chapter Five:
A Perilous Venture   47

Chapter Six:
A Demon Restrained   57

Chapter Seven:
An Appointment with Death   67

Chapter Eight:
The Battle of Crowtree   77

Chapter Nine:
In the Vipers' Nest   85

Chapter Ten:
A Secret Champion   95

Chapter Eleven:
Trial and Execution   103

Chapter Twelve:
Upon the Wall of Death   111

Chapter Thirteen:
Where Forty Dwell   117

Chapter Fourteen:
Divining the Riddle   125

Chapter Fifteen:
Journey into Danger   131

Chapter Sixteen:
Ledge of Frustration   139

Chapter Seventeen:
Angel of Mercy   145

Chapter Eighteen:
A Change of Heart   153

Chapter Nineteen:
Strange Landings   161

Chapter Twenty:
Searching for Bridges   169

Chapter Twenty-One:
Look East at the River   173

Chapter Twenty-Two:
Across to a Tower   181

Chapter Twenty-Three:
Where Once There Was Light   187

Chapter Twenty-Four:
From the Jaws of Death   193

Chapter Twenty-Five:
The Worst of Times   199

Chapter Twenty-Six:
Encounter With a Dragon   209

Chapter Twenty-Seven:
In a Northern Town   217

Chapter Twenty-Eight:
A Chance to Run   227

Chapter Twenty-Nine:
A Dragon Grins

231

Chapter Thirty:
A Sweet Reunion

237

Chapter Thirty-One:
Unlock and Enter

245

Chapter Thirty-Two:
An Auspicious Audience

251

Chapter Thirty-Three:
A Time for Hate, A Time for Love

261

Chapter Thirty-Four:
Digging for Treasure

273

Chapter Thirty-Five:
Awakening the Gods

279

Chapter Thirty-Six:
Beyond the Wall of Death

287

About the Author

295

CHAPTER ONE
WHEN A GOOD MAN COMES

Evening shadows joined hands and merged into dusk. Dominic Bradley stood close to the Wall, a speck at the foot of its massive stone face. He craned his neck back till it creaked, but still he couldn't see the top. A menacing sky cloaked the summit and melded with the heavens that had spawned it centuries before — or such was the belief of many. He finished what he'd come to do and buttoned up. His belly growled and a whiff of campfire smoke teased out a trickle of saliva. He spat and turned away, good and ready for a square meal after the long day's ride.

"Hey, Colby! Is supper ready yet?"

If Colby answered, Bradley didn't hear. But a sharp *smack* against the Wall above his head made him duck instinctively. Something touched his shoulder, light as a falling sprig of ivy. He looked down. The shaft of a spent arrow lay at his feet.

Senses sharpened, he scoured the looming darkness for the assailant archer, but only the dense forest glowered back at him. Then he heard a soft *thud* from the direction of the campfire. Crouching, he risked a few steps, but stopped short.

Colby sprawled face down, the crossed fins of an arrow's fletching protruding from his bloody tunic. Another bolt struck the ground beside him. There was no time to agonise. Keeping low, Bradley darted for the horses. They shied when the next arrow split a near-by branch. His mare's ears pricked up and he vaulted into the saddle. She squealed as he clutched the reins and squeezed his boot heels against her flanks. Then she reared and hurled herself into a frantic canter, his torso moulded to her neck.

Hooves thundered behind them and two more arrows whizzed past his head. He asked his horse for more and she responded with

1

a further burst of speed. Glancing back he saw four mounted raiders, barely twenty strides behind him. Foremost of these snarled a red-haired ruffian who rode with the fury of a hellhound. With reins fast beneath his knees, this devil drew back his bowstring. Nothing stood between the next arrow and Bradley's hide.

Just ahead the track twisted sharp right, offering the briefest cover. Instinct kicked in and he wheeled his mare blind into the undergrowth. Her right leg buckled at the awkward turn and he lost a stirrup. Desperately he struggled to regain control. She read his signals and righted herself and he drove her on. Thrashing through dense foliage she coughed and snorted, his sweating body pressed tight against her lathered neck, until at last they burst through to a deer trail. Now he pushed her to canter, urgently ducking and diving under whipping branches. Startled creatures fled screeching before their frantic onslaught. Ripping briars tore at his bare hands and cheeks till he tasted blood. But there was no stopping now. The overwhelming fear of death masked all present pain and discomfort. Horse and rider sustained this merciless lashing almost to the point of exhaustion. Then out of nowhere, a low branch swept him from the saddle and he hit the ground with a mighty *thump*.

He lay in a daze for a while, then checked his limbs. Finding nothing broken, he sat upright and took his bearings. They'd landed in a clearing. Scarlett panted urgently close by, head down, legs splayed and sides heaving. He strained to listen beyond the murmurings of the nocturnal forest — the teasing breeze in the branches above, the hoot of an owl, the ripple of a near-by stream. Only their laboured breathing sawed against these sounds. No hostile noises intruded. He offered silent thanks for his life to the Gods of the Wall.

Then he remembered Colby. Dead? That might have been him. The thought made his guts churn. He retched, but his belly had nothing to give up. His eyes scalded but yielded no tears. No relief, no redemption. What else could he have done? Four raiders were too many to face alone. Flight had been his only choice. To stay would have wasted both their lives — and their mission. He'd done well to save his own skin. Damn their eyes!

It would be fully dark soon. He staggered over to where Scarlett stood. She had some nasty scratches on her chest and legs. He took a rag from his saddlebag and led her to the stream, where he dampened it to wash her down with gentle strokes as she

2

drank. Then he knelt by the water and cupped his hands. The ripples settled to reveal his reflection. Only now did the sight of his bloody face alert him to the smarting cuts. He bent closer to the surface in the growing darkness, probing the wounds with his fingers till he winced. Though they smarted, they felt superficial and should heal in a few days. He plunged his head, glad of the soothing coolness. Then he sat up and rubbed the water from his eyes.

"Stand up and turn around with your hands in the air."

The female voice carried authority. Turning with arms raised, he fixed its owner with a sullen stare. The young girl who faced him wore dishevelled, mud-stained hunters' furs. Despite her youth, she had a fierce look about her, with ragged brown hair and a scar that ran from below her eye to her upper lip. A bag hung across her back and its strap dug deep into her sagging shoulder. Its weight told of a decent night's hunting and of her undoubted skill with that crossbow. Still, he wasn't about to let a mere peasant lass intimidate him.

"Be careful who you point your bow at, girl. They might be important."

Her lips moved, but he didn't hear her words, because something heavy then hit the base of his skull with a sharp *crack*. The girl's face was the last thing he saw before his knees buckled and he collapsed like a rag doll onto the forest floor.

* * * * *

A piercing light drove needles into his eyes. He didn't know who was drilling a hole into the back of his head, but he wished they'd stop. He wanted to reach up and push them away, but he couldn't because his wrists were bound. So were his ankles. And he ached with cold. His tongue felt numb and a rancid taste in his mouth made him want to retch.

His creeping consciousness brought thoughts of Colby, the companion he'd deserted and left for dead, far from home in a forest clearing. Fleeting wisps of hellish dreams floated across his mind — then vanished, forgotten — for the moment. The guilt would have to wait — he'd face it later. Right now, survival was all that mattered.

He set his jaw and opened his eyes again, defying the glare. Soon they acclimatised to the first rays of sunlight that burst

3

through a tiny window. He fought the brightness and looked for his weapons — short sword, arrows and bow.

But of course they'd been taken away.

Now he recalled the frantic chase, his capture in the forest, the female archer and then — nothing. But the throbbing pain at the back of his head could mean only one thing — the girl had an accomplice. They'd dumped him here and concussion must have given way to fitful sleep.

He took in his surroundings. The cell comprised a small wooden shed, with a flimsy-looking door and a roughly barred window. There wasn't enough floor space to lie down, so he'd been forced to spend the night with his back propped against the wall. The bare earthen ground smelled dank and musty, with a chill to drive sleep away. At least they'd tied his arms in front, but still he hadn't slept well. Why hadn't they killed him? In fact he was unharmed — apart from that damned blow to the head.

He tugged at his tight bonds, but they wouldn't give. His tongue had some feeling now and forced out bits of disgusting fabric, the remains of a gag. Probably the rag he'd used to clean Scarlett's wounds. The natural grinding of his teeth must have shredded it while he'd slept and at last he eschewed the foul piece of cloth, spitting out the remnants onto the earthen floor.

With wakefulness came anger, but extreme hunger and thirst called for more urgent satisfaction. He tried calling out, but managed only a lifeless cough that amplified the pain in his head a hundredfold. He didn't know who or where his captors were, but he had to get out of there. He shuffled around till he faced the door. His feet were almost lifeless from the cold and the tight ropes round his ankles, but he managed to draw in his legs. Then he summoned all the strength he had and shot them out towards the bottom lateral plank that held the uprights in place. The lower section burst outwards with a clatter, bringing one of his captors running towards the shed. Bradley lowered his head to view him from under the broken carpentry. The youth held a primed crossbow in his left hand, while his right reached for a bolt from his shoulder quiver.

"Stop that or I'll shoot!" he yelled.

But Bradley was in no mood to play the victim. He fought to find his voice.

"For the sake of the Sacred Wall, let me out of this place, you peasant, or I'll have the full force of the Council down on you!"

4

"Council?" The lad laughed mockingly. "Fellow raiders more like! Didn't we find you sneaking about in our forest?" Then a second youth approached and lifted the bar from what remained of the door. The first kept his weapon pointed at Bradley as the other drew the door fully open.

The realisation dawned that a village foraging party had taken him. The image of a girl with a hunting bag flashed across his mind again. He felt relieved, but also annoyed with himself, especially in view of their ages.

"Untie me, you young puppies and let me speak to an elder. I'll not bargain with children."

Then the girl appeared and said, "We may be little more than children, mister, but we have you as our prisoner." She stepped forward and knelt to untie the ropes from around his ankles.

With narrowed eyes he glanced at her face. She drew her hand in front of the scar on her cheek, blushing at the close attention. As the blood flowed into his feet, she helped him to stand. He held out his hands for her to untie them too.

"No," she said. "Not until you've seen our father."

"And who might he be?"

She looked at him coldly. "Village headman."

"Really? Of which village?"

He wondered why she furrowed her brow, as if surprised he didn't know.

"Crowtree, of course."

So, he thought, a girl and her two brothers. Three against one — that wasn't too humiliating, even if they were comparative youngsters.

The brother who looked the senior said, "He'll be well pleased with us for bringing in a raider."

Bradley looked him in the eye. "I'm no raider, lad. Let me talk with your father and we'll settle the matter."

The youth shook his head. "That can wait. It's early yet. We ought to eat something. I don't know about you lot, but my belly thinks my throat's cut. There's some food in my small sack, Sylvia."

The girl fetched the bag and shared out the rations. They weren't much, just goat's cheese and bread washed down with water from the stream. But he felt hungry enough to eat just about anything. He accepted a lump of bread, which he held awkwardly between his bound hands, managing to tear a chunk off with his teeth. In between chewing he asked the girl, "Where's my horse? Is she all right?"

"She's in the barn, fed and watered. I rubbed her down last night. She was all lathered up."

"Thanks," he said grudgingly.

She looked away saying, "She can stay there while we take you to the village."

He'd rather Scarlett came with them, but he wouldn't press the point. The girl said nothing more and for a while the four of them ate in silence.

He looked around to get his bearings. Dense forest dominated the north and west, with cleared ground to the south and east. Some of this was cultivated, mainly with ragged looking wheat. In the middle distance he counted a few cottages. The main village buildings must lie beyond them. Close by, apart from the demolished shed, stood a wooden barn that backed onto the forest. Four furlongs to the south, the Wall dominated the skyline and on a peaceful morning like this, he saw why many looked on it as a symbol of benevolent protection. Though a fair way off, he thought he discerned some shading to the lower half of the Wall that could be ivy growth. He made a mental note to confirm that later.

"Is that Crowtree over there?" he asked, nodding towards the cottages.

The younger lad looked at him coldly. "You should know. Your lot have been holed up in Ashwell for long enough now, waiting to make your move against us."

The other frowned at his brother then said to their prisoner, "You'd best keep any questions for our father. Finish eating, then we'll take you to him."

Bradley nodded towards the barn. "Did you stay in there last night? Why didn't you go home?"

"What's it to you?" asked the younger brother.

"Nothing. But it can't be too safe with raiders about."

The elder one said, "We have to hunt — raiders or no raiders. Anyhow, we know how to use our weapons. We can take care of ourselves. And if you must know why we stayed out here, we don't like to disturb our parents so late."

"Yeah — especially with a captured raider in tow," the younger lad chipped in.

"I've already told you I'm no raider!"

The elder one said, "Our father can decide that. For now, no more questions."

Bradley pursed his lips and said no more. These might only be youngsters, but they had spirit. That was just as well, because he knew that before too long their lives might depend on it.

* * * * *

As they entered the main village a boy and girl emerged from a chicken coop, put down their baskets and ran towards them. They stopped short when they saw Bradley, obviously wary of anyone they didn't know. One pointed at his bound hands and they trotted alongside the group, fascinated by the dishevelled, dark-haired stranger.

"Who is he, Jack?" the boy asked. "He looks fierce. Is he a raider?"

"Could be," said the older youth.

"Of course he is!" his brother boasted. "We caught him prowling around in the forest last night."

His sister scowled. "He means *I* caught him prowling in the forest."

Damn their childish squabbling. But he kept quiet. It was pointless arguing with a bunch of kids. Soon several other youngsters came up to inspect him, laughing and pointing and some even poking him with sticks. The brothers shooed them away, but they weren't doing any real harm.

They led him past several dwellings, mean and simple but neat and clean. Most were the repaired remnants of brick dwellings from the ancient times. Some were more recently built cabins, skilfully constructed of wood. A few adults came out to look, mostly only to stand and stare in stony silence. For peasants they didn't seem as primitive as he'd expected. They were poor, but civil enough and neatly dressed in trousers and tunics. Eventually the group stopped at the door of one of the larger cottages. A man, whom he took to be his captors' father, stood out in his yard, bending to feed a couple of pigs at their trough. He straightened when the group approached.

"Well now, what have you got there?"

"Morning, Father," said the younger son. "There'll be one less raider to bother us from now on."

Bradley sighed. "I've already told these young pups that I'm no raider. Surely you've the sense to see that."

The old fellow — Bradley estimated his age at about forty — looked him straight in the eyes, but he didn't flinch. Then he looked at his clothing and shook his head. "Untie him, you fools. Come inside, young man. Excuse the mess — my wife and I have just finished breakfast. Take a seat. Have you eaten?"

He recalled his recent snack and still felt hungry. But he returned the old man's good manners and answered, "Your children have fed me." The headman didn't look too convinced.

The younger son spoke again. "But Father, he must be a raider — why else would he be out in the forest at dead of night?"

"You talk like a fool, Liam. Does he really look like a raider? He's a bit ragged, I'll grant you. But see how he's clean-shaven, with trimmed hair and healthy complexion? And look at his clothes. They may be grimy from the trail, but even my old eyes can see they're all new this season. Why, the wool of his tunic shows hardly any wear. Nor do his trousers either. And as for those leather boots, I'd give my best sow for a pair so finely crafted and stitched."

The siblings looked at the floor, clearly embarrassed.

"Ah well, I suppose you did what you thought was right. I hope the rest of your evening's hunting proved as productive."

Proudly they showed off their combined haul of eight rabbits and a hare.

"Not bad. I reckon you've earned your keep for a few more days. But I'd sooner you kept closer to the village next time you go out."

He turned to the newcomer. "I'm Tom Storey, headman of Crowtree. And if you're not a raider, then what are you and what brings you to this forsaken corner of Fenwold? A trader maybe?"

He shook his head. "My name's Dominic Bradley. I'm Marshal for the south-west." He rubbed the back of his head and grimaced. "I'd just escaped an attack by real raiders last night when I bumped into your children."

Storey went over to him. "Here, let's see. Does it hurt much?" He parted Bradley's hair to get a closer look.

The lawman winced. "Not so much as it did earlier on. Is the skin broken?"

"No, but there's quite a bruise. I'll ask my wife to put something on it presently. You did well to escape the raiders if they got close enough to do this."

Bradley twisted his eyes towards Storey's sons and wondered which one of them had nearly caved his head in.

But the older one rubbed the back of his own neck in sympathy, shrugged with a grin and said, "Sorry, Marshal. I didn't know."

The old man sighed. "Jack, whatever did you hit him with?"

"Just a lump of rock. Remember, we thought he was dangerous."

His sister spoke. "You needn't have hit him so hard, Jack. I already had him covered anyway."

"Just a precaution," Jack said. "He could easily have jumped you."

"Not before I'd put an arrow in his gut."

The old fellow intervened. "All right, all right. Let's not have another fight. Be gone, the three of you and give your mother a hand skinning that lot."

When they'd left he sat down opposite Bradley. "I don't doubt your word, Marshal, but as headman of the village I have to be careful. Do you have proof that you are who you say you are?"

Bradley reached inside his tunic and took out an embroidered badge, which bore the emblem of Fenwold's government.

"Hmm, I know the token of the Council. And to be honest, I've little time for them. For years now we've been left alone to fight off the raiders with no help whatsoever. The swine took the village of Ashwell to the north only a few weeks back. For now, they're leaving us be, but when they've used up the entire store there I expect they'll turn on us. And now, when it's nearly too late to do anything about it, the Council sends us just one man — and a young one, too. Judging by the cut of your clothing, I'd say you're from a wealthy east coast family. Well I'm telling you, you won't find things too easy out here."

Bradley bristled and suppressed a flush of anger. *Ungrateful old goat!* But he must at least appear to be diplomatic, though his tone betrayed his irritation.

"I didn't come here alone, sir. I had a deputy with me."

Somewhere in his head he heard the mocking *screech* of the black hawk of guilt accuse him from some distant woodland glade.

9

He almost expected Storey to react, but the old man just looked at him calmly, waiting for him to continue.

"My clothing's new because I was only recently appointed. As you say, I'm young to be a marshal. But I've had four years' experience as a deputy back home in the East."

"Hah! Deputy marshals! Part-time farmers handed a bow and a knife and sent out on patrol! The cream of our youth cast empty handed into the jaws of danger!" For a moment his gaze turned inwards and he fell silent.

Bradley softened his tone. "You speak as if you had some direct experience, sir."

"Not I, but my elder brother. He was just eighteen when the recruiter came looking for young bloods. Twenty-six summers ago it would be — before you were born, I'd say. It was I who discovered his body, out in the forest while hunting, barely two leagues from home. I've never told anyone how I found him and what those bastards had done to him."

Bradley thought again about Colby and moodily stared at the floor. Tom Storey must have read his mind.

"You say you had a deputy with you? What happened? Did they capture him?"

"He took an arrow in the back. He was only nineteen."

"I'm sorry. Were you close friends?"

He hadn't expected to be drawn so soon into revealing his emotions to these peasants. He'd intended to stay aloof and just do his job. But perhaps they weren't so different from his people in the capital. The headman's pompous geniality even reminded him of his father's manner. He seemed genuinely concerned and Bradley thought he deserved honesty.

"We'd come through the Academy together. He turned down a marshal's post to ride as deputy with me. I feel bad about leaving him. I really need to go back."

Storey shook his head. "Not advisable, Marshal. Those woods near Ashwell are raiders' territory. You were lucky they didn't get you as well."

To a degree consoled by the old man's words, he said grudgingly, "I'm sorry about your brother. The Council admits they were wrong. The work of lawmen can't be left to amateurs any more, so now every new deputy gets proper training. I spent a year putting new recruits through their paces before accepting this commission."

"Forgive a bitter old farmer, Marshal. You sound sincere in what you say. But if you've come here recruiting and choose either of my sons, it won't be with my blessing. As for the other elders, that'll be up to them."

"That's fair enough. But I'm not here just to recruit deputies. First I have to help you get organised."

The old man puffed up his chest. "There are plenty of able men in this village — young and old — who are more than ready to fight to protect their own. When the time comes, you can be certain we'll stand our ground."

"I don't doubt that, Mr. Storey. But I'm sure the same can be said of your neighbouring village. Yet it fell to the raiders."

The headman sank back in his chair. "You're right. But what else can we do but wait and fight them when they come?"

Bradley looked him straight in the eye.

"With the right preparations, you can fight them — and win!"

* * * * *

The red-haired raider pushed aside his half eaten breakfast and gulped down the dregs of his tea.

"Clamp! Get your arse in here! I want a report on the prisoners — now!"

"Coming, Red!"

The outlaw who shuffled in had a stoop from an old leg injury. Red recalled the gang's discovery of a store of liquor in a midland village, taken a couple of years back. The resulting knife fight had been costly, leaving two good men dead and most of the others unfit for action for days. Since then he'd imposed tighter discipline. But he smiled to himself now because Clamp's limp always made him appear subservient, as if constantly bowing. He did so now, his eyes fixed on Red's leavings.

"All right, you can have it when we've finished. First though, what's the condition of the Ashwell prisoners?"

"Not too good, Red. Two died in the night — one kid crushed and an old biddy just pegged it, don't know what of. I got two of the lads to burn the bodies. There could be others. But none of us can stay in there for long, 'cos of the stench. That cottage we got 'em in's a right shit hole."

"Well, move them into another one then. The one next door, that's the same size, isn't it?"

"Yeah, just about. I'll get the lads to shift 'em."

"And get some of 'em to clean out the other cottage. We don't want disease spreading from all their filth. I shouldn't have to be telling you this, you know."

Clamp nodded vigorously. "Yeah, Red, I know. I was goin' to do all that. I just wanted to check with you first."

"See to it then. After that you can get 'em back to work in the fields."

"Okay Red, but..."

"But, what?"

"Well, only a few of 'em are fit enough for work. And even they're doin' less and less."

"Well, we can't spare any more rations. Tell the lads they'll have to use the whip more. But first, how about the new prisoner?"

"He's come round, Red. He's asking for water."

"Well, give him some then. I don't want him croaking on us — yet. Did you get the arrow out?"

"Nah, boss, we had to leave it in. He'd have bled to death otherwise. We sawed it off at the back, clean as we could and gave him some neat barley spirit. After that he slept like a baby."

"I'm amazed he's lasted the night — must be a tough bugger. Fetch him in here."

Red got up from the table while Clamp dragged the half-dead Colby in on a pallet. He went over and knelt beside him.

"Well, lad. Seems you're a hard one to kill. The arrow must have just missed your heart. Probably pierced a lung though. I bet that's painful, isn't it?" And he grinned callously.

The young Colby raised his head to look him straight in the eye and tried to spit at him through his teeth. But he lacked the strength and the spittle only dribbled down his chin.

"Ah! Some spirit, I see. I'll let that go, but don't test my patience, because I'm cursed with a short temper and you're not in much of a position to defend yourself."

Colby's head fell back and he mumbled unintelligibly.

"Eh? What's that you say?"

The deputy managed a weak cough that cleared his throat momentarily. "May the Gods curse you!"

12

Red's expression hardened and he fetched a sharp slap across the sick man's face. Though the blow wasn't severe, Colby's resultant gasp must have jarred his injured lung, for his upper body arched and his face contorted.

The raider shook his head. "I did warn you. Now, let's have no further nonsense and listen to me. There's nothing we can do for you, which means you're going to die soon, either from loss of blood or, more likely, infection. So you might as well cooperate."

He took a piece of fabric from his pocket. "This thing here — we found it inside your tunic. I've seen something like it before. On a dead lawman, as I recall. Now, I can't have Council lawmen prowling around on my territory."

Colby spluttered.

"What is it?"

Colby's question came in the faintest of whispers.

"Bradley?"

"Bradley? So that's his name, is it? Some partner, that one! Soon as he saw you were down, he rode off, quick as you like. Not a thought for your predicament — only for saving himself. We chased him into the woods, but he got lucky. We lost his trail in the undergrowth."

The lawman gagged again, but his eyes radiated joy at the news of Bradley's escape. "Good!" he said.

"You're too forgiving," Red sneered. "But I'm not. When we catch up with him — and we shall — we'll give him a little extra something for leaving his friend behind. That'll be my present to you."

"Won't catch him!" came the heartfelt response.

"Stop! Save your strength. I don't want you dying on us till you've given me some answers. You've not been thrust into our midst without some kind of a plan. And I want to know every detail. What exactly were you and your partner doing here? Tell us that and we'll make you as comfortable as we can — until you croak."

Colby said nothing, but just stared coldly into the raider's wild, bloodshot eyes.

"All right," Red said. "Let's make it easier for you." He beckoned Clamp to stop shovelling the remains of his breakfast and come over. "You've met Clamp. Though he's taken good care of you so far, he won't mind my telling you that he also has a bit of a cruel streak."

Clamp wiped the grease from his mouth and grinned at what he obviously took as Red's compliment.

"Clamp enjoys inflicting pain and suffering and he's good at it. To be honest, it sometimes turns my stomach to watch him at work. I usually go and do some fishing while he's about it."

Colby grew visibly paler and beads of perspiration condensed on his forehead. Nevertheless he tensed his jaw as if fighting for courage. Through gritted teeth he managed to hiss, "I'll not be a traitor, you lawless bastards."

"Hmm. Probably right on both counts there. But you might want to reconsider. You think you're in pain now? It's nothing compared to what Clamp can do. He's got a little tool bag where he keeps his equipment for cutting, peeling, gouging and — well, I'll leave the rest to your imagination. So, come now. What's it to be?"

Though Colby's voice was weak, there was venom in his response.

"A curse on you!"

Red stood up. "All right. I can see you're a man of principle, so I won't waste my breath. It doesn't bother me either way. Clamp, he's yours for the rest of the morning. You know what to do."

Then he walked towards the door, where he paused and turned.

"Send for me if he tells you anything."

"Where will you be, boss?"

"I'm going fishing."

CHAPTER TWO
THE FRIGHTENED VILLAGE

By the Gods, what had he let himself in for?

Here he was, as far from the capital as he'd ever been, away from the comforts of home and family, cast alone into the jaws of danger. Maybe those few doubting voices at the Academy had been right. Perhaps he really was too young for such a daunting commission. Though most of the High Council elders supported his appointment, there were a few hard men who looked forward to the news of his failure. How they'd crow to learn of the careless loss of Colby. And they'd be right. Though Colby had wanted to rest, he should have insisted they backtrack straight away and find Crowtree rather than give in to hunger and fatigue. To set up camp in such a vulnerable position went against all his training. It was a hard lesson, but he'd have to be more careful in future. Meanwhile he must press on with his mission and bear the burden as best he could.

"Ouch!" He winced at Mistress Storey's dabbing at his head wound, while her husband sat by and watched.

"I'm sorry, Marshal. It must be painful, but it's not a serious wound. It'll soon heal. There, that's done. Sylvia!"

Her daughter appeared directly, having been lurking in the hallway just beyond the kitchen.

"Yes Mother?"

"Sylvia, I'm going to heat up some water for the Marshal to wash with. Meanwhile go to your brothers' room and sort out some clean clothing for him. Something of Jack's should fit him."

Bradley said, "Thanks for that, Mistress Storey. I do have spare clothes in my saddlebags, but I need to go fetch my horse from where we left her. It would be good to clean up first though."

The girl left to do her mother's bidding. Then Tom Storey smiled and said, "You'll not start your day's chores without a proper breakfast."

After changing and wolfing down some eggs and ham, Bradley slaked his thirst with a mug of ale. Tom Storey had one too, 'just to be sociable'.

"Have another one, Marshal?" Storey asked.

"Thank you but no, Mr. Storey. I'd like to take a tour of the village, study its layout and meet your neighbours. Then tonight I'd like to address the elders." Storey nodded and Bradley got up.

Storey said, "Well, if there's nothing more, I've a few things to do just now. Sylvia can reunite you with your horse, then later I'll show you around the village."

The girl presented herself again and this time Bradley looked beyond the scar to see a pleasant and honest face, much improved by a recent scrubbing. She'd also changed into smarter clothes and brushed and fixed carved wooden combs in her hair. Whether this was her normal daily habit, or a gesture made in his honour, he didn't know. In any event, he could do no worse than to be civil towards her.

"Sylvia, I think we got off on the wrong foot at our first meeting." And for the first time he smiled, while he rubbed the back of his head.

"Can't be too careful in the forest — you might've been a raider for all I knew."

"You're right," he said. "Better to assume the worst. I'll not hold it against you, young lady."

He took her crooked smile to mean she wasn't used to being called a lady. But he realised his mistake when she said, "I bet I'm not that much younger than you, Marshal."

It was left to her father to break the ensuing silence. "Sylvia, I want you to take Marshal Bradley to collect his horse. Meanwhile you can return his weapons to him. Marshal, don't be afraid to ask for anything you need. We may not have made you welcome from the start, but you'll be our honoured guest for the time you're with us."

On their way back to the barn, the pair passed a fork in the trail, partly concealed by overgrown vegetation, which he hadn't noticed earlier. "Is that the main route out of the village?" he asked.

"Yes. It connects with the main trail — right if you want to go east, or left for Ashwell and the north. You must have come by this way yesterday."

"I guess we must have — and missed the link to Crowtree."

"We don't use these main routes any more. We keep more to the forest trails. It's safer. When did you realise you'd gone wrong?"

"We found an opening a bit further on, but it only led to a forest trail. We decided to camp overnight in the woods near the Wall and retrace our steps this morning."

He cursed their bad luck in missing the track into the safe haven of Crowtree. After that, their fates had been sealed — or rather Colby's had. His own too, if they'd gone further along the main trail, for then they'd have ridden straight into Ashwell — the vipers' nest. That they'd stopped short was of small consolation. Again his mind filled up with guilt and recrimination.

"You don't look old enough to be a Marshal."

"How old should a Marshal look? I could say you look too young to handle a crossbow, though I know you can."

"How old are you then?"

"If you must know, I've seen twenty-two summers. What about you?"

"I'm seventeen — I'll be eighteen later this year. Can I see your badge?"

He reached for it from inside his tunic and handed it over and she inspected it. "Hmm, it's well stitched. I'm not much good at sewing myself." Otherwise unimpressed, she gave it back, but her curiosity wasn't yet satisfied.

"Do you live with your parents? Or do you have a house of your own and a wife?"

He sighed. "I lived with my parents until I moved to the Academy. I grew up on their farm on the east coast, but..." He was about to say that his father was now a wealthy trader and Council member, but decided he'd told her enough.

"But what?" she persisted.

"But nothing. I don't have a permanent house of my own, nor am I married. There. I think that answers your questions."

They spoke no more until they reached the barn, where he helped her lift the heavy retaining plank from the big double doors. It was quite an effort. Once inside he went straight to his mare. He was surprised that, despite last night's ordeal, she appeared quite settled. Then on examining her scratches he noticed they'd been treated with a salve. Someone had also placed a hay net and water within reach.

Sylvia stroked her muzzle. "What do you call her?" she asked.

"Scarlett," he said, bending to examine the horse's feet. "This shoe is loose."

He looked around. He estimated forty or fifty hay bales were stacked nearby and there were more in the loft. And there were several barrels at ground level. He nodded towards them.

"What's in those?"

"Mainly oats and barley brought in by traders last autumn. What do you think I fed Scarlett with last night?"

He frowned, surprised that so much foodstuff was kept this far away from the main village. But he realised he couldn't blame her for that. He'd talk to her father about it later.

"What's the matter?" she asked.

"Nothing for you to worry about," he said. Her expression showed the hurt of his put-down. He'd better change the subject.

"Do you have a farrier in the village?"

"A blacksmith, do you mean? Yes. Dan Benson takes care of all that stuff. When I was a kid I used to hang around his forge quite a bit. I still do sometimes. We'll take her along there if you like. I'm sure Father won't mind."

Leading Scarlett away from the barn, his thoughts were drawn again to the general layout of the village and cultivated land. He acknowledged a group of villagers who were busy pulling weeds in the outer fields of ripening grain.

He said to Sylvia, "That's wheat, isn't it? The rows are straight. You must sow the seed into drills. Do you plough the ground?"

"Yes. We use horse-drawn ploughs. Most of us have a go at it. You see this section here?" She indicated an area to their right. "I did that bit."

"Hmm. Not bad. Where did your ploughs come from?"

"Some are really old, but we keep them in good order. Dan Benson's made others. He can make nearly anything."

He looked forward to meeting the blacksmith. Despite his fears, it seemed these folk weren't just simple peasants, but sophisticated farmers and craftsmen. He hoped his ideas for defending their village would be matched by their own ingenuity.

"Is it just grain you grow in these fields out here?"

"Mainly. We leave some areas for general grazing. But we don't grow anything here that might be easy to steal."

"I see. So, where do you grow your vegetables and root crops?"

"In the big open area between the Wall and the village. They're easier to defend just there."

"In the shade of the Wall?"

"Yes, that's a bit of a problem. But the crops get plenty of sun for ripening early mornings and forenoons in the summertime. It's enough to give us some decent potatoes, beet and green vegetables. There's a shaded strip though alongside the Wall. We keep that for our compost bins and some pig pens."

He made a feeble attempt at humour. "No sunshine for the pigs then?"

"Sometimes we take them to sunny areas where we want the ground turned over. It's not so miserable for them."

"Sylvia, I was only joking."

She grimaced awkwardly and they continued in silence back to the village.

At the forge she introduced him to Dan Benson, a giant of a man who nevertheless gently lifted Scarlett's hoof and pursed his lips.

"Been doing some heavy riding, haven't you, Marshal?"

"You could say that. We had to flee from raiders last night. Can you tap a fresh nail in?"

"No. If I do that, another bout of rough riding and she'll go lame on you. You'll have to be patient while I do the job properly."

Talking softly to the mare, the blacksmith removed the whole shoe, rasped and cleaned the hoof and re-fitted the shoe using a complete set of new nails.

As he worked Bradley said, "I expect you've heard why I'm here."

Benson had a mouthful of nails, so he just grunted and nodded.

"I hope you'll come to a meeting of elders at Tom Storey's cottage this evening."

The smith nodded again while he checked his work, put down the hoof and said, "Right. That'll catch raiders. She'll give you another thirty leagues if you don't overstretch her."

Bradley took a pouch of coins from his tunic pocket.

"You'll not be paying me with Council money, young feller. It doesn't count for much in these parts," Benson said.

"Well then, how can I pay you for your trouble?"

The blacksmith stiffened to his full height of two strides, his massive bulk towering over the younger man. "We get by with barter around here. If you're any good as a lawman, I reckon you'll repay us all in kind before too long. Now put your Council money away and we'll say no more about it. I'll see you at the meeting tonight."

Bradley thanked him and took hold of the mare's reins. Sylvia grabbed them from him, saying, "Here, I'll do that. And if it's all right, I'll exercise her for you later this afternoon."

He softened at the gesture. "Thanks. It's kind of you to offer."

"No trouble," she said, patting the mare's muzzle. "I've wanted to ride her since I saw her last night."

"Have you no horse of your own?"

"No. Mostly it's the boys who get the horses. That's why I had you leave her at the main barn this morning."

"What do you mean?"

"Well, if you really had turned out to be a raider, I wanted to be sure of having first claim to her."

"I see. Don't your parents mind you going out hunting at night?"

"Why should they? Anyone knows that's the best time for stalking rabbits and hares. Or is it because I'm just a girl — is that what you mean?"

He'd touched a raw nerve, so he backed off. "I'm sure you can take care of yourself."

"Yes, I can — as well as any man!"

And she led the lawman and his horse back to her father's house, without another word passing between them.

* * * * *

The elders of Crowtree assembled in Storey's kitchen immediately after supper. There were about a dozen of them, the blacksmith Benson being the last to arrive. He muttered an apology and eased his large behind onto a vacant window ledge, there being insufficient chairs for everyone. Storey nodded to Bradley, the signal that all were now present.

The young Marshal looked at their stern faces and took a deep breath.

"I know you've lost respect for the Council and you have good cause. For years now, they've all but forgotten you. They've sent me here to apologise for that." The hardest part done with, he paused to let his statement sink in. Many of the faces showed a grudging approval, but it was Benson who voiced their unspoken thought.

"An apology's a fine thing, Marshal, but it's only words."

"You're right. And it would be a waste of my time to come all this way only to say 'sorry'. I've also come to help you deal with the growing threat from the raider gangs."

Another elder spoke up. "And how do you intend doing that?"

"By showing you how to improve your village defences." He didn't insult them by correctly observing that they had none. "This afternoon Tom Storey and I surveyed the perimeter and we've come up with a few ideas, which with your help we plan to put into effect over the next week or so. At the same time I make no secret of the fact that I need to recruit deputy marshals — at least two from a village the size of Crowtree — to whom I'll give some basic training before I move on. I've lost my former deputy, so I'll need one of these to accompany me. The other will stay to keep order and uphold the law in my absence."

He took their silence to reflect a sullen resignation rather than a heartfelt acceptance. So he hastened to add, "I assure you I've no intention of forcing anyone to become a deputy against his will. I'll only recruit volunteers."

But this assertion was met with a wall of grim countenances.

Grim faced, Tom Storey sighed and said, "Marshal, we know you have your job to do. But don't forget we were all young men once and that our fathers stood where we stand today. To a man, we were all eager to answer the Council's call and offer ourselves as deputies. You know how that turned out. And now you're asking us to sacrifice our own sons. I can't deny that, by the law, you have the right. But don't expect our unqualified thanks for what you're about to do."

Then another stepped forward and declared, "In any case, how can we be sure this is necessary? Crowtree isn't an easy target, with the forest and the Wall to protect it. Besides, we have little that's worth stealing. We'd have barely enough to sustain ourselves, if it weren't for the hunting. If we keep our heads down, surely the raiders will leave us alone."

Several faces then turned towards the window, distracted by some disturbance outside. The Storey boys and two or three others were running towards the cottage. Then the door burst open and young Jack Storey almost fell in, yelling, "Father, neighbours, come quick! The outer barn's on fire!"

"On fire?" his father demanded, thrusting his way to the door. "But who...?"

Jack's response struck terror into every heart.

"Raiders!"

CHAPTER THREE
BAPTISM OF FIRE

"By the Gods, the grain! Everybody — get up there as quick as you can! If you've no horse, double up with someone who has! And take buckets — anything that'll hold water!"

Tom Storey spat out orders in rapid succession and each able-bodied member of Crowtree's community responded as fast as two or four legs could carry them. The headman was among the first to saddle up, while others chose to cover the nine furlongs bareback. His sons had their own horses, but the Marshal asked Jack to wait for him while he spoke to their sister.

"Sylvia, take Scarlett and pack as many blankets and hides as you can find into my saddlebags, then bring them to the barn. I'll ride with Jack."

The store was well ablaze before they got there. From two furlongs off they heard the loud *crackle* of the burning timber, as shooting flames and sparks lit up the evening sky. A smoky sweetness in the air told Bradley that the hay had already caught. Once at the scene of the fire, he sprang down and sought out the headman. He may no longer be a youth, Bradley thought, but old Storey could still shift on horseback.

"What's the damage, Tom?" he shouted over the roar.

"Looks like they fired the roof at the back — probably from the cover of the forest. It's already taken hold of the whole rear wall and must be well into the loft area."

"There's a stream close by here, isn't there?"

"Yes, but the fire's too strong to try and quench. We'll never save the barn."

"What about the grain barrels at ground level? Are they afire yet?"

"Can't see with the big doors closed, Marshal."

Folk were by now milling around aimlessly, gawping at the spectacle and unsure what to do.

"Mind if I try something?" Bradley asked.

The headman wiped sweat from his brow with the sleeve of his tunic.

"Be my guest."

Bradley's thoughts raced as he got his plans in order. He turned to the villagers nearest to him.

"This group here — clear away anything that might catch fire from around the front of the barn!"

For the briefest moment they looked at their headman, uncertain of this newcomer's authority. But Storey yelled at them, "Do what he says!" and a dozen or so men and women fell to it like worker bees to do Bradley's bidding.

While they were clearing the ground, he yelled to Storey, "I've got to see inside! We need to shift that long retaining bar from its brackets."

Storey rolled up his sleeves and spat into his hands.

Although the headman was fit for his age, Bradley would prefer a younger man to help him with this job. Besides, Storey was too important to the village to take unnecessary risks.

"No, Tom! It'll be scorching hot and the Gods alone know what inferno lies behind it." The briefest nod told him that Storey wasn't about to argue.

His eldest son stood to his right, so Bradley said, "Come with me, Jack and help me shift that bar." They ran forward together, feeling the fearsome heat building up behind the doors.

He turned to the crowd and yelled, "I want six strong volunteers to manhandle the barrels!" A group of eight young men stepped forward. "First go and drench yourselves in the stream, then get back here as fast as you can. Make sure you're thoroughly soaked." Quickly they moved off to do his bidding and Sylvia arrived with her cargo of skins and blankets. He yelled to the rest, "Take these and soak them in the stream! If there aren't enough, use your shirts and tunics! Everyone else, stand well back from the doors — it'll be like a furnace in there!"

He and Jack took some of the first wet rags to protect their hands, then grabbed the scorching retaining bar and let it fall to the ground. A blast of exploding air flung open the doors with a *crack* like thunder and a huge golden tongue of flame shot out towards the terrified villagers. Thankfully though, they'd heeded his directions and were beyond its reach. But the force hurled Bradley and Jack backwards, one to either side of the raging doorway.

Then just as fast the flame receded, for the moment apparently satisfied by its initial gulp of fresh air. Bradley got up and peered into the throat of the fire through a hot cloud of choking wood smoke. He narrowed his eyes to pick out anything worth saving. Barrels to the rear were already ablaze and the rapid *popping* of thousands of exploding barley grains filled the stifling air. But there were half a dozen large butts close to the front of the store, which, though smoking and steaming heavily, the hungry flames hadn't yet ignited.

Just then the team of youths presented themselves, thoroughly drenched as directed. Bradley didn't have to tell them what to do. Taking soaked cloths to protect their heads, hands and arms, they went in. Dense clouds of steam rose from their waterlogged protective rags and clothing as gingerly they approached the smoking grain barrels. Evidently handling and shifting heavy barrels was yet another common talent here in Crowtree. Now one by one the youngsters deftly tipped each barrel and balanced it on its edge, finding untold resources of strength to keep it from toppling, smashing and spilling its valuable contents onto the earthen floor. Then adeptly the lads rolled each one out into the cool evening air, after which they returned exhausted to the stream for a further drenching — this time though, to find sweet relief from the suffocating heat.

Tom Storey grabbed Bradley's arm. "Well done, Marshal! That's saved half the barley!" Sylvia stood beside him now and he also gave her a hug. "And well done, my daughter! That was a clever thing, bringing all those blankets!"

Embarrassed by her father's error she smiled and said, "It was the Marshal's idea, Father."

Bradley shrugged. He never could handle praise.

Then old Storey shook his head. "Though why those idiots should seek to destroy what they'd normally steal, only the Gods can say."

Bradley stared at him dumbly and smacked a palm against his own brow. "Fool!" he yelled.

Storey frowned and stammered, "Yes, I know, but..."

"No, no. It's I that am the fool! Why would they fire your secondary store, if not just as a distraction?"

The headman stood dumbfounded for a moment, until the full significance of Bradley's words sank in. Then the hot glow on his face suddenly yielded to a clay-cold pallor of doom. He turned to the all but exhausted crowd, yelling, "All you men, collect your weapons and bring them to the main barn — now!"

Even before he'd issued the order, Bradley was astride his horse, beckoning Jack to follow him. Then the two of them galloped back towards the village with all the speed they could muster.

They arrived outside the main barn to find the unconscious bodies of two elderly women on the ground. Bradley jumped from the saddle and checked them for vital signs.

He shouted to young Storey, "They're both concussed — but alive. Get someone to tend to them, will you Jack?" But women who'd stayed in their cottages to mind babies were already rushing to the scene to do just that.

He glanced at the ground. "Look here! Fresh wagon tracks!"

He went into the barn, not to assess how much produce the raiders had taken — he couldn't say, for he'd not seen its contents beforehand. In any case, Tom Storey and the other elders could do that later. It was to check if anyone else had been hurt that he walked cautiously between the open doors.

What he found there dropped him to his knees.

The body was badly mutilated, the face a bloody pulp. Several fingers were missing. There were other disfigurements too. But he couldn't bear to look any more. He thrashed around for some sacking to cover the wretched remains and in doing so he noticed a piece of embroidered cloth lying on the blood-soaked tunic. He picked it up and stared at it, fighting back the scalding pressure of recriminating tears. But the release of anguish by the simple act of weeping was to be denied him yet again.

If in his suffering Colby had broken and betrayed their plans, Bradley forgave him now without hesitation. Not for the first time he blamed himself for letting this happen. While he knelt there in his grief, Jack stepped up and stood beside him.

"Do you know this man, Marshal?"

In a broken voice Bradley said, "It's Colby, my deputy. Look what those animals have done to him!"

He pulled back the sacking for a moment. Jack recoiled and put a hand up to his face, but couldn't control the urge to be sick. Presently he recovered and turned back, ashen faced, and gently placed a hand on Bradley's shoulder.

"Even animals wouldn't do that to one of their own. Father told me they'd captured him. Why do you think they brought him here?"

Bradley got up and composed himself. He must try not to display weakness to these people. "To strike fear, for one thing. But mainly for my benefit."

Then he nodded towards the back of the barn. "Help me move him behind those straw bales before anyone else comes in."

Together they lifted Colby's mutilated body out of sight.

"Don't mention this to anyone, Jack. I'll tell your father myself tomorrow. But the villagers have enough to fear, without seeing what those swine are capable of. I'll want you to help me cremate the body later tonight. Can you manage that?"

White faced, the youth nodded.

"Good man. Now come with me."

Still in a storm of grief and rage Bradley turned and ran outside. Jack followed him and they both mounted up. They galloped out onto the linking track that led through the narrow copse towards the main trail. There was no moon, but here and there in the starlight they picked out the deep tracks of the raiders' laden wagon, clearly headed north towards Ashwell. Here Bradley hesitated.

Jack yelled, "Come on, Marshal, we might just be able to catch them!"

"No. Don't think I don't want to, but that's exactly what they expect of us. There'll be more of them waiting not far ahead. We'd be riding straight into a trap."

They stood still for a while, their horses panting in the darkness. Otherwise the night was deathly quiet now except, Bradley thought, for what sounded like distant chanting, away towards the north. Faintly, mockingly, he fancied he heard them calling.

"Marshal Bradley! Marshal Bradley!"

"Listen. Do you hear that?"

Jack strained to listen but shook his head.

Bradley sighed. "We won't go after them tonight, though I'm aching to give them a taste of my sword! But, by the Sacred Wall, I promise you they'll not enjoy their spoils for long! For now though, we'll have to be patient."

Then reluctantly he wheeled his horse around and Jack followed. With heavy hearts they returned, angry and disheartened, back to the exhausted villagers of Crowtree and to pay their last respects to what remained of brave young Deputy Colby.

* * * * *

"Tom, did you call a meeting?"

The headman looked at Bradley wearily and pushed away his untouched breakfast. "No, why?"

"Come and look out here."

Storey got up and joined him by the kitchen window, beyond which a sizeable group of Crowtree villagers had gathered.

"Yes, I see them," Storey said. "I'm not surprised they're here. After last night's fiasco they'll want an account of our losses and to hear my excuses. They see the raid as a collective failure, you see, and they expect collective punishment. They'll want to hear a scolding lecture from their pathetic leader. I've been dreading this. Are you coming out with me?"

"Yes, Tom. But... I want to ask you a favour."

"You're one of the few who came through last night with any honour. What do you want? Just name it."

"Let me talk to them first."

The old man rubbed his jaw. "That's a tempting offer. I can't deny this is a task I'd sooner be relieved of."

"Do you think they'll listen to me?"

"If they won't accept your authority now, they never will. Come on. Let's get it over with." And they went out to face the crowd.

The villagers' bleary eyes and pallid complexions told of a night with little sleep. Bradley knew how they must feel, for he'd lain awake most of the past night too. He didn't wait for any introduction, but jumped right in.

"I came to Crowtree expecting to find a bunch of simple peasants. I was wrong. I've only been here a day and already I know you people to be courageous and resourceful. When my deputy and I were attacked I thought our mission was doomed. But the cooperation I saw last night has changed my mind on that score. I now know that all of you have the guts and determination to see this fight through to the end. What I'm trying to say is this. Don't be hard on yourselves. The loss of the barn and the barley and other provisions is a big setback. I know it leaves you feeling frustrated and angry. But I want you to look upon last night as a turning point. Don't be frustrated. But keep a hold of that anger. Because it's that anger that's going to help you to win through and defeat the raiders! Together, I promise you we're going to crush them. Death to the raiders!" So saying, he stabbed an arm into the air.

For a moment they just stared at him. Then a few fists at the back jerked skyward and one or two voices echoed his slogan. "Death to the raiders! Death to the raiders!"

This was the catalyst needed to spread the fervour through the entire crowd, until the heartened villagers chanted repeatedly with one voice, "Death to the raiders! Death to the raiders! Death to the raiders!"

He looked sideways to see Tom Storey's face sporting a broad grin. Moments ago so downcast, he too had caught the mood of excitement and joined in the chanting. He turned to Bradley and slapped him appreciatively on the back. Bradley grinned and whispered to him, "Send them away, Tom. You and I need to talk."

Storey raised both hands to silence the villagers. "Well done, all of you. We'll speak again later. Meanwhile the Marshal and I have some business to discuss."

The crowd dispersed and the two of them went back inside. The headman put the kettle on the stove and said, "Marshal, I'm not sure what happened out there, but I like what you said. You're some talker."

"Not really. I've been rehearsing that all night. And it helped when I got some support with the chanting."

"I think I know who your supporters were. My three youngsters happened to be standing at the back. Now, what I want to know is this — and I want you to be honest. Were you sincere in what you said out there?"

He looked the headman in the eye. "Yes Tom, I was."

"We haven't given you much reason to have any faith in us, Marshal. I'm ashamed at our lack of preparedness. You warned me yesterday against storing the grain in the outer barn. I should have had it moved straight away."

"Tom, don't beat yourself up about that. I'm sure there are many things you can teach me. Just about everything I know I learned from older men, wise men back at the Academy. Not all of them were warriors. Some couldn't handle a sword, or even a bow. But they knew plenty about planning and strategy. One important thing they taught me is this. Don't dwell on past mistakes — only make sure you learn from them. If we're going to defeat the raiders, the villagers have to be resolute and confident. We've all got a hard task ahead, but we'll only carry it through if we believe in ourselves and in each other."

The headman grasped his hand. "All right, Marshal. I'm with you. What do you want us to do?"

"First, what about the two old ladies who tried to stop the raiders? Sorry, what were their names again?"

Storey said sadly, "Megan Beckett was one. She took a blow to the head and didn't regain consciousness. She passed away before daylight. The other, Megan's spinster sister Annie, still lies in shock and none can say if she'll recover. We all pray to the Gods of the Wall that she does. But she's frail and old."

"If only we could hear their accounts of exactly what happened."

"Forgive me, Marshal. You were off with Jack when the other eyewitness came forward last night."

"Eyewitness? What did they see, Tom?"

"It's probably best if you hear it from her yourself. I'll send Sylvia to fetch her. She only lives a few doors away."

When the witness came in, Bradley felt disappointed at first to see that it was a child, a young girl no more than eight years old. He wondered how reliable her account could be. Bleary-eyed, she looked as though she'd slept in the crumpled smock she wore. Though obviously well acquainted with the Storey family, her expression was fearful as she stood in front of him.

Tom Storey took pity. "Now, Lucy, this is Marshal Bradley. He's a very nice man and our good friend. You don't need to be afraid. He just wants to ask you a couple of questions about what you saw last night."

Bradley spoke as gently as he could. "Hello, Lucy. Why don't you sit down? That's it. Now then, I want you to think about last night. Most of the other children ran to see the fire. Didn't you want to go there too?"

She glanced at Tom who smiled and nodded. With wrinkled brow she said, "I was in the chicken house, feeding and cleaning out. The chickens were squawking and I didn't hear the noise. I'm sorry, Marshal."

"That's all right, Lucy. You've done nothing wrong. Can you tell us what you saw?"

"There were two men in the wagon. I stayed hidden in the coop, but Megan and Annie went to try and stop them. They got down and hit Megan and Annie and they both fell on the ground. I was frightened!"

"I'm sure you were. But you were right to stay hidden. What else did you see?"

"The men took lots of stuff out of the barn and put it in the wagon. Then they got into it and drove off."

She hesitated and corrected herself. "No. They put the other thing in the barn before that."

Tom Storey said, "This other thing — what was it, Lucy?"

With furrowed brow she concentrated hard. "A big sack or something. It looked heavy."

"Why do you say that, Lucy?"

"They both had to carry it. They were strugger..."

The headman helped her out.

"They were struggling?"

"Yes, Mr. Storey."

"But you couldn't see what it was?"

She shook her head. "Sorry, sir."

Bradley said, "It doesn't matter, Lucy. You've been very helpful. And you're a brave girl. Thank you."

She looked at Tom Storey with a silent plea to be excused and he nodded again. She turned to leave, but at the door she turned back and said, "One of them had red hair, sir." And she left.

The headman said, "I reckon the sods were waiting hidden on the link track until we'd all gone to the fire. They were taking a chance, but the moonless night lessened the risk we'd see them. They trotted up to the barn, unloaded all they could cram onto the wagon and then shot back to Ashwell before we even knew they were here. It's a pity Annie and Megan tried to stop them, poor things."

"It was brave of Annie and Megan to offer resistance, Tom, but they didn't deserve such a beating. We should honour them."

"And so we shall, Marshal. I'll see to that myself."

Then he looked puzzled. "But I don't know what Lucy meant about them carrying something into the barn. She said the same thing last night. Some of us scoured the place early this morning, but we didn't find anything. She must have imagined it. You know what children are."

"No, she didn't imagine it, Tom. And you have to forgive me this time, because I should have mentioned it to you. They dumped a body in the barn."

Storey looked bewildered. "A body? But no one else is unaccounted for. Whose body?"

Bradley saw Colby's laughing face dance in front of him and he choked, "My deputy."

"Your deputy? Why would they want to do that?"

"To draw me out, to make me go after them. They'd hurt him bad. His body was almost unrecognisable." He paused and stared at the ground. "Jack and I followed their tracks for a bit, but I decided to turn back. It had all the signs of a trap. It sounds cowardly, but I chose not to ride into it."

Storey shook his head. "Not at all cowardly. You did the right thing. The scheming swine! But what happened to your deputy's body?"

"Jack and I went out to cremate it in the woods before we turned in. I didn't want any of the villagers to see how they'd..."

"Leave it, Marshal. You don't have to say any more."

"Thanks. I need to put that behind me — for the moment. Now, do we know the extent of last night's other losses?"

"A couple of the elders will report on the main barn later this morning. A wagonload of root crops for sure — potatoes, sugar beet — probably a third of the stores that were to see us through till harvest time. They didn't take any of the seeds though — I checked that myself. The idiots wouldn't take seed when food's there for stealing."

Bradley bit his tongue. He suspected the red-haired raider boss wasn't so lacking in brainpower. If they did eventually capture

Crowtree, they'd need the seed for the newly conquered slave labour to sow for them.

Storey continued, "As for the totally destroyed outlying barn, we know we lost all our bartered oats and half our barley. The oats will be badly missed — mainly horse feed, especially important at ploughing time. Some of the weaker animals will have to go, but the extra meat will compensate a bit. Losing the barley means beer will have to be rationed. That won't go down well. Apart from herbal tea, weak beer's all that staves off hunger when other food's scarce."

He sighed. "So, we're going to have to step up our hunting and foraging in the woods to supplement our needs through the summer and hope for a decent harvest when it comes."

Bradley said, "Your hunters will have to be even more careful from now on. After the raiders' success last night, I wouldn't be surprised if they tried their luck in the woods closer to the village."

Storey nodded. "I'll tell them. And when the stocktaking's done, I'll work out a rationing plan to feed the village up to harvest time."

"Very well, Tom. Now, as headman I need your formal agreement to let me help you improve the village defences and to recruit at least two deputies. Do I have your approval?"

Storey stood up. "This time yesterday I'd have been sceptical. But after what's happened I realise we can't just sit and wait. I'm certain the rest of the elders will agree. Tell us your plans and we'll do our best to put them into effect."

"Good. Call the elders together later this morning and I'll explain what I've got in mind."

Chapter Four
A Call To Arms

"Clamp! Fetch me the headman!"

Red leaned over the ashes of the campfire, raking them with a stick to expose the last glowing embers. He covered these with a few dry twigs and blew on them to revive the flames. Then he warmed his hands while Clamp reluctantly pulled on his boots.

Last night's raid had ended in a celebration of sorts and so most of his men were still abed and hung over, either inside a couple of the near-by dwellings or, by way of a half-hearted watch system, out here close to the fire. Members of this latter group now shivered in the early morning air and either dragged on more covers or sat up, bleary eyed, while they rubbed their hides to get their circulation going. The sycophant Clamp could have managed another half hour's dozing, but knew by now that it was best to jump when his boss gave an order, so he forced his body into action to do Red's bidding. He kicked awake a couple of dozing outlaws to go with him. They complied under protest.

Clamp removed the retaining bar from the door of the newly designated prison cottage and limped in, followed by his two henchmen. All three were armed with stout blackthorn branches, bloodied from previous lashings out at slow or defiant village slave workers. The roomful of desolate captives recoiled when the door burst open to reveal the frightening spectre of the three brutish outlaws.

Clamp decided to have some fun.

"Right, you lot! Now we've moved you into this nice new cottage we've decided there's too many mouths to feed. So we're goin' to have to get rid of someone. Now, who's it goin' to be?"

Slowly he moved his stick around, pointing it in turn at one or other of the terrorised faces of the once proud citizens of Ashwell. In doing so, he relished their expressions, at first of horror when the pointer rested momentarily, then of relief when it moved on to some other anguished victim. The fear was tangible, a creeping demon known well to these pathetic folk since the raiders' invasion, yet never diminished by its familiarity. Several wept, even some of the older men, more from self-disgust than fear of death. For by now such was their lack of strength and state of health that none could lift a finger to save themselves or their loved ones.

Clamp lowered his stick and grinned callously. "Nah. Only kidding. This time, anyway."

His words were met by a collective sigh.

"Aaron Genney! You're headman of this rabble, ain't you?"

A gaunt figure rose from the group of prisoners and moved forwards. It took all of the elder's strength to respond.

"That's me," he said weakly, head bowed from shame and exhaustion.

"Boss wants to see you," Clamp said. Then he turned to his accomplices. "Better give him a hand. I doubt if he'll make it on his own pins." Roughly grabbing the old fellow's arms they dragged him outside. Clamp secured the door and they frog-marched the headman across the compound to where Red stood close to the now blazing fire.

Clamp said, "Headman here to see you, boss."

Red turned to face the elder. "Oh, yes." He sniffed. "You stink, old man. Stand a bit further a way, will you? That's right. Now, just a little chat is all I want. I would have come to your cottage but, well, it's not very pleasant in there. Still, I'm sure you're glad of a bit of fresh air."

Red's mock politeness brought no reaction from Genney. By now the headman was fully aware that the raider leader's demeanour could easily twist either into sudden violence or arbitrary humiliation. Stony faced, he stared straight ahead as defiantly as he was able.

"You needn't worry. It's nothing bad — quite the reverse. We've recently had a bit of luck, which means we're going to be able to increase your food ration."

The old man almost perked up at this, but still said nothing.

"But there's something I want in return. You'll only get the extra rations — three whole turnips a day — if you'll persuade your young folk to work harder in the fields from now on."

Now Genney broke his silence. "But they're doing as much as they're able already. I don't see..."

Red cut in. "But you'll be getting more food for them, so they'll surely be able to work harder. You can see the logic in that, can't you?"

The headman sighed. "I suppose..."

"Good. I'm glad you agree. Now, go back to your people and give them the good news."

Then he nodded to Clamp who ordered his helpers to drag the old man back to the prison cottage.

When they'd gone Clamp said, "Good haul last night, eh, Red?"

"Not bad. It'll keep us going a few more weeks."

"I can't see why we're keeping the Ashwell peasants alive though, boss. The food 'd go further without that lot to feed."

Red flashed him a withering look. Speaking slowly, he thumped the hard ground with his stick to drive his message home. "Because we have to look to the future. We can't move from village to village forever. Sooner or later the pickings are going to run out. And we're not the only band of raiders in Fenwold. We need a base we can defend and a slave labour force to grow food for us."

Backtracking, Clamp was keen to agree. "Yeah, I can see that, Red. And this isn't a bad place, I suppose."

"It'll do for now. But Crowtree would be better. It's easier to defend. It's got the Wall behind it. It's their position that made the Crowtree fools think they were safe. But last night proved them wrong. We can hold out here a bit longer with the stuff we took, but we can't leave it too long till we make our next move — as soon as their harvest's in anyway. Then with the two villages working for us, we'll be sitting pretty." He yawned and stretched. "Did the lads have any luck out hunting yesterday? I need some meat inside my belly."

"Yeah, I think so. There's a bunch of rabbit and some pigeons they netted."

Red smiled. "Rouse those lazy buggers and get something cooking then."

Clamp stamped around, shouting orders at the outlaws who were awake, and stirring those who weren't with jolting kicks to the ribs. Then he went over to his boss by the fire.

"Pity Bradley didn't take the bait, Red."

"Yeah. I thought the sight of his buddy with his guts ripped out might fetch him after us. But it seems he's not the hasty type."

"Star of the Academy, according to the deputy."

"For someone who wasn't going to talk, you got him singing loud enough." Clamp opened his mouth to speak, but Red held up a hand. "No, I don't want to hear all the gory details. You'll put me off my food. I saw the body — that was enough. Just go over again what you got from him. I want to be sure there's nothing you forgot to tell me."

"I told you everything, Red. His name was Colby, deputy to Marshal Dominic Bradley — some clever bugger from the capital. To hear Colby talk, you'd think this Bradley was a god or something. The Council sent 'em here to try and get rid of us."

"Did he say how they expected to do that? What tricks they had up their sleeves?"

Clamp shook his head. "Nah. He kept that to himself. I went as far as I could, but he pegged out. But what could they do anyway? I ask you, boss — two young colts against our numbers!"

Red threw his stick into the fire and then dipped a billycan into a bucket of water. He set it on the trivet, stared into the flickering flames and laughed.

"You mean, one young colt and a god."

* * * * *

Towards noon as arranged, Bradley addressed the Crowtree elders in the yard outside Tom Storey's house.

"I meant what I said this morning. We can beat the raiders. But it won't be easy and it's going to take hard work and careful preparation. I'll be asking a lot of all of you."

Storey said, "After last night, Marshal, you can count on our full cooperation, no matter what it takes." Several others quietly voiced their agreement or nodded.

"First task is to secure the village as best we can. To make it easier, we'll need to reduce the occupied area."

Tom Storey frowned. "How do you mean, Marshal?"

"It's a question of economy. To defend the whole village would take too much time and effort. Remember there's work to do in the fields as well. So I want those families occupying the northern outlying properties to bring their belongings closer to the heart of the village, where they'll share living space and stockades with households behind the defences."

The headman said with authority, "Like I said just now — whatever it takes." He looked at each man in turn and there were grunts of approval.

"Good," Bradley said. Then, picking up a stick, he scratched out a rough plan of the village on the dusty ground in front of him. "You've one important factor in your favour — and that's the Wall. Few villages nestle so close to it as Crowtree does. So that rules out any attack from the south. The fields and gardens between the Wall and your dwellings are thus protected, except at the east and west where their boundaries meet the forest. If you can sacrifice an open stretch of, say, ten strides on either side we can start our fortifications at the Wall, skirting your farmland and bring them round in a half circle to meet in the present centre of the village, more or less where we're standing now."

Every eye was on him, older heads cocked not to miss his words.

"You're all well used to hard labour. Soon it'll be time for harvesting, then ploughing and tilling the ground ready for planting again. But some of you need to get busy building the defences, because a further attack might come at any time.

"To achieve all this you'll need to divide the available labour. I suggest the older folk who are fit enough, along with the children, tackle the manual work in the fields. That'll free the young men and women to work on the defences."

Storey said, "Tell us more about these defences, Marshal."

Using his stick again, Bradley pointed out the east and west boundaries on his rough ground plan. "We'll fell trees along each edge of the village. This will create an open corridor to lessen the chances of a surprise attack. Also it'll provide timber to make impaling spikes for pits and barricades. And we're going to need to make lots of wicker screens — some to camouflage the pits and the rest set up as light fences along the perimeter."

Now Dan Benson spoke. "Hold on, Marshal. I'm trying to keep up with you. How will all this fit together?"

"Look. Imagine you're a raider attacking the village. You come out of the woods to find a gap of several strides, so you're immediately exposed to our archers. But let's say you cross it safely. Next you encounter a picket fence. 'Ha!' you say, 'Is this the best they can do to keep me out?' So you plough easily through the flimsy picket, only to fall into the spiked barricades just beyond it. But perhaps you manage to dodge or leap over these. In that case you rush across the wicker mats, not realising they conceal pits containing more of those lethal spikes. That takes some more of you out. Any that get through will have to deal with a small army of well-trained warriors, armed and ready to strike them down! The raiders won't stand a chance!"

He was heartened to see glints of excited approval in their eyes and sensed an air of hope that had been absent before. Tom Storey shook his hand, as did several others. The elders then dispersed to pass on his plans to the rest of the villagers. But when Dan Benson moved away Bradley called out to him.

"Dan, can I have a word?"

The blacksmith turned to face him.

"I'll be asking more of you than of anyone. As Crowtree's key craftsman you'll be central to the whole plan. For one thing, the village will need hammers and cutting tools, such as saws and axes. Do you mind if I come back with you to your forge, to see your store of materials?"

"Sure, Marshal. I've got plenty of stuff."

At the smithy, Benson unbolted the door of a large wooden shed. Inside it were heaped piles of metal of all shapes and sizes, the sight of which made Bradley gasp.

"Wherever did this lot come from?"

Benson beamed. "From generations of my forefathers scavenging and salvaging from the ancient brick dwellings. You've probably heard stories of the Ancient Ones and how they had water brought right into their homes, by a system of metal and other piping. Some call it a legend, but I know it to be true, because I've seen it. I have some of it here somewhere."

Shoving aside large pieces of wood and metal, the big man cleared a way towards the back of the store. Here he stooped and picked up a length of smooth metal tubing with a green corrosive coating, which he handed to Bradley.

The Marshal scratched off a bit of the oxide to reveal the smooth red copper beneath. "I've heard about such things, but I've never held a piece in my hands before." He put the end of the tube up to his eye. "It's perfectly round! How do you think they formed it?"

"Not by any human hand. They must have had machines to make something as perfectly circular as this. But I can't imagine how those machines were powered, or where the metal came from. In my opinion, it could only have come from outside."

Bradley would have liked to discuss Benson's theory further, but now wasn't the time to pursue it. He only asked, "Why do you keep it?"

"Good question. It may be perfect, but it's of little use to us in this form. Even if we made a system of pipes from a water source to our houses, we haven't the means to pump the liquid through the system. You could do it with a high tank, but then you'd have to raise the water up to it first. I daresay I could fix the pipe to a hand pump, but what would be the point, if someone had to pump away at the source, just to deliver it a few strides away? It's quicker and easier to fill a bucket."

"But the metal itself must be useful."

"Certainly it is. Just like any other, I can soften it in my furnace and shape it into anything you like. There's plenty of old metal here to make all the tools and weapons we'll be needing."

Closer inspection of the store revealed a treasure trove from the ancient times. Benson and his forebears had collected and re-used, or else meticulously stored for future re-working, every piece of iron, lead and copper that had come their way. The blacksmith's precious hoard would be more than adequate for their immediate needs.

"This is excellent," Bradley said. "I'll want you to make axes first, so we can start felling trees straight away. You'll also be busy sharpening existing tools. Then we'll need short swords for close combat and metal arrow tips, sharp enough to pierce the enemy's furs. And we'll need hammers and nails for building our barricades and knives and small axes for shaping hundreds of wooden spikes. The axes will double as hand weapons later. What do you reckon?"

"It's a tall order. I'll need help. There's my own son Ryan. And one or two other youngsters who've learned some of my skills, if they can be spared."

"Of course. Choose your apprentices and get to work straight away. Whom did you have in mind?"

41

"My first choice might surprise you. It's Tom Storey's daughter, Sylvia."

"That girl, a blacksmith? Surely not."

"Ah, now, don't write Sylvia off so quickly, Marshal. What she lacks in strength — which really isn't that much — she makes up for in keenness of eye and control of the furnace. She pays it great respect, but the fire holds little fear for her. I've watched her expression. She loves the glow of the scorching charcoal when the bellows breathe life into it and in bending and shaping the various metals to her will. Believe me, Sylvia will make as good a blacksmith as any young man in the village. She has a great deal of courage. Not even the accident kept her away."

"Accident? Ah, you mean, the scar on her cheek. Was that from working in the forge?"

"Aye. She was hit with a piece of spitting metal when she was no more than ten years old. It made her poorly for a few days. But do you know, she shed not one tear? She seemed more annoyed at her own carelessness than anything else. When she'd got over the shock she was back in the forge, begging me to let her get back to work. I tell you, that lass will never be beaten, not by anyone, or anything."

After leaving Benson, Bradley returned to the headman's cottage, by now his adopted headquarters. Over lunch, he and Storey discussed his plans in more detail.

"As well as the fortifications, Tom, I want to test anyone who can handle a crossbow and train them to improve their speed and accuracy. I'll also want to inspect every weapon for its precision and state of repair. That applies to spare bows too — I want each bowman and woman to possess a second weapon."

"A weapon can be lost or damaged in the heat of battle, I suppose."

"Yes, that's true, but having two bows means someone else can be reloading while the other's shooting. That way we can double our volley power."

Storey laughed and shook his head. "That's clever. It must be some place, that Academy of yours!" Then he pursed his lips. "We'll need a whole lot of arrows though. And who'll do the reloading?"

"We'll drill some of the stronger children in priming and loading the bows for the warriors. Those of any age who've the skill will be set to making a stockpile of arrows, reinforced with metal tips from Dan Benson's forge."

"You know, Marshal, the word's already spread through the village about your plan. People are setting great store by it."

"I'm glad morale's improving. It's good to see it in their faces. But the barricades and pits won't keep all the raiders out when the time comes. Some are bound to get through."

"Yes, I realise that. But, like I said to you before, none of us will flinch from defending our village against those swine."

"With all due respect, that might not be good enough."

Storey rubbed his chin. "I must admit, we've little experience of close combat. We're just farmers, after all."

"I know. That's why, each evening after supper, I'll be holding training sessions in combat skills for any who want to attend them."

"Ah! I wondered where the small army of trained warriors you mentioned was going to come from. Who will you invite to these training sessions?"

"Anyone who's fit and wants to learn, Tom."

"That'll be every able-bodied man, Marshal."

Bradley grinned. "Women too, Tom, if they're willing."

* * * * *

"A kill! An arrow to the heart! Well done!"

The Marshal had organised a shooting match between two teams of villagers who'd turned out in force to attend his first evening training session. They'd shifted some sheep and fenced off a patch of meadow for the purpose and fashioned a 'raider' target out of a sack of straw with a turnip for a head, suspended from a tree branch.

Not only had all the young men come for instruction, but also many of their fathers and some of the girls, too. Of the latter small group, it didn't surprise Bradley to find Sylvia Storey a keen and able member. Her brother Liam had just scored with an arrow to the suspended torso. Now came her turn.

"Come on, Sylvia!" Bradley urged her. "Let's see if you can do as well as your brother."

43

Deftly she drew back the taut string to set her crossbow and placed a bolt in the groove. Then, with confidence, she raised the weapon to eye level, steadily took aim and pulled the release trigger. The missile *swished*, but then there arose a disappointed moan from her fellow team members at the sight of the untouched torso. The turnip head fell away into the long grass.

"Oh, hard luck, Sylvia!" Colby said. Why not have another try?"

Sylvia turned to him with crossbow in hand and said sullenly, "I don't need another try, Marshal. He's dead."

"Dead? What do you mean?"

She walked over to the target and stooped to pick up something from the grass around the tree stump. Grinning, she held up the turnip 'head' with her arrow stuck firmly in its centre. She carried it back and handed it to him.

"That's what I was aiming for," she said quietly. "The torso's an easy target. But it doesn't always result in a kill. An arrow in the head's a lot more effective."

Bradley dismissed it as a lucky shot and put the episode out of his mind.

The following evening saw him sitting down to supper with his host family. Though subject to the same rations as the other villagers, he hadn't yet gone away from the table feeling hungry.

"I'm sorry there's not much bread, Marshal." Amelia Storey sounded genuinely responsible for this as she offered him the breadbasket.

He took just one piece — his daily ration. "Thanks, Mistress Storey. But you've no need to apologise. We all have to do our bit and what the table lacks in bread and vegetables is more than made up for in meat and game."

Tom broke his own bread and smiled proudly. "We've the hunting skill of our offspring to thank for that. Their efforts even provide for some of the less fortunate families."

Bradley looked across to Jack and Liam, seated opposite. He'd already made clear his intention to recruit deputy marshals from two different families and by now an air of healthy competition had grown between the two brothers. So with more than a hint of mischief in his voice he asked, "And which of you two is the Storey family's finest marksman with a bow?"

But neither of the youths seemed keen to claim superiority and for a while they looked at one another uncertainly. Then Jack said,

"Well, there's not much to choose between us. We're both pretty accurate."

Then there came a loud cough from his right. He'd hardly acknowledged Sylvia so far during the meal, except for exchanging the usual social niceties. Now she glared at her brothers and gripped her dinner knife — a bit too tightly, in his opinion.

Jack spoke again. "If I'm honest, Marshal, I'd have to say that the ablest archer here — excluding yourself, of course — is sitting just there." He nodded towards his sister.

Bradley showed no reaction. But Sylvia blurted out, "That's right. Not that anyone will consider me for deputy marshal because, after all, I'm just a girl!"

There followed an embarrassing silence. Although Bradley couldn't think of a single reason why a capable girl shouldn't aspire to the position of deputy, he knew he had no intention of appointing one.

It was left to Tom Storey to assert his authority. Clearly the old man was fond of his daughter. Like any devoted father, he'd consider it unthinkable for her to take up arms as a career. But though his tone was considerate and tempered, his words were forthright enough.

"Sylvia, you know very well that the idea is preposterous. I've never heard of any woman becoming a deputy marshal and I don't intend to allow my daughter to be the first to do so. Why, I'd be thought a heartless and uncaring parent even to consider it — and quite rightly, too. So, if only for my own and your mother's sake, let's hear no more of such silly notions."

Bradley hoped she wouldn't cause a scene. He knew the girl was headstrong, but doubted if she was also disobedient. She proved him right, for she only pouted and went back to finishing her meal in silence, after which she asked to be excused.

Her father's assertion couldn't have dampened her spirit though, because she showed up as usual later that evening for combat training. In fact, she and her two brothers all showed exceptional adroitness and were quick to learn whatever he could teach them. He was pleased with their keenness and amazed at their inexhaustible stores of energy. They worked hard at their tasks during the day and yet were still willing and eager for combat practice each evening.

But then this was the case with virtually all the young warriors. Their skill in handling bow, knife, short sword and axe improved with every day that passed.

And he knew — though he wished it not so — that the fruits of his tuition would all too soon be put to the test.

Chapter Five
A Perilous Venture

The heavy axe blade smashed into the log, splitting it as clean as if it had been a block of Mistress Storey's cheese. Bradley leaned on the shaft while the headman stooped to pick up the pieces and placed them on the woodpile.

"It's plain you're no stranger to hard work, Marshal."

"Like you, Tom, I grew up on a farm. You soon learn that you either work or go hungry, don't you? Having a good, sharp axe is half the battle though. Dan Benson and his crew are doing a fine job making and mending the tools and weapons."

"Nobody's shirking their duties. This plan of yours has breathed new life into the village — given us all a sense of purpose."

"It's good to see spirits so high. I'm especially pleased how well the defences are coming on. All the pits are dug out and most of the barricades are in place. By the end of today we'll be just about done. And I've been thinking. I reckon we can take time out for a punitive raid on the enemy camp."

Storey straightened. "A raid? What do you have in mind?"

"I was thinking of a quick strike to get some of your provisions back. I want to give them a taste of their own medicine."

"But I thought..."

"I know. You thought we'd wait for them to attack us."

"I suppose so, yes."

"I'd assumed that too at first. But then I thought: why leave it to the enemy to dictate the timing? They're probably happy to sit tight until you've got your harvest in. No, I'd rather provoke them to act before they're ready. A short, sharp strike should weaken them and lift the villagers' spirits into the bargain."

The old man scratched his stubble and frowned. "What if things don't go to plan?"

"They won't be expecting a raid. Our foraging parties have seen or heard no sign of them in the forest since they took your provisions. I reckon they're content to gorge their way through the supplies they stole. They'll think we're too scared and weak to retaliate. We'll have surprise on our side. Trust me, Tom. The time is right."

The headman gave a shrug of resignation. "It seems to make sense, the way you put it. What's your plan?"

"We'll use their own tactics against them. Fire one or two of their buildings to create a diversion, then raid their barn, just as they did ours."

"It sounds risky. You don't know Ashwell's layout, do you?"

"I won't be alone, Tom. I'll be taking five young warriors with me."

"Of course. I wouldn't expect you to do it alone. Still, it's bound to be dangerous."

"We'll stick to the edge of Ashwell until we locate their store, so we can retreat quickly into the forest if necessary. But, yes, there'll be some risk."

Storey coughed nervously. Bradley knew the old man couldn't bring himself to ask the question that was uppermost in his mind. So he answered it for him.

"I want to take Jack along. He's one of my best warriors and I know he'll not want to be left out. I've spoken to him about this and he knows his way around Ashwell, so he'll be a useful guide as well."

"Yes, I see," said Storey. "You know that doesn't please me, but I can't forbid it either. I can't protect my own brood at the expense of others'. When will you ride?"

"Tonight, after dusk. I don't want to make things easy for them by attacking in daylight. And if they do have lookouts posted in the woods, it'll be harder for them to detect us. We should arrive there after they've eaten and their bellies are full."

"Very well," said the headman. "I pray that the Gods of the Wall will be watching over you."

* * * * *

Just after sunset the raiding party saddled up and trotted out of Crowtree along the main track north towards Ashwell. Four other youths who'd also displayed courage during training completed the team, riding in pairs behind the Marshal and Jack Storey.

Moving cautiously along the trail, Bradley sensed the menace of the thick, dark forest that loomed on either side of them, contrasting with the pale light of a rising moon. He narrowed his eyes to peer beyond the shapes of the outer trees and bushes, but even his keen vision couldn't penetrate the blackness for more than a few strides. The darkness itself didn't bother him. He was well acquainted with the cold, eerie atmosphere of the woodland at night. Nor did he fear an attack by wild animals, for generations of settlers had long ago banished the most fearsome creatures far from the areas settled by men. No, it was the two-legged variety of beast that he was wary of, especially since he knew just how brutal these raiders could be.

He hoped his trepidation wasn't too obvious. He glanced at Jack and knew from his expression that he too was trying hard to conceal a genuine fear of their situation. He turned in his saddle and noted the same look of concern on the faces of the other four young warriors.

Forcing a smile, he tried to quell their anxiety with a few well-chosen words. "It's a fine night for hunting, lads! Mind you, I'm betting the outlaws are still feasting on their plunder from Crowtree. They'll not be venturing into the forest for a while. I reckon a chance encounter's unlikely. Still, we need to be vigilant and watch and listen for any commotion."

Jack shuffled in his saddle. "That's right, Marshal. Those swine took enough food to keep them going for weeks. And they won't have the sense to ration it. They may have hunters out closer to the village though. We'd best be careful as we approach. There are forest trails we can take, so we won't be so conspicuous."

"All right. We'll dismount well before we're in sight of Ashwell."

"Ashwell," Jack repeated glumly. "I find it hard to speak the name, when I think of what might've happened to its people. I knew many of them well — hard-working, peace-loving folk, much like our own."

"I hope we'll discover their fate tonight. And if we can, we'll at least let the raiders know they can't always have things their own way."

"What's your plan, Marshal?" asked Archie Forrester. Just turned seventeen, he was the youngest of the group, overtly excited at the prospect of exacting revenge on the enemy.

His companion and senior by barely a season, Rajeev Shah, turned to rebuke him. "Don't be so inquisitive, Archie — Marshal Bradley will reveal all in good time."

Bradley blessed the dusk for hiding his blushes on realising the degree of trust these youngsters placed on him. Thanks be to the Gods that none had ever asked him how much real action he'd seen. He hoped he truly possessed the qualities needed to earn their respect. While they rode on, he outlined his plan, largely based on Jack's reported knowledge of Ashwell's layout.

About a couple of furlongs off, they dismounted quietly and tethered their horses far enough into the gloom of the woodland not to be visible from the track. Taking their weapons they chose the cover of a forest trail suggested by young Storey.

Jack whispered to the others, "This one leads to the main village stockade."

Soon they emerged alongside the stockade's eastern fence, where Bradley stopped and spoke softly to them. "There must be twenty horses here and I see only one man guarding them. Wait here and cover me."

He drew a short knife from his belt and crouching, silently skirted the vegetation to a point where the disinterested guard had his back to him. He darted towards the outlaw and grabbed his head from behind, covering his nose and mouth with his hand. Then in one swift action he drew the blade across the exposed neck, thrusting deep to slice through veins and windpipe. Wiping and replacing his knife, he dragged the lifeless body into the undergrowth and returned to his men. He felt both repulsed and exhilarated by this necessary action and wondered how much of it they'd witnessed in the gloom. One look at their gaunt, blank expressions told him it must have shocked them to some extent. But this was the stark reality of war. He gave them no time to dwell on the matter.

"See over there?" He pointed to the far side of the enclosure, where an empty four-wheeled cart stood alongside its main gated entrance. "I'm pretty certain that's the wagon they used in last week's raid. And listen."

Laughing and shouting came from the centre of the village and surges of sparks from their fires were visible just above near-by rooftops.

"Good, it's suppertime. Now — Jack, Archie and Rajeev, I want you three to find the weakest section of this fence, then wait for us in the shadows here."

"All right," Jack said. "But where are you going?"

"We three will make our way around the back of the first house over there. I thought I saw a child's face at one of the windows. Don't worry — we'll be careful. Just find a way into the stockade and wait for us there."

The house he'd indicated stood right next to the stockade and also backed onto the shrubbery at the edge of the forest. He and his two companions were able to sneak around behind it without having to cross open ground. The door at the back was barred from the outside, but he easily lifted the securing timber and laid it gently on the ground. Then quietly he opened the door, which led straight into the main room of the dwelling. They went in.

A sickening sight greeted them. The room was crammed full of people — or more accurately, of people and bodies — for it was obvious through the gloom that some of the poor souls lacked the spark of life. The stench was almost unbearable. He held up his emblem to show them he meant no harm. One or two faces looked up at him, their eyes begging for what he couldn't give them — not yet, at least. Others murmured pleadingly when they sensed his presence, clearly desperately in need of food and medical attention, but they obeyed when he put his index finger to his lips to signal the need for silence. He guessed the room contained what remained of Ashwell's inhabitants — about thirty of them, he reckoned. Their captors — for whatever purpose — had kept them barely alive with the minimum of sustenance, while they greedily consumed the villagers' store of provisions.

He paused to take stock. He hadn't known what he might find if and when he came upon the defeated villagers, but never had he expected anything so terrible as this. And because — selfishly, he now acknowledged — he'd wanted only to give the raiders a bloody nose for the crime they'd committed on his watch, he had no contingency plan for what confronted him now. He'd come with neither food nor medicine. But he couldn't walk away from these pathetic people. He must revise his plan — and fast.

He gestured to the wretched captives for their attention. "Those of you who can, please stand up," he urged. Thankfully, most were able — with a struggle — to make it to their feet, Bradley's companions helping where necessary. One of the villagers pushed forward to address him.

51

"I don't know who you are, friend, but you're welcome. I'm Aaron Genney, headman — to my great shame." He bowed his head, raising a hand to his eyes and sobbed silently.

Embarrassed, Bradley laid a hand upon his shoulder. "Marshal Dominic Bradley. I'm based at Crowtree." Then he addressed the pitiful group. "There's no shame for the people of Ashwell for what's happened here. I see only bravery and courage. Take heart and listen to what I have to say. We're going to try and get you all to Crowtree, but you must use only the forest tracks. Some of you will have to walk. If we can, we'll take the raiders' horses, but there'll be places where you'll need to dismount and lead them. Do you think you can make it that far?"

Genney straightened and composed himself. "I'm sure those of us who can stand will find the strength that's needed, if it means freedom from these devils. But what of those who can't walk?"

Bradley fixed his jaw and made a solemn promise. "If the able-bodied can make it on foot, we'll find a way to move the rest. First though, I need to go and tell our companions, Jack Storey and the others, what's happening. Meanwhile, I need you to examine the infirm and separate the living from..."

Genney stopped him in mid-sentence. "Go, young man and speak with Jack — a fine boy, I know him well. I'll do what's needed here."

When they returned to the stockade, Bradley saw that young Storey and his companions had done as he'd asked and now waited patiently in the cover of the undergrowth. He told them what he'd found and detailed his revised plan. Then he asked, "Can one of you harness two horses to that wagon?"

"My speciality," said Rajeev. "I think I can see the harness laid across the seat. Leave it to me. Where shall I bring it?"

"Leave it there for now. Secure the horses, then come back and meet us here." Rajeev moved off. To Jack and Archie he said, "Cover him from the far corners of the stockade. And if any of the raiders show, don't hesitate to shoot. Meanwhile be as quiet as you can."

Jack said, "All right. But what are you going to do?"

Bradley allowed himself the ghost of a smile. "We three are going to give those bastards something to think about."

The three of them quickly skirted the forest around the edge of the village until they came to where Jack had said the main barn was situated. With tinderboxes and prepared arrows they soon had the roof alight and Bradley sank a couple more burning arrows into the rear wooden wall of the building, just to be certain. The trio didn't hang around then to witness the reaction, but raced back to where the others were waiting.

"That's going to put them off their supper," young Archie said. And he pointed out the flame and smoke that even now showed above the other rooftops.

Bradley grinned. "It should distract them long enough for us to do what we have to do. But watch out in case they guess it's a diversion — this was the trick they used in their raid on Crowtree, remember. Be prepared for armed men very soon. Did you find a weak point in this fencing?"

Jack nodded and between them they easily removed a full section, so that the horses could be led out into the forest. By now some of the disturbed animals were whinnying, but the growing commotion from the vicinity of the burning barn was enough to mask their alarm.

Bradley said to his men, "Give one each to the able-bodied. There's room here to help the weakest to mount up. We've no saddles for them, but at least they'll be able to cover the journey in some comfort."

As the last few were mounting Bradley said to Archie Forrester, "You and the other two, accompany this group to where we left our horses. Take your own and escort them back to Crowtree, but keep to the forest trails until you're well clear of Ashwell. Jack, Rajeev and I will take care of the infirm."

But then he noticed that the headman hadn't mounted up and gone with the main group. A young man stood beside him.

"Please, Mr. Genney, take a horse and follow the others."

"Thank you, but my son Adam and I can't leave until all of our people are safe. You must understand that."

Bradley thought to argue with the headman, but time was short. "All right. You can help us move the lame into the wagon. Rajeev, bring the cart over here."

They moved the remaining starved, crippled villagers into the waiting wagon. Then Genney and his son went back into the cottage and after a few moments emerged, both of them weeping silently.

"Sorry," the old man said. "We wanted to say a final farewell to Isabelle, my wife. She passed away with a fever a couple of days ago."

Bradley bowed his head out of respect. "I'm truly sorry, sir. I wish we'd enough time to take proper care of all the deceased, but..."

Genney shook his head. "We might all have perished in that hell-hole, if it hadn't been for you and your young comrades. Come, what's..."

Swish! He was stopped in mid-sentence by an arrow that pierced his neck, a great spout of blood gushing from his jugular that made Jack flinch and all three rescuers reach for their bows. Young Genney stooped and cradled his dead father's head as his limp body slumped to the ground, while the rest took cover behind the wagon. Bradley hoped the sick and lame would have the sense to keep their heads down. In the faint moonlight they saw the two assailants, crossing the open ground on the far side of the stockade. All three swiftly let fly and two of their arrows found their marks, his own striking the breast of one of the bowmen, while Jack's took the other in the thigh. This one immediately dropped his weapon and fell to the ground, to writhe beside his colleague who must already be dead.

"Quick, Jack, into the wagon! It's time we were gone! Adam, take a horse and catch up with the main group. Rajeev, follow the forest trail back to our horses and lead them back to Crowtree — you should be all right using the main track. With luck, we'll not be far behind you."

Rajeev vanished into the forest with young Genney, while Jack and Bradley jumped aboard the wagon, Jack taking hold of the reins. Bradley primed his crossbow, ready for any further attack, as Jack urged the horses across the now empty stockade. When they reached the spot where the two raiders had fallen, Bradley told him to stop. He leapt down and stooped to examine the injured man, now unconscious, and smiled. The red hair and beard told him this had to be the barn raider who'd also attacked him and Colby. The devil inside him gave a little *whoop* and Jack helped him drag the outlaw onto the wagon seat between them. Then young Storey applied the whip, just clearing three more arrows that hit the ground only a few strides behind. Half a dozen screaming outlaws now ran towards them from the centre of the village.

"Jack, let's get out of here!" he yelled, as two of the raiders took aim and let fly a pair of whistling shafts. These thudded into the woodwork of the wagon seat just beside him. But under Jack's mastery the horses sped them away from their angry pursuers. Then, while Bradley tied the hands of the wounded raider and with no further opposition to hamper their escape, they raced out onto the main track that took them away from the occupied village and back towards the safety of Crowtree.

Chapter Six
A Demon Restrained

Sylvia peered along the moonlit trail towards Ashwell, her eyes fixed on the unyielding horizon. Other young warriors waited here too, some on horseback, some on foot, but all of them eager to witness the raiding party's safe return. She turned to her brother who stood beside her.

"Liam, what could have happened to them? They should be back by now!"

"Don't worry. The Marshal knows what he's doing. I'll bet you any moment they'll come riding down the road with our wagonload of supplies."

But others echoed his sister's concern. "We've been waiting here for ages. They've had more than enough time," said one.

Another spread his hands against the sky. "The moon's moved two spans since we came out. It must be close to midnight now."

Sylvia strained her eyes northwards. "There's nothing, Liam! If they don't show up soon, I think we should ride out to Ashwell and help them."

"No! The Marshal made it clear we mustn't follow them. He discussed all this with Father. On no account are we to place any more lives at risk! We need every able warrior to stay and defend the village in case of a counter-attack!"

"But we can't just leave them to the raiders' mercy!"

Liam gritted his teeth. "We'll do exactly what the Marshal said!"

She grabbed his arm. "Oh, if I only had a horse of my own!"

Then one of the others shouted, "Someone's coming! About a furlong down the track!"

There was a buzz of excitement and a murmur that could have developed into a cheer. But as its outline sharpened the reality of the approaching vision quelled any surge of joy that might have been welling inside of them.

Sylvia groaned, "There's only one horseman and he's leading two riderless horses!"

As the lone rider drew closer someone else cried out, "It's Rajeev!"

Sylvia ran out fifty strides to meet him and grabbed at his tunic before he had a chance to halt. She turned and ran alongside while the horses trotted towards the reception party. His horse was skittish because of her proximity and she took hold of its halter.

"Rajeev! What happened? Where are the others?"

Straight-faced, Shah looked down at her and shook his head. "I'm afraid we didn't achieve what we set out to do."

She stared at the horses that trailed behind him. "Wait a bit! That's Jack's horse — and Scarlett!" She tugged hard now at his leggings. "What's happened to Jack and the Marshal? Where are they?"

He relaxed his grave expression and his face cracked into a broad grin. "Stop pulling, Sylvia, please! You'll have me off! And cheer up! They're not far behind me with the wagon — see!" Then he twisted in his saddle and pointed.

She looked along the track and just discerned the outline of a wagon in the distance, the silhouettes of three figures on the front seat becoming steadily clearer against the moonlit sky.

"You devil, Shah! You lied! You were successful!" she shouted through tear-dimmed eyes.

"I didn't lie," he insisted. "We failed to recover the provisions."

"What's in the wagon, then, Rajeev?" Liam asked.

"Some very poorly Ashwell folk. They'll need care and attention. Send word to the village so they're ready to receive them. And after that, the rest of the Ashwell survivors."

The news of the raiding party's return soon reached Tom Storey, who was ready to greet Jack and the Marshal when his son brought the wagon to a halt outside his cottage.

"Well done, well done!" he said, giving Jack a hand down. Then he asked gravely, "Any casualties?"

Bradley answered, "Not among our party. But Ashwell's headman took a fatal arrow."

The old man looked grim. "Poor Aaron! He was a good fellow. I know Rajeev's arrived with your horses. What of the other three warriors?"

"They're escorting the Ashwell villagers back here, using forest trails for cover. I expect they'll arrive in dribs and drabs through the night. With luck it'll be a while before the raiders realise they've gone. They were more interested in stopping us from taking their wagon." Then he laughed. "And right now they'll be busy searching for their horses."

"Why? Did you release them?"

"Better than that. The Ashwell folk who are fit enough are riding some of them here. You can tell Sylvia she might be getting that horse she's been wanting."

Storey's face cracked into a smile. "Splendid!"

Then he nodded towards the unconscious figure that slumped across the wagon seat. "Is that one of the Ashwell casualties? I don't recognise him."

"No, Father," said Jack. "The Marshal believes that this one's the raiders' leader."

Together they manhandled the unconscious Red down and laid him on the ground.

Bradley said, "Tom, I want your people to give the Ashwell sick and wounded priority, but he needs some attention too. The arrow's pierced his thigh muscle and he's lost a lot of blood. It would be useful if we could bring him round, so I can interrogate him."

Men and women were already helping the sick and crippled down from the rear of the wagon and guiding them towards a cottage that would serve as a makeshift hospital.

The headman looked sternly at the unconscious raider. "I wouldn't blame you if you did more than just talk to him, Marshal."

"Don't tempt me. And don't think I haven't thought of a hundred ways to torture the swine. But if a Council marshal can't keep to the rule of law, there's not much hope for any of us, is there? No, after I've questioned him, I'll turn him over to you for trial and punishment, according to your custom. Is there somewhere secure we can keep him after his wound's been tended to?"

"There's an old stone shed with a bolt on the door just behind my cottage. It should be sturdy enough to hold him. We can put a double guard on it, just to be sure."

Through the second part of the night most of the Ashwell refugees emerged from the forest, but even as dawn broke a few exhausted stragglers still trickled in. The whole of Crowtree busied itself comforting and feeding the refugees, or gathering and tending to the captured horses. No one had much of a chance to rest.

* * * * *

Later in the morning Bradley sat down to breakfast with the headman and his wife. He could scarcely keep his eyes open, but Storey was still full of the recent events.

"This has been a night to remember, Marshal. I must admit I had reservations when you told me of your plan. But you've exceeded all our expectations. You may not have retrieved our stolen supplies, but you've done far better. You've rescued our friends and neighbours and given those outlaw scum something to think about!"

Storey's repeated praise embarrassed Bradley, but he felt too tired to argue. He finished his meal and sat back, letting his eyelids fall momentarily. But then he forced them open, gave his head a shake and said, "Tom, you do realise they'll retaliate as soon as they can get organised?"

The headman rose from his seat, simultaneously yawning and nodding. "They'll be bent on vengeance, I agree. But your actions last night effectively put them to rout. Not only that, but you've robbed them of their horses."

"Maybe not all of them. They could have others stabled elsewhere in the village. And some of the loose horses might've found their way back to Ashwell."

"But they've lost their leader. They'll be nothing but an aimless rabble."

"It'll only take a new leader to step forward, then they'll regroup and strike back. What's more they'll be angry and desperate."

Storey shrugged. "What do you advise?"

"The raiding party needs to rest. Meanwhile, I want you to assemble the other warriors and organise them into three platoons. We must have a waking watch of two platoons at all times from now on. And for the least disruption of household routines, allocate family members to the same platoon. Then I'd deem it a favour if you'd stay by my side until the fighting's over."

"Willingly! And I assume you'll want the watches to continue through the night?"

"Especially during the night — that's when they're most likely to attack. Have each platoon rest in shifts, while the others go about their normal duties. But ensure everyone stays on full alert. I've no idea what the raiders are capable of, but we must assume they'll retaliate very soon."

"I'll pass on your instructions right away," said Storey. "You look tired out — you ought to get some rest."

Bradley nodded and said, "Have someone wake me at midday." Then he dragged his weary body up the cottage stairs to bed.

* * * * *

It wasn't easy to get off to sleep. The excitement of the recent raid still quickened his blood. More important, the enormity of events now unfolding was unnerving. And he wondered if the Crowtree trainees were ready yet for real action. Only a few days before, they'd no immediate fear of a provoked attack, though sooner or later the raiders' ill-gotten stores would have run out and they'd have turned their weapons on Crowtree out of desperation. He'd merely brought things forward a little. Still, he felt a sting of regret for having overturned the lives of these good folk, no matter how necessary his intervention.

And then there was Colby. No amount of logical reasoning could wipe the slate clean of his responsibility for his friend's death. Battling with such doubts and recriminations, he'd eventually drifted off for what seemed only a few moments when he felt a gentle hand shaking him awake.

"Marshal," a soft voice whispered. He opened his eyes to see Sylvia's cheery face smiling down at him. "It's a little past noon — you asked to be awakened. I've brought you some tea."

He sat up and rubbed his eyes, then took the mug she offered him. "Thank you, Sylvia. You're a good girl." For a moment he expected her to retaliate at what must sound a condescending remark. But she can't have taken it as such, for she only smiled.

"Has your father organised the platoons as I asked him?"

61

"Yes. Everyone knows what's expected of them."

"Good. I'll take some lunch, then spend the afternoon inspecting the weapons and fortifications."

He expected her to go, but she hung about looking dejected. He recalled her disappointment at being left out of the raiding party. He knew she'd have played her part as well as any of the young men. He felt mean in treating her now as a mere servant sent to wake him.

So he said, "If you can be spared this afternoon, I'd like you to accompany me. I must admit I don't feel thoroughly refreshed and an extra pair of eyes will make certain everything's as it should be."

Her mood lifted and she smiled back at him. "Finish your tea then," she said. "I'll be waiting for you downstairs when you're ready."

She was an unusual girl, he thought. At one moment she was morose and touchy like any teenager, the next intelligent and adult, with a strong sense of responsibility. Not a bad warrior too — for a girl. And though he'd asked her to come along mainly to please her, he couldn't deny that she really would be useful. Yes, she tended to be outspoken, but she was pleasant to have around when in her "grown-up" mood and would probably help make the day's work less tedious. He finished his tea and met her downstairs. Then they went outside.

"Right then — defences first," he said. "We'll start here in the middle of the village and check the trenches on the western side, come back and examine all the barricades, then return alongside the eastern trenches to bring us back where we started. We can inspect the picket fences as we go. Ready?"

She stood to attention. "Yes, Marshal."

He wondered whether to suggest she try to relax, then thought better of it. They began with the trench right outside her father's cottage. "Any observations here?" he asked.

She knelt down and felt each impaling spike, checking that it was firmly set. "These seem sharp and solid enough. Should make quite a mess if any of the enemy falls in. And the trench looks about the right width."

"Good," he said. "But what about the wicker covers? I know they should be off now, for general safety. But they should be close by, ready to go back on. I don't see them."

She pursed her lips, clearly annoyed to have missed something so important. "No, you're right. Someone must have moved them. There's a lot of coming and going here and I expect they get in people's way." She looked around and then pointed towards the cottage. "There they are. Someone's stacked them against the wall."

"All right," he said. "That's something to mention to the platoon leaders after the inspection. All the covers must be in place before sunset. After that, everyone stays inside the fortifications."

They continued their review of the trenches, barricades and outer fences and most were in good order. Where they found a chipped or insecure spike, a section of barricade not fixed firmly enough, or part of the wicker fence missing or fallen, warriors were summoned to make them good. As planned, completion of this part of the inspection brought them back to the cottage.

He said, "I'm really pleased with the work everyone's done here."

She nodded. "The sharpened spikes and barricades are a great idea. Were they effective the last time you used them?"

He'd hoped the subject of his previous active service wouldn't arise. Why did she have the knack of asking the most difficult questions? He took a deep breath.

"You're the only one who's asked me about my experience, Sylvia." She looked hurt. "No, it's all right," he said. "You're naturally inquisitive — there's nothing wrong with that. I'll tell you this because I know you have the maturity to understand." She looked straight at him and her eyes didn't flinch. He hoped she didn't think he was patronising her. He carried on anyway.

"All the new peacekeepers were chosen for their agility and alertness — and that ruled out most of the older men with experience of major campaigns. Very few of the new marshals — myself included — have seen active service at this level. But those seasoned lawmen drilled us well and without them we'd have been poorly prepared. It was one of them who told me about these devices."

"I understand. This older marshal — did the spikes work when he used them?"

Oh, Gods of the Wall, have mercy! Why must her questions be so probing? And why was he so ready to be candid with her? He fought to match her stare. It wasn't easy.

"To my knowledge the devices were used — or rather, prepared for use — on one occasion. But the raiders they were intended for were intercepted and defeated before they could attack the target."

He waited for her to question the use of untested defences, but instead she only said calmly, "Oh, I see. Still, I'm sure they'll work for us. Then we can show other villages how to use them. It's weapons inspection next, isn't it? But I'm really thirsty. Do you think we've time for some tea?"

He smiled. "All right. I could do with a short break."

Inspecting everyone's weapons took them until mid-afternoon and the few defects found were quickly rectified. When they'd finished, he thanked her for her help.

"Oh, that's all right. Any time. What's your next job?"

"I'm going to interrogate the prisoner."

"Oh? Can I help you?"

"I'd sooner do this alone. But thanks for the offer."

"It'll be dangerous on your own. He might have worked his fetters free and try to jump you. I can go and get my bow if you like. It won't take long."

"It's all right. I have my own weapons. And I won't be alone. Your father placed a double guard on him, remember."

Still she tarried. "Oh, yes. Am I dismissed then?"

"Yes, Sylvia, for now. Thanks again."

He stared after her momentarily while she marched away. Then he shook his head and turned his attention to the next task in hand.

At the shed that now served for a cell he approached the two guards, who straightened and nodded formally. He ordered the shed to be opened and one of them followed him inside. Red had been set down on a settle strewn with straw, arms and legs bound as a precaution. Now roused from his sleep by the noise of their entry he tried to raise himself, then winced from the pain of his leg wound.

His deep-set black, bloodshot eyes darted shafts of hatred at Bradley. He said nothing, but his contemptuous sneer spoke volumes. When he tried to move, the pain of his injury forced him back and he glared at his captor with an arrogant defiance.

"Well," Bradley said, seizing the initiative, "I see we didn't manage to kill you, then. How's your injury?"

"Your witches did a good job with their herbs and potions. It still pains me but I'll survive to cut you down, lawman."

"I doubt that. The arrow didn't pierce anything vital, so yes, you'll live. But only long enough to face trial by the people you've terrorised these last few months."

As he'd hoped, his statement provoked an outburst.

"Before that happens, my men will come and wipe these pathetic peasants off this land as I might wipe my arse with a handful of tussock grass."

"Ah, then you are — or should I say, were — as I suspected, the leader of that rabble. In which case they'll be squabbling among themselves just now to fill your wretched place. I doubt they'll have the time or intelligence to organise themselves for a further attack."

Red narrowed his eyes and spat out one final threat.

"They'll organise, have no fear. And when they do, you'd best prepare yourselves for slaughter, the lot of you."

Bradley looked straight into his evil eyes and said, "That's precisely what we are doing."

Then he turned to the guards, saying, "Make sure he gets regular food and water. I want him fit to stand trial."

Then he turned to look back at the prisoner and added coldly, "And execution."

CHAPTER SEVEN
AN APPOINTMENT WITH DEATH

Clamp looked across at Riley. They hadn't exchanged a word all morning. Yet each blamed the other for aiming just too short by the stockade last night to stop that wagon. As a result Bradley and his sidekick had sped off, taking the injured Red with them. A moment sooner and they'd have had them. Riley blamed Clamp for being too slow. But that wasn't true and he knew it. Even with his lame leg, Clamp could still keep up well enough with anyone on foot. They'd just been too late, that was all. So they'd had to watch the two blasted rescuers speeding off with their prize, and laughing as they fled.

Then he and Riley had found the stockade guard's body in the long grass. Clamp knew the gash of a quick, clean killing when he saw one. Whoever did that knew what he was doing. They'd looked around for the missing horses, but there were none to be found. Then he'd wandered over to the prison house, not really surprised when he found it empty apart from a few corpses.

So they'd tramped back to help the rest of the gang finish dowsing the fired storage barn and salvaging what they could of the stores. After that, the exhausted outlaws had drifted to their beds.

The morning saw little action. They assumed all the horses were lost and no one volunteered to go looking for strays. Most feared snipers posted in the forest to pick off anyone who might try. So the crumpled raiders passed their time eating, drinking and throwing dice. Clamp sat by watching, listening and sharpening his knives, always with an eye on Riley. He'd never liked the man and saw him as his main rival as Red's successor. As far as they knew, Red was still alive, though his absence was tangible. But it looked as if nobody was going to step forward to take his place, even just as temporary commander till they could organise his rescue.

By noon Clamp's patience had run out. He had to establish his authority. He stuffed his dagger into his belt, got up and stood more or less in the middle of the indolent crowd. He pointed at men indiscriminately.

"You and you! Get out in the forest and round up any stray horses those bastards might have left behind! You two over there go and burn Ned's body before the wild dogs smell his blood! And the rest of you, gather up all your weapons!"

Riley said, "Hang on Clamp. Who says you're in charge?"

With a twisted grin Clamp snarled back at him. "I do! Until we get Red back anyway. Anybody want to argue?" He scowled at the desperate band of outlaws, of whom only Riley offered opposition.

"How by the Gods are we goin' to rescue Red? You saw how well organised the Crowtree lot were! Maybe that lawman Bradley is some kind of god, anyway. I say we clear out of here before they come back and finish us all off!" He looked around at a few half-hearted shrugs and nods of approval.

Clamp's face contorted into a withering scowl. "You bunch of snivelling cowards! Do you really think if we clear out that they won't come after us? We don't have any choice but to stand and fight. But first we need to be ready, by checking all our weapons and catching any horses that are still around."

A man next to Riley said, "Maybe Clamp has a point. If Bradley's so good he'll try to hunt us down anyway. We might as well make a stand. We're still a fair sized gang. We're bound to have more fighting men than they do."

Riley stood up. "All right. So we fight. But I still don't see how that makes Clamp our leader." Then he grinned cruelly. "A leader with a limp!" Some of the men sniggered at this, but clammed up when Clamp's stony glare settled on their faces.

Clamp did some quick weighing-up: the value of an able man against the risk of a knife in the back. He didn't hesitate. In an instant the haft of his dagger protruded from Riley's breast. Riley's shocked eyes looked briefly at Clamp's cruel scowl, then he felt the creeping warm stain of blood on his tunic and he slumped to the ground.

All were silent. Then Clamp stood as tall as he could and said, "Here's another corpse to burn. Let's make sure the next one's a lawman. You've had your orders. Now get to it. We strike back tonight!"

* * * * *

All day long Crowtree was busy as an anthill, with fortifications, positions and weapons being checked and re-checked. With physical defences now pretty much taken care of, Bradley's mind focussed on communications. Late in the afternoon he visited the forge and found the blacksmith, his son and Sylvia still busy making arrow tips and sharpening swords and axes. These were conveyed by a procession of youngsters, fetchers for their older brothers and sisters now manning the barricades.

"Dan, I need a signalling device for when things start happening. Something that'll be heard right across the village when the time comes. Got any ideas?"

"Hmm. Only thing I can think of is the old bell from the ancient gathering house. It was dismantled in my grandfather's time, but I think it's still intact in my store. It'll take five or six strong men to shift it and fix it up though. Given time we could raise it up high."

"How much time?"

"A couple of days at least."

"What can you do in a few hours?"

"With stout wooden beams I could set it just above head height. But it won't be a permanent job."

"If it works for a day, that'll be enough."

Benson supervised a group of volunteers to transport the bell to the front of Storey's cottage. They cut and dragged heavy timbers to the spot and constructed a sturdy support from which they suspended the bell using strong rope, having raised it into position with pulleys. By late afternoon it was in place and could be rung easily with a sharp strike from a hammer.

Benson surveyed the device. "I doubt if this is how it was supposed to work, but let's give it a try." Then he grabbed the hammer and struck it hard against the body of the bell. It gave out a clear peal that appointed warriors soon reported as audible throughout the village.

In the early evening at change of watch Bradley called the platoon leaders together to explain the signalling system.

"A repeated pattern of four quick peals means I want to see you three straight away. Several peals at short intervals means all warriors should assume battle positions. No action is to be taken then until you hear repeated rapid peals. Is that clear?"

They all nodded.

Sylvia stood close by and asked, "Who'll ring the bell for you, Marshal?"

Almost without thinking he said, "You can if you like, Sylvia. I'll need to keep my mind alert and hands free."

Jack Storey asked, "Do you really think they'll come tonight, Marshal?"

He looked back at him gravely. "It'll be tonight or not at all."

It was obvious to Bradley that these brave young warriors had reached a watershed, the sudden reality of imminent battle reflected in their serious faces. For his own part, the responsibility of command had never weighed so heavily upon his young shoulders. Not for the first time, he silently sought the blessing of the Gods and his departed friend, Colby.

* * * * *

Waiting. This was the worst part.

People had to eat and the weather being fair, families gathered outdoors to take their evening meals, all platoons now being on full alert.

The Storeys had moved out table and chairs to take supper under the bell. The ground around them bristled with weapons, ready to be grabbed when needed. Lookouts were posted along the perimeter so the word could be passed quickly to the command centre if the enemy attacked. But in any case all eyes were on the forest and vacated village areas beyond the defences.

The aroma of Amelia Storey's freshly baked loaf filled the air and stimulated everyone's taste buds. The headman broke off a piece and passed the loaf on to the Marshal.

"Thank you, Tom. It's good to be doing something as normal as taking supper at the family table. Something the Ashwell folk won't have enjoyed for several weeks. Thanks be to the Gods they're able to share a simple meal with their hosts around the village."

Tom Storey rubbed his chin.

"Marshal, you'll have noticed we've none of our friends from Ashwell here. I'm afraid it's impossible because we're five adults already — six including yourself. Of course the boys would willingly have moved to an outhouse had dear Aaron and Isabelle Genney survived, but..." He bowed his head, deep in sorrowful memory of the absent Ashwell headman and his wife. Then he added, "Perhaps you wouldn't mind if we dedicated this meal to their memory?"

Bradley broke off a piece of the loaf and passed it on. "Of course not. And there's no need to apologise. I only appreciate your putting up with me and my erratic comings and goings. Besides, there's been no shortage of offers of hospitality for all who need it. The survivors from Ashwell owe Crowtree a great debt."

Storey, now with carving knife in hand, handed him a plate with almost half a chicken on it. "They're good people. I'm sure they'd have done the same for us, had our positions been reversed. Some of their boys are already offering to lend a hand in defending Crowtree. Of course I've told them it's impossible, given the state they're in. But they might only need a couple of decent meals to bring them up to strength."

Bradley helped himself to potatoes and vegetables. While he ate, he felt a twinge of homesickness for his own parents' hearth and kitchen, many leagues away near the east coast. But he forced a smile and said, "This food's wonderful, Mistress Storey. As usual, you set a fine table."

The lady of the house, clearly unused to receiving such praise, merely smiled and passed him the beer jug, saying, "You're very welcome, I'm sure, Marshal."

Young Liam then grinned mischievously. "Father, don't you think, in the circumstances, the occasion calls for a bottle from Grandfather's store?"

Tom Storey smiled wryly and Bradley made a puzzled frown. The headman explained, "My dear old father — the Gods bless his memory — had an ancient contraption for refining wine that some of our villagers occasionally make from potato water. You must have seen such devices, for removing much of the liquid and leaving the intoxicating liquor behind. Those who've tried it reckon it to be highly potent. It's vile stuff in my opinion — I never took to it. When the old man died, he left a store of about thirty bottles in the cellar, *which we seldom touch*."

He emphasised these last few words, glancing pointedly at his two sons, who appeared at once to be studiously interested in their cutlery.

Bradley smiled. "I think that degree of celebration would be premature just now," and the brothers grinned and shrugged.

Tom Storey's face also cracked into a smile, but after a short silence his expression grew more serious and he turned to Bradley. "What do you think the chances are they'll come tonight?"

The Marshal put down his mug and looked out at the tranquil twilight. "Very high. They'll want revenge for what we did to them last night. They'll have had time to re-group by now and an attack in the dark's bound to be their best hope."

The younger Storey brother chipped in, "But they're leaderless, Marshal and they haven't any horses."

"They were leaderless, Liam, but a day's long enough for one of them to have established his authority. And short enough for their anger still to be burning. As for horses, Ashwell's barely two leagues away. Even on foot through the forest it's less than half a day's trek. My guess is that they're out there in the forest even while we sit here eating, just waiting for nightfall."

For the first time he saw a pallor of fear wash over the young lad's face, though he was clearly trying hard to suppress it.

"Don't worry. We're ready for them. We hold the superior position. We're as well prepared as a village can ever be to repel an attack. Our warriors are well drilled and know exactly what's expected of them. The enemy, on the other hand, is nothing more than a rabble. We'll defeat them, for sure." He hoped his words were convincing. He also prayed that they were true.

Tom Storey said, "Marshal, there's one thing that's been troubling me."

"Let's hear it, Tom. If there's something I've overlooked, don't keep it to yourself."

"Tell me, what was the successful opening action, both in the raiders' attack on Crowtree and in your own assault on their encampment at Ashwell last night?"

He didn't feel a need to respond, but Jack voiced the undeniable answer.

"Flaming arrows!"

"Yes lad," his father acknowledged. "Flaming arrows — a most effective and destructive means of causing major havoc and mayhem. And though I've racked my brains I can think of no certain method of thwarting such tactics."

Bradley sat back in his chair and nodded slowly. "I've thought about that as well, Tom. But I didn't raise it because, like you, I know of no defence against the firing of village buildings. Even though our fortifications should do their job, the raiders might still inflict untold damage on your homes and storehouses."

Then Sylvia said, "If only the heavens would deliver a downpour, the roofs and walls would be too wet to catch fire."

Tom Storey looked up at an almost clear sky. "There's no chance of that today, I fear."

"No, Tom," Bradley said, rising urgently from his seat. "But your genius of a daughter has just given me an idea. Eat up, you young warriors. There's more work to be done!"

* * * * *

"But Marshal," Sylvia protested, "there's not enough cloud for a downpour." Then she gasped and added with wide-eyed innocence, "Do you know a way to make the rain fall?"

He smiled and replied, "No, Sylvia, you'll see no acts of wizardry from me this evening. But what you said suggested something that might give us at least a little extra protection and perhaps work some magic in the minds of the enemy."

Standing by the bell, he looked out across the clearing into the swiftly falling darkness. Just like the night before, a near-full moon was rising and would later provide sufficient light for both sides to see each other's blood stain the village ground. As ever though, the lowering woods looked dark and sombre, revealing few of their secrets and providing ideal cover to any potential attacker.

She followed his gaze and gave voice to his thoughts. "They're watching us, aren't they?"

"Yes, I believe so. And if they are, I think we should put on a show for them. Ring the bell for me, will you — four quick peals to summon the platoon leaders."

Jack was already close by and his father only a couple of strides away, watching and listening while he wiped some chicken grease from his lips with the back of his hand. The other two lieutenants, Rajeev Shah and the blacksmith's son, Ryan Benson, had soon joined them and all three stood attentively to receive their orders.

Bradley's first thoughts were for his troops' well being.

"Has everyone eaten?" All nodded.

"Good. We're still on full alert, of course. I want half of each platoon to take ladders to the thatched or wooden dwellings and stores closest to the barricades. But only those that are visible from the forest. Collect as many buckets as you can, fill them from the stream and dowse the rooftops with water."

The three looked at one another in puzzlement and Ryan Benson voiced their concern. "But we haven't the manpower to drench all the vulnerable buildings. And when they see what we're doing, won't the raiders be provoked to attack straight away?"

Tom Storey nodded thoughtfully and spoke up to dispel their doubts.

"I suspect that's exactly what the Marshal is trying to do. Am I right, Dominic?"

"Yes. In the cover of a moonless night and with more warriors, we might dampen the roofs sufficiently to thwart a volley of flaming arrows. But I'm tired of playing this waiting game. It's time we took control. If they're going to attack, let's force them to do it soon, while we're fully alert. Let them think we're trying to protect our buildings. If they're planning to use fired arrows, they'll have to do it before we can finish. As soon as they make their move, Sylvia will ring the bell for battle stations. That'll be the signal to stop drenching and take up positions."

"What if they don't rise to our bait?" Jack asked.

Bradley allowed himself a vengeful sneer. "Then we'll hook our line with a bigger worm. We'll haul out their leader and make as if to execute him. That should be enough to provoke them."

The headman frowned at this suggestion. "Would you really do that?"

"If I thought it would save the village, Tom, I have to say — yes, I would do it. But if the pretence of finishing him doesn't flush them out, I'd sooner save his live hide so he can stand trial for his crimes."

Storey looked relieved.

Bradley went on, "Get some of your other warriors to check that no foodstuffs are stored in the buildings along the perimeter. They should have been moved away to the interior of the village anyway. We can't afford to lose anything of value apart from the buildings themselves. I don't want anybody to waste time and effort trying to put out fires. That's what they'll expect us to do — that, after all, is the reason for such a distraction. We must conserve our resources and energies to fight off the outlaws, even if that means sacrificing some of the buildings. And once everyone's taken up battle positions, I want no action from anyone until you hear the attack signal — repeating rapid peals on the bell."

Ryan asked, "Should we start shooting as soon as the raiders emerge from the forest?"

He shook his head. "No. I'd rather we conserve our arrows till they're closer — those who don't fall foul of the stakes and pits anyhow. Nobody shoots until they hear the rapid peals."

The implications of this strategy told on the face of each young warrior, and he realised that probably none of them had killed a human being. Now they waited, thoughtful and attentive, for his remaining orders.

He spoke quietly. "I want you all to know that I'm proud of you, whatever happens tonight. But I don't doubt the outcome. You're better equipped, better trained and better prepared than that gang of thugs hiding in the woods. Let them come now, because we're ready for them!"

They grinned at his words of cheer.

Then he said, "If I'm killed or badly injured, Jack will assume battle command, then Rajeev, then you, Ryan. Of course, you'll look to Tom Storey for your overall leadership. Is all this clear?"

Now with serious faces, each of them nodded.

"Then go now, and prepare for battle."

Chapter Eight
The Battle Of Crowtree

Appointed warriors busied themselves with ladders, shields, buckets and wheelbarrows, while others assumed battle positions and prepared for the attack that they all now knew must come soon. Bradley made one final check of the perimeter, finding each stationed warrior ready and nothing out of place. Making his way along the trenches, he met Jack.

"Don't you find this waiting nerve-wracking, Marshal?"

"It won't be long now, Jack. The trick is to keep busy. Remind your warriors to use the protection of walls, fences and buildings till the action starts. It's probably unnecessary but it'll give them something else to think about."

Jack nodded and went off to re-check his platoon's positioning.

Bradley joined Sylvia at the alarm bell, where they waited for the enemy to make their move. Behind them knelt the young boy whose job it would be to prime and re-load their crossbows once the battle started. An uneasy proposal, but the elders agreed that the whole village would be fighting for its life and everyone who was willing and able should play their part. For protection, these "arrow urchins" crouched behind wooden barriers fashioned out of thick planks.

Bradley turned and winked at their urchin. "All right?" he whispered.

The lad, who couldn't have been more than nine years old, nodded excitedly, while he and Sylvia exchanged nervous glances.

Bradley looked across the open ground between the barricades and the forest, wondering what terrors the eerie blackness might hold. The sky was darkening now, with clouds building from the east, threatening to obscure the light of the rising moon. Would the raiders launch their attack while they could at least see what they were doing? Or would they take their chances in the confusion of darkness?

All that afternoon and still even now, an intricate web of tactics and strategy crisscrossed his racing mind. He wondered whether a similar process occupied another brain somewhere out there in the forest. Had someone managed to impose his will upon the remaining rabble and if so, did that person command the loyalty of his troops, as he believed he did of his own? And had the new raider leader set up lines of communication so that all would act as one — a difficult task when your fighting force is spread out in uncharted woodland? Or would the attack be a random confusion of brute force, to smother and overwhelm his loyal but unproven army of otherwise peaceful farmers? But he realised such questions were futile, so again he resorted to a prayer that the Gods of the Wall would be with the villagers of Crowtree this night. There was nothing more he could do.

A cloud passed across the moon.

His eyes were drawn towards a glow in the sky above his head and a mocking *swish* as a burning arrow sped towards the nearest rooftop just behind him.

"Sound battle stations, Sylvia."

She'd kept a tight grip on the hammer since they'd taken up their position and now determinedly struck several repeating series of strikes against the ancient metal.

On hearing the signal, the bucket brigade ceased their roof dampening and rushed to their battle positions to take up arms. Several more flaming arrows flew hissing from the forest and Bradley turned and raised his head as much as he dared without breaking cover to check on their effect. So far he detected no telltale glows of ignited thatch. The drenching must have had some practical use after all. But then he heard the loud *whine* of a more organised volley of arrows, whose burning cargo took hold of the roof of one of the taller barns, too lofty for the platoons to scale with their ladders. The fire soon had the dry thatch well ablaze and without dousing would quickly spread to the wooden walls. Thankfully, due to the young warriors' efforts, it was now empty of valuable foodstuffs, except for a few bales of last season's rotting straw.

Above the crackle of the inferno that issued from the burning barn, Bradley thought he heard a cheer rise up from the forest.

The outlaws must be thinking they'd scored a major strike and that the villagers would divert their energies to fighting the fire.

Not so. Instead, all remained calm within the barricades and, as instructed, not one of the villagers stirred.

He blessed them for their obedience and almost smelt the seething indignation of the confused outlaws. He hoped doubts would be arising about their new leader's abilities to predict the villagers' reactions. He heard shouting and tones that he hoped implied dissent and he guessed that, whatever orders their new leader was now issuing, it was going to be a case of every man for himself.

There were no more flaming arrows. Peering through the darkness to his left, Bradley made out the forms of three raiders charging out of the shadows. Then, over to his right, four more emerged, running and yelling and brandishing short swords. Others followed from various points along the forest rim, waving their weapons, screaming and cursing for all they were worth. Still his warriors made no move.

Now the darkness afforded by the cloud cover began to work in the villagers' favour. The rabble army rushed headlong into the flimsy wicker fencing, trampling it down with contempt. But what met them then came as a complete surprise. Bradley smiled with satisfaction when he heard first one, then another of the ragged vanguard fall with a sickening *squelch* onto the sharpened business end of well-sited clusters of stakes. The pinioned victims struggled and groaned, but stayed firmly impaled while guts and blood oozed out and the last dregs of life drained away. In his immediate sight Bradley counted five or six who thus either perished outright or were mortally wounded.

Then another wave of raiders ran out of the forest. With eyes more accustomed to the darkness, they carefully skirted around the bodies and barricades. This second front seemed equally resolute, now deftly dodging the villagers' clumsy defences.

But they were in for a different surprise. All along the village boundary, where more wary attackers avoided the spikes, groups of them suddenly disappeared from sight, swallowed up by the trenches. Again there were splintering crunches, howls and cries as the attackers fell foul of the lethal spikes awaiting them at the bottom of the pits. Bradley reckoned half the opposing force had already been immobilised — and the defending warriors had so far not let fly one single arrow in defence.

From the disastrous progress of their vanguard, the remaining raiders must know by now to avoid the barricades and pits. A few chose to slink silently away into the forest at the sight and sound of the carnage before them. But the rest — twenty or more — now rushed out, mad with anger and baying for blood, across the open ground towards the village dwellings.

It was time for action. Bradley nodded to Sylvia to strike the bell rapidly, so that every warrior knew that the real battle had at last begun. Almost immediately, he shot one raider and was already taking aim with his second bow, while the arrow urchin just behind him primed his spent weapon. If he'd ever doubted the worth of using these youngsters to keep the crossbows charged, now in the fury of actual battle, he realised just how indispensable they were.

Sylvia next claimed her first enemy casualty, a wild-eyed, ugly brute of a man who'd leapt to the spot in front of her with an axe aimed directly at her head. The figure looked stupefied in its collapse, arm still raised but letting fall its weapon, the flights of Sylvia's arrow festooning its open mouth. The metal-tipped shaft, now clogged with bits of brain and bone, protruded from the back of its open, bleeding skull. The ruffian's expression was one more of surprise than of pain, as if the man were amazed to perish at the hand of such a young girl.

Similar scenes were acted out across the compound, as the disciplined Crowtree warriors applied their well-honed skills against the desperate rabble.

Inevitably, the villagers suffered some casualties, where a wildly aimed axe found yielding flesh and bone, or a thrashing knife sliced into an exposed limb. But each assailant paid dearly for his luck, either with an arrow through the heart, or by swift decapitation from a sharp sword wielded by some other Crowtree warrior. It wasn't long before what remained of the marauding band realised that for them the battle was lost. Some dropped their weapons and fell to their knees pleading for mercy. Others made their escape and retreated, cowed or injured, into the relative safety of the black, all-enveloping forest.

As the last retreating raider fled into the night, Bradley ordered Sylvia to sound the alarm to muster the platoon leaders.

"Jack, I want you to position your warriors around the edge of the compound. Have them watch out for any returning attackers. It's unlikely they'll try anything, but you never know."

He looked around. "Wait. Where's Ryan Benson?"

A member of young Benson's platoon approached, a lad of no more than fifteen years, who blurted tearfully, "He's been hit, Marshal! He's over there!"

The boy pointed to where a group of villagers were huddled. Bradley rushed across and pushed his way through to see. The warrior lay face down, the haft of a large knife protruding from the middle of his back. He knelt and felt Ryan's neck for a pulse, but slowly shook his head. He heard a commotion behind him and moved aside to make way for Mistress Benson. The distraught mother fell to her knees, wailing loudly over her son's body, while her husband stood ashen-faced and silent behind her. After a while he gently raised her up, then bent and effortlessly lifted the fallen warrior to take him home.

News of Ryan Benson's death soon spread through the village, quelling any rejoicing for the victory and laying a shroud of gloom over the community.

Tom Storey approached Bradley and placed a hand on his shoulder. Neither of them spoke. They just stood and watched the villagers quietly clearing away the carnage, the mess and detritus that would forever be remembered as the Battle of Crowtree.

After a while Bradley said, "The Benson family should be honoured for their sacrifice, Tom. Will you organise a ceremony tomorrow?"

"Of course."

"Any other casualties?"

"Thanks be to the Gods — very few. The Ashwad boys took a couple of nasty gashes — they're being tended to. Otherwise, just minor cuts and bruises. Few of the hand-to-hand conflicts lasted long. None of the raiders who made it through the fortifications was a match for our warriors. They showed little skill in close combat beyond their brute strength."

"They got more than they'd bargained for, Tom. All credit to our young men and women."

An arrow urchin ran excitedly past them, whooping and yelling in accompaniment to an improvised victory dance. Tom Storey grabbed his arm and gathered him in for a hug.

"And children, Marshal." He released the lad to continue his celebration. In other circumstances his dancing and shouting might have been infectious and indeed a few other boys and girls did join in the game. But the hearts of the older warriors and villagers were too heavy to rejoice in their victory on account of the loss of Ryan Benson.

The third platoon leader Rajeev Shah approached them. "You summoned us, Marshal. Jack's posting his people around the perimeter, just like you said. Have you any orders for my platoon?"

"Yes, Rajeev. There's still plenty to do. Some of it can wait until tomorrow. But we ought to clear away the raiders' bodies — at least those that have fallen inside the compound. If Tom can allocate a suitable store as a morgue, tell your troops to drag them in there for the time being. And place a guard. I don't want any of the children stumbling across them."

"Yes, Marshal," said Shah. "And what of the bodies on the barricades and in the trenches?"

"If you can, remove the corpses from the perimeter spikes and take them to the morgue for now. But take care in the dark to avoid the pits. The bodies in the trenches will have to wait till daylight. We'll need ropes to lift them safely. When you've moved the others your platoon can stand down and get some rest. But I want you to muster again at first light."

Shah nodded that he understood. While he moved away Bradley added, "Rajeev, ask one of Ryan's warriors to come and see me, will you?"

"Yes, Marshal."

Bradley turned to the headman and said, "Poor young Benson's troops will be harbouring vengeful feelings after losing their leader. And there's one last unpleasant job that needs taking care of before we can turn in."

As soon as he'd said this, two members of Ryan's platoon came forward and stood attentively to receive their orders.

"I want your platoon to break into groups of three, with a good archer in each group for protection. Take torches around the perimeter and look for any wounded raiders whose lives might be saved. If you find any, bring them into the village to be tended. If any are close to death, put them out of their misery. But on no account are you to enter the forest. Is that clear?"

The teenagers nodded and scurried off to muster their comrades.

Tom Storey said, "Marshal, how will those boys know which raiders' lives might be saved?"

"I doubt they'll find any, Tom. But I don't want to send them off to bed only feeling an empty grief for the loss of their platoon leader. If a sword through a dead man's heart relieves them of their pent-up thirst for vengeance, it'll have been a useful exercise."

The headman looked perplexed. "Marshal, I'm not sure I can condone…"

Bradley grabbed his arm. "War is a journey of self-discovery, Tom. The hearts of these youngsters have to stay hardened, for they may have to fight again before peace returns to Fenwold. If they find wounded raiders still breathing, they'll have to decide for themselves what to do. Whatever their choice, I don't think we should interfere."

The perimeter guard having been posted under Jack Storey's command, his father organised the other platoons to take their turn on watch through the night. Bradley then announced that little more remained to be done and that everyone else should rest until morning. Without commotion, then, the villagers went off to their beds in anticipation of some well-earned, restful sleep.

CHAPTER NINE
IN THE VIPERS' NEST

"By the Gods, whatever is that?"

Amelia Storey awoke later than usual and prodded her husband to sample the strange aroma that drifted in through their open bedroom window.

Many of the villagers slept in and awoke feeling ravenous. But in most cases regal appetites weren't just the result of the previous night's exertions. Rather it was the delicious smoky smell on the air that set hunger pangs twitching and taste buds salivating. It had about it the salty sweetness of barbecued pork. Several heads of household stuck their noses outdoors to discover the source and then upon realising its nature, drew them swiftly back in again. Once folk had had the source explained to them, stimulated appetites gave way to feelings of nausea and a widespread reluctance to face any breakfast at all.

Tom said to his wife, "Surely you know the smell of human cremation, Amelia. The Marshal told me last night he'd be organising the disposal of the raiders' corpses early this morning. Better that than risk disease and infection from putrefying flesh. After all, we all end up on the funeral pyre sooner or later."

His wife grimaced and said, "Oh, Tom, please don't..." And she reached for a kerchief to hold up to her face.

Later there'd be a more solemn, formal cremation of the body of brave young Ryan Benson, fallen in battle. Meanwhile Bradley wasted neither time nor formality in getting rid of the bodies of the slain attackers. Everyone understood and was grateful for this, but the sickly sweetness would hang over the village as a morbid reminder for several days afterwards.

85

At breakfast, while the Storey family picked at their food, the subject of cremation was carefully avoided. In any case the headman was still crowing over their success in battle, much to Bradley's embarrassment.

"Marshal, I don't need to tell you how grateful we all are to you for leading us to victory last night. But tell me, what will you do now? Are you planning to move on and help other villages?"

"Not yet, Tom. I do have other assignments planned, of course. But my work here isn't finished yet. When they're fit and able, we have to prepare the young people of Ashwell to re-take their village and clear out what remains of the raider rabble. After that, we'll see."

"You're a good man, Marshal. We'll not forget what you've done here."

Feeling his face flushing, Bradley shook his head and looked around the table. "All I've done is to show you all what you're capable of."

It fell to the mistress of the house to spare him further embarrassment, by bringing in a foaming jug of beer and demanding, "Come on now, if you can't eat, then surely you must be thirsty?"

* * * * *

Just before noon, Bradley approached Tom Storey while he mended a fence in the yard.

"Tom, I've been thinking about the pits and barricades. I hope you'll keep them in good repair, in case of any future attack?"

"Of course. I'd no intention of dismantling them. We invested much time and toil in their making. We'd be fools to waste all that effort."

"Good. But, as we've seen how lethal they can be, I think they should be fenced off from children and straying animals."

"That makes good sense. I'll get some of the warriors onto it right away. And while we're at it we'll repair the camouflage fencing where it's been breached."

He turned to resume his work, but Bradley didn't leave, still having something on his mind. The headman must have sensed this, for he stopped what he was doing and leaned on a spar of the repaired fence. For once the Marshal had trouble framing his words and it was left to Storey to fill the silence.

"Marshal, you'll recall that I didn't extend you a particularly warm welcome when you first arrived here."

He dismissed the elder's comment with a wave of his hand. But Storey ploughed on.

"I believe I made my reasons clear. I was concerned about the potential danger to our young people. As village leader and a father it's my duty to be protective. But now I see how misguided I was. I'm truly proud of the qualities you've brought out in our sons and daughters in the short time you've been here. It's an honour to me that my own son, Jack, has achieved high office among the ranks of your volunteers. I know he'd be proud to become one of your deputies. And I want you to know that — if that's your wish — I'll not stand in his way."

Bradley hadn't planned to be drawn just yet on the question of selection of deputy marshals. But he'd intended discussing the matter soon with Storey before making his final choices. He looked around and since no one appeared to be in earshot, he saw no harm in sharing his thoughts with the headman.

"As you've guessed, I'm thinking of offering Jack one of the positions," he said. "But I think it best for him to remain here as resident deputy for the district. His first task will be to show the Ashwell youth how to defend and fortify their settlement. From the day I leave he'll exercise my authority and represent the Council's law in the vicinity of the two villages."

"I'm certain Jack will accept your offer — except that..."

"I know, Tom. He probably hoped I'd ask him ride with me. Believe me, if I let my heart decide, your son would my first choice. He has the makings of a first class warrior. I'm sure he'd accept if I asked him to come and I'd be glad to have him as my companion. But, being your son, he already carries some authority — enough for the villagers to accept him as resident peacekeeper. There can be no better choice. Honestly, this is a big sacrifice on my own part, but my head tells me over and over again that it's the right decision."

"As usual, Marshal, your reasoning is impeccable. And I don't deny that — speaking for my good wife and myself — this is the best possible outcome. And I'm sure Jack has the maturity to accept your judgment. So, whom have you in mind to ride with you?"

"As headman, that's something I'd like to have your advice upon," came the diplomatic response.

"My advice?" The old man took time to collect his thoughts. "Well, until yesterday I'd have recommended young Ryan. But that's not an option any more. He'll be a great loss to the village in many ways. He was skilled in the blacksmith's trade and, like his father, could turn his hand to making just about anything out of next to nothing. He was a big youth and perhaps not so swift in action as some of the others. The Shah boy is a little younger, but he's a capable lad — quick, keen and intelligent. Rajeev's also a brilliant horseman, though he's not much of a talker. With Ryan out of the picture, I can think of no one with better qualities."

He paused just then and a mischievous smile lit up his face.

"Wait though. Now that I think about it, I do know of one contender who'll be mightily disappointed when they learn they're out of the running."

"Oh? Who's that then? Ah, you must be referring to Archie Forrester. He performed well on our raiding mission, but I'm afraid he's not confident enough yet to ride out as a deputy. In time, maybe..."

Storey chuckled. "No, it's not young Forrester. Mind you, the person I'm thinking of is about the same age — in years, at least. And confidence isn't a quality this person lacks to any degree."

Bradley shook his head, confounded as to who this mystery candidate might be.

It seemed Storey was enjoying the game and keen to prolong the agony. "Tell me, when you're out and about on your inspections and duties, whose face do you see whenever you turn around, ready to give advice — whether asked for or not? Who's often at your side and taking mental note of nearly everything you say and do, for reporting back to the family kitchen each evening?"

The dawn of enlightenment illuminated Bradley's face.

"What? You can't mean Sylvia. She isn't... She's only... She's just a..."

"Just a girl, Marshal? Only seventeen? Not strong enough?" Storey laughed again. "I'm sorry, but if you're going to leave here in one piece with anyone but my daughter at your side, you're going to have to come up with a far more plausible excuse than any of those!" And he emitted a devilish chuckle that was infectious, causing Bradley's pained expression to give way to an embarrassed smile and then to an outright belly laugh. He grabbed the headman's arm and snorted, "Well, Tom, that's a problem I'll have to sort out nearer the time!"

Storey offered some tongue-in-cheek solace with the suggestion, "I suppose when you want to leave you could always slip away at dead of night. We'll have to keep her tied up for a couple of weeks though!"

Bradley let out a heavy sigh. The joke was wearing a bit thin, but he didn't want to show his annoyance to his host. "If all else fails, I hope I can rely on you to forbid any such notion on Sylvia's part. You've done as much before in my presence."

"True. Trouble is, to forbid my daughter to take any course of action always seems to result in her striving even harder to persuade me to change my mind. But I promise I'll be firm with her. Don't worry."

Bradley's relief was visible. "Thanks for that, Tom — and for drawing the matter to my attention. It just goes to show, even a marshal can't be expected to notice everything."

The headman turned to take up his work again, but Bradley still lingered, so he stopped and said, "Is something else bothering you?"

"Well, yes. There is one practical matter we need to talk about."

Storey leaned on the fence again. "Of course. What is it?"

"It's to do with the raider leader. What do we do with him now?"

"Well, he'll have to go on trial — that goes without saying. Apart from leading that criminal gang, we know he caused the death of Megan Beckett during his raid on our store. He must at least answer for that."

"Yes, I agree. Justice has to be done, for the sake of the rule of law." Then he hesitated, finding it hard to put directly into words the question foremost in his mind. "I've not travelled extensively, Tom. I know the customs of my own region naturally, but since I've never visited the southwest before now, I'm not sure how..."

Storey allowed himself a broad grin when it dawned on him just what was troubling Bradley.

"Ah, you mean, what's our established method of execution?"

"Yes, that's it. Is it hanging, decapitation, or what?"

"It's been many years since we've had to execute anyone round here, I'm glad to say. Local folk are, in the main, law-abiding and don't go around killing one another. There's been the odd child molester. I recall when I was a young man a little girl was abducted and the culprit turned out to be a chap from Ashwell. He confessed, soon after the poor kid's body was found. Pathetic character, he was. There was no question about it — he would have to forfeit his life. In the end he was locked up with a knife and he had the decency to open a vein."

The Marshal shrugged. "Hmm. I doubt if our red-headed raider's the suicidal type."

"No," Storey agreed. "I suppose not. Well, before the child molester, there was a vagrant who killed one of the villagers for his horse. The horse was lame, so he was easily caught. He was executed the old-fashioned way."

"Old-fashioned way? What? Hanging?"

"No, no. We've never favoured that. It can take far too long. Unless done skilfully, you end up leaving a half-dead man dying a lingering death in the forest. It upsets the children. No. The murderer was lashed to a plank that was then up-ended and plunged into a barrel of water."

"Ah, that'll be it then. Execution by drowning."

As he walked away, more or less satisfied with this important if gruesome item of local knowledge, Storey called out to him, "Of course, he can always opt to take his chances on the Wall. No one can be denied that, wherever you go in Fenwold."

"Ah, yes." Bradley stopped, turned back momentarily and nodded to acknowledge that he understood. "The Wall."

* * * * *

After lunch, the villagers gathered to pay their respects and cremate the remains of Ryan Benson. Following the ceremony, Bradley called a meeting of the village elders, to which those Ashwell counterparts who were fit enough were also invited. Without beating about the bush, he outlined his plans for the next few days.

"I'm sure you'll all agree that our next objective must be to reunite the people of Ashwell with their homes and property."

There were nods of approval all round.

"Now I know — and fully understand — that some of the younger people of Ashwell in particular are impatient to act straight away. That would be a mistake, because we've no idea of the strength of the remaining raider force that might still be holed up there. An indiscriminate attack could prove disastrous for us. So I want you to ask your people to please be patient and allow me to make the proper preparations."

One of the Ashwell elders called out, "What preparations do we need? We've sufficient warriors to ride in and wipe them out now!"

The Marshal held up his hands when other Ashwell elders murmured their agreement. "Yes, you're probably right. We've killed several of them, so their numbers can't be great. But an ill-prepared raid, even if successful, could cost us lives in the process. I'm sorry, but I'm not prepared to sacrifice a single young warrior just to satisfy everyone's natural impatience — which I share, believe me. Let me explain what I want to do."

"All right, Marshal," said the same man. "You've not let us down so far. Explain away."

"This morning, I sent out patrols along the woodland tracks between here and Ashwell, to find and eliminate any stragglers from last night's battle. I expect them to report back here by dusk. If I'm satisfied that we can ride freely between the two villages, I'll lead a reconnaissance party to Ashwell later this evening. This will be simply to establish the strength of the raiders' presence in the village. Based on this intelligence, I'll determine what size of force is needed to launch an attack tomorrow."

"Good," said the Ashwell elder. "Our young men will be more than willing to play their full part in your mission tonight and in the re-taking of our village tomorrow."

Bradley rubbed his chin and thought for a moment. Then he said, "All right. Select your two best men. I'll brief them later this afternoon."

After the elders dispersed he took Tom Storey to one side.

"Tom, I'm not at all happy about this. However keen their boys are, I'm afraid they'll be a hindrance on this mission. It won't require a large force. Three at the most would be enough. But I need trained warriors alongside me, not raw recruits."

"It's a matter of diplomacy, Marshal. It's important to involve the people of Ashwell in the liberation of their own properties. I already know young Adam Genney is expecting to be involved. You can't blame him either, since he lost both his parents in the siege. It's understandable if he's bitter and angry."

"Yes, I can see that. But I've heard some of the young Ashwell lads talking. Their language is over-zealous and in some cases downright belligerent. Don't get me wrong, Tom. After the atrocities they've witnessed and their foul treatment at the raiders' hands, I can forgive them for that. But in a delicate reconnaissance mission, any careless action could prove disastrous."

After some thought Storey said, "Why not take the two Ashwell lads as well as two of our own? As it's strictly a reconnaissance mission, tell them they're only to observe and to do nothing provocative. That should work, shouldn't it?"

"I hope so, Tom."

* * * * *

As he led the reconnaissance party towards Ashwell, Bradley still wasn't sure he'd done the right thing. Four horsemen rode with him: trusty Crowtree lieutenants Forrester and Shah and the two Ashwell volunteers, Max Reynolds and Adam Genney. Their induction had comprised a short lecture on the importance of discipline and adherence to his orders at all times. The two were by now passably fit, after some decent feeding at the tables of the hospitable folk of Crowtree, and keen to the degree of razor sharpness — almost too keen, in fact. They weren't bad bowmen either, each having hit their mark when put to the test. Perhaps his worries were misplaced.

The patrols sent into the forest earlier in the day had reported no contact with remnants of the previous night's defeated raiding party. So Bradley figured that all of the survivors must have returned to Ashwell to regroup as best they could. He now needed to know their number and what weaponry they possessed. That would be enough for now. Based on the intelligence they'd collect tonight, he'd work out a strategy for moving in and re-taking the village tomorrow.

He turned in his saddle to address his small troop. "It's dusk now, so it'll be dark when we reach Ashwell. There's not much cloud and there'll be a moon to help us see what's going on. To cause the least commotion we'll approach the village on foot via the forest track, leaving our horses tethered away from the main bridleway and well out of sight. The plan is to skirt the village in two groups: Shah, Forrester and Reynolds in one, Genney and me in the other. All we're going to do tonight is observe the strength of their force, so it's vital we keep out of sight. On no account are we to engage the enemy, unless attacked first. Is that understood?"

All four nodded, but then Genney drew a large hunting knife and boasted, "Let them attack us and they'll feel some of this cold steel!"

Bradley bit his tongue and only said, "That's not going to be necessary, lad. Put that blade away."

When they reached the empty stockade, the group split up and went in opposite directions. The idea was to maintain cover well within the confines of the forest undergrowth and meet on the other side of the village, observing as they proceeded.

About halfway, Bradley caught sight of an outlaw kneeling to light a fire in the clearing just beyond the stockade. As the man reached for some dry sticks to feed the flickering flame he happened to turn his head so that they had a better view of him. Genney stopped in his tracks and pulled out his knife.

"That bastard slew my cousin!" he hissed. Then, to Bradley's dismay and amazement, the youngster dashed towards the figure, with his arm raised and ready to exact revenge.

But before he could make contact, an unseen raider shouted, "Clamp! Look out!"

The kneeling outlaw turned and rose to meet his attacker, at the same time drawing his own knife from the belt around his waist. The two stood locked in combat, Genney struggling for supremacy in the face of Clamp's superior strength.

Bradley acted instinctively then. Drawing his own knife, he ran straight to Genney's aid and pulled the raider away, allowing the lad to run off into the undergrowth. But at that moment two more outlaws appeared, crossbows loaded, barely four strides away from Bradley. He was outnumbered. The bowmen had him in their sights and he knew there was nothing he could do. He released his grip on Clamp and let his weapon fall.

"Hands in the air — now!" one of the raiders yelled.

He complied. Then Clamp turned around to face him, drew back his arm and fetched him a blow squarely on the jaw that sent him sprawling to the ground. Clamp knelt and grabbed his arm, roughly rifled through his tunic and withdrew his embroidered emblem of office. He stood up and showed it to the others.

As Bradley's consciousness faded, the last thing he heard was Clamp's voice crowing, "Well, look here now! Looks like we've caught ourselves a real live Council Marshal!"

CHAPTER TEN
A SECRET CHAMPION

Clamp leaned over Bradley's unconscious body and squinted in the firelight to check out his features.

"Let's have a good look at him. Yeah, I thought so. This is definitely the bastard who was yellin' out the orders to the Crowtree peasants last night. Bradley, they call him. Well, he's yelled his last order. Where did my knife go?"

The weapon glinted a couple of strides away, where he and the Marshal had struggled moments earlier. One of the other outlaws reached over to pick it up and handed it to him. Clamp grabbed it, then placed the blade close up against the lawman's throat, ready to drive it in and sever his windpipe.

With a sneer he said, "Pity he's out. I'd sooner let him have some of what I gave his snivellin' deputy."

The second archer, silent so far, coughed and said, "Wait though, Clamp. He might be worth more to us alive."

Clamp turned his head. With some of his authority eroded after last night's failed raid, he'd found it expedient at least to feign interest in ideas other than his own. "Eh? What do you mean? Are you crazy, man? We'll have to clear out of here soon. We can't leave him loose to follow us! I say we slit his gullet here and now!"

But the man pressed his point. "Look, if we play this the right way, we might not have to clear out of here. That'd be better than a life on the run, wouldn't it?"

Clamp was only half convinced. "I don't know. I reckon with their marshal dead, the Crowtree lot won't have the stomach to follow us anyway. We'd be free to set up somewhere else."

"That's a big gamble to take, though, don't you think? I reckon, if we had something to bargain with, we might just be able to work out a way to stay here and..."

"And what?" Clamp sneered. "Become bleedin' farmers?"

"No, I don't mean that. But we've got a Council marshal here and when he's dead, he's worth nothing to us. If he's alive, he might be worth something to us. Listen, if he's been such a big help to those Crowtree peasants, they might want him back, or at least want him alive. And if they want that bad enough, well, maybe there'd be something in it for us."

Clamp paused. "A ransom, d'you mean?"

"Who knows? All I'm sayin' is — chances are they'll try and run us out of here soon. Except that now, we've got something to bargain with, see? And yeah, they might even pay to get their precious marshal back."

Clamp sheathed his knife. "All right, but if nothing comes o' this, I want to finish him personally. After last night, I want to see this lawman suffer. Help me tie him up meanwhile — out in the open, so we can all keep an eye on him. From what we've seen so far, he's a tricky sod. Here, I'll knock a stake in near the fire if one o' you two lazy buggers 'll chuck some more wood on. Bring that rope over here. I want a guard on him tonight. Looks like his mate ran off. Get the boys to check round and make sure there's no more of 'em snoopin' around."

"What if we catch any, boss?"

"Kill 'em."

* * * * *

"What do you mean, the Marshal's been taken?" Jack Storey couldn't believe what he was hearing.

"Just that," Rajeev Shah admitted. "When he and Genney didn't rendezvous as planned, we went on further around the village perimeter till we saw some of them armed and standing over him. He looked unconscious. We stayed in the shadows as long as we dared — long enough to hear them talk about holding him for ransom. But we had to come away or else we'd have all been captured."

Sylvia pushed past her brother, bristling with indignation. "Why didn't you do something? How could you just leave him there?" Her red-rimmed eyes were filled with anger. She pounded her fists against Shah's chest.

He grasped her wrists as gently as possible and tried to console her. "Please, Sylvia, we were helpless. We'd finished our reconnaissance and counted at least fifteen of them, all armed to the teeth. For the three of us to have gone in would've meant suicide for us and certain death for the Marshal."

This didn't satisfy her. "What about Genney? What happened to him?"

Archie Forrester said grimly, "We never saw him again. His horse was where he'd tied it, alongside our own. We suspect they got him, though."

Jack Storey spoke for all of them. "What a bloody mess! Well, we're going to have to do something — we can't just leave him to their mercy. After all he's done for us!"

Rajeev said, "Looks like you're in charge, Jack. What do we do now?"

Jack took Forrester and Shah aside and there was much muttering and nodding of heads, as the other young warriors of Crowtree and their hotheaded Ashwell counterparts stood by waiting for Jack's orders.

After a while the three rejoined them and Jack gave his assessment. "For some reason, they're keeping the Marshal alive. But there are at least fifteen of them — all armed and desperate. They'll be on the alert right now and have him well guarded. They'll be more vulnerable early in the morning though. Besides, some of us are bushed and need to rest now. So I want everyone to assemble here just before dawn. Crowtree platoons, the three commanders will carry out a thorough weapons inspection before we all turn in. Rajeev will place two members of his platoon on guard. Ashwell contingent, you may as well retire now. Thanks. And don't worry, we'll all ride in at dawn, rescue the Marshal and clear that rabble out for good and all."

* * * * *

Red's mind was in turmoil. After the living hell of hearing the noise of the battle without being able to lift a finger to help his men, he'd spent all that night wondering if he was going to be left to rot in that stinking shed. Then in the morning the Crowtree swine had given him the gloating news of his gang's defeat. But around midnight he'd heard voices outside planning a dawn assault on the remnants of the Ashwell camp. So, some of his forces must have survived the battle. That was heartening. But were there enough to try another assault? Then he'd overheard a couple of the Crowtree kids bemoaning the capture of their precious Marshal. Having not had much to look forward to except his own trial and presumed execution, he now felt elated that all might not yet be lost. If only he could do something to help his men put these peasants back squarely in their place!

Tantalised by these thoughts, he'd drifted in and out of sleep.

He woke when he felt someone's hand gently touching his shoulder.

As the blurred recollections of hopeful dreams faded, he opened his eyes to see the vague shape of a human figure leaning over him in the darkness. The vision leaned close and held a single finger to its lips, indicating the need for silence.

Nevertheless, he gasped, "What's this? What do you want?"

A hand was placed over his mouth and a voice whispered urgently, "Quiet! We're leaving. No noise now! Can you ride if I support you to a horse?"

Now fully alert, he made no sound, but simply nodded his head. Then, with his rescuer's aid, he limped out of the makeshift cell, noting the prone body of the guard on the ground nearby, a large rock lying beside the bloodied head. Together in the silence the pair hurried to where two steeds were tethered and he was helped up into the saddle.

Moments later the sweating horses were galloping through the forest at breakneck speed, their fugitive riders dodging low branches and briars. Then, when they were far enough away from the village to be out of sight or earshot, they transferred onto the main trail where they made easier progress. With renewed confidence Red wondered if he might shake off his rescuer, but the sight of a loaded crossbow made him think again and he found the shouted instruction "To Ashwell!" acceptable enough for now.

* * * * *

About the raiders' campfire two sentries lolled drowsily at their stations, while several other sleeping figures snored on bedrolls not far away from Bradley, forming a rough semi-circle around him. Coming to, he'd heard them boasting of their atrocities —

especially Clamp, who seemed to relish the re-telling of his cruel torture of Colby. He wished he had his hands around that devil's neck just then. But his wrists were tightly bound and he could do nothing but listen to their bragging and bickering until at last they nodded off.

Now all was silent, save for the occasional spit and crackle from the fire. The night was still gloomy, but the moon broke through occasionally and in the half-light they might have seen that he was now awake, vainly tugging at his fetters. But they all still slept on. For a moment he fancied he heard the sound of distant riders, but he was unsure because his head still spun from the recent blow to his jaw.

Then without warning, the peace of the camp was shattered by the clatter of hooves as the raider leader and a second rider raced into the clearing, abruptly bringing up their steeds within a couple of strides of where he lay tied and gagged.

Muffled in hunters' furs the mystery figure swiftly dismounted and pulled Red from his saddle. He winced when his injured limb struck the hard dusty ground, but his companion didn't release him, now holding a glinting knife blade close up against his throat. Bradley was confused at the sight, but his heart sank to see the monster being returned to his gang.

Several of the disturbed outlaws reached instinctively for their weapons, rising in disbelief and muted excitement.

Then Clamp cried out, "Red! It's Red!" And he hobbled towards his old boss.

"Shut up and stay where you are!" shouted his deliverer. "And put down your weapons, or he gets it — now!"

Clamp turned around and nodded. They did as they were told. But from where he stood he must have noticed something odd about the warrior who so coolly held their leader at knifepoint.

"It's — it's a girl!" he sneered and again limped forwards.

"I may be a girl," Sylvia said, "but I'm still a blink away from ending his life! Now back off! All I've come for is to make an exchange — his life for the Marshal's. You there!" She addressed the sleepy guard nearest to Bradley. "Untie his hands and give him your knife — and no tricks or I'll let your boss have it!"

The bemused guard looked across at Clamp, who nodded again. So he complied and with the knife Bradley cut the fetters binding his feet, then removed the gag from his mouth. Free to speak now, he couldn't help but give voice to his thoughts.

"Sylvia! By the Gods — what are you doing? Are you mad, girl?"

"There's a primed bow and some bolts in the nearest saddlebag, Marshal. Get them, please and mount up. Then lead my horse back towards the main track."

Now she addressed the outlaws again. "I'm going to back up to the gateway over there with your boss so we can get clear. I'll release him then."

Clamp murmured, "If you don't, missy, you're dead for sure."

"All right," she snapped. "But touch your weapons before I release him and I'll slit his throat. And don't think I won't do it."

She forced Red to back up with her until she reached the spot where Bradley held her horse. He then covered the outlaw with the bow she'd brought for him while she mounted, whereupon she took her own weapon to hand once more. Then she reached behind into her saddlebag, handed down three bottles to the outlaw boss and shouted so that everyone heard her, "Just to put a seal on our exchange, here's a present from my grandfather's liquor store. You can drink a toast to your leader's return. Then if you've any sense, you'll all clear out of here!"

In an instant, she and Bradley wheeled the horses round and galloped off up the track before any of the outlaws had a chance to pick up their weapons.

* * * * *

With the best of his unspeakable teeth Red eagerly pulled the stopper from one of Sylvia's gift bottles. He took a generous mouthful, swallowed and then drew a cooling breath to quench the liquor's scorching flame.

The look of rapture on his face contrasted with thirsty grimaces from the gang members who crowded round him. When he raised the bottle for a second pull, murmurs of dissent and jealousy arose from the rabble. So he flung the other two bottles in their direction.

Before his turn came for a taste of the nectar, Clamp said, "Do you think we should do like she said and clear out, Red?"

"Nah!" he slurred, wiping his mouth with the back of his hand. "I overheard 'em planning their next move. They're going to make a panic attack at dawn — they were all turning in before this girl took it on herself to make the swap with her precious Marshal. I

100

wouldn't be surprised if she's got her own plans for the lucky sod tonight!"

As their ribald laughter died down, he added, "We can get some sleep now, but when these jumped-up farmers ride in at first light, we'll be waiting in the trees with our crossbows to pick 'em off like rabbits!"

* * * * *

Barely two furlongs down the road and safely clear of the raiders, Bradley reached over to pull up Sylvia's mount, forcing her to slow to a trot beside him.

"What in the name of the Sacred Wall did you think you were doing back there? Don't you realise you might have got us both killed? I've never seen anything so stupid!"

Then came the sound of hooves from behind and he turned in the saddle to see Jack and Rajeev trotting their own horses out of the forest to join them.

Jack drew alongside them, laughing. "It's good to see you, Marshal. And don't be too hard on Sylvia. You don't really think we'd let her try this without backup, do you? We've merely put into practice the things you've taught us. We've two platoons waiting in the woods back there. When we get the signal that the raiders have had a good drink and are asleep again, we're going in. We wanted to get you back first though and Sylvia volunteered to perform the exchange. It was my decision to let her do it, so yell at me if you must. We made the pretence of a dawn attack at first for the benefit of the Ashwell boys — we needed to ensure they didn't come with us on this one — they're good lads but we couldn't afford any more blunders. Then Sylvia suggested we let Redhead overhear the same plan, stage a fake rescue and throw in the liquor just to be sure. When we go in we'll not only have the element of surprise on our side, but I reckon they'll have trouble finding their weapons, never mind hitting anything with them! So, Marshal, is Sylvia forgiven?"

Bradley shook his head, shrugged and allowed the hint of a smile to break his otherwise fixed expression. Then he sighed and said, "I think we'd better talk about this in the morning. Meanwhile, let's get tonight's job over with. Since this is your operation, Jack, you'd better retain command for now. Just tell me what you want me to do."

The Fenwold Riddle

When the outlaws were sleeping soundly, the platoons went in on foot. With little time for any serious opposition, the two raiders who managed to grab their crossbows were shot dead before they could take aim. The rest, including their now thoroughly confused, drunken and dishonoured leader, were taken prisoner and marched back to Crowtree in a cowed and beaten procession.

Young Adam Genney, whose misplaced enthusiasm had been the cause of Bradley's capture, was never found and all assumed he must have been hit while running off into the undergrowth and his body returned to the earth via the natural habits of the innocent creatures of the forest.

CHAPTER ELEVEN
TRIAL AND EXECUTION

A great weight had lifted from Bradley's shoulders. For the first time he could enjoy his breakfast with Tom Storey and look out of the kitchen window, to see villagers going about their daily duties, happy and smiling, finally free from the threat of attack by desperate outlaws. It was a picture of mundane, blissful normality and it gave him an overwhelming sense of relief. From the look on his face, Storey felt it too.

"Marshal, I always knew that right would prevail in the end."

Bradley nodded and smiled. There was no point in disputing the headman's statement, in spite of his own doubts. It seemed these people were just naturally optimistic. Even so, surely dark premonitions of defeat must sometimes have haunted their dreams? Or maybe the human spirit wouldn't let them imagine such dreadful consequences. He swallowed a mouthful of tea and then lied diplomatically.

"I never doubted it either, Tom."

"Mind you," Storey went on, "I never thought we'd kill or capture the entire gang of 'em, nor that we'd come off so lightly. Of course, any loss is one too many and young Ryan will be honoured for many a year to come."

"I don't believe that glory can ever compensate for lives lost in battle. I suppose you have to witness that to know it's true. I find it hard now to look Dan Benson in the eye without feeling somehow responsible for the death of his son."

"We're all of us responsible. Dan and his wife will pick up the pieces and carry on in the knowledge that young Ryan's name will forever be linked with our victory."

"As will those of the Ashwell villagers who perished, either through wilful neglect or outright violence."

The headman nodded slowly.

Then he said, "I suppose your work's pretty much done here in Crowtree."

"Yes, I reckon it is. I want to thank you and Mistress Storey for the hospitality you've shown me here. You've been like parents to me."

"And will continue to be, Dominic. You'll always be welcome here — you know that. But do you have to leave so soon?"

"Well, I..."

"If I can make a suggestion — why not take a break for a few days? Jack and the others have things in hand now. And the Ashwell folk are beginning to tidy up and re-establish their village. I think you've earned a bit of a rest. In any event, you'll stay for the trial?"

"I wouldn't want to miss it. What's the procedure?"

"What do you do with a half-demented tyrant and thirteen ragged members of his rabble army? We asked the Ashwell survivors to point out the main villains, but only one of the thirteen was identified as an outright murderer — the one they call Clamp."

"I know the man. When they captured me, I overheard him boast about torturing Colby."

"Will you testify to that?"

"Surely."

"We also have witnesses who'll confirm Clamp slaughtered two unarmed Ashwell youths, just because of their misplaced bravado. He and his boss will be tried and, if found guilty, face retribution."

"When will you hold the trial?"

"As soon as possible. We haven't the resources to keep and guard fourteen outlaws for more than a few days. We're keeping Clamp and Red under constant guard, but we've chained up the other twelve and put them to work making repairs and installing fortifications in Ashwell. We've formed a tribunal, consisting of two Ashwell elders and myself. It'll be our job to interview the accused and decide what should be done with them all."

* * * * *

Three days after the raiders' capture, in the early afternoon, the tribunal convened a court in the clearing in front of the Storey household and no able-bodied member of either community failed to attend to hear the verdicts and sentences. The fourteen accused were brought out in their fetters and stood, for the most part cowed and frightened, before their accusers.

Clamp was an exception. In spite of his limp, his eyes were fiery, his head held defiantly upon his square shoulders, contemptuous of the authority of the court that now dared to judge him. He struggled and argued with his guards. Beside him Red, the raider leader, still had difficulty walking and standing because of his thigh wound and had been allowed a makeshift crutch to support his weight. But he showed no emotion and kept silent, as if resigned to his fate.

Tom Storey spoke on behalf of the tribunal, while Bradley looked on, hoping their decisions would be sensible. But he knew he had no authority to argue with them, whatever their verdicts.

"Neighbours, we three, the elected tribunal of the villagers of Crowtree and Ashwell, have interviewed the fourteen raiders before you and will now announce our findings. The two accused of murder — known as Clamp and Red — we'll deal with shortly. I shall turn first to the twelve facing lesser charges, serious though their crimes are. We find these twelve guilty as charged of theft and brutal behaviour towards our good citizens. Lately these men have been put to work in chain gangs rebuilding and fortifying the village of Ashwell. This arrangement has been working well, so it's the tribunal's decision that they'll remain thus enslaved for as long as the elders deem necessary. As a precaution they will each forfeit their index and middle bow fingers."

At this pronouncement there arose some understandable unrest among the twelve men and Clamp smiled while the serious-faced Red only nodded slowly.

Storey raised his voice above the murmur of the crowd. "We stress that this operation is to be performed as humanely as possible and without undue ceremony. If we're to go on record as people concerned with justice, we mustn't demean ourselves by exacting unnecessary revenge. Our punishments must be appropriate and practical."

The hubbub subsided.

"I now turn to the two accused of murder. In each case the tribunal has reached a unanimous guilty verdict and the sentence in each case is execution by drowning, to be carried out immediately."

He then addressed Clamp directly.

"Have you anything to say before the sentence is carried out?"

The cruel outlaw sneered and — so far as he was able — acted out the motions of his next hate-inspired statement. "I violated six of your daughters, Ashwell peasants! I piss on your tribunal! Do your worst, old women!"

The angry crowd hurled shouts and threatening gestures at the outlaw and tried to surge towards him, but was held back by members of the platoons.

Tom Storey only shook his head and intoned sadly, "I accept those as your final words on the subject. Take him away." Three young guards then pulled the struggling outlaw away from the enclosure to his execution and some of the gathered spectators turned to follow.

"Everyone else please remain here!" he ordered. "All deaths are tragedies and the tragedy of that man's fate won't be diminished by making it a public spectacle. His guards know what to do and will carry out the tribunal's sentence forthwith. Besides, we've unfinished business here."

The crowd turned its attention to the redheaded raider leader, to whom Storey now directed his words.

"Have you anything to say before the sentence is carried out?"

Red said nothing for a few moments, as if calmly gathering his thoughts. Then he spoke.

"Looking at your faces, I see your anger, feel your hatred. But I also see that you're men of honour. Not like me. No. I chose my path in life a long time ago. Why waste my breath trying to justify that to the likes of you? Yes, I am guilty of killing that old woman. She got in the way. She was unlucky and, as it turns out, so was I. Your law calls it murder, so what defence do I have? Besides, I've killed people before and I always knew there'd be a day of reckoning. I deserve what's coming to me, I know.

"But I had time to think while I lay festering in that filthy cell. I'm not stupid enough to believe I can throw myself on your mercy. But the old laws allow me one slim chance to save my skin and if you really are men of honour, you won't deny it to me. So, as a citizen of Fenwold, I elect to take my chances on the Wall!"

The crowd was hushed. Although they'd all heard of the option, none present had ever witnessed it — including Bradley.

And if pleasure had any sort of a place at that gathering, he was pleased with the raider's choice, if only because it had to do with the other part of his mission, which as yet he'd disclosed to no one. In fact it presented him with a welcome opportunity, for here was his chance to learn something about the object of his secondary assignment.

The Wall.

* * * * *

Early the following morning, Bradley visited Red in his makeshift cell.

He entered flanked by two armed guards and watched the outlaw rise unaided from his couch.

"I see your wound's healing well," he grudgingly observed.

"Well enough for me to make the climb. How will you get me to the top?"

"You'll get yourself to the top and it won't be easy. There are no trees even half as high as the Wall, nor that can grow close enough in the shallow ground next to it. Its surface is smooth, so attaching anything to it is out of the question. Around here some ivy plants have grown up its face in places, but none reach right to the top. So we've come up with the idea of an extended ladder."

Red raised his eyebrows. "A ladder? How will you make it long enough?"

"By tying shorter ladders together with rope. We've no way of knowing if it'll support your weight. It may well buckle as you climb higher and deliver you to certain death on the forest floor below." And he smiled.

But the outlaw only said calmly, "I reckon I'd prefer that to being up-ended in a barrel of water. And anyway, what if I decide to run for it when you untie me to start the climb?"

"I'd advise against it. The elders have given specific instructions that, should that happen, you're to be shot in the legs, then immediately taken away for drowning. So don't hope for a quick despatch. I hear the gambling men of the community are accepting short odds in favour of that possibility though."

"Really? I hope to disappoint them. I intend to make the climb as best I can. But what help can you give me?"

"Help? I don't know what you mean."

"Well, do I get any food to take with me? And how about some rope?"

"Sorry, no food — and definitely no rope. If we gave you that and you did make it to the top, you might just walk on a few leagues and lower yourself down again. It defeats the object. You'll get a water bottle, but that's all."

"Fair enough. You can't blame me for trying, can you?"

Then he looked thoughtfully at Bradley, almost as if they were acquaintances having a cosy chat over a drink. "Tell me, Marshal, what do you think I'll find up there?"

"I've no idea. To my knowledge, no one who's tried to scale the Wall and made it to the top has ever come down again — on this side anyway. And it's said the top is laid with spikes and traps to stop anyone getting over."

"Have you ever wondered why that might be?"

Bradley suspected the outlaw was trying to establish some empathy with him, by drawing him into a discussion of this nature, probably with a view to changing his mind about the food and rope. Still, guardedly but courteously, he said, "Haven't many men?"

"What's your theory then? Come on, you must have one."

He didn't want to indulge in rash conjecture, especially with a condemned man for whom he had little respect. Every child in Fenwold had silly notions about witches and warlocks and other such theories and he wasn't about to be drawn into listing such ridiculous fantasies. Instead he said, "I keep an open mind. Only the Gods who built the Wall centuries ago knew why it was important to keep us in."

"Or to keep us out."

"Yes, well, in or out, I'm sure they had good reason."

"Hmm. But what if the reason doesn't apply any more?"

Bradley thought it best to close the conversation, so he rose, saying, "You'll be fed for the last time at mid-day. Make the most of it. And be ready to make the climb soon after."

The raider leader's expression changed to a sneer, the time for bargaining for any favours now passed. "All right, Marshal. I suppose I should admit that the better man won. But I'm not dead yet and I promise you this. Whatever your plans and wherever they take you, if I survive I'll hunt you down and kill you if I can. I've a feeling your interest in the Wall's more than just a passing fancy. And who knows, maybe we'll meet again some day on one side or the other."

* * * * *

None of those present had ever seen such a long ladder. Each section had to be attached in turn at the bottom and the whole structure nudged farther up the smooth surface of the Wall, until it reached the top. The faces of the strong young warriors tasked with the nudging looked more and more strained with every addition.

At last the length was judged sufficient and as warriors held firmly to the bottom section, Red started his ascent, which looked ever more doomed to failure the higher he progressed. Bradley doubted that he'd reach the top, both because of the inherent instability of the structure and also due to the leg wound that he was sure must be affecting the raider more than he was letting on. But he noticed that, wherever the ladder passed some ivy, the outlaw stopped and pulled out a tendril, which he would knot to the ladder to help make it more secure. The man might be evil, but he clearly didn't lack intelligence. After an age, to everyone's amazement Red's struggling form gave a final push and he disappeared from view.

A silence borne of anti-climax came over the many spectators who still peered up to the top of the Wall. The realisation was dawning that, barring the outlaw tumbling to his death in their sight, they would probably never know his fate.

Red's ascent completed, warriors took hold of the structure to lower it for dismantling. But Red's impromptu knots of ivy made this impossible straight away. After a brief discussion, one of them placed a sheathed knife between his teeth and took hold of the lower section to commence climbing.

But before he could do so, Bradley spoke. "Stop. Don't do that!"

The warrior looked around, removed the knife from his mouth and said, "Sorry, Marshal?"

"I said, leave it, please."

"But, Marshal, the ladder's of no use now, is it?"

"Yes, it's of great use. Move out of the way, please."

Then he stepped forward, placed his hands on either side of the lowest section of the rickety ladder and his right foot on the bottom rung.

"Right," he said. "Hold it nice and steady. I'm going up."

And he started climbing.

CHAPTER TWELVE
UPON THE WALL OF DEATH

The climb seemed endless. Rung by suspect rung he made cautious progress, checking the ladder's integrity with each step. He fought to clear his mind of all but the task at hand. Only one unwanted thought intruded and though it started as a single cloud of doubt, it quickly grew to a size that threatened to dominate his otherwise clear blue sky of concentration. And strangely it took him a while to identify the nature of the dark intruder. Then he realised what it was — fear, pure and simple.

Fear was no stranger. He knew it was essential to survival, a natural reaction that prepared one's body to deal with danger. A man without fear would soon become a man without life. But thoughts of fear were usually outpaced swiftly by events, when natural instincts drove the body and mind to do what they needed to do to survive. For a man in his position, fear was something the body reacted to automatically, but on which the mind had no time to dwell.

But just now, as hand over hand his body moved slowly towards its objective, there was little else to think about but the concept of fear. What if that fear should grow to the point where his body and mind ceased to react rationally? That way lay madness, he supposed, for what was madness but the triumph of the irrational? Sanity depended on rationality, therefore he should think about rational things. If he felt afraid now, there must be a reason and to deal with his fear he must determine the cause.

He took stock. Here he was, half way up a very long, flimsy, almost perpendicular ladder. If the structure should fail now, or if his weight moved it too far to one side or the other, it might easily collapse. If it did, he would fall with it and he'd climbed far enough from the ground now for the fall to prove fatal. That must be reason enough to be afraid. But one man — bigger and heavier than he was — had already made this climb and the ladder had neither buckled nor swayed during his ascent. In fact he'd seen Red making the structure more stable as he climbed, using strong fronds of ivy to secure it in places. He found these ties as he climbed and they certainly helped to steady the device. He even added a few more as he progressed. Unless Red's weight had weakened the ladder in some way, then he, Bradley, should also be able to complete the climb safely. Nearer to the top, he found it even more stable. Perhaps the outlaw had taken some strips to secure it up there somehow.

But he hadn't quite reached the top yet, and his mind returned to the subject of fear. He felt he could trust the ladder and if he took care always to hold on with one hand and be careful with his footing, he should be all right. But something else was affecting his mood, some other stimulus that made him feel jittery, something that grew inside him with each step that he took. Just then his foot lost its purchase on a rung and an enormous adrenaline surge flushed through his body, making him tighten his grip and check his foothold. He fought to steady himself and looked down at his feet. Had his gaze rested there, merely made a quick visual check of his footing and returned to his right hand when it reached for the next rung, then all would have been well. But he let his focus readjust onto the ground below him, where the crowd of anxious villagers, their tiny heads straining ever upwards, must be desperately willing him not to falter and fall. At once he felt nauseous and he heard a thousand bells ringing inside his head. He felt giddy, as though his head were spinning. One part of him told his hands to retain their grip, another to let go, allowing him to lean back and fall into space. Thankfully the former voice prevailed, the spinning and the ringing ceased and he regained his senses. And then he realised what this other aspect of his fear was all about. It had to do with his height above the ground.

This was a new experience for him. Most of Fenwold was flat — a large river plain with some low hills running more or less north to south down its centre. Of the "old time" buildings, if there'd been any of more than two storeys, none had survived. There simply were no opportunities to view his world from such a perspective as this. And having this view just now produced in him an extraordinary feeling. Why should this be?

Perhaps it was the novelty of the situation. For example, he'd never before looked down over the treetops. He'd climbed trees as a boy, but there were none that grew to this height. Now, close to the top of the Wall, he gazed out across the broad expanse of the forest canopy and it looked as if it stretched on forever. To his left and to his right, the great, grey bulk of the Wall looked like the never-ending rim of some gigantic cooking utensil, from which he, a tiny fly, was trying to escape. The thought amused him and suddenly the enormity of the situation enveloped him and he felt that irrational part of his fear erupt and transform into an overwhelming exhilaration. He was privileged to be here and he was now eager to complete the climb and possibly witness what no man had ever seen and returned to report — that other world on the far side of the Wall.

But when his hands found the final two rungs and he pulled his body as far as the ladder would support him, he saw that this wasn't to be. For the top of the Wall comprised a huge rounded lip, more than two strides high — too high to see over. An agile man might scramble to the top of this, except that it was festooned with closely spaced metal spikes of varying length. These were fixed firmly into the concrete giving the impression of a huge, never-ending spiny-backed centipede bristling along the entire length of the Wall, away off both ways into the hazy distance. The spikes were carefully arranged so that any attempt to scramble over them would result in impalement upon their sharp, unyielding shafts. It occurred to him that much thought had gone into keeping this barrier impenetrable and that, behind this thought, lay an intelligent mind or minds. This was something that he — and other thinking men of Fenwold — had long believed. Though his own eyes confirmed it, he still found the thought both amazing and exciting. No wonder the Wall was commonly held to be the work of the Gods.

His mind cleared and reminded him that his present position — however tenuous — was also highly fortunate and not to be wasted. He must use this opportunity to gather whatever information there was to take with him on the quest that lay ahead of him. He trained his eyes on the spikes and followed their deadly pattern away to the north and south along the top of the Wall. He detected no breaks and this lethal arrangement held true wherever he looked along its visible length. However, there was an outer ledge of sorts (his elbow now rested on it), flat and about a half stride in width, again extending to the horizon in each direction. He realised a man might walk along this ledge, for a while at least. Red must be doing just that right now, unless he'd already lost his balance and tumbled to his doom in the forest below. He looked along the ledge more carefully, first to the south, where he saw no one. But when he looked northwards his eyes were drawn towards a tiny figure that might have been a man, about five furlongs distant. Could Red have walked that far during Bradley's climb? Why not? And though a mere speck, if his eyes weren't playing tricks, he fancied the outlaw sat resting on the ledge, dangling his legs over the abyss and waving — yes, waving — in his direction.

What harm could it do?

Gripping the top rung tightly with his left hand, he let go with his right and waved back.

* * * * *

"Dominic, how could you do this to us? Put your life in danger for us all to see? Please, don't ever do anything like this again! I'm asking for your promise on this!"

Bradley stepped off the bottom rung, smiled and rested a filial hand on Tom Storey's shoulder.

"There really wasn't any danger, believe me. I apologise for giving no warning, but I saw the opportunity and acted on impulse. I had to climb that ladder."

"Well, I'm glad to see you safe here on the ground again. Come to my house and at least have some beer to steady your nerves."

Laughing now, Bradley said, "All right. But, honestly, my nerves are quite steady. Maybe it's you who needs a drink though, Tom. But first, there's something that needs to be done."

"What's that?"

"Our red-headed friend wasn't stupid. He managed to make some rope out of strips of ivy he gathered on his way up. He used it to tie the upper rung of the ladder to one of the metal spikes at the top of the Wall. So we won't be able to remove the entire ladder from down here. He may have been planning to return later to try descending — perhaps in the hours of darkness. By now I reckon he'll see the futility of this. But as a precaution I suggest you place a guard here for the next few days. I suppose I could have undone his handiwork while I was up there. Call me selfish if you like, but I was rather glad he'd done it. It meant I had a better chance of returning to the ground in one piece. On my way down though, I cut away the bindings between the fourth and fifth sections. The last four were steady enough for the rest of my descent and these can now be removed. If he should return and try to climb down, he'll get an almighty surprise."

"What about the ivy? Would it hold his weight?"

"Good point. Possibly. I suggest you organise a work party to strip it away."

Storey grinned. "Yes. Some of the raider slaves, I think."

Bradley appreciated the irony in this and nodded slowly. But he found it hard to concentrate because his mind was still exhilarated from his climb. Also by now a small crowd of villagers had gathered round him, so far waiting politely until he'd finished speaking to the headman. But when he turned to face them, their questions came thick and fast.

"What did you see, Marshal?"

"How did it feel? Weren't you scared?"

"Please, Marshal, tell us — did you speak with the Gods of the Wall?"

He knew that to some — especially the very young and the very old — the Wall had an almost religious significance. Apart from the life-giving sun and rain, it was after all the one physical thing that contained and controlled their lives. Traditionally the children were warned to stay away from it, as if it held some dark and ancient secret power. Whatever his personal beliefs, he'd always respected the feelings of others and avoided decrying or belittling their taboos or legends. So he weighed his words carefully before replying to the wide-eyed young warrior who'd posed this latter question.

"I neither saw, nor spoke with the Gods. If they knew of my presence, they chose not to acknowledge it, or to make themselves known to me."

Hungry for knowledge, they asked him about the appearance of the Wall and how the world looked from up there and whether he could see over to the other side and all of these questions he answered as fully and truthfully as he was able.

"And what of the raider leader? Did he make it over the top?"

"No. There's no other safe way down on this side and the top of the Wall's crowned by a deadly array of sharp metal spikes. If a man tried to scramble over them they'd tear him to pieces. In any case, I caught sight of the outlaw some distance along the ledge. He's steady on his feet — I'll give him that, for the rim's barely a man's width. I expect he'll try to keep walking north. But without food and not much water, I doubt if he'll keep his balance on that narrow lip for long and sleeping won't be easy either. My guess is that he'll either roll over in his sleep, or eventually falter while walking. In either case he'll fall to his death."

Then from the back of the crowd came Sylvia's unmistakable voice. And typically, hers was the hardest question for him to answer. It didn't help that she addressed him not coldly as "Marshal," but by his given name.

"Dominic, why did you climb that ladder?"

He wondered whether to repeat what he'd said earlier to her father, about having acted on impulse. But even that hadn't been the whole truth. He opened his mouth to speak, but realised the question was too big and the answer too complex to attempt here and now. Dismissively he waved an arm at the crowd.

"I'm sorry. I'll try and answer your questions later. I don't want to keep you from your work."

CHAPTER THIRTEEN
WHERE FORTY DWELL

There was much work to be done. Work in the fields, weeding and preparing for harvesting, repairing burned and battered buildings and fortifications. All that was necessary to restore the depleted resources of Crowtree and Ashwell after their ordeals. So, satisfied or not with the Marshal's answers, most of the witnesses to his climb soon dispersed to resume their various duties.

But these were intelligent people. Many of them would remember Sylvia's question and be puzzled by his apparent inability to make a clear response. She alone hung back, looking morose and disappointed and making him feel inadequate. He turned to her father.

"Tom, can I talk to you? It's important."

"Of course. Let's go into the kitchen. We'll have that drink we spoke about."

As they turned towards Storey's house, Sylvia strode towards them and said, "Can I come too?"

Her father said tetchily, "Haven't you some chores to attend to, young lady?"

But Bradley took pity. "It's all right, Tom. Let her come. Nothing I have to say is so confidential."

Seated at the kitchen table, they waited for Amelia Storey to pour them some beer, thanked her and took long, quenching draughts of the ale.

Storey said, "Now then, what's troubling you?"

He coughed and gathered his thoughts. "Tom, your young people have worked wonders here — far beyond my expectations."

"Only with your help. No, don't protest. I know you're going to say you were only doing your job. But it's a job that not many people could have done. If the Council hadn't sent you, we'd all have been slaughtered or enslaved by now."

Bradley scratched his head. "Well, let's say it was a team effort. Everyone played his or her part. It's still true that what I did, I was trained to do. But let's leave that aside. The thing is, I haven't been entirely open with you about the extent of my mission."

Storey stroked his chin thoughtfully. "I realise you'll want to go on and clear out more raider gangs beyond Crowtree and Ashwell."

"Yes, there'll be some of that. But other marshals have been sent out to different parts of Fenwold with the same objective. If they find the same heroism and determination that I've found here in Crowtree and Ashwell, I'm sure the enclave will soon be cleansed of this plague of outlaws."

"Then your task will be completed, won't it?"

"That's just the point. No, it won't. Earlier Sylvia asked me why I climbed that ladder. I could have told you that I did it on impulse — for who wouldn't like to know what's on the other side of the Wall? But that wouldn't be entirely true. You see, defeating the raiders is only one half of my mission. I've been charged with another task, which in a way is more important."

"More important? What can be more important than ridding Fenwold of those thugs?"

Bradley took a deep breath.

"Tom, I'm a soldier, not a scholar. But as part of my training I spent time under the instruction of several wise men and women. We people of Fenwold have always wondered about our origins and why this Wall surrounds our land. My teachers have made it their business to collect all the knowledge and thinking passed down and see if there are any patterns or clues that might help answer our questions. I don't know or understand how they work these things out, but their belief is that our society has been like it is now for something like eight hundred years."

Storey said, "I have no idea where this is leading, Marshal. But to start with, you'll have to help me understand such an extraordinary length of time."

"Well, if we think of it in terms of family trees — grandparents, parents, children and so on — it might represent something like forty generations."

The headman gave a low whistle. Sylvia stared wide-eyed at Bradley, as she'd been doing since the start of his discourse.

He went on, "So it's a very long time. And my learned tutors have made a further observation. They believe that our society was enclosed for reasons of protection. From what or from whom, they don't know. That knowledge has been lost. But we've enjoyed a fairly good, simple life in the meantime, if not always easy."

Tom nodded.

"One thing's clear. Whatever the Wall was intended to protect us from hasn't harmed us. But during recent generations our numbers have increased to an unsustainable degree. Very soon we'll see real hardship and possibly famine. And in such adversity some desperate people have chosen to steal rather than work. This can't be allowed to continue."

Storey grinned. "Well, if as you say there are more lawmen like you, we're sure to rid ourselves of that problem."

"Maybe. But our population still continues to grow."

"I suppose that's only natural, when communities are settled and law-abiding. What do your wise men suggest we do about it?"

Bradley looked him straight in the eye. "The obvious thing, Tom. Break through to the far side of the Wall."

The headman looked aghast. "But how? And where? We both know it's impenetrable. And besides, wouldn't that be foolhardy if it's there to protect us?"

"That's an excellent question and one that the thinkers have been pondering for several years now."

Here Sylvia jumped in. "And what's their answer?"

"Answer? Nobody can have an absolute answer. But they've applied reasoning and weighed up the relative likelihood of various possibilities."

"All right then," she said. "What's the most likely possibility?"

He paused then to recall the hardest lessons his teachers had tried to drill into his mind. "Their reasoning goes like this. Consider the Gods of the Wall. Think about what they achieved. Look at the Wall itself. Don't you think that, whatever power knew how to build and contain our society within such a fantastic structure and to protect us from danger for so long, would also foresee a time when we'd need — and be able — to break free?"

"Yes!" This exploded from Sylvia, who then looked sheepish and put a hand to her mouth.

Her father frowned at her, but only said, "Go on, Dominic."

"Well, that's my teachers' reasoning. They argue that the Gods wouldn't want to keep us caged behind the Wall forever. There'd come a point in time when the danger ceased to exist and we could safely pass through or over the Wall."

He paused, feeling the intensity of their excitement.

Then he said, "I can tell you now that the wise ones believe we've reached that point in time."

Sylvia coughed and said, "Excuse me."

"What is it?" her father asked with a sigh.

"Well, if all that the wise ones say is true, that the Gods planned our survival and they now expect us to break through the Wall — well, then, wouldn't they also have left instructions as to how we should do it?"

Bradley gasped. "Yes! This is what the wise ones believe too. They've reasoned that somewhere within Fenwold there must be a message, a clue, or a sign that will lead us to the new world beyond the Wall. And that's the object of the second part of my mission. The Council has charged me with the quest to find that message from the Gods."

Then his serious expression gave way to a boyish grin. "They've even honoured me with a title to go with the job."

Tom Storey raised his eyebrows. "Which is...?"

Still smiling, he folded his arms and looked at each of them in turn.

"Surveyor of the Wall."

* * * * *

Bradley remained in the southwest corner of Fenwold for the rest of the summer. Using Ashwell as a base, he and Rajeev Shah ventured out north and east to seek out and assist other villages that had been suffering from harassment by gangs of plundering raiders — or what remained of them. They'd become increasingly desperate because of the return of law and order to the area — and, by all accounts, across the enclave. Their reign of terror was nearing its end and those with any sense of the inevitable were inclined to surrender to the elders of their nearest village. Rather that than risk the same fate as their counterparts who'd perished at the hands of the merciless citizens of Crowtree, under their ferocious warlord Dominic Bradley.

It was a bright autumn morning when Bradley and Shah saddled up to ride out on a routine patrol from the village. As in several nearby settlements, fortifications at Ashwell were all but completed, as were repairs to damaged buildings. The crippled village society was, with the help of their neighbours from Crowtree, beginning to re-form itself and face a more hopeful future.

This hadn't been an easy season for any of the communities, with stores of food seriously depleted and rationing harshly enforced. But much had been accomplished in the fields, the weather had been kind with a good mixture of sunshine and rain and the harvest had exceeded all expectations.

Before the two lawmen could begin their journey, they were aware of a commotion in the village centre, from where a wagon drawn by a single horse sped towards them.

Bradley signalled Rajeev to wait and turned as the wagon came to a clattering halt beside him. The driver was a young lad, no more than eight years of age. His open wagon contained an aged person, who must be either sick or infirm, for she was trussed up on a makeshift bed of blankets and straw.

"Marshal!" the boy called to him. "Are you the one they call Slayer of the Wall?"

He didn't bother to deny it. He'd lost count of the various titles and tortuous misnomers bestowed on him by grateful villagers and defeated raiders. "Yes," he replied. "That's me. And who might you be, young man? I've not seen you in Ashwell before, have I?"

"No, sir. I've driven overnight from Roundhill, over to the east. I didn't want to come — I was afraid. But we've nothing any raiders could want and besides we didn't run into any. My great aunt told me it was important I bring her to you. We heard about your great victory and she demanded to be brought here. Honestly, she's given us no peace these last few days. She says she must speak to you. The future of Fenwold depends on it."

Bradley was intrigued, but as usual, his first thoughts were for these people's welfare.

"Have you eaten, lad?"

"Not since yesterday. But I had to get her here. She was desperate to see you."

"All right. If she can be moved, let's get your great aunt indoors and we'll see you're both fed and given something to drink. Rajeev, take care of their horses, will you?"

After a while, in the cool of an Ashwell cottage kitchen, Bradley sat down next to the old woman, while the mistress of the household spoon-fed her some hot broth.

"Mother," he began respectfully, "I am Dominic Bradley, whom you know as the Surveyor of the Wall. I believe you've something to say to me."

Up to this point, the old woman's eyes had been closed, though she'd managed to take a couple of mouthfuls of broth. On hearing his voice however, she opened them and looked almost lovingly into his face, resting a feeble hand on his.

She spoke in a whisper and he had to draw his face closer to her lips. "Dominic Bradley. Yes, I've heard of you. You're the Good Man. You must be. I'd begun to fear you'd never come. I thought I should die and take the knowledge with me. It's getting beyond the time, you see."

"Beyond the time, Mother? How so? What have you to tell me?"

"Listen," she whispered, "and listen well. I haven't much strength."

There was some noise outside and he signalled to the headman to close the door. Then he returned to the old woman. "I'm listening, Mother," he said.

And then she recited to him a piece of doggerel that might have been learned in childhood, yet seemed to have its origins in a much earlier time, so that its simple recital sent shivers down his spine. These were the old woman's words:

"When a good man comes where Forty dwell,
It will be time these words to tell.
Look east at the river as far as you might
Across to a tower, where once there was light.
Inside that tower a key hangs down
That opens a door in a northern town.
Above that door a dragon grins.
Unlock and enter — the quest begins."

After this short recital she smiled, more or less satisfied her message had been delivered, though leaving its recipient perplexed. And she went back to consuming her broth — now, Bradley smiled to observe, with great relish. But, her work clearly done, she seemed unable or unwilling to divulge any further information.

So he went over to the boy, who was also enjoying a good feed, to try and extract any morsel of knowledge that might help him better understand the message — if indeed that's what it was.

"You say this old lady's an elderly relative of yours, lad?"

His mouth full of potato, the boy just nodded.

"Has she ever recited this riddle before?"

The boy shook his head. Then, gulping down his draught of watered ale, he added, "She always said she learned a riddle from my great grandfather, Thirty-Nine, but never told us what it was. Most people thought she was crazy. But she fell sick a few weeks ago and said she must speak to you before she died. I had to bring her. Did I do wrong, sir?"

He placed a friendly hand on the boy's shoulder. "No, son, you did no wrong. But tell me, how did you say your great grandfather was called? Did you say his name was Thirty-Nine?"

"Yes, sir. Great Aunt always said there'd been a line running through our family where each one learning the riddle took the next number for their given name. That's why it was so important for her to see you, because she said that, according to the riddle, she was the one who had to pass it on to you."

Bradley nodded. And though it wasn't anywhere close to the entire truth, he said, "I see."

Then, frowning and scratching his head, he drawled, "So you're telling me that you great aunt's name is..."

"Her name sir? It's Forty."

CHAPTER FOURTEEN
DIVINING THE RIDDLE

"Mother, did your uncle say the riddle came from the Gods of the Wall?"

The old woman's message had become a worm inside Bradley's head. So much so that he delayed their patrol by a whole day in case she should expand on its meaning. He tried nearly every trick he knew. Repetitive questioning, wheedling, cajoling, feeding her with the best of fare — he stopped only just short of outright interrogation. But, try as he might, he could get nothing out of her, save for the tedious repetition of her rhyme. Once, out of desperation, he tried offering her some coins, but she shook her head disdainfully and dashed them to the ground. It was as if, in advanced age, her senses all but gone, her mind clung only to this one coherent stanza, intent on playing out the role assigned to her in early childhood.

The poem's repetition came so often that he had the lines completely to heart by evening. In fact he felt sure that, had she breathed her final breath there and then, the verse would be locked forever safely inside his head.

Far from her strength failing, however, the joy of its successful delivery seemed to refresh her spirit. The good food and care given by her Ashwell hosts must also have aided her recovery. So the following morning saw the wagon pull away, the young boy beaming a sunny smile at the whip and his great aunt displaying a broad, toothless grin of fulfilment from the seat beside him.

After they'd gone Bradley briefly considered breaking off from his mission to report this development to the Fenwold High Council and discuss it with the scholars. But he wasn't inclined to run back to base whenever a problem came up. One of the central tenets of his training had been the importance of self-reliance and the ability to make use of whatever resources were to hand. Intelligence wasn't something magical, he had learned, but a matter of separating fact from fancy, of carefully weighing probabilities and proceeding step by considered step to a logical conclusion.

Still, he thought he should discuss the matter with someone with a clear mind whose judgement he respected. So he had Shah ride back to Crowtree and ask Tom Storey to come urgently and speak with him.

* * * * *

It was just after noon when two horses trotted into the clearing in front of the Ashwell stockade. Crowtree's headman dismounted and approached Bradley with the awkward gait of an old man challenged by the onset of arthritis. But his daughter leapt easily down from her horse's saddle and skipped lightly to where the Marshal stood to welcome them.

She reached him first, her hands stretched out towards him. He accepted them with a puzzled grin, saying, "I'm pleased to see you, Sylvia." Then he greeted her father. "Thanks for coming, Tom. I'm sure you've plenty to do in Crowtree."

The old fellow smiled and his daughter said, "Rajeev said there was something important you wanted to discuss. We came as soon as we heard."

He led them into the Ashwell headman's cottage, where they could speak in private. If the truth were told, it annoyed him that Sylvia had invited herself to the meeting, but seeing the doting expression on Tom's care-worn face, that pleaded, "How could I stop her?" he relented and told himself her presence was of no consequence.

Once settled at the kitchen table, each with a mug of tea offered by the mistress of the house, he told them about the message delivered by the old woman called Forty.

"I can't sort this out on my own, Tom. I'm not sure if this is just the nonsensical ranting of a crazy old woman, or something I should act upon. I'd value your opinion."

Storey scratched his head. "I don't know that I can help much, Dominic. This needs some thinking about. Many of these children's rhymes contain some sort of meaning."

But Sylvia jumped in. "Let me see if I understand. The basic question is: could this be the message from the Gods that we spoke about after you climbed the Wall?"

Bradley nodded and said curtly, "That's it." Then he looked back at her father, who from his furrowed brow still struggled with the problem.

"And, if it is," she continued, "how is it to be interpreted?"

He forced himself to look at her again and acknowledge her contribution. "Well, yes, Sylvia. But I really wanted to ask your father..."

"Oh, sorry," she said. She sat on her hands, pouting at his indifference towards her and clearly bursting to pour out her thoughts on the matter.

Then her exasperated father shook his head and said, "It's no good. You'll have to let her have her say. I'll never hear the end of it if you don't."

Bradley sighed. "All right. Go on then, Sylvia. Let's have the benefit of your unquestionable wisdom."

She wrinkled her lips with an air of superiority, clearly unaffected by his patronising sarcasm. "Look, the old woman learned this rhyme as a child and was given the enormous responsibility of passing it on to somebody important, right?"

He nodded.

"If her name's Forty and the relative who taught her the rhyme was called Thirty-Nine, that suggests it's been passed down through forty generations, from the time Fenwold was created. This ties in with what the scholars told you. The rhyme could have been planted by the Gods, intending it to be repeated to this 'good man' who'd then have the job of interpreting its clues."

He nodded again. "Yes, I see that, but I'm still sceptical. I mean, how could the Gods have got the timing so perfectly right? How could they have known the Council would appoint a Surveyor just when this old woman with the rhyme was about to take it with her to the funeral pyre?"

She shook her head. "I don't know. I suppose they reasoned that by now somebody would turn up who was inquisitive enough to make some use of the rhyme. In all probability the old woman would've found someone to tell before her time came, if only out of desperation. It just happens that she heard about you and decided you must be the one. And is it possible that your wise scholars got the timing right due to some clever planning by the Gods? You

127

said yourself they used knowledge passed down through the generations. Maybe there were two threads of knowledge designed to come together at the right time."

Both Storey and Bradley were speechless for a moment. Storey presumably because he was amazed how he'd sired such an intelligent child and the Marshal because he was searching frantically for a flaw in her argument.

Then he thought he'd found one.

"All right," he said. "Let's assume the Gods did arrange the perfect timing that would bring together the Surveyor and the old woman. But the rhyme says that the 'good man' has to come to the place where she dwells. The old woman came to me here at Ashwell."

"Oh, come on Dominic! Even the Gods of the Wall couldn't predict exactly how you two would meet! Anyway, you did come to her corner of the enclave and would've visited her village eventually. She just sped up the process because she heard about you, put two and two together and was afraid to wait any longer in case she died without delivering the riddle. If you're looking for exact symbolism in the rhyme, I think you're expecting too much." Here she hesitated for a moment, as if unsure of her ground. But then she gritted her teeth saying, "And I think I know why."

He grinned. "Oh, you do, do you, you little squirrel?"

"Yes. You said it yourself when you spoke to Father before about your mission. You're a soldier and you love it. You don't want to be distracted so soon from doing what you most enjoy. You've had some success in this corner of Fenwold and thought you'd spend a couple of years riding around sorting out raiders all over the place."

Her father said angrily, "Sylvia, don't be impertinent to the Marshal!"

Bradley shook his head. "No, it's all right, Tom. I want to hear this. Go on, young lady."

In deference to her father's annoyance, she was more subdued, but by no means deterred.

"The Council gave you two jobs. You had no idea when the opportunity would arise to follow your quest to conquer the Wall and it's come a lot sooner than you thought it would. This means you'll have to give up your soldiering and leave it to others, who are quite capable — thanks to the training you've given." This had the ring of a tactical concession. "But this quest is by far the more important part of your mission. And if you accept the old woman's rhyme as genuine — which I believe it is and as you do too, I think — then you can't justify putting it off any longer."

He was almost speechless, but managed to say, "Is that so?"

There was fire in her eyes now and he saw that there was no stopping her, so he let her finish. She rose from her seat and, with both hands on the table, looked him squarely in the eyes and concluded, "Yes, it is. You'll have to put up your sword, Marshal Dominic Bradley, and take up this greater challenge. The future of Fenwold depends on it — and on you!"

Her enthusiasm spent and energy drained, she sat down again and took on the worried look of a confused teenage girl, who was afraid she'd spoken out of turn.

Her father said quietly but seriously, "Go and wait outside, Sylvia. I'll speak with you later."

She rose and obeyed.

Tom Storey rubbed his face with his hands and issued forth an exasperated sigh. "I must ask you to forgive my daughter's outburst. I'm afraid we've never been able to restrain her in that respect, though in most other ways she's a good and dutiful daughter. I promise you I'll take her to task for it later."

"Don't worry, Tom. It's not the first time I've seen that precocious girl open her mouth and heard words of wisdom pour out. It can be annoying, I'll grant you. But she does appear to have a gift for getting to the root of a matter."

The headman frowned. "You're not telling me you agree with what she said to you just now? I'd call it impudence."

Bradley shrugged. "Impudence, confidence — call it what you like. The truth has many names, Tom." He paused thoughtfully. "Yes, I think she's right. I was inclined to accept the riddle at face value — I only needed a reasoned second opinion. And now that I have the clues to hand, I have to agree that it would be insulting to the Gods to delay the quest any further. My work's done here. Jack, Liam and the rest are more than capable of handling any trouble that might arise locally. And together with the work others are doing elsewhere, I'm sure the last of the raider gangs will soon be overthrown. I intend to ride north-east across the central uplands with Rajeev in the morning, to look for the first objective mentioned in the riddle."

Storey cocked his head to one side. "Remind me?"

"The river — its eastern extreme, where the estuary meets the sea. And the tower where once there was light."

Chapter Fifteen
Journey Into Danger

Bradley and Shah rose early and made ready to ride out in the mid-morning sunshine with the minimum of ceremony. But when word spread that they were leaving to head north, a sizeable contingent arrived from Crowtree to join the Ashwell villagers and pay their compliments. It seemed some kind of semi-formal send-off wasn't to be avoided and as the two lawmen saddled up the excited villagers gathered round them, all wanting to shake their hands and wish them luck on their journey.

A committee of village elders presented the Marshal with an embroidered saddlecloth, with a motif to commemorate the victory over the local raiders. It depicted a gruesome (and wildly inaccurate) scene that featured Bradley on horseback with Red's head on the end of a sword. He took this to be symbolic and tried not to look too embarrassed as he accepted it with gratitude. The departing lawmen then said their farewells and headed off along the track leading northwards.

Bradley looked back at the dispersing group of villagers and a mood of disappointment hung over him. It took him a while to figure out why.

"I wonder why Sylvia didn't turn up to see us off, Rajeev," he grizzled.

The deputy shrugged. "I suppose she must have had something more important to see to. Why, does it bother you that she stayed away?"

He bristled and snapped, "No, of course it doesn't bother me, man." Then he relented. "Sorry, Rajeev. I didn't mean to yell at you. It just seems a bit discourteous that she was too busy to leave her chores and bid us goodbye. After all, I stayed with her family for some time and her father and brothers found time to come and wish us well."

"The womenfolk tend to stand aside on official occasions, Marshal."

"Really? I've never noticed Sylvia standing aside on *any* occasion that I can remember. Anyhow, it doesn't matter. Let's put it from our minds. There's no reason why Sylvia's absence should dampen our enthusiasm. I'd appreciate it if you wouldn't mention the matter again."

For some reason, Shah put his hand up to his face.

"No, Marshal. I won't."

Young Shah did little to help lift the Marshal's morose mood. Not that Bradley had had any reservations in appointing him deputy. He'd proved entirely dependable and courageous whenever the need arose. But unlike himself he was a quiet, taciturn lad. It had been easier to strike up a friendship with the more outgoing Jack Storey. And though he felt certain his decision to appoint Jack local lawman had been the right one, he regretted the loss of his company. Jack was talkative, amusing and socially stimulating. Rajeev, on the other hand, seldom bothered with idle conversation, but used his words sparingly. Come the second day of their journey, Bradley found the lack of exchange between them frustrating and tedious. He didn't place any blame on Shah. It wasn't every person's lot to be socially confident and talkative. Yet he felt at times that the silence they shared might soon become unbearable.

They were approaching the range of low hills that ran from south to north almost along the centre of Fenwold, when Bradley decided he'd try and strike up a conversation. Here earlier generations had cleared away much of the forest, but found the ground too congested with roots and rocks to be easily cultivated. Having exhausted the timber they'd felled, the farmers had moved on and left the disturbed ground to the voracious spreading gorse and low shrub. The old tracks remained clear due to frequent use, however and Bradley for one enjoyed the openness afforded by the absence of the familiar, lowering forest. Gone was the concealed threat of a thousand potential dangers, replaced by unhindered visibility for several furlongs in all directions. It was late afternoon, the weather was kind and a soft bloom of rustiness in the western sky promised a fine evening. There'd be sufficient daylight for them to ride a couple of leagues further before setting up camp.

He looked about him and said, "Ah, Rajeev! Isn't it a fine afternoon?"

Shah's response was positive, but economical. "Hmm."

Bradley persisted. "We're lucky, you and I. We've full bellies, two good horses, a splendid day and a mission before us. It's good to be alive, don't you agree?"

There came a pause, which made him think the deputy was giving more thought to his answer this time.

But "Yes, Marshal," was all he said. Though he did at least make the effort to turn his head and emit something resembling a half smile in Bradley's direction.

What could he do to prise the youth from out of his shell? Then he recalled something his teachers had told him — it had been to do with the subject of successful interrogation and the way a question should be framed to elicit the maximum information, with more than a simple answer of "Yes" or "No."

"Rajeev, I've always admired your ability with horses. How did you come by such a skill?"

"Skill?" came the response, then silence. Bradley thought that was to be the extent of his answer. But then to his surprise Shah continued, "I suppose it's a skill — I've never given it much thought. My Dad was a horseman and his father too. I grew up with horses around — they were part of the family. I can't remember when I couldn't ride. I like being near horses — the sound, the smell of them."

"I know what you mean," Bradley said. "There's something special about the relationship between a man and his horse. But often it's just a master and servant relationship. For you, I get the impression it's more than that."

"I've never thought of a horse as a servant. Yes, they'll do things for you, but it's only because they want to. Unless there's cruelty involved, naturally. I won't stand for that."

"Me neither," Bradley said. "But even though I respect them, it takes me months before I can win their trust. Take Scarlett here. Two years we've been together and we're as close as man and horse can be now. But she didn't like me at first — wouldn't even let me mount her. It was ages before she really took to me. But I've seen you handle horses you've never seen before — those raiders' mounts for instance. They were like babies with you. That's what I meant by skill."

Rajeev beamed a broad smile. "That's not skill, Marshal. It's love. I love the little darlings and they know it."

"Well said, Rajeev!" At least here was one subject sure to loosen the deputy's tongue. After a short silence, Bradley decided to capitalise on his success.

"Have you travelled any distance from Crowtree before, Rajeev?"

"When the traders came to our village, they used to tell us of their life travelling around and bartering different goods. It got easier when the Council introduced their coinage — even if our elders say they don't approve of it. The traders did a useful job — and made a decent living from it. But mostly they said it was the freedom they enjoyed, the new places they'd seen and the life on the open road. They made it sound exciting — a lot more fun than village life. I wanted to try it. My father amazed me by giving his blessing, even though he could have done with my help with the livestock and everything. But he said it would broaden my mind. So I went along with them for the summer — three years ago, it was. I made myself useful with the horses, helping with rounding up and breaking in some wild ones. They reckoned I might have become a successful horse trader."

Bradley was impressed. "I'll bet they had cause. I suppose the raiders put paid to those ambitions?"

"That's right. The raiders destroyed most things of any worth — until you came to help us."

In all humility Bradley felt he must protest. "Not just me, Rajeev. We've the Council to thank for training up their force of lawmen. And none of us could have done it without the bravery of villagers such as you, Jack and the others. So, is there a chance you'll be taking up horse trading when these troubles are over?"

"It's possible. But so many things are changing just now — who knows what other opportunities might arise? Especially if we're successful in our mission and discover a new world on the far side of the Wall."

It was Bradley's turn to be pensive now and as if reading his mind, young Shah asked, "What do you think we'll find, Marshal?"

"On the other side? I've often wondered. Who hasn't? A land of plenty, perhaps — or more of this?"

He gestured to indicate the scrub and forest that covered the greater part of Fenwold.

"Whatever lies in store, I reckon there'll be a whole lot of work involved in winning a livelihood, just as there is for us here. Though — and I can't tell you why I think this — I believe, whatever we find on the far side, that it'll be so different and new that we'll be absolutely amazed by it."

"You make it sound exciting. Aren't you impatient to go there? I know I am."

Bradley laughed. "Yes, Rajeev. I can hardly wait. But we've much to accomplish before we see what lies beyond the Wall. We've the old woman's riddle to decipher for a start. And by my reckoning we're still four or five days from the river estuary. Time enough for news of our journey to have spread to other raider gangs. There are sure to be some still at large and a conquering marshal and his deputy will be fair game. We'll be all right moving through this open terrain in daylight, where we can see well enough to take evasive action. But when we've to travel through woodland again, we'll need to be especially watchful."

Reminded now of the potential danger they were in, Shah became noticeably twitchy, frequently peering into the distance, or looking behind them to check for outlaws. Bradley approved of his deputy's vigilance and wasn't of a mind to discourage his dedication to duty. He had to admit he felt more apprehensive, too. For one thing, he knew of no village hereabouts where they might pass the night in safety. He reflected on their recent conversation and the likelihood that their fame might attract the unwanted attention of any remaining raiders — whether out of revenge or sheer bravado. He made a decision.

"Rajeev, I reckon we should turn off this track and head towards the low hills. It's too exposed down here for setting up camp. There'll be better shelter up there, in the folds of the uplands."

"Wouldn't that be good hideout country for raiders too though, Marshal?"

"Possibly. But generally raiders prey on villages and stick to the cover of the forest when moving from one target to another. There's not much for them out here. That's not to say we won't encounter the odd fugitive, but we'll take turns on watch while the other rests, just to be sure. We'll be fine."

"Right you are, Marshal," Shah replied. And they turned their horses eastwards for the gentle ascent while the declining sun stretched out their shadows in front of them.

After a while they reached a vale where the scrub gave way to grassy banks and clusters of sheltering trees. Here and there were great white gashes in the hillside, exposing the underlying rock.

Shah observed, "That's something I've not seen before. I wonder what it can be?"

"What you think it is?"

The young deputy looked thoughtful.

"It looks like the soil's been ripped away and the rock left exposed. I recognise this rock — it's chalk. We find lumps of it in our fields when we turn the soil over after harvest, before the frosts come. But I've never seen such great swathes of it, open to the elements like this. It's as if great chunks have been gouged away, leaving huge holes all over the hillside. That's strange. I can't imagine what could've done that."

Bradley said, "You're right, Rajeev. It is chalk. It's quite a sight. I've not been here before, though my teachers told me what to expect. They think this must be where the Gods took the materials they used to build the Wall. They're not sure how they dug it out, moved it and altered it to form the smooth concrete we're all familiar with. But the fact that so much of this rock's been stripped away is evidence that can't be ignored. There isn't much doubt — it's places like this where the Wall was originally spawned."

* * * * *

They passed through more of the scarred landscape, their horses showing signs of nervousness in the unfamiliar terrain. The trail here was less well defined, with broken pieces of loose chalk on the narrow track, causing the horses to pick up their feet and tread more carefully. The rapidly fading daylight didn't help either.

Then immediately after the next turn on their left they were presented with the sight of an enormous open chasm of exposed rock. The horses, unused to so much white in their field of vision and sensing the danger of the precipitous edge of the gaping chalk quarry, recoiled momentarily with eyes bulging. Then among the brush on the slope just above them some startled animal scurried away up the hillside, dislodging a small avalanche of rocks that spilled out onto the track ahead. This spooked the horses even more and their riders fought desperately to retain control.

Shah was easily the better horseman. Out of the corner of his eye he saw that Bradley was having trouble and that at one point Scarlett went up on her hind legs. But he was too busy controlling his own mare to offer any help and with concentration he managed to steer her away from the edge and into the bushes, where he coaxed and spoke softly to her until she quietened down. He was relieved when in the half-light the form of Scarlett trotted up beside them. But his initial relief was short-lived.

The Marshal was no longer in the saddle.

CHAPTER SIXTEEN
LEDGE OF FRUSTRATION

"Marshal! Marshal! Are you all right? Where are you?"

Shah drove his nervous horse to pick her way up and down the narrow, stony track, screwing up his eyes to search for Bradley's fallen body in the spreading gloom. His companion's horse whinnied and danced at a lone tree branch some way along the track where he'd secured her, her confusion spreading to his own mount, now more skittish with each passing moment. He twisted in the saddle and peered each way along that rocky trail, but still in the fading light his tired eyes couldn't see where the Marshal had been thrown. After a while he pulled on his mare's reins to steady her, stopped and took some deep breaths.

He realised he was panicking and that this would do him no good whatsoever. He was scared, he didn't mind admitting it. But he must clear his mind and take stock of the situation, just as Bradley had taught him. He knew the Marshal had fallen when his horse had been spooked, but he was nowhere to be seen on that part of the track. That meant only one thing. But the young deputy didn't want to acknowledge the most likely conclusion. On the far side of the track yawned the gaping quarry. Bradley must have gone over the edge. Now Shah must take control of his fear, dismount and go and look.

He'd never seen terrain like this before. Even during his season with the traders, he hadn't encountered quarries such as these, great excavations in the ground, with steep, rocky sides and unfathomable drops. He tethered his own horse alongside Bradley's and shuffled slowly to the edge of the precipice, where he crouched and looked over into the void. The light now almost gone, even the whiteness of the chalk rock was all but obscured and he found it hard to focus upon anything solid, anything that might serve as a reference point. Then he noticed a small bush with a broken branch growing out of the chalk cliff about five strides beneath him and using this as a visual anchor, he carefully and methodically made a detailed search of every square stride of rock within his field of vision. But there was still no sign of the Marshal.

Then a thought crossed his mind. What broke the branch?

He shifted his position a stride to the left, squinted and peered down below the damaged bush. Then his heart sank.

Bradley lay on a ledge about three strides below the bush. His fall had split its main branch. It was hard to tell from where young Shah crouched, but he saw no sign of any movement. At once his mouth became dry and he said a silent prayer to the Gods of the Wall. With great effort he uttered a feeble call to his companion.

"Marshal! Marshal! Can you hear me?"

Silence.

"Marshal! Dominic! Try and tell me if you're conscious!" Then he realised how stupid that sounded.

Silence again. Shah was distraught. He covered his face with his hands and fought back tears of despair. Then he heard something that made his heart beat faster.

"Rajeev!"

It was faint, barely a whisper, almost inaudible. For a moment he wasn't sure he'd heard it at all. Then it came again.

"Rajeev!"

There was no doubt about it. Bradley was calling to him.

"Marshal! It's all right — I can hear you. Now don't worry — and don't try to move. I can see where you are. You're on a ledge. Don't roll — just lie still while I work out..."

"Arm hurting — could be broken. Cold!" The words came clearly and urgently.

"I hear you! If I lower down a blanket do you think you can pull it across you with your good arm?"

There came a muffled response that he took for affirmation. Swiftly then, he tied a rope to one corner of a thick fur bed-cover. By now his eyes were better adjusted to the darkness and with skill he was able to swing the animal skin towards Bradley without entangling it in the bush. When Bradley had caught it with his free hand and pulled it over his body, the deputy wrapped his end of the slack rope around a nearby boulder, lest the blanket fall off into the abyss during the night. Out here in the wilderness such commonplace articles as ropes and blankets were precious, potential lifesavers that you couldn't afford to lose.

"Are you warmer yet, Marshal?" he called after a while.

"Yes, thanks. The fall must have knocked me out. I'm all right — only... Ouch! Sorry, got to be careful — this blasted arm! Look, you're not going to be able to do anything while it's dark. I'm warmer now and easy as I can be. Make camp, get a fire going and if you can, lower me down something hot to eat and drink. I'll sleep here till daylight. You'll see better then what's to be done."

Shah hesitated. "I don't know. I don't like leaving you like this."

"You're not leaving me. I hope not anyway!" At least he still had his sense of humour. "Do as I say, please Rajeev. And don't think of trying any heroics in the dark — it's too dangerous. You'll be no good to me if you fall over the ledge as well. By the way, are you all right yourself — and the horses?"

He thanked the Gods that Bradley was in good spirits and thinking clearly despite his predicament.

"Yes, we're fine. You rest now and keep warm. I thought I heard the trickle of water close by. I think there's a spring behind the rock just along the trail. I'll water and feed the horses before I do anything, then I'll make camp and get some food prepared for us. Come first light, we'll get you out of there."

It didn't take him long to make a shelter. It was rough, but would do for the night. In no time he had a small fire blazing. On this he set a pan of water to boil. From his saddlebag he took a two-handled can, which he filled with hot tea and lowered down to Bradley without too much spillage. Then from their rations bag he cut up and cooked some vegetables, which together with dried meat and bread made a sufficiently satisfying broth for both of them. Bradley gulped this from the same can.

In between slurps he managed to say, "Well done, Rajeev. You'll make some woman a good house husband one day!"

Shah only hoped the warmth and nourishment of that simple supper would give Bradley some comfort through the night. And soon the low, regular drone of the Marshal's snoring reassured him of that.

His relief gave way to concern, though, when he remembered Bradley's earlier comment about taking it in turns to stay awake on watch. This would now be impossible and he sagged at the realisation that the responsibility for their safety this night was going to be his and his alone. He looked about him — as best he could, for the night now shrouded everything with its eerie darkness. And it was so quiet. With Bradley now fast off, there was nobody to distract him from his natural fear of this place. Normally he'd be happy with his own thoughts for company, but the circumstances and the unfamiliar territory gave him the jitters. Even if there were no raiders in these inhospitable hills, he'd no idea what wild beasts might be lurking in the shadows on their nightly hunt for food. He yawned. He needed to rest. His eyelids felt so heavy. He knew he couldn't stay awake for long, especially with a full belly. There was no time to lose. He must take precautions before his body succumbed to the perils of unprotected sleep.

He thought of Bradley lying injured and helpless on the ledge below and tried to recall elements of his invaluable training that he should now employ.

Fighting his tiredness, he worked skilfully with lengths of twine, setting trip wires and traps along the trail ahead and behind, connecting them to suspended cans with loose stones that would rattle and arouse him if disturbed. He then spread out several weapons to hand where he lay, including a couple of primed and loaded crossbows, as well as plenty of spare bolts and knives for throwing (a skill at which he was especially adept). He could do no more. His mind ranged for a while, wondering how he might safely raise Bradley from that ledge come daylight. But after only a few moments of undisciplined thought, exhaustion overwhelmed him and took him off into a deep, embracing slumber.

With both warriors now asleep, the environs of the ancient quarry were quiet and still. Light clouds had gathered over the hills, helping to keep in the warmth of the day and there was only a gentle breeze. There was just a small drop in temperature, not enough to waken them. No wolves or other nocturnal predators chose to come near them. There were countless sleeping animals in these hills — goats, rabbits, hares and even a few wild horses.

But, save for the initial recognition of the humans' scent on the breeze, the wild creatures of this hillside paid them little attention for the rest of the night. There was now hardly a sound, except for the gentle sighing of the breeze, the trickle of the nearby brook and the soft, steady snoring of the sleeping lawmen.

But in the cover of the bushes above the trail a short distance behind them, downwind of their campsite, a pair of eyes peered out into the darkness, watching the glow of their fire as it died down.

And waited.

CHAPTER SEVENTEEN
ANGEL OF MERCY

A raucous clattering shattered the peace of the hillside, abruptly dragging Shah from the comfort of an otherwise restful sleep. Instinctively, before his eyelids were open, his hand reached for the nearest loaded crossbow. He blinked. The dawn had scarcely broken. He raised himself swiftly but silently to a kneeling position and, lifting the weapon to eye-level, prepared to shoot at whatever or whoever had disturbed the tripwire. Moments later he collected the freshly killed rabbit that would feed them that day and laid its carcass beside the ashes of the campfire. Then he walked across to the chasm's edge to check on Bradley.

In the growing visibility of the blessed daylight he saw that the Marshal was awake too, no doubt roused by this activity. He must have felt a spasm of pain on waking, because his first word was an obscenity, uncharacteristic of his usually civil tongue. He looked up apologetically at Shah's concerned face.

"Sorry, Rajeev. Still painful."

"That's all right, Marshal. How are you otherwise? Did you manage to get any sleep?"

"Some. I don't think my arm's broken. It feels more like a dislocation. Still hurts like hell though. But apart from cuts and bruises I don't think I've any other serious injuries. I might be able to stand, if I lean on my good arm."

"I wouldn't risk that if I were you. You wouldn't be able to climb back up on your own, not just with one useful arm. I'm going to have to haul you up somehow, so you might as well relax until we're ready. What do you want to do? Shall I make us some breakfast first, or should we get on with the job?"

"Unless you're really hungry, Rajeev, I'd sooner not delay this while the weather's in our favour. If it rains and this rock gets wet it's going to be that much harder. Now, I've been thinking. This blanket you lowered is made of pretty tough hide. You could use a sharp knife to cut holes and weave a rope through either end and that ought to make a cradle strong enough to take my weight. What do you reckon?"

"Sounds like a good plan. But I've another skin up here, so keep that one over you for now. I don't want you getting cold. The sun's only just risen."

It didn't take Shah long to prepare the leather skin as a rescue cradle, with sufficient lengths of strong rope threaded through the slits he'd made to lower the blanket to the ledge. As before, he swung it to one side of the obscuring bush and looped the rope ends around a rock to secure it.

Bradley nodded at the bush. "That's going to be a problem. You're not going to be able to swing the cradle around that so easily with my weight in it."

"Hmm. Yes, you're right. Look, I think I might be able to scramble down and cut it away. I can secure myself with a rope to one of these outcropping rocks up here. It'll take a bit more time. Shall I do it?"

"I think you'd better. But be careful."

Shah took a machete from his saddlebag, looped the end of a rope around a nearby boulder and with the other end around his waist climbed gingerly down the rock face towards the bush. He hacked at it savagely, flinging each cutting away to one side so that it plummeted safely to the bottom of the deep quarry with a resounding *thud* fifty or more strides below. Eventually he'd removed most of the obstacle, leaving only the main trunk. This was too thick even for his machete, so he trimmed it short, leaving just a stump and hoped it wouldn't get in the way of the hoisting.

Then he scrambled back up the rock face, the machete tucked in his belt, using the securing rope to aid his ascent. He now had a much better view of the ledge below, where Bradley had managed to shuffle onto the makeshift cradle, ready to be hoisted to safety. Now came the hard part.

Shah took the four ropes in his hands. "Marshal, are you ready? I'm going to try and take your weight."

But with the first tug he realised it was impossible. The two men were of roughly equal weight and although by no means a weakling, the deputy was wiry rather than muscular. As much as he wanted to, he just hadn't the strength to raise the Marshal unaided.

Bradley yelled up to him. "Rajeev, why don't you use one of the horses?"

With uncertainty Shah replied, "All right, Marshal. I'll give it a try. But I'll need to rig up a makeshift collar. It might take a while."

Bradley called to him, "Don't worry about that — I'm not going anywhere!"

But after reviewing the terrain and relative pulling opportunities, Shah knew he must admit defeat. He called down to Bradley with undisguised frustration in his voice.

"It's no good, Marshal. The track's really rocky and narrow just here, with steep rising ground beyond it. I could harness up a horse but there wouldn't be enough room for a straight pull."

Bradley called back to him. "Isn't there anything you can loop the ropes around if you're short of space? How did you tie off the one you used when you trimmed the bush?"

"The nearest tree is too far along the track — the ropes aren't long enough to reach it. And this boulder here has too many sharp edges. When the horse starts pulling I'm afraid it'll cut the ropes and..." He held his palms to his temples. "I'll have to try again on my own."

"No, wait. It's only my shoulder that's injured. I can use the strength of my legs against the chalk face to make it easier for you to lift me. I'll walk up while you pull."

So the deputy took up the rope ends again and gave them a few turns around his wrist.

"All right, Marshal. If you can get yourself in position, let's go!"

Shah's face contorted and sweat oozed from his brow in spite of the cold, as he mustered every morsel of physical strength he possessed. With gritted teeth, he took the strain and slowly pulled the ropes towards him, gathering them in hand over hand. But even though the Marshal took some of his own weight through the contact of his legs with the quarry wall, Shah still struggled. It didn't help that Bradley, weakened by his injury, was clearly having difficulty maintaining a steady climbing motion and Shah heard scrapes and curses when he lost his footing against the rock face. Whenever this happened his residual body weight transferred to the ropes in erratic spasms, making the deputy's task that much harder. It was exhausting for him and when Bradley reached the stump of the bush, Shah gasped, "Marshal, can you hold on there for a moment?"

With an extra push with his legs Bradley managed to angle his good arm over the stump and take his full weight for a while. "All right, Rajeev. Take a breather. We're half way. Tell me when you're ready. But don't leave it for too long."

Concerned that the Marshal's strength might give out before his own, after only a short rest Shah called out, "Ready, Marshal!" and resumed hoisting on the ropes. But even after this brief respite, he couldn't muster the strength he needed. Bradley's legs were clearly getting much weaker too. At the first stride he missed his footing completely, taking the deputy by surprise so that the ropes slipped from his grip momentarily. Bradley fell back with a howl of pain, only just managing to regain his earlier position, clinging to the stump and hanging against the chalk face like a fly on a wall.

Anxiously, Shah shouted down the obvious question.

"Yes, I'm still in one piece," came the reply. "Look, this stump's pretty solid. It's holding my weight. Give me some slack and I'll wrap the rope around it a couple of turns. If you want to secure your ends, I can hang here for a while longer while we both rest and regain our strength."

The deputy gladly complied and fell back on the rocky track, gulping in mouthfuls of air to replenish his bursting lungs.

He worried now that he might lack the stamina to finish the job. He knew they must resume soon, for Bradley couldn't be left hanging on that stump indefinitely. So he took up the ropes again and checked that he was ready. But at the very first pull, he knew it was hopeless. The task was too much for him, no matter how hard he willed his overtaxed muscles to do his bidding. His mind was in turmoil. He didn't want to fail the Marshal, whom he respected and to whom he and his people owed so much. A surge of despair and shame overwhelmed him and resignation to failure seemed to be the only option.

Then he heard a noise behind him and saw another pair of hands take one set of ropes from his. Together the two of them pulled, the task now much easier and the additional muscle power enabling a steady gathering of the ropes. At last Bradley finished the scramble with a final push and with astonishment accept four helping hands to lift him by his good arm to the safety of the narrow track.

Exhausted, none of them spoke for a moment, until at last their unexpected benefactor broke the silence.

"I came as soon as I could," she said.

* * * * *

Sylvia knelt beside Bradley, now lying on the grassy bank beyond the chalk track above the quarry.

"I'll have to strip off your tunic and shirt if I'm going to get a good look at your injuries. I'll try not to hurt you."

He was in too much pain to even consider feeling bashful about this. He was only pleased that she seemed to know what she was doing. If he felt embarrassed at all it was because he, the great warrior and saviour of threatened villages, was now the helpless one, relying on his friends to tend to him.

"I'd have come down sooner, but I only caught sight of your campfire just before dusk," she explained, while her shocked expression told him the bruising around his shoulder must look as bad as it felt.

"I thought it best not to show myself till morning, so I slept on the hillside up there. I didn't know you'd taken a fall until I woke up to hear Rajeev struggling with the ropes."

Bradley didn't answer. He was more concerned with his immediate discomfort, which he reckoned she wasn't helping to relieve much, what with her poking and prodding.

"Hmm, you've a few cuts and bruises from your fall," she observed, casting aside his bloody shirt. "This gash across your chest is fairly deep."

"Ouch!" he protested. "You don't have to prod every one of them, do you?"

"Sorry," she said with a grimace. Then she glanced at Shah. "Boil up some water, would you, Rajeev? And I don't suppose you've any clean cloth that I can tear up to bathe his wounds with?"

The ever-resourceful Shah fetched a shirt from his saddlebag. Then he went to re-kindle the fire and heat up the kettle, while she attacked the woven shirt with her skinning knife.

"Now, what have you done to your shoulder? Does it feel broken?"

"I don't think so. More likely dislocated. I only know it hurts like hell."

"Dislocated? All right. I'm going to have to feel around a bit. I'll try to be gentle." She looked at him kindly and nervously he returned her smile.

"If you know what you're doing, go ahead. I hope your hands aren't too cold, though."

Self-consciously she breathed on her fingers to warm them. Then, carefully, she placed them on his injured shoulder and made a brief examination.

"I think you're right," she said. "I can't find any break. It's definitely dislocated though. I think I can fix it."

"Whoa! Hold on!" he protested. "You only think you can fix it? Aren't you sure?"

"Well... I've never done it myself. But I've seen it done. I'm pretty sure I can." Then before he could argue about it she shot another order at Shah. "Rajeev, pass me that crossbow, will you?"

Bradley frowned and tried to turn his head to see what she was up to. "You're not going to put me out of my misery, are you?"

She took the proffered bow from the deputy, placed her foot on one side of its stirrup and pulled hard on the string to prime it. Bradley knew this couldn't be easy, because her muscles must still have been aching from the effort of hauling him up that cliff face. He saw her glance in Shah's direction, but it was obvious her pride wouldn't let her ask him for help. Besides, Rajeev must be even more exhausted than she. Bradley had to admire how she gritted her teeth until she'd bullied the bowstring into the set position.

Gasping she said, "Rajeev, can you cut a strip of hide and fold it four times to make a thick pad, about the size of your palm? And give me a blunted bolt — just slice the end off." The deputy took his sharpest knife and set about doing what she'd asked.

Taking the thick wad, she placed the bolt in the bow's groove and said to the Marshal, "I want you to sit up straight if you can. Rajeev, can you help him?"

The deputy knelt beside Bradley, holding him upright.

"Now I'm going to try and align your shoulder with the other one. It might hurt a bit."

He felt her hands grip his shoulders and a lance of intense pain shoot through his body.

"Sorry," she said. But she didn't waste any more time apologising. "Keep still now and brace yourself while I manoeuvre the bow into place."

He looked away into the distance, trying not to think of what she was doing to him, but he felt her place the wadding between the blunt bolt and his skin. Then without warning she pulled the trigger that would normally have sent a lethal arrow speeding deep into the flesh of some unsuspecting enemy or animal. Instead the immense thrust of the pent-up string drove the bolt into the wadding, transmitting its force through his muscle and driving the displaced limb back into its socket. The jolt induced a surge of excruciating agony and straight away he emitted a howling scream that echoed across the silent hills. Then he flopped over.

* * * * *

He was unconscious for only a short while. When he opened his eyes, it was to see Sylvia carefully attending to his superficial wounds. His shoulder felt different. It was still painful, but less awkward than it had been before. He guessed her skill with the crossbow had done the trick.

She dabbed at his face with a clean, damp rag. Amidst all his other pain he'd failed to notice that he'd scraped his face during the fall, but now it smarted badly.

"It's cut deep," she said. "There'll be a scar. Just think — you'll look as hideous as me." He appreciated her amusing remark, so he reciprocated with a smile and a shake of the head. He was ready to refute her self-criticism, but before he could put his thoughts into words a sudden shaft of pain seared his recently injured shoulder. He recoiled automatically and then enjoyed the relief when the pain subsided.

"You'll need to be careful for a while," she said, genuinely concerned. "I did my best, but there'll be torn muscle that needs a chance to mend."

He nodded, then carefully turned his head to indicate the now improving shoulder. "Where did you learn to do that?" he asked. "In the village?"

"Not exactly..." She stared across at Shah, who was fetching some hot food over, as if to seek an answer to an unspoken question. He nodded and she went on, "I expect Rajeev told you that he went off for a season with the traders a few years back.

Well, I followed him and joined up with them too. That's where I learned some of the skills of the travelling folk."

"So, you make a habit of running off on your own without being invited."

He regretted at once having said it. It was now clear why she'd been absent from the leaving party. She'd been busy after all, preparing her horse and provisions to follow them out here into the wilderness. For whatever reason and however misguided he believed her to be, he had to admit that her presence here had proved more than helpful, even indispensable. And he realised how ungrateful and ungracious his unkind words must sound. But the damage was done and he despised himself for it.

She said nothing, only pursed her lips, got up and walked over towards the fire, where she helped herself to some food and sat down to eat, staring off into the distance.

CHAPTER EIGHTEEN
A CHANGE OF HEART

"I'm all right, Rajeev. I can easily ride one-handed. Stop fussing now."

Those were the last words to pass between them for the rest of the day.

Bradley was determined not to let his injury delay the mission. Against Shah's advice, he insisted on pressing ahead on the chance of sighting a free village where they might get some proper rest. Once the decision was made he didn't feel much like talking anyway, due mainly to his own low spirits. Having complained of Sylvia's absence from the farewell ceremony back at Ashwell, he should be glad to see her now — but not under these circumstances. She'd virtually run away from home and he needed to decide what to do about that. Certainly not waste precious time accompanying her back to her family. Neither, with all the attendant dangers, was he inclined to send her packing on her own — not that he thought for a moment that she'd go. No, he'd see what could be done when they reached civilisation. And then on top of everything she was in a foul mood because of his thoughtless comment. She rode a few horse lengths ahead, unwilling to talk and indulging in a female sulk of unfathomable magnitude. By the Gods, there were times when she got on his nerves!

He looked across at his deputy. Shah didn't seem to mind the silence. He looked quite happy to fall back into contemplative mode. And, if it wasn't Bradley's imagination, he fancied he caught the glimmer of a grin cross the deputy's lips whenever their eyes met. Well, he saw nothing even slightly amusing in the situation. Even the sky had taken on a murky greyness to match his mood.

Towards dusk they crossed the scarred, rolling hills and descended to a village on the leeward side. He was glad, not just because he didn't relish the prospect of another night camping out, but also because a steady drizzle had set in, drenching their clothing and making riders and horses feel uncomfortable. A couple of young village hunters rode out to meet them and soon they were drying themselves in front of a newly kindled fire in the kitchen of the headman's cottage.

"It's welcome you are, Marshal."

The speaker was the headman himself, one Hal Carter, who stoked the fire with logs to help the three young visitors dry out their wringing clothes and wet bodies. Sylvia was escorted away by one of his daughters, towelled and returned cocooned in a huge woollen blanket, in which she now snuggled on a bench, making the most of the welcoming heat of this kindly hearth. Her male companions were more or less naked, still drying themselves and relishing the enveloping warmth. She politely averted her gaze, though there was no shame attached to male nudity in such innocent circumstances. In any case, the two young men were soon handed dry clothing, which they gratefully pulled on before accepting jugs of mulled ale from the lady of the house and taking their own places by the now roaring fire.

"We'll not be demanding of your hospitality for long," Bradley assured their host. "Just warm, dry beds for the night and we'll be on our way again. Tell me, have you had any trouble from raiders?"

"We have that. But one of your colleagues, Marshal Barker, helped us organise and drive them out, a couple of moons ago. We thank the Gods for sending him to us. Life's been good since we got rid of that rabble."

"Barker, you say? I know Gerry Barker well. We were cadets together. He's a brave man and a fine warrior. Has he moved on to another village?"

"I wish I could say so. But I'm sad to report that your brave friend gave his life in battle on our behalf, a sacrifice for which we'll be eternally grateful."

Bradley was shocked to hear this news and let his face fall into his open hands.

"I apologise for springing it on you so suddenly, Marshal. I know of no other way to..."

Bradley sat up and shook his head, his face drained in spite of the heat from the crackling fire. He said sadly, "No matter, sir. Thank you for telling me. In the morning, I should like you to show me where his ashes have been scattered, if that's possible."

"Of course." Clearly embarrassed, Carter put another log on the fire.

"What of his work?" Bradley asked. "Is there still any danger from raiders in these parts?"

"Rest assured, Marshal. During his stay here, he created a miniature army. Four of our young men were appointed deputy marshals and I'm proud to say that my own son took Gerry Barker's place to carry on the fight after his death. The news we hear is that the Council's initiative is having similar success right across the enclave. I'd even venture to say it's safe enough for our traders to take up travelling again."

"In that case," Bradley said solemnly, "Gerry's death won't have been in vain."

* * * * *

Just after dawn of the following day, Bradley went into the nearby woods to the place where the ashes of his old friend and brother cadet Gerry Barker had been scattered.

He'd no sense of what might lie in store after death — if anything at all — but somehow he found comfort and solace in this peaceful place, where he could reflect on the good times they'd spent together while learning the skills and crafts of their honoured if bloody profession. Gerry had been a carefree type, always one to joke about danger, but more than adept at its avoidance, though frighteningly able to deal with it whenever necessary. In every practical sense his loss was great. But the loss to the world of his presence, his laughter and his courage was a harder thing to bear. He also thought again of his other lost companion, Colby. For a moment his spirit diminished at the futility of their chosen path and a feeling of profound weakness overcame him, so that he had to put out his arm for the support of a nearby tree trunk.

"Dominic, are you all right?"

It was Sylvia.

He steeled himself and tried to stand upright, letting go the tree's support. Almost instinctively she ran to him and took his arm in both her hands.

"Come over here and sit down for a moment," she said while leading him to a fallen trunk. "I told you it would take a while for your shoulder to heal. It's left you weak. You mustn't overdo things." Then she took a bottle from her tunic pocket, uncorked it and handed it to him. "Here, have a sip of this. It's some of my grandfather's store — I keep it for emergencies."

He sat down on the log, took a mouthful of the strong liquor and at once felt its warmth and his strength returning. Then he smiled at her, saying, "Dear Sylvia, how is it you're always around when I need you? Come to think of it, you're also often around when I don't need you. Still, I'm glad you're here now."

She looked astonished. "Are you really? I thought you were going to give me another telling-off for following you."

"I was. I'm sure your father doesn't approve of you going off on your own. But if you hadn't turned up to help us just when you did, I don't know what we'd have done. I reckon Rajeev would have had to leave me and go for help. I'd still be lying in agony on that ledge now, waiting for him. So, under the circumstances, how can I be angry with you?"

The smile that rose in her eyes quickly waned when he said, "But you must understand that we can't take you with us. I've asked Hal Carter to let you join a trading party that'll be heading south in a day or two."

There was fire in her voice as she stood up and said, "What do you mean, you can't take me? Didn't you just say that I'm always there when you need me? I don't want to crow about it, but it seems to me I'm pretty useful to have around whenever you get into scrapes — which is often. Leaving aside my helping pull you off that ledge, not to mention curing your dislocated shoulder — tell me, who rescued you from that raider camp? And who helped you plan the village defences and stood next to you in battle?"

Her eyes welled with angry tears, but through their veil she managed to complete her tirade with a defiant declaration. "And I rang that bloody bell for you!" So saying she turned away from him.

But he caught her shoulder and swung her to face him and although he gritted his teeth to avoid raising his voice, he couldn't conceal his rancour.

"All right! Have it your own way! Your father warned me you were headstrong. In any case, why am I worrying about your safety? Now I'll have to pay a trader to call by Crowtree and tell your family that you haven't been snaffled by brigands!"

As if by magic his words stemmed her tears and she beamed a happy smile.

"So I can come with you, then? Oh, thank you, Dominic, thank you. I promise you I won't be any trouble."

He only growled, "You'd better not be."

* * * * *

Later that day, humans and horses well fed and rested, the travellers said their farewells to the helpful villagers and continued on their journey north.

Bradley wondered if he'd been wrong to give in to Sylvia. For one thing, he hadn't realised just how talkative she could be. Barely a league into this stage of their journey, she'd rattled away since mounting her horse, hardly hesitating to draw breath. He compared this with the quiet and solitude of riding just with the taciturn Shah for his companion. How peaceful it had been then! But after a filling breakfast and still feeling weak from his injury, he now lacked the strength — or courage — to ask her to be quiet. So instead, he endured her chatter.

"Needless to say, Father didn't approve of my following after you. Not at first, anyway. But I made Jack tell him just what I was capable of and in the end he had to agree that I could handle myself as well as any man. I can hunt, ride and fight and I'm good at planning and strategy. If I weren't a girl, I bet you'd have made me a deputy. Father said so too, and Jack said there was no use trying to make me stay anyway, unless they tied me up and locked me in the shed where we kept that raider leader. Anyway, I told them I had to help you — destiny brought you to our village and intended me to go with you."

This made him smile. "You believe that, do you? In destiny, I mean. I'd have thought you too practical to think these things are mapped out for us."

"Why shouldn't they be? Who's to say? You may be a Council marshal, but that doesn't mean you know everything. Other people are entitled to an opinion, too."

He looked across at Shah, who was smirking — even on the verge of laughing outright. Bradley wasn't too pleased that his deputy was enjoying seeing him submit to this lecture from a teenage girl. Well, he wasn't going to submit. After all, who was in charge here?

"I've never claimed to know everything, young lady." He knew she didn't like being referred to in this way. "And while we're at it, what makes you think destiny chose *you* to help me in this quest? I don't recall the old woman's riddle mentioning a mischievous squirrel playing any part in the Gods' great plan."

She narrowed her eyes and gave him a wincing look, then kicked her horse into a canter that carried her well ahead, where she subsided into a trot to match theirs, retaining a good sulking distance between them.

"Ah well," Shah observed. "At least we'll have some peace and quiet for a while again."

Bradley laughed nervously. "I don't like falling out with her, Rajeev. But I just can't help rising to her bait. I've got to admit I think she'll be an asset to us. I wouldn't say so to her face, but as a warrior she's equal to any man I've trained. I hope you don't mind me saying that."

"If it were any other girl, Marshal, I might take it as criticism. But don't forget, I grew up alongside Sylvia Storey. She was always one of the boys — and not just that — she always wanted to be leader. She was never content to be told what to do. And she was hungry for knowledge. She's the only girl I know who insisted on spending time in the forge."

"Yes, I heard about that. That's where she came by..." For some reason, he didn't like to say it.

"The scar, you mean? That's right. I remember the incident. We were just children when it happened, but she took it so bravely. And it didn't put her off. I'd say it only made her more determined, as if nothing was going to stop her. That's what she is, you know. Unstoppable."

"Hmm, I reckon I'm learning that. So, you don't disapprove of my giving in... I mean, to my allowing her to come along?"

Shah smiled again. "Marshal, did you honestly ever have any choice in the matter?"

Whatever misgivings Bradley may have had about his decision, he didn't deny that Sylvia proved useful to have around, in all sorts of ways. For, despite her wanting to be one of the boys and prove her equality in what might otherwise be considered masculine tasks, she also insisted on playing the role of mother hen. It was she who prepared their food, chivvied them to keep the camp tidy (though in Shah she already had a convert in that department) and tended to any medical needs. For if a briar should scratch their cheek or a knife should slip while skinning a rabbit, she'd be there with gathered herbs, bandages and her grandfather's liquor, practical and comforting.

Nevertheless, for much of their onward journey there existed a grudging tolerance between Sylvia and Bradley, with Shah treating their relationship, with its occasional eruptions of froth and venom, as a distracting entertainment. Strangely though, whenever she was out of earshot Sylvia would often be the main topic of conservation, invariably at Bradley's instigation. And if she rode too far ahead during one of her sulks, he'd react tetchily.

"Where by the Gods is she, Rajeev? Why doesn't that girl have the sense to keep in sight? Doesn't she know how it annoys me when she does that?"

"I'm sure she does, Marshal. I suspect that's why she does it."

It was a crisp autumn morning when at last they topped a ridge of low hills providing them with an expansive view of the river estuary. None of them had seen such a sight as they now beheld and the beauty and majesty of the vista that stretched out before them rendered the three of them speechless.

Below and directly ahead, as expected, lay the river. But it was much wider than they'd imagined it to be, here more than five furlongs from bank to bank. Its swirling brown waters seethed with a life of their own, carrying silt and flotsam out towards the Great Sea that they knew lay away to the east, some several leagues distant. But from where they stood the river continued on, virtually as far as the eye could see. Below them spread a broad coastal plain, mostly wooded and with no obvious evidence of human habitation. From the west flowed the river and through a fine mist appeared the distant outline of a huge structure that seemed to span the two banks, causing them to gasp in amazement. Then still further west ran the faint but unerringly solid line of the Wall. It was difficult to tell because of the haze and its distance, but they thought it stretched right across the river and away to north, where it continued ever onwards and over the far horizon.

159

Shah broke the silence. "What a sight! I could stay here and watch this forever. But I suppose we ride eastwards from here, Marshal?"

"Well, I'd have agreed with you, before we reached this place. But I'd no idea just how wide this river would be. According to the old woman's rhyme, we should go east and then 'across to a tower.' Looking at the river, it gets broader as it flows east towards the Great Sea. Its waters don't look particularly friendly, either. If we're going to pass over it safely, we'll have to find a narrower crossing."

Sylvia said, "That means we'll need to ride west."

"That's right. And even then I suspect the crossing won't be easy. But look. Can you see that big structure up-river? I've never seen anything so huge."

Shah said excitedly, "It can't be a bridge, can it? No man could have constructed such a thing!"

"None that we know," Sylvia suggested. "Might it have been built by the same people who made the Wall?"

Her companions were silenced, even shocked, by her statement. The words she'd just uttered would have been considered, at the very least, disrespectful in ordinary polite society. Bradley gave her a chance to correct her mistake.

"You mean the Gods who made the Wall? You're saying that they may have built this bridge too. Right?"

"I know what I said. Just because we lack the skill and knowledge, that doesn't mean that men and women weren't once able to make such enormous structures, nor that they won't be able to again. How do we know that those we call the Gods of the Wall weren't just men and women like us? And why is it considered impolite to suggest the possibility?"

They had no answer for her. Bradley shook his head and resolved to put her outburst aside and pretend it had never occurred. It was just Sylvia being Sylvia, he told himself.

"Come on," he said, taking up his reins and turning Scarlett's head towards the west. "Let's see if we can reach that bridge before nightfall."

Chapter Nineteen
Strange Landings

The little boy knelt at play in the grassy meadow, plucking the last of the season's daisies to make a chain for his grandmother, who tended her little flock of sheep close by. All at once he felt a cool breeze gently stir the soft, long hair that nuzzled the back of his neck and he laughed at the funny tingle that ran down his spine. Free of care, he rolled over onto his back, supported by his elbows and raised his head, eyes shut, face to windward.

Even at five years old, these habits were as natural as life itself. Already he was used to the changing elements that ruled his little world, had learned to read their signs and knew when they were good-humoured and trustworthy, or when they were angered and deserved to be feared. At the feathery sting of this new cool air upon his cheeks, his nostrils dilated and drew in its richness, letting the raw taste of late autumn fill his throat and lungs. When he opened his eyes they smarted, but not unpleasantly. As the cloudiness cleared, he felt a single warm tear slip down his cheek and savoured it for a few moments before sitting up and raising an arm to wipe it away on his sheepskin sleeve.

He glanced across the hillside and saw that his grandmother had felt it too. She rubbed her hands with gusto and sniffed the air. Then she spoke and confirmed his thoughts, if confirmation were needed.

"Winter's calling, Toby my boy!" Her voice rode the breeze that rolled across the patches of straggly grass, driving wave upon wave before it. "Can you smell the snows to come? They'll not be far behind."

He recalled only briefly the initial pleasures of those early snows of the previous winter. Then at once his thoughts moved

161

reluctantly to the harsher face of that season. There was the never-ending toil to shift the drifting cliffs of snow that tried their hardest to smother the village. Then the raging storms that frightened all the children (and some adults too), rocking and shaking the wooden shacks that nevertheless refused to fall in around them. He shuddered to recall the fear for their men folk — his father, uncles and male cousins — whose lot it was, as stores of food diminished, to drive their tiny boats into the fury of the storm-torn estuary in search of fish to feed the village. And there was always the sheer hard struggle against the biting, menacing cold.

Toby didn't like to be reminded of those dark winter days and nights. He wished the milder weather would go on and on. He glanced across at the sheep that huddled as best they could on this leeward side of the hilltop. They knew what was to come well enough.

The hummock on which the sheep now grazed was hardly high enough to call a hill. It was little more than a bump of lush grassland standing barely a hundred strides downriver from Nearbank. That was the name of their village — although if, when rarely, he was away from the bank (say, in his father's boat on the river during calm, sunny afternoons), then the whole of this shore was known by that same name. For Toby — and indeed for most of the villagers (barring the men who must venture towards further horizons for fish) — Nearbank was the world, or at least the only part of the world that counted. Because of a local outbreak of plague early in the village's history, first necessity then superstition had caused them to dig in and shun most contact with the world outside. As years went by, dense forest enveloped the coastal plain along this south bank of the river, effectively isolating the village except for its access to the muddy waters of the estuary. By now, with the rare exception of the odd stray traveller, the villagers of Nearbank neither knew of, nor were known to the other inhabitants of Fenwold. Beyond the outskirts of the village and its grazing lands their forefathers had constructed a fence, now dilapidated and overcome by the forest, but still a visible marker beyond which it was deemed too dangerous to venture.

The old woman walked across to her grandson and smiled at the thoughtful eyes and wrinkled brow that caused him momentarily to appear far older than his five years. Then her smile gave way to a worried frown and she cocked an ear to the wind.

"Listen, Toby. Was that thunder in the distance?"

Together they looked out from their vantage point across the white-crested, murky waters towards the far bank and the dreadful country beyond. Above it approached the black and purple, almost chillingly beautiful mountains of storm cloud, stealthily mustering to do battle with those who had no means of fighting back.

She turned to the boy saying, "Come on, young man. Get your stick and we'll take this lot to the fold. Count as we go."

Obediently, the lad helped her drive the little flock downhill towards the village, checking their number on the way. The child had by now learned the old counting method — relic of an old, forgotten language. "Yan, chan, tether, mether, pip," he chanted softly.

Smiling once more, she joined him now in his counting with, "Azar, sazar, akka, cotta, dik!" and he giggled, begging her to let him count the next five. She shook her head, saying, "No. I'll do four — you do the fifth."

He gleefully nodded then, both knowing how much he loved to shout the word for the fifteenth sheep. So she began, "Yan-a-dik, chan-a-dik, tether-a-dik, mether-a-dik..." and without a moment's pause he yelled out, "Bumfit!" to the great delight of them both.

"Same again for the next five?" she asked. Again he nodded cheerfully and she continued, "Yan-a-bum, chan-a-bum, tether-a-bum, mether-a-bum..." leaving him to finish the twenty with a resounding, "Jiggit!"

At this, he looked to the ground for a small stone, which he picked up and clutched in his little hand, but taking care not to lose sight of the last sheep counted and the pair of them began again in unison, "Yan, chan, tether, mether, pip..."

On reaching the village clearing they finished their counting and agreed on thirty-four (one stone and a mether-a-dik), this being the required total; not a large flock perhaps, but precious to the last old yowe. There came a more persistent rumble of thunder — though still mercifully distant — and the sheep-minders hurried their flock towards the wicker-fenced fold. Here the old woman held open the gate while the boy gently ushered the animals into their enclosure. Finally he helped her by securing the gate and he watched her lips muttering a prayer that the morning would see all thirty-four still safe from harm.

She deposited the lad at his parents' cabin, where his mother came out to gather him in at the door. Then with kisses, nods and waves, they saw her sniff the air once more and shudder, pulling her shawl right up over her head before turning towards home.

* * * * *

The old woman shuffled towards her cabin, humming a fragment from some old, half-remembered tune, dodging geese and chickens as she crossed the little crew yard. By now the sky above the village had darkened menacingly, its threatening mass making her hurry towards her cabin door. She was cheered though by the little curl of smoke that rose from the cottage chimney and looked forward to warming her old bones in front of its log fire.

Her man — the village headman — was inside, seated at a table close by a window and peering out at the gathering storm. She knew his look — it spoke of a deep concern. "What is it?" she demanded, barring the door and wiping her muddy boots on the doormat.

He was a taciturn fellow and wasted no words. "Boat put out this afternoon." Then his tired grey face flexed and he said, "Sean saw some flotsam over near Farbank. Thought it worth taking a look. They had to follow it downriver a way. Got a hard row back. Might manage to make some sail, if they can hold the boat steady."

"Who's out there?" she urgently demanded.

"Sean, Chris, Luke — all three."

Her hand went instinctively to her mouth and she bit on the back of her wrist. These were nasty, treacherous waters. In far off days, or so it was told, boats of a size beyond her imagination had navigated the river's narrow channels and tormenting currents, though how they'd done it none could say. For the estuary silted up regularly and their men needed intimate knowledge of the waters to find a safe channel that wouldn't ground them and crack open their puny timber craft. The storms that swelled the river sometimes helped to clear away the silt, but always changed the underwater landscape with their ferocious scouring, so that the location of safe navigable lanes had to be learned all over again.

"Oh, Reuben!" she sighed. "Will we ever endure the hardships this world piles upon us?" Then, in her practical way accepting there was no future in despair, she softly enquired, "What are their chances?"

Her husband pulled on his boots and answered with as long a speech as she'd heard him make in many a day.

"Slim. They'll have seen the storm brewing and would've started back by now. But it's come on sudden and they're still downriver. They'll have to face up to it. Mind, they're river men, best we've had — better than I was or any of the old 'uns. They've got the knowledge. Aye, lass — they've got it in 'em to ride the storm when it hits 'em. They'll know to use just enough sail to tack with the wind against the current — they just need to stay in the channels and mind the banks, that's all."

"That's all," she echoed quietly, almost absently. Then, seeing that he was now fully kitted up for venturing outside, she observed, "Starting a fire? I'll come and help."

"Best if you rouse the other villagers to fetch plenty of dry timber from the woodpiles, bring it up to the top of the hill and then gather some brush. Tell them to make sure it's dry, mind. I'll fetch some embers."

Then he took a small metal shovel from the hearth, dug into the turf and scooped up a small pile of glowing sticks.

* * * * *

The headman stooped at the base of the little mound of dry kindling. Toby his grandson stood by his left elbow and even at his tender age he must know well the purpose of this activity — to provide a beacon to help guide the boatmen home through the approaching night. The hubbub of the chattering crowd subsided. He placed the hot embers under the kindling and blew on them to draw a flame. He'd skill enough to make fire in the old way, using flints or wood and yarn. But there was no time for that.

The fire flashed into life and the villagers stepped back.

"Gather more brush!" he yelled above the crackle of burning wood. But many were already busy collecting dry twigs and sticks from among the undergrowth surrounding the village.

Used to working closely together, the good folk of Nearbank moved quickly and industriously to maintain a steady supply of fuel for the all-important beacon. There was little chatter. The gusting wind from across the river challenged the loud *smack* of the flaming timber, at once fanning and then threatening to snuff out the first tenuous flickers. But soon the gatherers' work was rewarded and the crackling pile of burning wood countered the anger of the howling storm with its own fiery rage.

The heat was impressive and welcome to the workers who could at last slow their pace and enjoy its radiant embrace in the chilly evening. The sky was darker now and the storm clouds drew their menacing curtain across the sunset, driving parents and children alike to seek one another's comfort as the tempest approached.

Though expected by all, the first mighty roll and clap of terrorising thunder, preceded only briefly by a frightening shock of brilliant lightning, made each heart quicken and little hands tighten their grip on their mothers' clothing.

But there was no time to reflect on their fear. Nor would the fire maintain its life unaided. At the first signs of hesitation the old man drew a breath and yelled across the roar of wind and flame, "Don't stop! Fetch more wood! Keep it burning!"

Every pair of feet then scurried from the fire and into the hedgerows and little clumps of undergrowth to gather dry dead branches of elder or laurel. As he waited for more fuel to feed the hungry inferno, old Reuben peered out from the hilltop across the expanse of the river. Through the darkness he saw the white tops of dancing waves whipped up by the gale and the bank of rain steadily working its way across the estuary towards them. He averted his gaze from the stinging glare of the fire long enough for his eyesight to recover, clearly making out the coast downriver for a good half league and the thrashing waters out there too. But — though he tried hard to make his eyes pierce the shroud of darkness creeping over the water — he saw no boat. The faces of those brave young men danced tantalisingly before him, but their vessel failed to come into view. Something clouded his vision — smoke from the fire, he lied to himself — and he turned without further hesitation back to the stoking, now voicing the little prayer that had been forming in his mind.

"Gods of the Wall, let them see it!" he willed, with gritted teeth. "For the sake of us all — let them see the fire!"

Then at once a cry went up from Toby's mother. "Sail! Sail!" she cried. "I can see them!"

All eyes now turned towards the water. Soon, the headman saw it too — the familiar white square that only moments earlier he feared he'd never see again. He urged it to catch the wind while it slowly cleaved the air, dragging the dark hull of the puny boat towards the little jetty.

The fire now forgotten, its task completed, the throng of relieved villagers hurried down to the waterside to greet the brave crew. None dared contemplate that any of the men might have come to any harm in the storm — though many a private prayer was uttered in that short journey down to welcome the storm-tossed craft. But when the boat drew up to the jetty it was apparent that all were safe, if close to exhaustion. Sean, the leading boatman, managed to toss a rope to his father, who swiftly made the bow secure. He then stepped ashore and wrapped the aft rope around the stout pillar of oak that served for a shore bollard.

No words were spoken then. There was only the clasping of hands, the exchange of glances that spoke of thanks and love. Chris and Luke dragged something heavy from the darkness of their little hold — the precious flotsam whose getting had brought them all so close to disaster. They struggled to manhandle their catch over the side and onto the jetty and when they'd done so the headman stood dumbfounded. For when his weary eyes cleared he could hardly believe what it was his kinsmen had fetched back from the jaws of hell.

It was a half-drowned, half-starved, spluttering, wreck of a man with dark, steely, piercing eyes. He had little clothing and the Gods alone must know how he'd survived those raging waters. And even though clogged up with muck and debris from the swollen river, it was clear for all to see that his face and head were covered with a thick, bushy mass of fiery red hair.

CHAPTER TWENTY
SEARCHING FOR BRIDGES

They were well into the forest when the storm struck. Progress had been slow enough all day, owing to the absence of clear trails through the dense woodland. Shah did most of the hacking with his machete, because Bradley's shoulder still throbbed, and Sylvia had the job of leading the horses in the rear. But by now the lashing rain and formation of puddles in the sticky clay ground made it impossible to go any further.

"By the Gods, I've never seen such foul weather!" Bradley shouted. "We've no chance of reaching that bridge tonight. We should use this last bit of daylight to make camp. Let's find somewhere to sit it out till the storm passes."

Shah looked around and found an area of scrub that they could clear to serve as a resting place. Now the clouds burst with a vengeance, soaking them all and their clothing despite the usual protection of the forest canopy.

Sylvia said, "I hope somebody remembered to bring along some dry brush to start a fire."

Shah nodded towards his horse. "You'll find some in my saddlebags — left hand side. They're of good leather so it'll be dry enough. But don't open them till we get some hides up. How are the horses?" Though usually placid animals, they snorted their disapproval at the rainwater now drenching their backs.

"How do you think they are? They're fed up, just like us. Hurry up and sort out some shelter, will you?"

Bradley and Shah set to work using branches and skins to make a covered camp area with room for a fire and a space dry enough for them all to rest in relative comfort overnight. Sylvia rigged up some protection for the horses, then rubbed them down and gave them dry feed and water. The day's trek had been tedious, but soon the travellers were sitting around a cheery blaze and enjoying some hot food and a swig from Sylvia's little store of liquor, their wet outer garments hanging up to dry on some nearby branches.

"These woods are a lot denser than we thought," Shah said as he picked the last bit of meat from a leg of rabbit. "When do you think we'll reach that bridge?"

Bradley shrugged. "Not sure. If these were anything like the woods we're used to, I'd say we'd have been there by now. Trouble is, I don't think there are any settlements hereabouts. If there were, this forest would be crisscrossed with cleared trails. Looks like it'll be slow going all the way to the bridge."

Shah said, "You know, we'd move faster without the horses to slow us down."

"Hmm. I've been thinking about that too."

A loud sneeze escaped from the tent-shaped blanket under which Sylvia huddled. Then came the muffled comment, "I bet I know who'll be left behind to look after them."

Bradley winked across at Shah, who quietly chuckled.

"It's not a laughing matter," came another mutter from the blanket.

"Actually," the Marshal said, "I was thinking of going ahead alone on foot in the morning. There'd be little point in us struggling there with the horses if we were wrong about it being a bridge. I'd make better headway if you two stayed here with the horses for a day or two."

Shah said, "Wouldn't it make more sense for me to go? Your shoulder's not properly mended yet. With all due respect, I'm better placed to use the machete than you are just now."

"Hmm. I must say I was hoping to get a look at that bridge myself. But I can't deny you'd get there quicker, given the state I'm in. All right. We'll kit you out for a foot journey and you can get underway first thing in the morning. You'd better leave markers as you go. But whatever happens — even if you haven't reached the bridge — I want you to start back the following morning at the latest. If you haven't returned in two days from now, I'm coming after you. Is that clear?"

"Clear."

* * * * *

170

"Dominic, I don't suppose it even crossed your mind, but I could have gone and got there quicker than Rajeev."

It was mid-afternoon of the day that Shah was due to return. Bradley wasn't too worried. By now his deputy had shown himself to be capable enough. Still he couldn't help imagining a variety of mishaps that might have befallen him. He didn't give voice to his thoughts, and besides, his sole companion for the past couple of days had already established a vigorous monopoly of the conversation.

Sylvia was giving him some earache concerning her favourite subject — how she was as good as, if not better than, any man. He didn't want to encourage her, so he said nothing and continued cleaning his crossbow.

"You know, ever since we were children, I could outrun Rajeev — not that he isn't a good athlete. It's just that I'm a faster one. And I'm a better horseman. I mean horsewoman. And I'm better at survival skills. You should've sent me. Why didn't you send me?"

Just now he almost wished he had. But he kept his own counsel. Still, he knew he had to say something. "Look, Sylvia, I know you're good. Don't forget, I trained you — for a while, anyway. But when you're a leader of men — and women — you don't always choose your best warrior for every job that comes up."

"Don't you?"

"No."

"Why not?"

"Because... because, if you did, that would be a sure method of getting rid of all your best men, or women, wouldn't it?"

She looked pensive for a moment. "Oh, I think I can see what you're getting at. You sent Rajeev to look at the bridge, because you considered him expendable."

He bristled. "No, Sylvia. I don't consider Rajeev expendable at all. I didn't say that. I mean... I just thought it was more appropriate to send him on that particular mission."

"And it wasn't because he was expendable?"

"No."

"Why, then?"

"Because... Now, look here, Sylvia. You're going to have to get used to the fact that a marshal doesn't have to justify every decision he makes to his subordinates."

"Well, what good's that?"

"What do you mean, what good's that?"

"Well, if you can't explain your decisions, how are you ever going to train anyone to step into your shoes?"

"What's training got to do with it? Let's get this clear, Sylvia. This isn't a training situation. This is real life. And in real life, someone has to be in charge and if those who aren't in charge continually insist on questioning their leader's authority, the result's likely to be chaos."

There was silence for a moment. Then she said, "Oh. I see. Yes, I can accept that. What you say makes sense."

He smiled. "Good. I'm pleased you can see what I'm talking about."

She pursed her lips. "Only..."

"Only what?"

"Well, I still don't see why you sent Rajeev instead of me."

He stood up and walked slowly along the track that Shah had taken the day before.

"Where are you going?" she asked.

"I need to think — straighten out some plans — in my head."

"I'll come with you."

"No, no. It's all right. You stay here and... tidy up the camp. Or better still, check the horses — you're good at that. I mean to say, that's one of the many things you're good at — excellent, in fact. You're a first class warrior, Sylvia."

And she watched him in bemused silence as he turned and walked off down the trail.

CHAPTER TWENTY-ONE
LOOK EAST AT THE RIVER

"Rajeev! Well met! I was beginning to think you'd got lost."

Laughing, Shah extended a hand. "Come on, Marshal. You know me better than that. I might have fallen in the river and drowned, or been killed by raiders, or even eaten by some ferocious animal. But never lost."

"All right. Point taken. So what kept you?"

"It took me longer than expected to cut a trail through to that bridge. If you can believe it, the forest gets thicker the further west you go. It would have been impossible without the machete. Here, I brought a couple of rabbits as compensation for keeping you waiting."

He untied the carcasses from his belt. "It was so dense that I didn't find the old roadway till it was nearly dark last night. By the time I'd made camp, there wasn't enough light to get a good look at the bridge — I had to spend time at daybreak doing that. So it was mid-morning before I started back. I didn't sleep too well overnight. You know how it is when you're camping alone, always with one eye open. So when I stopped to rest at mid-day, I grabbed a bit of a catnap."

Bradley grasped his shoulder and said, "I'd have done the same, Rajeev. It's good to see you back safe and sound. Come and tell us what you saw over supper."

The Marshal had wandered some distance from the camp after his earlier discourse with Sylvia and as they walked he brought up his right palm to gently massage his injured shoulder.

Shah asked idly, "Been giving you some pain, Marshal?"

"How did you guess? I've never known such a talkative woman."

"I meant your shoulder."

"Shoulder? Oh. It's just a minor irritation. It's that girl Sylvia that's getting to me. She won't give me any peace, man!"

They still had some little way to go till reaching camp. Though obviously tired from his mission, the flicker of a mischievous smile crossed the deputy's face.

"Well, if you ask me, Marshal, I reckon she's in love with you."

Bradley stopped and scowled. "Don't be ridiculous, man. She's constantly at my throat."

Still grinning, Shah nodded. "Yes, I know. That's Sylvia's way. As I said before, I grew up with her. I know how she ticks. And believe me, she's absolutely besotted. You're all she talks about when you're not around. Gets rather boring, if you want the truth."

Bradley shrugged and resumed walking. "Well, she's shown no sign of it to me."

"Really? I'd thought something might have happened while I was away."

"Oh, I see. So that's why you insisted on going to the bridge instead of me. Playing the matchmaker, eh? Well, I can assure you, you've got her all wrong. Sylvia has no affection at all for me. She makes it pretty plain that she resents my authority."

Still smirking, the deputy said, "Well, I wouldn't let it bother you, Marshal."

Not far from the camp now, Bradley halted again and took hold of Shah's sleeve. "Why should it bother me? It's just a leadership issue that I'll have to deal with, that's all. It's nothing I can't handle."

"Hmm. Well, I can understand you'd find it a problem, if she did take a fancy to you. After all, she's not much to look at, what with that scar and those cold, blue eyes."

The bait was taken. Bradley bristled. "Look, Rajeev. I'm surprised to hear you make such comments as these. A mature man sees through such superficial blemishes. Besides, if you disregard the scar, Sylvia has very pleasant features. She's got a kindly face and these funny little wrinkles next to her eyes, whenever she laughs or frowns. And her eyes aren't cold, nor are they blue. They're a soft brown and quite warm..."

He stopped in mid sentence, because his deputy's face had broken into a broad smile. Then he thought about what he'd just said and bit his lip.

"Not a word more, Rajeev," he said, scowling. "You know, you're a dangerous friend for a man to have. Come on, let's go back and see what's for supper."

* * * * *

"Right, Rajeev. Let's have your report."

The Marshal had insisted they finish their meal before hearing what Shah had to say. Besides, he wanted to put some time between this and their earlier conversation. This, after all, was more serious business.

"Well, as I said earlier, it was hard going and nightfall by the time I reached the road leading to the bridge. It was weird, because one moment I was in the dense forest and the next on this old metalled road. You know, there are remnants of some of these old roads in our part of Fenwold, though over the years we've used most of the surface material for building and repairing our houses. This one was different though, because it was completely intact — seemed to be, anyway. None of it had been removed. Oh, it was well broken up by who knows how many years of frost and the vegetation growing up through the cracks. But it was still recognisable as a complete road. And looking north, I could see the structure of the bridge through the trees.

"So this morning — as early as possible, as soon as it was light — I picked my way through the vegetation, following the old roadway. It was a weird sensation as the gradient increased and took me up above the tops of the trees. The road was still cracked, but virtually free of vegetation here. That's apart from a fungus that grew on the exposed roadway. I tried a mouthful of it — smelled all right, so I didn't see any harm in it. It had an unusual taste, but there were no ill effects."

Sylvia butted in. "That was stupid, Rajeev. It might've made you ill."

Bradley said, as kindly as possible, "Let him finish, Sylvia, please."

"Sorry, Dominic." And she blinked both eyelids in his direction, which for some strange reason he found unnerving.

"It's all right," he said, returning her glance.

"Anyway," Shah continued, only pausing to check that he still had their full attention, "I kept going until the road levelled off and I was at the start of the bridge itself. The views were fantastic. Hard to describe really." Here he paused and stared into the smoky night air.

"Try," said Bradley.

"Well, from the west, the river flows in across a plain, pretty well covered with woodland on both banks. The Wall stretches out across the western horizon, running northwards without a break. I'd say it's about five leagues off upriver from there. To the north, all I could see was the rust of the autumn canopy, so much colour, spreading way off into the distant hills."

"That's poetic," Sylvia said.

"Thanks," he replied.

"Did you say 'hills'?" Bradley asked.

"Oh yes — definitely hills. Not big ones, but the northern terrain is definitely dominated by higher ground."

"And to the east?"

"To the east, yes. Well, much the same as to the west. Except that the river... gets wider and..."

Sylvia helped him. "It would be flowing away from you."

"Yes. Right. Well, it's almost completely wooded on both sides, though the forest thins out further to the east, towards the main estuary."

"Ah, the estuary." Bradley stopped him here. "Could you see the actual river mouth?"

"Well, not entirely."

"How not entirely?"

"I could only see one side of it, because of the bend in the river."

"Which way does the river bend?"

The deputy paused again and then said, "South."

"So, did you have a full view of the northern bank?"

"Oh, yes. I had a good view of it right to the tip of the northern bank. It sort of tapered off to a point."

"A point?"

"Yeah. The land kind of gets thinner and thinner and takes a sort of twist southwards, then comes to a point."

"And... did you see anything on that point?"

"Well, it was a long way off."

"Rajeev…"

"All right, all right. Yes, I thought I saw something that might just possibly be the remains of some kind of a…"

Sylvia couldn't help herself. Nor could the Marshal, for they both declared in unison, "A tower!"

"Yes," Rajeev said, beaming. "I'd guess it was a tower."

There were yelps and howls of delight then and the three of them got up and danced around the fire, with twirls and three-handed reels, until they all fell down breathless with delight at the news.

More than likely it was entirely accidental and the result of the liquor, but when they all collapsed in a giggling heap, the Marshal and Sylvia happened to fall quite close together, facing one another. What happened then was so quick that later each would wonder if it had happened at all. But Rajeev Shah knew and felt a warm glow to witness that first brief kiss between his childhood friend Sylvia Storey and Marshal Dominic Bradley, Surveyor of the Wall.

* * * * *

"Marshal!"

It was just before daybreak when Shah shook Bradley's good shoulder to wake him, but with lowered voice so as not to disturb Sylvia, still asleep on the other side of the glowing remains of the campfire. "Marshal! Wake up!"

Bradley's eyes opened and instinctively his right arm moved straight to his crossbow. Then, seeing Shah's concerned face looking at him, he relaxed his grip on the bow and merely said softly, "What's the matter, Rajeev?"

"I need to talk to you." Then he glanced across the fire to check his actions hadn't wakened Sylvia. "I need to tell you something I should've told you last night."

"All right," he said, slipping from under his blanket as quietly as he could. "Come for a walk up the trail and you can tell me whatever it is that's bothering you."

He picked up his blanket and wrapped it around his shoulders to retain some body heat, for the morning air was bitterly cold. The two lawmen walked a short way along the trail, out of sight and earshot of the camp, where Bradley stopped at a thorn tree. Here while emptying his bladder he said, "Come on then, Rajeev. What did you forget to tell me?"

"Well, you have to admit, we all got fairly merry on my news about the tower."

"So? Why shouldn't we? It was good news."

"Yes, I know. But when I hit my bedroll, I was so bushed that I fell asleep straight away. It wasn't until I awoke that I realised I hadn't finished giving you the whole of my report."

"I don't understand. What else is there to tell? You had sight of the tower. Now all we have to do is cross the bridge and make our way along the north bank, get into the tower and find that key."

"That's just it," Shah said glumly. "We can't cross the bridge."

"Pardon?"

"We can't cross it."

"Why not?"

"After a half furlong the road surface suddenly ran out. From that point it vanished."

"Vanished? How? You mean, it had been broken up and used for building?"

"I don't know, but I think not. It was a clean break, right across from one edge of the road to the other — just as if it had been sliced with some great machete."

"Weird. All right, we'll never know what happened to the road. But a structure of that size must have a strong framework of sorts. What of that?"

"Yes, I saw as I approached that there was an enormous metal framework and it was pretty solid right up to where the roadway stopped. But from that point the metal was rusted and flaky and when I put some weight on one bit of it, it just broke off and fell away into the river below. I don't mind admitting it gave me a fright. I tried in three or four different places and the same thing happened. It looked to me as though the whole middle section of the bridge was as brittle as an old man's bones. Believe me, it's not passable."

All Bradley could say was, "Oh, bugger!" He drew a breath and exhaled it in a long drawn-out sigh, as he raked his fingers through his tousled hair.

"Yeah, I know," said Shah and shrugged. "That's what I thought. I reckoned we were just about stuffed. So I turned round to walk back and happened to glance east along the south bank and saw the village."

"Saw the what?"

"The village. A settlement on this bank."

"What do you mean, a settlement? There's no sign of habitation hereabouts. No forest trails, no scavenging of the road surface, not a sign of human presence. Are you sure, man?"

"I'm only telling you what I saw. And I saw a cleared area about two leagues along the bank and — though I'll grant it was a long way off — I'd swear there were huts or cabins there."

"Are you sure they weren't deserted?"

"The thought did occur to me. Then I saw the boat."

"Boat? You saw a boat? What, on the river?"

The deputy grinned. "I don't think it was in the sky, Marshal."

"All right — very funny. I don't suppose you noticed if it was manned."

Shah shook his head. "Nah — too far away. But it did have a big white sheet thing sticking up."

"Sail, Rajeev. It's called a sail."

"Yeah, well, it had one of those. Does that suggest it could've been manned?"

"Almost certainly. And if it was, we might persuade whoever was sailing it..."

"To take us to the tower?"

"Who knows? One thing's for sure — we're not going to find out standing here. Let's get some breakfast, then we'll go and ask them."

Chapter Twenty-Two
Across To A Tower

"By the Gods, Marshal, this is tough going. It must be nearly mid-day and I'd be surprised if we've come more than half a league! And still no sign of that village."

"I know, Rajeev. And I'm sorry I'm leaving most of the work to you and Sylvia. But with this shoulder, I'd never get any force behind the machete."

Sylvia said, "Someone's got to lead the horses. Anyway, I can swing a machete as well as..."

"I know. As well as any man."

She smiled back at him. "You're learning. But maybe we'd have done better to backtrack along the trail we'd already cleared?"

"I thought if we cut eastwards and in towards the riverbank we should hit upon some local trails. But as yet there's been no sign of any."

Shah said, "I'm beginning to wonder if I imagined that village, by some trick of the light."

"Let's not be negative, please, Rajeev."

"Well, I told you I didn't get much sleep the night before. My eyes were a bit bleary. It was a long way off."

Sylvia said, "But you said you saw that boat, Rajeev. Aren't you even certain about that?"

Shah slashed through another branch. "I've never seen a boat before. You thought what I described to you was a boat, didn't you, Marshal?"

"I'm sure it was," Bradley lied. Though he wouldn't voice his doubts, he didn't hold out a great deal of hope. He was thankful for

Shah's strong arm and skill with the machete though. Even so, with the horses and everything their progress was painfully slow. At noon they rested. But with each day growing rapidly shorter, their remaining travelling time was brief and unproductive and by dusk they'd barely covered a full league in Bradley's estimation.

There were two consolations though.

First, the weather had quietened since the terrible storm of five days earlier. Winter's chill had set in with a vengeance, but they were clothed well enough, even though all would have killed for a hot bath. For the present, it was enough that they managed to stay dry. There was nothing worse when on the trail than being constantly rained on, with no possibility of properly drying out.

Second, these woods were teeming with wildlife, so they were eating like gods. Rabbits, hares and fowl here must have encountered few humans, for they almost froze and watched with a quizzical look when the hunters raised their bows. A soft-hearted person would have found it hard to take even a rabbit's life in such circumstances. But they had to eat.

As they set out the following morning, Bradley was almost convinced that his deputy had been mistaken and that the settlement he thought he'd seen had been nothing more than a hallucination caused by eating those mushrooms.

But they'd hacked through only about thirty strides of undergrowth when there came a pleasant shock. Shah, being out in front, slashed with his machete and found resistance.

"Hello, what's this?" he said.

Sylvia looked where his blade had met thick wood. "It's a fence. Or at least, the remains of one."

Bradley came forward to examine the obstacle. "Well, whatever its original purpose, it's virtually useless now." He leaned his entire weight against it and it splintered. They walked through easily.

Then he said, "You now what this means, Rajeev?"

"I know it's the work of men," Shah said. "But the makers must be long dead. This must have been put here before any of us were born."

"Yes. But what if those men had descendants and what if those descendants have survived?"

Sylvia followed his logic. "Yes and if they did, they might be in a position to help us."

It wasn't long before they came to the settlement. But when they walked into a clearing by the river's edge, they weren't prepared for the reception they received — or rather, the lack of it.

"Look at these people," said Sylvia. "What's wrong with them? They're ignoring us, as if we weren't here."

The villagers went about their business, hardly acknowledging them, even though they must have seen them enter. And yet, apart from sideways glances and stares from some of the children, nobody approached or challenged them.

"I don't understand," Bradley said. "From what I've seen of this area so far, it's unlikely these folk have seen outsiders in many a year. So our arrival should cause some kind of a stir. It's weird."

When it was obvious nobody was going to approach them, Bradley realised he must make the first move. He cast his eyes around for a male villager who looked as if he might carry some authority. He found such a man, attending to a boat down by the jetty, so he walked up to him openly but carefully and stood within a stride of him while he finished securing the craft.

The man eventually turned from what he was doing and looked straight into his eyes. He uttered a short phrase that, on first hearing, meant nothing at all to him.

"I'm sorry?" Then it occurred to Bradley that their isolation must have prevailed for far longer than he'd supposed — so long that they'd developed a dialect that was at first hard for him to understand. And the same must be true of his speech for them. He held up his hands and took a pace slowly backwards, to show he meant no harm. He then spoke as slowly and as clearly as he could. At the same time he used what small amount of signing he'd picked up during his training.

"My name is Dominic Bradley. I am a Council Marshal." So saying, he reached carefully into his tunic and pulled out his emblem of office, which he handed to the man.

The man stared at it and slowly turned it over in his hand, carefully examining it, front and back. Then he gave it back, repeating, "Dominic Bradley. Marshal." As he spoke his eyes darted nervously towards a cabin at the east end of the village clearing, but when Bradley looked in the same direction, the man quickly returned his gaze to the Marshal's face.

There was something odd here. But Bradley also decided that there wasn't much to fear from this man. For the time being, that was all that mattered. He gave his next question some thought before he spoke.

"Can you take us..." and here he indicated his two companions "...in your boat..." pointing to the craft before them "...to the big tower?" Now he looked and pointed downriver, towards its mouth, in the direction where he knew the tower to be. And he was betting that these sailing folk would know where it stood too.

The man looked at Shah and Sylvia and then at his boat, then downriver in the direction the Marshal had indicated. Then he looked back at him.

"Why?" he asked. The long vowel of the word had an unusual quality, so that it sounded more like "Whey?" And for a moment Bradley didn't understand him.

He scratched his head. "Whey?" he repeated. "Oh, yes. You mean, why? Why do we want to go there?" Then, half to himself, he muttered, "By the Gods, where do I begin?"

By now, many of the village children had gathered to take a closer look at them — or, more specifically, at their horses. Then Bradley noticed there were no horses to be seen in the village, other than their own. He deduced that they had none and so the children especially would have no knowledge of them.

He turned and spoke softly to Sylvia. "Why don't you let the children sit on the horses? You could walk them around for a while. They might enjoy that." She nodded and stooped to smile at one of the little ones. Soon the children were laughing and touching her clothes and a couple of them let her lift them gently onto the horses' backs and to lead them on a ride around the clearing.

Bradley turned back to the man and said slowly, "Can we go somewhere and talk?"

The man seemed to understand and led the lawmen towards the cabin he'd stared at earlier. But he didn't ask them in. A rough table and some stools were arranged outside and he invited them to sit. Then he called to a woman nearby, "Beer en brid!"

As expected, beer and bread, plates and mugs were brought to the table and the man said, "Tek en spick." By now the Marshal was growing used to the dialect, realising that it consisted of essentially familiar words made to sound slightly strange by nothing more than strong vowels.

He picked up some of the bread, broke it and offered a piece back to his host, who accepted it. He then raised his jug and nodded to the man, advancing it in his direction. Shah imitated his actions and Bradley was pleased to see their host do the same.

After these social niceties, he recalled that he'd been invited to speak, so he took a deep breath.

"You know about the Wall and that no man can go through it, or over it?"

The man nodded.

Bradley knew he must engage this man's attention, so he said, "We seek treasures beyond the Wall. First, we must find a key hidden in the tower at the north end of the estuary." Here, he pointed in the tower's general direction. "This key opens the door to a building in an ancient town to the north. That house holds the secrets of the Wall, offering freedom to everyone in Fenwold from their present toil and poverty."

He wondered if he'd sounded convincing. His summarisation must have seemed trite and stilted. For a moment he wondered whether he'd been understood. Then the man got up from his seat and approached the cabin, opened the door only just enough to slide in, then shut it firmly behind him.

Shah gave a puzzled look and Bradley shrugged, meaning they'd no choice but to wait. After a while the man emerged from the cabin, accompanied by a second and said, "We will take you." Then he pointed to Sylvia and the horses. "They stay here — you two come with us."

The Marshal went over to Sylvia and asked if she was happy to stay and wait for them. By now the children — and some of the village women — crowded happily around her and the horses and she enjoyed being the centre of attraction. Aside from the disinterested attitude of the villagers at their arrival, there was no real sense of hostility here. So she merely said, "I'll be all right, Dominic. You two go and I'll wait for you."

Reassured, he and Shah followed the two men down to the boat, which they boarded clumsily like the landlubbers they were. Then their host cast off, while the other fellow took hold of the tiller at the rear end. The first man picked up a couple of oars to pull them away from the shore and then pulled on some ropes to raise the sail. Before long they caught the wind and the current, taking them out into the river for their first ever experience of sailing on open water.

CHAPTER TWENTY-THREE
WHERE ONCE THERE WAS LIGHT

Bradley was amazed at the speed with which the craft now carried them towards the sand spit on which the tower stood. He understood that this was because of the river currents, but didn't realise how complex these were until they got out into the deeper water. For here, banks of sand and silt appeared without warning and the murky waters swirled and turned violently in places, causing the little craft to rock and roll until both lawmen felt queasy and clung ashen-faced to the wooden sides. But the turbulence evidently had little effect on their hosts, well used as they were to navigating these waters. And, seeing the worried looks on the gaunt faces of their passengers, their stern expressions for once turned into grins.

"Don't worry. We know what we're doing. You're in no danger." The first man then put a reassuring hand on Bradley's shoulder and he thought for a moment that the boatman wanted to say more to him. But then he looked away worriedly, back towards the village.

"Is anything wrong?" Bradley asked.

"No... nothing. We have some... sickness. My son, Toby, has a winter fever. Don't let it concern you."

"I'm sorry to hear that," Bradley said with sincerity. "What do we call you?"

"I am Sean, son of the village elder. This is my cousin, Luke. We know these waters — and the tower you seek. Though it's nothing but a derelict building with an inner staircase leading to an empty room."

"You've been inside?" Bradley asked flatly.

187

"Why, yes. All children are curious, aren't they? But our forefathers removed everything of use years ago. It's just a shell. If there were a key there, we'd know about it."

The boatman's words made perfect sense, but Bradley found them disappointing and he was annoyed with himself for not having considered this likelihood. Of course something so obvious as a key would have been removed by now, if only by mischievous children playing in the ruin. He tried not to show it, but by the time the little boat ran up on the beach close to the tower, he was in low spirits and fully expected their quest to end in premature frustration on this desolate shore.

As Luke secured the boat and Sean led them up the stony beach, Bradley asked a question that he realised should have been put to his host earlier. "What exactly was this tower used for, Sean?"

"Many, many years ago, when big boats moved about these waters and into the Great Sea beyond — so it's told — at night or in foul weather a great light shone out from inside the tower, visible for many leagues. It marked this place of peril and sailors knew to keep to the southern channel. How the light was made we don't know — it was one that didn't burn, that wouldn't destroy the tower. It doesn't concern us these days though, because ours is the only boat hereabouts and we try to stay at home at times of danger."

This piece of ancient knowledge interested Bradley, having grown up on the coast. But it was the landsman Shah who wanted to know more.

"And what about the Great Sea? Do you ever go out on it?"

Sean laughed. "Of course. The fishing is much better out there."

Rajeev's eyes lit up with inspiration.

"Then — if you wished — you might sail on and find other lands, or even sail north or south beyond the Wall!"

Sean was already shaking his head. "No. That's not possible. A few leagues out lies a great metal mesh barrier, buoyed to float but still so strong that we haven't the means to break through it. Believe me, it's been tried. We think it extends to meet the Wall, to the north and south. This our forefathers knew, before the plague outbreak caused us to isolate our village."

"Plague?" Shah asked. "But we know of no plague having visited this region."

Sean looked at Luke and then explained, "Then our forefathers' precautions were effective. The plague was among our own people. It killed many, but then mercifully left us. As a precaution we've remained enclosed ever since, in case we carry it in our blood."

Bradley observed, "That was a selfless thing to do. Is that why nobody approached us when first we entered your village?"

At first Sean looked puzzled. "What? Oh, yes. That would be the reason. Well, it was a concern to us — for your sakes. But you're here now and must take your chances."

Bradley looked across at the deputy and realised he wasn't the only one to be unnerved by this revelation, but there was nothing they could do about it, other than get on with the task in hand. "Let's look inside the tower," he said.

Sean opened the door and led the way up the steep circular stairway. He must have made the climb several times before, for he did it effortlessly and with confidence. The lawmen, though, made unashamed use of an inner handrail, occasionally risking a giddy glance over it, down to the concrete bottom of the stairwell. On reaching the room at the top level, they looked out and gasped at the astonishing vista, accompanied by an eerie east wind that howled through the now unglazed window openings. But, just as Sean had said, the room's contents (if there'd been any) had long ago been stripped by generations of indiscriminate scavengers. This was to be expected — it was the way throughout Fenwold. The two lawmen scoured every corner of the room, but nothing resembling a key was to be seen anywhere and after Sean's earlier comment this came as no real surprise to Bradley. His disappointment, though, was obvious.

For a few moments he sought consolation in the wonderful views from this newly found vantage point. Never before had so much of the world been spread out before him. For the first time he had a real sense of the full extent of the Wall — and of the sea barrier that Sean had described. These were truly feats of skill, power and intelligence beyond his understanding. And at that moment a vivid chain of logic began to form in his mind. This wasn't the work of gods. Gods would have applied miracles and magic to prevent the people's exit from Fenwold — fantastic monsters and howling demons. Only men would have constructed forms known to men, making use of familiar materials and physical structures. Maybe Sylvia was right. Perhaps it had been men and women after all who'd built the Wall, the sea barrier, this tower and the big bridge upriver.

Then he voiced his continuing thoughts saying, "Wait a moment. They wouldn't have just left a key hanging here for all to see. They'd have made it more difficult. They'd expect some intelligence to be applied. Look around — the room looks empty — anything that's useful has been removed. If a key were hanging here and it were visible, we'd see it, wouldn't we?"

Shah said, "I suppose so."

"If it's here then, the only reason we can't see it is because it's hidden. What is there in this room that might conceal something that's hanging down?"

Shah said, "There's nothing. Like you just said, it's empty. We've looked in every nook and cranny. I think we should give it up." As he turned to descend the staircase, he casually grasped the top of the inner handrail.

"Stop!" Bradley commanded.

He stopped.

"Now lift up your hand."

Again he did as he was asked. "What now?"

"Can you pull that handrail away from its support?"

"Eh? Do you mean this tube that's secured to the top step? I don't know. I'd need something heavy to whack the rail from underneath."

Sean now showed some interest. "I have tools in the boat. Wait here."

He returned with a hammer, which he handed to Shah. Taking it in both hands, he swung it upwards as hard as he could towards the underside of the rail. It didn't move. Two further strikes produced a tiny displacement. But with the fourth blow, the rusty joint gave way and the end of the rail moved off its support. He was about to give it another *whack* with the hammer when Bradley said, "Hold it a moment, Rajeev. Let's have a look."

He took hold of the loosened rail with his hand and slowly pulled it further off the metal tube that had supported it. He was amazed at what he saw.

"There's a chain attached to the rail by a hook and it's hanging down the inside of the supporting tube. Here, give me a hand, will you? Mind though — it's weakened by rust."

The astonished deputy took the rail and coaxed it further upwards, creating a wide enough gap for the Marshal to hook a finger around the chain and then close the grip with his thumb.

"I've got it!" he gasped. "Bend the rail up more if you can — go carefully now!" And as Shah strained to give him greater clearance, he carefully released the chain from the hook from which it had hung for centuries and slowly drew it out to reveal the prize attached to the end of it.

"That's not a key," said Sean.

Bradley frowned. "Well, I agree it's not what we'd recognise as a key. It's not one that's likely to fit any lock that I've ever seen, anyway. But let's take a closer look at it."

When fully withdrawn, they saw that it was made of a hard, shiny but non-metallic material unknown to any of them. It had been folded in the middle to fit into the tubular handrail support and when Bradley carefully unfolded it he was surprised that it showed no sign of wear or deterioration from its centuries of concealment. Opened up, it comprised four squares on which were engraved four symbols — a six-pointed star, a circle with a point at its centre, a square with a diagonal line running corner to corner and a triangle.

"This is a kind of a key," he said. "I'm certain of it."

Sean asked, "But a key to open what? Where is this town in the north you spoke of?"

"I don't know," he had to confess. Then he turned the object over in his palm, to reveal some more engraving on the reverse. This time the design covered the surface of all four squares, as if to depict one single item of information.

He stared at the engraving for a few moments and then looked out of the open window of the tower, upriver. He looked again at the engraving.

"I think this is a plan. It shows the river estuary and the north side of Fenwold. See, here's the tower, on the spit across the river mouth and there's the bridge — except that the middle part's missing. Here's the Wall — look how it goes north, then turns east and out towards the Great Sea. There's even a line here that must represent the sea barrier. And it shows the road that runs northwards from the bridge. Then look what lies on that road, further north."

It was a smaller depiction of the four symbols engraved on the other side of the tablets.

"This has to be the location of the town."

"How far?" Sean asked.

"If the plan is to scale, judging by the relative distance from the tower to the bridge, it lies roughly three days' journey directly north of the bridge."

"I can't believe it," said Shah. "You've found it, Marshal! You've found the key! The rhyme must be genuine after all! This is wonderful!" Grinning, the two lawmen grasped each other and danced for joy around the top floor of the old lighthouse.

But when they stopped dancing, it was to see the stern-faced Sean pointing a loaded crossbow directly at Bradley. Behind him, just two steps down the stairway, Luke stood poised with his bow aimed at Shah.

"What's this, friends?" Bradley demanded. "Is it some joke?"

"No, Marshal," Sean murmured solemnly. "It's not a joke. Hand over that key please. I am under orders to kill you now."

Chapter Twenty-Four
From The Jaws Of Death

Bradley's heart and mind were racing as he stared open-mouthed at the weapons now pointed directly at him and his deputy. How could he have been so stupid as to trust these two turncoat fishermen? Only moments earlier they'd shown nothing but kindness, but now their set jaws and fixed eyes showed them all too capable of carrying out their threat. Any moment might see the lawmen killed and all their efforts wasted. Trapped in this room at the top of the tower, their exit barred by two armed assailants, their only chance of escape meant a suicidal leap through the open window onto the compacted sandbank far below. But any sudden movement on their part meant their being shot instantly. Their single remaining hope was to try and reason with these assassins.

"Under orders? What do you mean? Under whose orders?" Bradley felt the blood drain from his face, knowing the fear and chill of his own mortality. Yet he fought for inner strength to inject some authority into his voice. "Who could possibly order a free man to commit murder?"

Sean turned his head slightly towards his cousin, as if to confer silently. The other, however, maintained a steady glare, never taking his eye off the two lawmen, and was evidently more than ready to carry out their terrible commission.

Sean said, "Huh! Would we were free men! But we're not. Don't think we want to do this to you, Marshal, but we've no choice."

Luke said morosely, "Come on, Sean. Let's get this damn job over with and return to the village. You know what he said if we were too long away."

"Who said?" Bradley demanded desperately. "What are you talking about? Was there someone inside that hut where we were sitting? Come on, man. If you're going to kill us, at least don't let us perish without knowing the reason!"

"All right," Sean agreed. "Why should we keep it from you? Not that it'll make any difference. About a week ago we rescued a drowning man from the river — the worst day's work we ever did. Our women fed and nursed him till his strength returned, then he repaid us..."

At this point, Sean lowered his weapon and showed every sign of breaking down. But Luke didn't drop his guard and prodded his bow in Bradley's direction, while urgently addressing his cousin.

"Sean! Sean, we have to do this — think of little Toby!"

At the utterance of the name the boatman regained his determination, steadied himself and held the primed crossbow firmly once more. This time he aimed it directly at Bradley's heart.

"All right — wait just a moment!" Bradley pleaded. "If you've got a raider in your village, we can help you. We've experience of dealing with these men. They're ruthless and you can't defeat them on your own. Whatever deal they've offered you, you can't trust them. At least let's talk about it! What has this man told you to do?"

"He overheard you telling us about the key and how it could lead to treasures on the other side of the Wall. He said we were to take you and find the key, then kill you and bring it to him."

Shah asked the obvious question. "But you're good men. What hold does he have over you, to make you kill us against your will?"

Sean only looked away, though his bow was still aimed steadily at Bradley. Luke answered for him.

"The bastard has Toby — Sean's son — and his parents — the village headman and his wife. He says he'll kill them if we fail. We're sorry, Marshal, but it's either your lives or theirs."

"Not so," Bradley argued. "If he's there with your family as you say, then he can't know exactly what's happening here. Here..." He handed the key to Luke, who lowered his bow to accept it. He hoped Shah would realise that they must make their move now, or never. Swiftly, each grabbed the right wrist of his assailant, while deftly removing their weapons from their grips. The action — honed and perfected during their weeks of training — was so quick and effective that it left the two cousins standing gawping, clearly at a loss to see how suddenly their positions had been reversed.

194

There was silence for a moment and then Luke shrugged morosely and offered back the key. But Bradley shook his head.

"No. Keep it — for now. We said we wanted to help you and we meant it. And for the time being, that means — as far as the raider's concerned — that we're dead men and you have the key. Let him believe you've carried out his instructions. Is there any way you can put us ashore on the south bank, as close as possible to your village, without this outlaw knowing?"

Sean scratched his chin. "There's a bend a couple of furlongs east of the village. We could make it appear the current was dragging the boat inshore, drop you off without being seen and tack up to the jetty along by the bank. The channel's deep enough there. But, what do you intend? He says he'll kill them if there's any attempt to storm the cabin. Marshal, whatever you do, please promise me you won't put our families in danger."

"I won't — you have my word," Bradley said and smiled grimly, hoping he'd be able to keep such a rash promise. But his motives weren't entirely altruistic, for he was now desperately concerned for Sylvia's safety.

* * * * *

Reuben, headman of Nearbank, tugged at the tightly bound leather straps that cut deep into the flesh of his feeble wrists. He cursed the bleeding sores and felt a single stinging tear slide down his grimy cheek. He bowed his head to hide his silent sobbing. But the cause of his grief wasn't physical pain. Nor were his tears for his own pathetic weakness at the hands of his cruel, deceiving guest, who had mocked and held him hostage here these three long hellish days and nights. No, it was for shame that he wept now — the shame of failure.

He had failed his village, his lifelong friends and relatives, once a free people, but now reduced to slavery and compelled to submit to this fiend's every whim. He had failed his dear wife, only just now finding brief respite from her ordeal by snatching a few moments of fitful sleep in the chimney corner, where she lay curled up in a wretched heap with a leash around her neck like some old, worn-out dog. And he had failed his poor little grandson Toby, bound like himself and threatened with sudden death should each command of the wild-eyed monster not be speedily obeyed.

And all this had happened because of the abundance of trust of a foolish old man and of his affable stupidity. This was the cause of his shame. Also, kept so long bound and confined, there was now the added humiliation of the three of them having to lie here in their own filth, so that even their stinking, soiled clothing could no longer afford them any semblance of dignity. If there were such a place as hell in Fenwold, it was here in this kitchen.

In a moment of bitter reflection he cursed the two days his old wife had nursed this devil in the shape of a man, to snatch him skilfully from the brink of death. How amiable and grateful he had seemed to them then in his recovery. In his renewed state of health he had joked and laughed and charmed them all. In particular he had quickly impressed young Toby, who soon hung onto every word that slid from his silver, lying tongue. On the third day, early in the morning, the lad had come in to play before breakfast and in the guise of playmate the outlaw had swiftly bound him while his grandparents slept. By then he had the headman's weapons to hand — his crossbows, sword and daggers — and must have gloated in the knowledge that now, through the boy, he controlled the entire village.

Bound as they now were, the raider could easily kill the old man and the boy at any moment, while the elder's wife was made to convey his orders to the rest of the community. If he wanted food, he'd yell at the old woman, "Tell them to bring meat, bread and beer, old hag!" And he'd let out just enough of her leash to allow her to the door, which she'd open gingerly to pass his demands to the group of anxious women waiting outside. Once delivered, he'd make little Toby taste some of the food first, as insurance against their tampering with it. The headman was at least glad of his wife's advanced years and wondered how long it would be before their jailer bade her fetch him in one of the young girls to satisfy his baser desires. He'd hoped the younger men might overpower him whenever he grew tired, but he didn't sleep as ordinary folk did. He catnapped, always half awake, his weapons close by, at once fully alert at the slightest sound or movement. There was no surprising him. Tired of life and his grief, the old fellow closed his weary eyes and found some respite in a shallow but comforting sleep.

* * * * *

Red looked across at the old man and sneered at his weakness. Then he looked out of the window again at the Crowtree girl who'd humiliated him in front of his men months before. Why fate should bring her and that jumped-up puppy of a marshal to this God-forsaken hole, to amuse the village children with her horses, he could only conjecture. Well, there were better games to play. He cast his mind back to a day or two after his rescue, when from this window beside the bed on which they'd laid his exhausted body, he'd seen the wisp of campfire smoke, curling high above the forest barely a league to the north. By then they'd told him of the settlement's isolation and it was evident from the villagers' reaction to the smoke that visitors were a rarity. They'd been both apprehensive and excited and although he didn't believe in second sight, he had an extraordinary feeling that whoever was out there had come looking for him. His paranoia was rewarded when they appeared and he was unfazed when he peered out to see Bradley from Crowtree walk into the village clearing followed by his lapdog and bitch.

It was a fateful deliverance. Since his capture he'd nurtured a growing hatred for the man who'd sent him — or so his twisted logic reasoned — to perish on the Wall. He'd expected to die by falling at first. Then he found he had a talent for keeping his balance on that narrow ledge, whether awake or asleep. Like some scavenging rat he was forced to eat the foul fungus that grew along sections of it and to drink the rainwater that collected in its occasional shallow depressions. At first this diet made him retch violently, but with nothing else to sustain him, he forced himself to persevere till his palate and gut grew accustomed to its awful taste. Eventually he managed to catch some gulls that used the Wall's summit as their roost. Though he preferred his meat cooked, the raw flesh at least made a change from the disgusting fungus. He had to live like an animal, but discovered that he could survive. So he kept on walking, all the time allowing his anger and hatred for Bradley to fester and feed on itself. Whenever it seemed his trek along the Wall would never end and his resolve threatened to falter, a single thought kept him going: the thought that some day their paths would cross again.

On the day he reached the river crossing, he realised this was the only chance he'd ever get to descend. The domed, armoured capping to the Wall had continued without a break and at no point had there been any possibility of breaching it. Neither was there anywhere that the tantalising ivy grew more than half the height of the Wall. So his only hope was to try a descent back into Fenwold and the outlaw life that was all he'd known since his youth.

He stared down into the swirling brown waters, knowing neither their depth nor what obstacles they might conceal, but only that the fall would probably kill him. But he had no choice — this place was going to afford him the nearest thing to a soft landing and there'd be no second chance. Tucked inside his dirty tunic he still had a few strands of ivy collected from his original climb, but now that he examined them he found them too dried up and brittle to be useful and threw them angrily into the river far below. So he stripped off his filthy clothing and tore it up to make as much length of makeshift rope as would support his weight — by now, much reduced — and secured it to one of the metal spikes that was just within his reach. It wasn't much, but would have to do. He grasped the end firmly and lowered himself over the edge. But he barely made it three strides down before it tore with a loud *rip* and dropped him like a stone into the raging torrent below.

The force of the fall, his physical weakness and the shock of the cold water combined to render him immediately unconscious. The river was swollen by a violent storm, whose fury buoyed up his body and draped it across a floating timber, which it tossed and propelled several leagues downstream. Somewhere in the estuary those two fishermen had hauled him out almost lifeless, and dragged him aboard their little craft. He was lucky no bones had been broken. After coming round, his strength returning in the care of the village women, he felt not just fortunate, but special. So special that when he saw Bradley enter the village he felt a perverse empowerment, a sense that destiny had somehow intended their reunion.

And now the lawman was chasing some treasure on the far side of the Wall — supposedly for the good of these stupid people. Well, he believed none of that. This marshal was like any other man — out to increase his own wealth and status at everyone else's expense. How satisfying it would be to shatter those ambitions! Red's life as a warlord may have been abruptly snuffed out by this upstart lawman, but here now was a chance to regain his former position of authority and to teach the young whelp a lesson he'd never forget. He'd turn the tables on the proud Marshal Bradley, snatch from him the title of King of the Wall and place that precious crown upon his own exalted head.

Chapter Twenty-Five
The Worst Of Times

Sylvia sat by the little jetty and peered out ever more fretfully across the murky waters of the river. The village children had long since grown tired of being led around the stockade on the horses and had gone off to play other games. Now with time on her hands she felt alone and vulnerable. The villagers had been kind enough, but the novelty of her arrival having subsided, they now paid her scant attention. She had no idea how long a journey it was to the tower and back — or if it even existed at all. She spent the rest of the afternoon huddled on the bank, her gaze trained on the far shore.

It was well into the early evening when the white sail appeared from around the nearside bend barely two furlongs downriver. Several villagers came down to meet the vessel and its two sailors who jumped ashore and tied it up to the quay. The women of the village had few words of greeting for their men folk, only barely acknowledging their return with a quiet nod and a worried glance. Then the blood drained from Sylvia's face as she saw that Dominic and Rajeev weren't on board.

She stood up. "Where are my friends? What's happened to them?" Hers was the only voice to rise up out of the silence in undisguised concern for her missing companions. She threw herself towards Sean and grabbed at the sleeve of his tunic, now tearfully pleading for a response to her questions.

"Answer me! What have you done with them?"

As the boatman regarded her, his lips framed a reply, but the words didn't come. Instead he merely shook his head and looked shamefully at the ground, pushing her away and hurrying towards the cabin.

Unsatisfied, she followed him and was about to grab again at his coat, when she was stopped in her progress by the shock of what she saw next. The red-haired raider leader, he whom she'd seen condemned and set high upon the Wall for punishment, emerged from the hut with a frightened young boy in front of him. The little lad was cruelly constrained by a tight rope about the neck and threatened by the outlaw's sharp knife at his throat.

"You!" she cried out.

Then the still air was suddenly rent by his cruel laughter. "Ha! Why, if it isn't the scar-faced Princess of Crowtree! How nice to renew your acquaintance, young miss! I'm sorry we didn't know you and your friends were coming to see us — had we done so, we'd have made preparations to celebrate your visit. I must also apologise that I can't greet you with a genteel bow, or a kiss on the hand, but as you see, my own are rather full at the moment. Perhaps we can re-kindle our friendship later, when there aren't so many people around." Again his laughter rent the air.

Before Sylvia could respond, he turned to Sean and gruffly demanded, "Well, did our clever Marshal find what he was looking for?"

At this, the boatman reached inside his tunic and took out an object, which he offered to the wild-eyed ruffian. The latter shook his head and said, "Like I said — I have my hands full just now. Bring it nearer and let me see it."

The wretched man obeyed, his eyes on the terrified face of the captive child, who she guessed must be someone dear to him.

"Hmm — a strange thing. Show me the other side."

Sean turned the object over to reveal the design on the back.

"The Marshal thought this showed a map of the estuary and the northern part of Fenwold."

"Huh!" Red sneered. "Is this what the great Marshal Bradley came all this way to find? It doesn't make any sense to me — hardly worth laying down his life for, at any rate. By the way, did you carry out all my instructions?"

Sean nodded sadly and again cast his gaze downwards.

The outlaw looked at the boat and growled, "Where are the bodies then?"

On hearing his words Sylvia's face turned pale and she spoke with a terrible coldness in her voice. "What are you saying? You can't mean that..."

Sean murmured, "I am sorry, lady. Yon raider had my young son's life in his hands. I had to do as I was told."

Enraged, she raised her claws to attack the poor fisherman, but then, knowing her anger was misplaced, she hurled herself towards the red-haired raider. But by now he was restored almost to his former strength and, without letting go of the rope, easily knocked her to the ground with one sweep of his powerful arm. Some of the village women went to her aid, gently helped her to her feet and led her away with words of comfort, while Sean responded woodenly to Red's question.

"We tricked them into standing up in the boat half way across, shot them and then they fell overboard — the current was too strong for us to fish them out. Their bodies will be in the Great Sea by now."

Apparently satisfied with this explanation, the outlaw shoved the boy back towards the cabin and bellowed at his father to follow them. Red paused at the door, only turning once to yell at the village women, "Fetch me some food and something to drink and be quick about it! And no tricks, remember — the lad tastes it first!"

* * * * *

Once inside the cabin, now a prison for his loved ones, Sean went over to the side of his aged parents and tried to comfort them as best he could, restrained and distraught as they were.

"Leave them alone!" Red spat out. "They're all right — and will remain so as long as you do as I tell you. Now then, what did our clever Marshal say about these markings here?"

He answered sullenly. "Like I said, he thought them to represent a plan. Look — here's the great bridge. The key has something to do with an ancient town some three days' journey northwards. It's supposed to unlock a door to be found in that town."

Red looked sceptical. "This doesn't look anything like a key. How does it work?"

Sean replied, "He didn't seem to know. He thought it might be a different kind of key from those we're used to."

Red nodded. "Hmm — brilliant man, our Marshal. Or at least, he was. But he was too good for this world. What a waste — between us, we might have controlled the entire enclave. Well, never mind. When I've unlocked that door with this key, all that he was seeking will be mine. Did he say what kind of treasure the door concealed?"

"Not exactly," Sean said. "It was more to do with knowledge — about how to break through the Wall — to find all manner of wonderful things on the other side."

"All right," Red said then. "We'll see. Put the key on the table there. And tell that girl Sylvia to prepare the horses for a journey. Watch her though — she's a sly one. I want provisions for at least a week — enough for three people. She, I and — oh, yes — your little Toby here. We've grown close these last few days, haven't we lad?"

The poor frightened little boy glanced first at his father — who gave him an almost imperceptible nod — then up at his captor and mouthed a feeble, "Yes, sir."

"There's a good boy!" Red said cynically. Then he motioned to the dejected parent to leave and execute his orders, the outlaw's cruel laughter ringing mockingly in his ears, followed by a final proclamation.

"We'll be leaving first thing in the morning!"

* * * * *

The following day after dawn the raider leader, young Toby and Sylvia set out with the horses towards the bridge back along the trail that she, Bradley and Shah had recently created in making their way to the village.

By mid-morning the villagers were in a sullen mood. Everyone was naturally relieved that Red was no longer there to mete out his terror. In particular Reuben and his wife were recovering from their days of imprisonment, enjoying hot baths and some decent food. Though the experience had scarred them severely, nevertheless Sean, Luke and all of the other villagers were now glad for their release. But any rejoicing for the outlaw's departure was subdued, for everyone was intensely sad that the cruel raider had taken young Toby as a hostage. There was also some sympathy for the pleasant young girl who'd amused the children with her horses — but as she was unknown to them, their feelings for her weren't so intense.

Sean, his cousin Luke and several of the other villagers were helping to clean up the mess in the elder's cabin, when a silhouette appeared framed against the bright morning sky at the open doorway.

"How long have they been gone?" came the Marshal's urgent demand.

Sean rose from sweeping out the fireplace to greet Bradley, now warmly grasping his arm.

"They left just after dawn. Didn't you see?"

"No. We had to camp a fair way away. Even then we daren't risk a fire, in case he saw the smoke. We've spent a cold night out there in the woods. Can you spare something to eat and drink?"

Sean felt his hands. "By the Gods, man — you're icy cold." Then he shot out instructions for food and fresh clothing to be brought for the two lawmen, as well as hot water for them to bathe.

Later, as the lawmen greedily devoured their meal, the two cousins sat down with them and Sean wasted no time in asking them about their intentions.

"We'll not be following them too closely, will we, Marshal? He still has my son, you know."

"Yes, I know. No, we won't risk following straight away — mainly for young Toby's sake. But there's another reason."

"Oh? What's that?"

The lawmen exchanged knowing glances and Bradley let Shah explain. "He's followed our trail because he thinks it'll bring him to the bridge — which it will. But I've been up on the bridge — that's how I caught sight of your village — and I know it to be impassable."

The fishermen both looked astonished. Luke said, "I didn't know that. Because of the plague, none of us has journeyed there — and no such knowledge has been passed to us by our forefathers."

"That's right," said Sean. "But we always assumed that it offered a way across the river to anyone foolhardy enough to want to go there."

Bradley nodded. "We thought so too. But why do you say 'foolhardy'?"

Luke said, "The forest on that side has never been inhabited by men — it's home to ferocious wild animals — wolf and wildcat. Legends say there are even dragons."

"Dragons?" Shah scoffed. "Don't tell us you place any belief in such children's stories?"

Sean's expression was deadly serious as he said, "Don't be so quick to dismiss such tales. Haven't you two come all this way on a quest that's based on little more than a nursery rhyme?"

The young deputy looked ashamed and Bradley was forced to concur. "He may have a point there, Rajeev. Let's not be unwilling to expect the unexpected."

After a short pause, he continued, "But as for the bridge, it looks like the Ancient Ones saw fit to disable it. According to Rajeev, from a certain point the road surface has been carefully removed and the structure of the bridge made brittle, so that it gives way under any kind of pressure. We don't think it'll bear a person's weight."

"Why do you suppose they did that, Marshal?" Luke asked.

"I'd guess they didn't want to leave an easy access to the north — to discourage settlement, maybe. They couldn't prevent someone sailing over in a boat, but to leave the bridge intact would have eventually invited large-scale migration by people from the south bank. I think they wanted to delay discovery of the town in the north until the time was right."

"And you think that time is now," Sean observed. "It's an interesting theory." Then he frowned, adding, "But if the bridge is useless as you say, then the raider and Toby and the girl are going to have to..."

"That's right," said Shah. "They must turn back."

Sean's head drooped and he rubbed his hands ruefully over his face, saying, "What's to be done? So much do I want to see my son again and yet the prospect of the village suffering more of that bastard's domination is more than I can bear. And what of your friend, Sylvia? She must know that they can't cross the bridge — do you suppose she'll tell him?"

Bradley thought for a moment, then said, "I can see no advantage in concealing it. But if she were ever going to tell him, why put it off? Why go to the trouble of packing and preparing the horses? No, she'd have done so before they set off this morning, or not at all."

Shah suggested, "Perhaps she didn't want to make the swine's progress any easier than it need be."

Bradley nodded and said to the fishermen, "By the way, I hope you were able to make her understand that you only feigned our deaths?"

With shamed expressions, the two men shook their heads.

When Bradley took in the immensity of their silent disclosure, he turned his burning eyes towards the heavens.

"Oh, my poor Sylvia! Your mind must be in turmoil!"

Clearly also moved at the thought of Sylvia's suffering, Shah said sadly, "Poor girl. Whatever are we going to do?"

Bradley fought hard to overcome his low spirits. "I don't know. Let's think this through. He's taken the horses because he thinks he'll make better progress with them. He would, if he could cross the river with them, but he can't do that, because the bridge is impassable. It's more than likely he'll return and get you to take him across in your boat, Sean — without the horses, I assume."

Sean nodded. "The boat won't carry such big animals."

"In that case he'll be forced to leave them here. If we're lucky, he'll leave Sylvia too — I'm hoping he only wants her to look after the horses."

Shah nodded as he picked at the remains of his chicken meal, while Bradley thoughtfully took a swig of beer from his mug. For a few moments Sean and Luke watched their guests' faces in silence. Then almost simultaneously the two fishermen's faces assumed expressions of horror.

Bradley asked nervously, "What is it?"

"Marshal..." Sean began. "We thought you knew, but..."

Bradley didn't hide his impatience. "Come on, man. You thought we knew what?"

It was Luke who said, "The raider and your friend, Sylvia... they seemed to know one another. And there was bad feeling between them."

"Knew one another? Bad feeling? Whatever do you mean?" Then he went cold, as his tormented mind slowly yielded to the unthinkable. Before Luke or Sean could say anything else, he demanded, "What did this raider look like?"

Only a few words of Sean's description were necessary. The red hair and beard, the wild, dark eyes — these were sufficient for Bradley and Shah to recognise the outlaw Red, whom they believed had perished on the Wall.

The lawmen sat in silence as the implications sank in. After the way Sylvia had humiliated the outlaw, she'd now be in unimaginable danger. Yes, he needed her to control the horses, but when she ceased to be of further practical use, what then?

Shah offered some words of consolation, placing a comforting hand on Bradley's arm. "Without the horses he'll need someone to carry his stuff, cook his meals and..."

"All right, Rajeev. I appreciate your intentions and there may be a lot in what you say. But I can't help thinking what that mad bastard might be capable of. I suppose we could take the initiative. If we were to set up some kind of ambush when they return, we might kill Red and rescue Sylvia."

Sean said desperately, "But Marshal, such action would endanger my son. I can't allow it."

Bradley saw his point. If Toby were harmed because of their fouling up, they and Sylvia would face the rightful wrath of Sean and the other villagers. For the moment, he felt powerless. This was a dilemma that wouldn't be resolved using mere logic and reason. It was a position he was unused to and he didn't like it one bit. For once, he'd have to place trust in one slim hope — that the outlaw Red would indeed see Sylvia as a useful, if abrasive, trail slave.

Sean said solemnly, "For my own selfish reasons, I hope he does take her along. Though it breaks my heart to think of it, he'll doubtless keep my little Toby as hostage and if your kind-hearted friend is there too, I pray she'll watch out for the boy."

"If I know Sylvia, you can be certain of that. You're sure he believes you killed us?"

"Yes, I'm convinced he does."

"Good. Then we have surprise as a possible weapon — though as yet I don't know how or when we'll use it. But here's what we must do now. At this moment, he's following our forest trail, so he'll be out of sight of the river. Therefore, I want you to take Rajeev and me over to the other side now and put us ashore as near to the bridge as you can. Is that possible?"

Sean nodded. "Yes. And you're thinking that he'll want me to do the same for him when he returns here?"

"Exactly. He'll want to take the quickest route to the northern town. If you get the chance, tell Sylvia we're all right. But not if he remains in earshot. I can't risk his getting to know. We have to maintain the element of surprise at all costs. If necessary, much as it grieves me, let her go on believing you've killed us."

"All right," Sean agreed. "Then, after I've landed him, I'll wait for a while and follow."

Bradley shook his head. "No, Sean. I can understand why you'd want to, but you mustn't do that. He'll expect it and your little boy's life would be in danger if he found out you were following. Besides, you're unused to travelling in the forest and believe me, he'd soon know you were there. The river estuary and the sea are your domain. Rajeev and I are used to the woods. We know how to follow without giving ourselves away. We'll conceal ourselves until you've landed them on the north bank. You must leave it to us from that point. I know it's hard for you, but you must come back and take care of the villagers. Your poor father's spirit is broken by his ordeal. You're needed here."

Desperately the boatman pleaded, "But what of my son? There must be something I can do, man! My wife is sick with worry and has taken to her bed. I need something positive to tell her."

Bradley placed a friendly hand on Sean's arm, saying, "Tell your wife this — though it's the hardest thing I can ask devoted parents to do. You must wait and be patient. Accept this promise as from one friend to another. Rajeev and I will follow this raider and return your son to you. Each evening, you must look to the opposite shore. When we're ready to return, we'll make our campfire there. Then on the morning after you see our smoke, you can put your boat out and come for your son."

CHAPTER TWENTY-SIX
ENCOUNTER WITH A DRAGON

Bradley had no concrete plan for rescuing Sylvia and young Toby from the clutches of the cold-hearted raider who held them hostage. All that he and Shah could do for the time being was follow the group as closely as they dared to avoid discovery. He felt a mixture of relief and revulsion that Red had kept Sylvia with him as well as Toby. Relief that he hadn't considered her dispensable on their return to Nearbank and revulsion at the mistreatment he knew she'd have to face from the cruel ogre.

From the ample cover of the forest, the two lawmen watched them land on the north bank from Sean's fishing boat. It was good at least that both hostages appeared to be unharmed. But it was one of the most frustrating moments of his life to watch Sylvia and the boy being pushed and prodded onwards by that merciless devil, while he must stay hidden from view, seething but powerless to raise a finger to help them.

Despite his assurance to Sean about their woodland skills, it was as much as they could do to maintain a safe distance, because they were eager to seize any opportunity to surprise and overcome the outlaw. But they daren't risk breaking their cover for the hostages' sake, so they forced themselves to hang back by at least a half-day's walk. Thus they were able to light an evening campfire — essential at this time of the year for bodily warmth, but equally necessary to ward off the wild animals that Luke and Sean had warned them about. More than once Bradley, by nature a light sleeper, was roused from his slumber by the distant howling of a wolf pack and both he and Shah assured one another that heavy rustling in the adjacent undergrowth was just the product of the breeze and an over-sensitive imagination.

As he expected, the raider chose the way of the old metalled road surface that led directly northwards from the bridge. He might be evil, but he was no fool and must realise this would be the easiest route. Just about everything else this side of the river was completely overgrown by dense vegetation. The road surface had kept its integrity to a surprising extent, being thick enough not to have cracked completely except here and there. Over the centuries, successive leaf-falls and layers of lighter rotted vegetation had covered it with ragged topsoil, but this supported only small shrubs and grasses. In addition, the indigenous wildlife had adopted the old road as their natural highway, so that well-worn animal tracks and pathways made progress easy, without too much recourse to the knife or machete.

"The horses would have made light work of this trail after all," Shah observed.

Even under these desperate circumstances, Bradley nodded and smiled. "Right, Rajeev. And won't that swine be cursing his bad luck in having been forced to leave them behind?"

Then, after a half-day's walking, an amazing change occurred along their route. Over a distance of barely twenty strides the vegetation covering the road surface — sparse as it had been up to this point — diminished gradually until it died out altogether, leaving only a clear, open mossy surface that was soft yet firm underfoot. From this point there was another substance mixed with the moss and Bradley crouched down to sift it through his fingers.

"What is it, Marshal?" Shah asked.

"I think it's ash. It's as if the emerging vegetation had been consumed by fire." He sniffed the air. "Smell that?"

"A hint of wood smoke," said the deputy.

Looking ahead along the track, the way before them now took the form of an inviting tunnel through the forest, overhung only by the colourful autumn canopy through which the dappled sunlight glinted playfully upon the mossy trail before them.

"I've never seen anything like this before. It's beautiful," Bradley said.

"A bit spooky though," said Shah with a shiver. "It's unnatural. And incredible! How do you suppose it's kept so clear?"

Bradley stopped and looked around, then pointed to something at the edge of the roadway. "I don't know, but that might have something to do with it."

What they were looking at now was equally astounding. From where the clear trail began, running parallel to the ground at about knee height, a single rigid metal rail extended onwards as far as they could see along the roadway. The rail was supported at intervals of about ten strides by sturdy metal pillars, by way of brackets that protruded from their nearside edge. These small stanchions rose up from beneath the moss. Bradley knelt and scratched some of it away.

"By the Gods, Rajeev! These structures go right through the road surface. They must be fixed below. And look at this." On top of each one sat a cluster of shiny black squares, made of an unfamiliar substance that had the appearance and texture of glass.

"What in the Gods' name...?" the deputy gasped. Then he bent down to examine the rail more closely. "If this was put here by the Ancient Ones, why isn't it brittle like the bridge, or rusted and corroded like the metal pieces that Benson our blacksmith hoards in his store? It looks almost new. I wonder what it feels like?"

"Don't touch it!" Bradley yelled.

Shah recoiled at the urgency of this order and straightened up immediately, standing almost to attention.

"Sorry, Rajeev. I didn't mean to yell, but we don't know if it's safe to touch. Stand back." He picked up a small branch from the side of the trail and lobbed it at the metal rail. A flash of light cracked from where the branch had struck it. The stick burst into flame and was flung by the force of the flash four or five strides along the track, where it lay smouldering and smoking.

Both lawmen instinctively raised their arms to shield their faces from the flash, turning their bodies away as they did so. However, seeing that there was no danger, they cautiously approached the smouldering stick. Bradley turned it over gently with his foot while Shah knelt down to sniff it and examine it more closely.

"Hmm. I see what you mean," the bewildered deputy muttered. Then he pointed at the rail. "But what do you think this thing is?"

"I think the Ancient Ones did put it here — but it's not just something left over from their time. I think it was intended for some purpose that involves us, here and now. I've never seen this kind of metal before, but it must be very special to have stayed unblemished for all these years."

Shah said, "I hope Sylvia and the boy have the sense not to touch the rail. Do you suppose it carries on all the way to the town?"

At the mention of Sylvia's name, Bradley's eyes clouded. He visualised her as little more than the outlaw's packhorse, or even worse — though he tried hard not to dwell on that thought. He imagined her loaded up with all the supplies, struggling to keep up with her abductor and worrying on account of little Toby. And all the time she'd be distraught in the false belief that he and Rajeev had been killed. The vision of what she must be going through disturbed him and depressed his spirit.

Shah must have caught the look of anguish on his face, for he made a clumsy attempt to cheer him. "I think we're privileged to look upon such wonders, Marshal. And we're making good progress, don't you think?"

"Eh? Oh, yes. And look here — their tracks are clearly visible on this ashy surface. He hasn't even considered trying to mask them, which means he's confident he's not being followed. And I'm fairly sure we're holding ground with them — with the little boy to slow them down, they can't be outpacing us. From the remains of the last campfire we came across I'd estimate their position as still about half a day ahead. That's close enough not to lose them, but far enough away to stay undetected. It's the best we can hope for."

"Hmm. What plans do you have when we reach the town?"

By now Bradley had accrued enough respect for his deputy not to be anything but completely honest with him, so he told him the plain truth.

"At the moment, I don't have a clear plan. What we do is going to depend on what happens when we get there, the layout of the place and how our red-haired friend decides to play it. Our only constraint is that I've given my word to do nothing to endanger that young child's life — and I don't intend to break my promise. But we still have the element of surprise and we have to use that to our full advantage."

Shah nodded thoughtfully. "That's fair enough. And there's another unpredictable factor that may work in our favour."

"Oh? What's that?"

"Why, Sylvia, of course. Don't forget how well I know that girl. Oh yes, she'll be in pretty low spirits just now, but she's a survivor, you know. Don't you worry — when the time comes, she'll play her part. I'd stake my life on it."

* * * * *

Sylvia's spirits were about as low as they'd ever been. She and Toby were so laden with supplies that the boy had already collapsed once out of fatigue and she'd taken as much of his burden as she could cope with on top of her own. Red wasn't exactly travelling light, the major part of his load consisting of his personal stuff — mainly spare food, clothing for his own use and assorted weaponry. He had a slight limp just now, the result of an earlier incident when he smacked his blackthorn stick experimentally against the strange metal rail that ran alongside the track. The rail emitted a blinding flash and the heavy stick was violently repulsed, striking him hard on the shin, making him yell out in pain and hop about to the accompaniment of foul utterances and curses. Sylvia smiled inwardly at the spectacle and in a better frame of mind she might have laughed out loud. But on swift reflection she saw this merely as just one additional danger, one more source of potential pain and anguish for herself and the little lad who now looked to her for protection. She made certain from that point that both she and Toby kept well away from the rail.

To help combat her misery she resorted to playing games in her mind. One of these was to look for any signs of goodness or caring in her captor's behaviour. But try as she might, she found no redeeming features, nothing to suggest that he gave a thought for anyone except himself. Certainly not for their comfort or welfare, beyond the minimum practical regard you'd have for any useful beast of burden.

Sometimes she wondered what evil forces had produced such a vile personality, one so capable of inflicting the utmost cruelty upon his fellow men. Was his uncaring character the product of a neglectful upbringing, the result of a clutch of misfortunes that had forced him to become brutal simply to survive? Or did he just derive an unnatural pleasure from dominating and humiliating those who were weaker than he was? She'd seen evidence of this — in his apparent lack of concern for the feelings of animals he hunted, often killing more than necessary and leaving wounded ones to die slowly in pain and terror. From her childhood she and the other village children had learned to be considerate, even when it was necessary to kill. Was it only the teaching that made such things appear natural, just as revulsion to cruelty seemed natural to most people she knew? If she hadn't been taught to be kind, would she also be as cruel as he was? And if disregard for the feelings of other creatures and people became habitual, could such casual cruelty eventually grow to become a pleasure, as it patently was for him?

But there was no use in trying to excuse his brutish behaviour. There was one act for which he deserved never to be forgiven and that was ordering the cold-blooded murder of her dear friends, Rajeev and Dominic. When she thought about them, hot tears of anger welled up in her eyes and hatred consumed her tormented mind. In this state she knew she was capable of grabbing the nearest sharp object to hand and piercing the filthy swine to the heart. But there was Toby, a truly innocent hostage for whom an undeserved end might be only a blink away. She daren't risk the life of the child. She must wait, allow her anger to subside and bide her time. The right moment would come. During the previous night she'd lain awake for a long time, waiting to hear him snore. When he was asleep, she thought she might make her move. But he'd forced Toby to bind her wrists before bedding down and though her bonds weren't tight, the small amount of wriggling required to try and free herself was always enough to disturb him. "Be still there!" he'd growl. And she'd have to obey or risk a blow from the thick blackthorn that he kept within his grasp even as he dozed.

It was obvious that he cared nothing for their comfort. He drove them — and himself — extremely hard, with an undisguised urgency to reach his goal, though she was still unclear as to its precise nature. She knew he'd forced the fishermen to take the key that Dominic had found in the tower and that they must now be heading for the northern town mentioned in the old woman's riddle. What they would find there, she had no idea. By this madman's actions he must believe it was something of great value. But although he was relentless, he obviously wasn't entirely stupid, for he allowed them to rest and take food and water at reasonable intervals. He was also canny enough to know that you didn't try to make progress in the dark, but stopped short of nightfall, so as to allow time to gather brush and make your campfire.

It was on the evening of the second day that she was cured of any sympathy or compassion for the hard, uncaring man that the world had made him. After devouring the meal she'd prepared (she and Toby were still eating, for Red insisted on being fed first), he'd emitted a long, loud belch that echoed around the forest canopy. This to him must have stood for humour, for he followed it with a peal of loud, resounding laughter that disturbed the slumbering birds and made little Toby whimper with fear. As he ate, he kept the child under his control by way of a noose around his throat, tied so that a powerful tug might either choke the boy or even break his little neck. Still holding on to the end of the rope, he sidled over to Sylvia's side.

"You know, you're not a bad cook, girl. I reckon I could get used to your looking after me."

She said nothing, only wishing he'd get back to his side of the campfire. Then she froze as he roughly placed a grubby finger on her cheek, saying, "This scar — it's not so bad, you know. Makes you look sort of — like a wildcat, that's had a few scrapes, but come out of 'em with even more spunk and spirit."

She stared angrily into his lust-filled eyes with a withering look, loaded with spite and venom. Then she whispered coldly, "Get your hand off me, or I'll bite your filthy finger off!"

Undeterred he laughed again and snarled, "That's what I mean! You're like a wildcat! Oh, if I could tame you, girl, you and I might have some fun, don't you think?" And he moved his hand down to rest upon her breast, which he squeezed clumsily. At the same time he brought his face close to hers, so that their lips almost touched.

She made no motion to resist, but simply gritted her teeth and sneered, "Do you honestly think I could fancy a monster such as you, with the face of a rabid dog and the stinking breath of a goat?"

Her words had the desired deflationary effect and he withdrew, declaring, "Huh! Just having a joke, I was! You'll never get a man with a scar like that — unless he's either mad or blind!"

She turned away and lay down her head, quietly sobbing, not just for the element of truth she believed lay in his cruel insult, but because it made her think of the only man to whom she'd ever been attracted and would now never see again.

* * * * *

"Get away! Get away, you devils!"

Sylvia woke abruptly to Red's shouts and curses and saw half a dozen pairs of glinting black eyes surrounding their little camping place. The outlaw lashed out with his stick at the nearest wolf, which yelled in pain as the blow struck home. But the animal didn't run off, nor did the rest of the pack, for they must know that they outnumbered their prey. He reeled around and lashed about some more, with little result and Sylvia shook herself to clear her mind and think how they might be saved from being savagely attacked right there and then.

First she grabbed the remains of the supper and threw them into the brush. This succeeded in distracting three of the animals momentarily. The other three still snarled and growled and were closing in on the weakest member of the group — young Toby who, though wide awake, was rigid with fear. She got up and waved her arms at them, then desperately shoved some dry sticks on the embers of the dying fire, fanning them with the empty dish until the first few flickers of flame took hold and the fire crackled urgently into life again.

"More wood! More dry wood!" she yelled at Red, who followed her lead and helped stoke up the flaming fire. But the pack was persistent. Though they retreated a short distance while the fire grew in intensity, still they stood slavering at the prospect of the new taste of human flesh on their palates. There was little more either Sylvia or Red could do to disperse the pack and send it scurrying off into the night.

Then they heard what sounded like a deafening "Roar!" coming from the roadway some fifty strides ahead of them. The flash of an enormous flame accompanied the noise, followed by a loud humming from the metal rail. Then out of the darkness, floating (or so Sylvia thought) along the rail, a strange, ferocious form approached and emitted two or three further bursts of flame in the direction of the remaining wolves. As one, the heads of the animals went up and the whole pack ran off yelping into the darkness of the forest. The fire-breathing creature, its task completed, floated back away along the rail and into the black tunnel as swiftly as it had first appeared, leaving the three travellers astonished and shaken, wondering why and whence it had come to their aid. Whatever it was apparently had no intention of harming the three of them and as it sped away, the humming of the rail gradually subsided, until at last they heard it no more.

After a while Red broke the eerie silence.

"What in the name of the Sacred Wall was that?" he gasped.

Sylvia had no answer. But then she realised that Toby's young mind drew most clearly on the imagery of stories heard in the nursery, for he alone could readily put a name to what it was that had just saved their lives.

"That," he declared with confidence, "was a dragon!"

CHAPTER TWENTY-SEVEN
IN A NORTHERN TOWN

The pursuers' first sighting of the dragon was less dramatic — chiefly because it took place in broad daylight. It was mid-afternoon on the second day of their trek and the two were making good progress, Shah walking ahead and nearer to the rail, when he signalled to Bradley to stop.

"Can you hear that?"

Bradley strained an ear to listen. "No, I don't think..." Then he cocked the other ear and said, "Wait. Yes, I think I can. There's a sound coming from that rail. It's humming!"

The low drone from the metal rail was unmistakeable now, though the cause of the emission wasn't evident. Gingerly the pair walked on, towards a slight left-hand curve in the road ahead. When they'd rounded the bend, the road straightened out for at least a couple of furlongs in front of them. About half way along, hovering above or upon the rail was one of the strangest visions that either of them had ever seen.

"Well, I'll be..." Shah gasped. "It must be one of those dragons the fishermen told us about!"

Bradley stood and looked at it open-mouthed, then said, "I couldn't suggest a better name for it."

"What do you think it's doing?"

On the face of it, this question needed no answer, for it was obvious what the creature was doing. It was breathing fire. But it did this without any show of ferocity, but rather in soft, gentle bursts along the surface of the roadway. Sound carried easily in the tunnel of vegetation, so the spit and crackle of burning twigs and smouldering bracken drifted back to them with clarity while the dragon went casually about its business. Curls and wisps of smoke rose from where its fiery breath ignited the kindling before it moved slowly further along the rail to repeat the process. What they were witnessing was, on the face of it, strange in the extreme and yet Bradley was convinced it had a logical explanation.

"I think it's keeping the roadway clear," he said.

"Keeping the roadway clear? But you couldn't train an animal to do that, could you? What's going on here, Marshal?"

"Rajeev, if — when — we reach the town, I suspect that's a question we'll be asking ourselves time and again. Right now I have no answer. But let's see if we can approach the creature and get a closer look at it."

It wasn't difficult, for the dragon made slow progress and showed no sign of having noticed them, ostensibly engrossed in its task of ridding the mossy floor of weeds and seedlings. As they drew closer, both men instinctively loaded and aimed their crossbows, ready to shoot. But when they came within five strides of the creature, it seemed somehow to sense their presence, because it stopped what it was doing and turned its head towards them.

Now they had a really good view of it.

"Hmm," Bradley said. "No hairs or feathers."

Shah said with authority, "Of course not. You must recall from childhood stories that dragons are supposed to be covered in scales."

"Yes, I remember. But look. Nothing about this dragon is remotely natural — it's completely metallic."

The deputy carried the observation to its conclusion. "Then it must be man-made."

It was true. The head was nothing more or less than a swivelling dome attached without the benefit of a visible neck to the creature's body, which was about a stride long and balanced lengthwise on top of the metal rail. As to how it was held on the rail, they couldn't make out, because instead of legs the dragon had a skirt comprising a sheet of solid metal that hung down over each side, obscuring the point of contact.

"How do you suppose it moves along the rail?" Shah asked.

Bradley crouched and looked up under its skirts.

Shah said, "I hope it's not female, Marshal. There's probably a law against that sort of thing."

218

Bradley glared up at the smirking deputy. "Please, Rajeev, no jokes. Not now."

Shah fought to make a serious face. "Sorry, Marshal. Can you see any mechanism under there?"

"None. When it moves, its body seems to rise up — as though it's floating on a cushion of air."

"Floating on air? Now who's joking?"

Bradley got up and rubbed ash from his hands. "Well, I can't see any wheels or legs. No visible means of propulsion at all."

The creature's head had no mouth and the feature that earned it the name of "dragon" was surely the cone-like shape of the front of its head, from which the bursts of flame were emitted.

"How did it hear us approach? It hasn't any ears."

"No, but look closer. It's got two raised areas, one on each side of its head and pierced with tiny holes. The ears must be under the metal. Perhaps for protection."

There was just one eye, in the centre of the forehead of its hairless dome. When in motion, this eye flashed with a yellow light, but now the dragon was at rest, it had stopped flashing and turned completely white except for a small black iris in the middle.

With its head swivelled towards them, the dragon now had them in its view and they kept their weapons pointed in case it made a hostile move. Bradley knew a wooden arrow would do little damage to the creature's metal body. Still, he hoped it might yet perceive the threat as real. The iris of the big eye flickered first up and down and then from side to side.

"What's it doing now, I wonder?" Shah said.

"I think it's weighing us up and working out what to do next."

Shah gasped. "You mean, it's thinking?"

"Looks like it to me."

But after a short while, it seemed to lose interest. Not only that — it must have found their presence so tedious that it fell asleep. That is, it settled lifeless upon the rail, where previously it had floated along smoothly like a leaf on a gentle breeze. Once at rest, the single eye now lost its brilliance and turned completely black and shiny. The lawmen lowered their weapons.

"It isn't really a dragon, is it?" asked Shah.

"Call it a dragon if you like, but it's definitely not an animal, though it's been fashioned to appear as one from a distance."

"So you agree that it's man-made? That must be right, because everything about it is metallic. But which men made it?"

"We can't know for sure, Rajeev. But I suspect, the same men who made the Wall and planted that riddle to persuade us to make this journey."

"You agree with Sylvia, then? The Gods of the Wall were nothing more than mortal men?"

"Perhaps. But men so far advanced that they *seem* like gods to us."

"All right. But that means this dragon — or whatever it is — must be forty generations old. I find that hard to swallow. Eight hundred years is longer than I can grasp the meaning of. We've seen how metal from the old days rusts and turns brittle when exposed to the sun and rain. And now you're asking me to believe that this rail and, I suppose, the thing that rides along it have been here for all those years and yet neither shows any sign of deteriorating. How can that be?"

Bradley shook his head. "Honestly, Rajeev, I haven't the knowledge or education even to guess an answer to that. But, consider what we do know about the capabilities of the Ancient Ones. They made the Wall, didn't they? And that's stood undamaged for all this time, hasn't it? You've lived close to it for much of your life. Though forbidden by your parents, I'll bet you and your friends have been right up to it and even touched it. Am I right?"

Shah's face took on the expression of a small boy caught stealing a neighbour's vegetables. "Well, I suppose I..."

"It's all right, Rajeev. We've all done it. We're too curious not to."

Then Shah laughed. "I don't know why I'm feeling so guilty — you're the one who climbed up it not so long ago!"

"Right. So we both know how resistant it is to the forces of the weather. Each winter we have driving rain, strong winds, hail and snow, while the mid-summer sun sometimes threatens to bake the soil. Yet the Wall still stands and remains sound. If we were able to build a wall like that using only the materials we have readily to hand, do you honestly think it would last as long?"

"No, I don't suppose it would. So, do you think the Gods of the Wall — I mean, the Ancient Ones — had some special substance to make the Wall last longer?"

220

"Yes, I do. And if they could do that for something as huge as the Wall, it wouldn't be beyond them to make a metal with similar properties. It's as if they built the Wall to last and keep us confined, yet left us also with the means — tools if you like — to leave Fenwold when the time came. Until that time, those tools would have to be kept in perfect condition."

"And the way to assure that would be to make them out of something that wouldn't rust or break because of exposure to the weather," said Shah. Then he pointed at the dragon. "Like our new friend here. He's just one of the tools, I suppose?" The creature was still completely motionless, as if unconscious. "Why do you think he went to sleep so soon after we approached him?"

"I can only guess that it's not inclined to harm us. I believe it's been working all this time to keep the way clear, ready for the day when someone came along in search of the town."

Shah frowned. "But it can't know that's what brought us here, can it?"

"Who can tell what it knows? Perhaps it was just meant to carry on working here patiently for as long as might be necessary. Sooner or later someone would come through armed with the rhyme and the key. But no, I don't believe it can possibly know our true intentions."

"How can you be sure of that?"

"Because it's already allowed our red-haired friend to pass this way unharmed. If it could see the evil in his heart, it would surely have taken steps to prevent him."

"Thank the Gods that it didn't try, or else Sylvia and Toby might have been harmed as well."

"That's true. So at least we've good reason to believe they're still safe. Come on. Let's get going. If that plan on the back of the key was anything like true to scale, then I reckon we can't be more than a day's trek from the town."

So they left the dragon to sleep, until it decided to carry on burning away any new growth that nosed its way through the surface of the mossy track.

* * * * *

It was mid-morning on the third day of the lawmen's journey northwards from the bridge. On finding the key at the tower, Bradley had held it in his hands for only a moment, yet every detail was committed to his memory. From the brief study he'd been able to make of the plan on its reverse, he'd reckoned three days should be sufficient to reach the town. Thanks to the housemaid dragons, the going hadn't been difficult and they'd made good time. So, unless the entire quest had been a cruel hoax to amuse the Gods, today should be the day. The town, if it existed, must lie only a short distance ahead.

His fertile imagination had conjured up countless alternative images of the town and how it would appear to them at first sighting. But by now he'd learned enough about the Ancient Ones to know they couldn't always be relied upon to produce exactly what was expected. Shah described his own vision of a large golden gate, possibly guarded by a phalanx of friendly dragons, which would open as they approached and welcome them into a glistening metropolis of metal and stone, full of magical wonders and towering buildings.

In fact their entry into the town was something of an anticlimax, marked by the termination of the metal rail and consequently the limit of the dragons' ability to keep the way ahead clear for the travellers. Suddenly they were faced by a wall of unchecked vegetation that grew up through the cracked roadway in front of them. This had the immediate and annoying effect of seriously impeding their progress.

Shah's reaction was to utter a coarse expletive, which was out of character. Bradley fought the urge to do the same and instead, using his good arm, took up his machete and began hacking.

"Careful, Marshal," Shah advised him. "Are you sure you should be doing that after your injury? Why don't you leave the chopping to me, while you keep a watch through this thickening vegetation? After all, where there are no dragons to breathe fire, we're in more danger from wolves and wildcats."

"I doubt if they'll attack us in the daylight. In any case, my shoulder's much improved. But I take your point. I promise I'll stop at the first twinge. Meanwhile we'll make faster progress if we both work at it." And he carried on swinging his machete.

But after a few more swings he stopped and said, "Stupid!"

The deputy also put up his weapon and looked bemused. "Sorry?" he said.

"No, not you Rajeev. It's me. I'm not thinking clearly. Where in the name of the Gods has their trail gone?"

The dawn of enlightenment broke upon Shah's face. "Ah, yes, I see what you mean. We shouldn't be having to do this, should we?"

Bradley sighed. "Not if he's been this way before us — which, as you've correctly observed, he hasn't. I think both you and I are getting careless. We must be tired from all the walking we've been doing. Let's go back and see if we can pick up their tracks again."

When they did, it was obvious what had happened. At the point where the vegetation thickened, the raider hadn't continued forwards along the original roadway. Instead he'd taken his hostages away to the right, where he'd noticed (as the lawmen had failed to do) another metalled surface leading off. This was less densely overgrown than the way straight ahead. They saw plainly now where the outlaw had cut through to ease his passage and with a foolish grin Bradley signalled to Shah to follow him through.

"I won't tell anyone if you don't, Rajeev. Come on. But we'd better be as quiet as we can now. They'll have slowed down, or may even have stopped." And cautiously they followed the trail of broken vegetation created by Red, Sylvia and little Toby just a short time before them.

It wasn't much later that Shah halted and whispered, "Marshal! What's that?" He peered into the darkness of the vegetation to his left, at something straight and tall and very bulky.

Bradley gasped. "It's a building! We must be in the town!"

Shah said, "But it's completely overgrown. And look — there are more buildings covered by the vegetation on the other side and up ahead — see!"

It was true. Wherever they looked, there loomed the overbearing shapes of ancient buildings — even behind them, where they'd failed to notice them before. And in each case the forest had established its mastery, shrouding the masonry in a tangle of branches, fronds and the all-pervasive ivy that obscured and clung to every surface.

Bradley trained his eyes ahead along the trail they were following and into the dense growth on either side. "I'd say the town extends in all directions from here. It must be huge!"

Then Shah put into words what Bradley had been wondering. "How are we ever going to find the building we're looking for among all this lot? It's like searching for a single apple seed in a dung heap!"

"Let's not panic. We should reason this out. Now, let me think. We're following where Red's gone before, but he's merely taking what he thinks is the line of least resistance. That's just a matter of chance, for without dragons to keep the way clear, there's no controlling where the forest grows thickest. By taking such a route he's simply going to wander around aimlessly."

Shah said, "And if we follow him, we'll be doing the same. Maybe we should have continued straight on back there and not followed his trail after all."

"No. We have to find him first. Even if we do manage to stumble on the door we're looking for, we're going to need that key to open it. And then there's Sylvia and the boy to consider."

"Yes of course."

"Still it would be useful to know if we were heading in the right direction. Now, I can understand the Ancient Ones making this difficult for us. But I can't believe they'd have set us an impossible task."

Shah stared glumly at the ground and muttered, "You know, there's always another possibility."

"What's that?"

"Well, I don't want to sound negative, but you said yourself that Sylvia might be right after all. The Ancient Ones might not be Gods, but men and women made of flesh and blood."

"Ah, I follow your train of thought. They could be fallible and might've got this part of it wrong. Is that what you're saying?"

"Well, it can't be ruled out."

"I can't argue with your logic, Rajeev. I agree that has to be a possibility. But we can't give up now. Look how far we've come. I still believe there's much to be gained for our people if we can complete this quest. While ever there's the slightest chance of success, we owe it to them to carry on. Now, help me look around for the tallest tree we can find."

"Tallest tree? Why do you want...? Oh, I see. You want to get a better view. Well, you'll need one that's taller than the buildings and I can hardly see the tops of some of those."

"All right. Then let's look for the tallest building hereabouts."

They clambered through a broken ground floor window of a near-by building, to see if there was any means of getting to the top using internal stairways, like the one they'd used in the tower. But the inside was riddled by invasive vegetation. It comprised mainly roots and runners, but so dense as to be impenetrable after centuries of creeping and twisting. They hacked their way through and found a staircase of sorts but the steps were too fragile to be trusted. They soon realised they'd need to find another way to attain a high vantage point.

They wandered among the undergrowth for some time, craning their necks until they ached. Eventually they selected what they thought was the highest structure in the vicinity. Bradley judged it to be about eight levels in height and almost entirely enveloped in dark green ivy.

"Right," he said. "I reckon this is the one."

"Yes," said Shah. "I think you're right." And he stood looking at Bradley.

"Well?"

"Well, what?"

"Well, you don't think I can do it, not with my shoulder injury?"

"I thought you said it was getting better?"

"Not that much better."

"But, Marshal, I've never... I mean... I don't like... Please..."

"There's nothing to it, Rajeev, honestly. Just keep going, always keep your feet on a sound branch, hold on with at least one hand and don't look down. This is strong stuff." He tugged on a skimpy frond of the vine, which immediately broke away from the main plant. Then he gave the worried-looking deputy a boyish grin and pulled hard on a main stem, which this time held its purchase.

He wondered whether it was the green of the creeper reflected on Shah's sallow skin, or if his face really had turned that colour. But he smiled with relief — and no small amount of admiration — when the young deputy gulped, turned towards the wall of ivy, grasped it with both hands and started to climb.

Chapter Twenty-Eight
A Chance To Run

"For the sake of the Gods, let us rest, will you, you brute! This boy's nearly exhausted! If you keep driving us like this, you'll kill us!"

Sylvia glared with unmitigated hatred at the outlaw. The swine had swung his machete continuously ever since they'd left the cleared roadway, pushing himself and his hostages ever harder to make headway through the unrelenting jungle. From the outset, he seemed to enjoy the physical exertion of fighting a pathway through the dense vegetation. His big jaw, hard as granite, was gritted with resolution and beads of sweat ran off his bulging neck muscles as he hacked and slashed for all he was worth. His crazy eyes looked ever forwards, his mind no doubt fixed on the prize that was now only just within his grasp. But lately Sylvia thought his strength showed signs of fading, his determined look giving way to momentary scowls of frustration and he must be wondering where this trail was leading. In spite of all their hardships, she allowed herself a brief smile. Red must surely see Toby as an encumbrance now, having to be pulled ever harder as he repeatedly stumbled and delayed their progress. And her own constant complaining was probably getting on the outlaw's nerves as well. She hoped so anyway. She'd take another shot.

"Why not just cut us loose if we're slowing you down?"

He turned and yelled, "Shut your mouth, or I'll knock your ugly little head off! We'll stop here for a bit. Get me something to eat and drink. And no tricks, mind, or I'll snap this puppy's neck!"

Toby collapsed in a dishevelled heap and Sylvia shot him a sympathetic smile. His look told of sweet relief from the exertion of just keeping up and the constant tug of that rope around his throat. Now it was loosened, she noticed a nasty rash beneath his left ear where the noose had rubbed and chafed as their brutish captor dragged him along. There was little chance Red would allow her to collect healing herbs to treat Toby's wound, but she'd do what she could when she found a chance. She wondered if he understood the reason for his suffering or the nature of the outlaw's quest. He must know Red was a bad man, from his behaviour now and earlier during those long days of imprisonment in his grandparents' cabin. And he would have heard him boast about defeating Marshal Bradley and how he'd forced Toby's father to slay him in exchange for his son's life. He'd already told her how wretched this made him feel. If not for him, his father wouldn't be a murderer and that good lawman would still be alive. She fought back welling tears for the mountain of guilt piled onto such innocent young shoulders.

Toby was now the focus of her attention. Her personal grief was with her constantly, but she carried it deep within her, a dull cloud in the abyss of her mind, that she had resolved would stay there until this ordeal was over. For the present, she must do everything possible to relieve the little boy of his pain and suffering. She was surely a poor substitute for his natural mother, but just now she knew she was his only comfort. Throughout their ordeal she'd tried to show him tenderness, cheering him with words and raising his spirits even in these dreadful circumstances.

She took out some food from one of the bags she'd been carrying and said flatly to the outlaw, "Shall I light a fire?" She wouldn't usually have asked, but where they'd stopped there wasn't much clear ground.

"Why not? I could do with something hot to drink. No, wait. You sort out the food. The boy can light it. Can you make a fire, lad?"

"Y-yes sir," Toby whispered. "B-but I'll need to gather some dry grass and sticks."

Red let out some more of the rope to let him forage for what he needed. "Well, go on then! And don't try anything — unless you want an arrow in your belly!" So Toby set about looking for kindling.

Sylvia had given up trying to make allowances for Red. Now as far as she was concerned he was pure evil, with no redeeming qualities. Fortunately he hadn't tried to force himself on her again and she put this down to the fact that he found her unattractive. But she could also deal him withering words that seemed to quell his animal desire — for a while anyway. This was a dangerous game though. She'd already borne more than one blow from his stick or the back of his hand. Still, that was preferable to the prospect of surrendering herself to the beast. As she handed him a plate of hard, dry bread and rancid cheese, she wondered what she might say to him now to drive that imaginary knife further into his gut.

She simply said, "You've managed to get us lost, haven't you?"

Though he said nothing, she knew her accusation rattled him, so she twisted the blade some more.

"I said, you haven't got a clue where we are, have you?" Then she deftly raised her forearm to deflect the flying plate that would otherwise have struck her fully in the face.

"Shut your mouth! I know where you'll be if you don't mind your business! We're in the town we set out to find. All I have to do is find the door that this key belongs to." He slapped the breast of his tunic. "When I've found your dead Marshal's treasure, if you behave yourself, I might let you go! Now, get some water boiling and make me a drink!"

Watching the water come to the boil, she thought about their chances of surviving this ordeal. Despite what Red had said, she knew there was scant likelihood he'd ever release them. If he found the treasure he sought, he'd do better to kill them, to prevent their running back to Nearbank and organising a posse to bring him to justice. Even now their value as hostages was in doubt, for by this time he must know Toby's father wouldn't follow and jeopardise his son's life. Their only use to him was to carry his gear and prepare his meals. Sooner or later, she reasoned, they'd become too much of a burden on him even for this and he'd have to get rid them.

So she made a decision. As she'd done several times before, she now put some leaves of herbal tea in his mug and poured the scalding water over them. Then she moved slowly towards him in pretence of handing him the drink. But at the last moment as he looked towards her to take it, she flung the hot liquid into his face, aiming it directly into his eyes.

"Ayah!" the outlaw screamed. "What in the name of the Gods? You've blinded me, you flaming witch!" Both his hands went straight to his eyes in a useless reflex action, dropping the end of Toby's rope as they did so.

She seized the opportunity and yelled, "Run, Toby, run! Back along the trail — I'll catch up with you!"

Toby turned and ran. While Red lay yelling and writhing in agony, Sylvia knew she'd only a few moments to gather a handful of items that might be useful — food, water and a knife. Picking one up, she considered for a brief moment sliding its blade under his tunic and into his flesh and imagined the satisfaction this would give her. But she hesitated. She'd taken a human life in battle, but never before in cold blood. Besides, if she didn't do it properly and he survived, he'd kill her for certain. He was stronger than she was and might even be so with a knife blade sticking in him. Then what would become of little Toby? She just had time to escape now and put enough distance between them and him to assure their safety.

But in the short time she took to consider all this, he reached out and grasped her tightly by her right wrist, pulling hard to force her off balance. She saw the blackthorn stick lying beside him and reached for it with her free hand. She grabbed it, drew it back as far as she was able and brought it down with a satisfying *thud* across his face. Immediately he let go his grasp and fell in a writhing heap, leaving her trembling with the now bloody weapon still in her hand.

She shook herself to regain her senses, dropped the stick, gathered some scraps of food and fled after the boy, leaving the outlaw to curse and swear in his temporary agony. But only the echoes of his oaths and foul threats followed her down that dark and dismal forest trail.

Chapter Twenty-Nine
A Dragon Grins

"Ah, tea! It's good to see you've made yourself useful while I've been risking my life up there."

Shah jumped the last half-stride to the ground. Bradley said nothing, but handed him a steaming cup and a chunk of roast rabbit.

"Thanks, Marshal. I'm ready for this. Ouch! My palms are so sore from all that pulling on those vines. They can give you a nasty rash, you know. Still, they did their job. They cling to a brick wall like — well, like ivy, I suppose. This tea will go down a treat. And the rabbit smells delicious, man! Just let me get my teeth into it!"

Bradley watched him patiently for a few moments and thought he caught the glimmer of a cheeky smile.

"All right. You've made your point. You're a hero. Now, tell me — what did you see from up there?"

"Up there?" He gnawed greedily on a rabbit bone and then slurped his tea.

"Yes, up there. From the roof."

"The roof? You wanted me to go onto the roof? I wish you'd said so. Fancy letting me climb all that way and not telling me you..."

"What did you see?" Bradley's patience was running out.

Shah chuckled. "Sometimes, Marshal, you can be too serious, you know. All right. I'll tell you what I saw. Well, there were lots of trees..."

Bradley sighed. "Rajeev..."

"I haven't finished. I was going to say that there were lots of trees, as you'd expect. But I guess you want to know if there was anything different, other than trees, that is?"

Bradley didn't answer, only stared at him seriously.

"Yes, well, I did see an area that might have been a clearing of sorts — a fairly big area, it was. It lies about a furlong to the north-west of here."

"And it's cleared of vegetation?"

"Yes, it looked clear."

"And were there any other clearings to be seen?"

"No. I reckon that's the only one."

Bradley clapped his hands. "Right! That's it, then. It has to be the place we're looking for. The Ancient Ones wouldn't have let the vegetation smother it. Only a furlong, you say? If it's that close, we should be able to reach it before nightfall."

"There's something else. I saw a plume of smoke."

"Smoke?"

"Yes. Campfire smoke."

"Are you certain?"

"Couldn't be anything else. I reckon they've set up camp, or are making a meal, just under a furlong away."

"That close? In what direction?"

"North-west."

"North-west? So they must be close to that clearing you saw."

"Within spitting distance, I'd say."

"Come on then. Pack up and make it quick. You can finish that rabbit later. Lets go get them."

* * * * *

When Red had uttered every oath and foul curse he knew, he lay on his back next to the fire and collected his thoughts. His first instinct was to catch that girl and beat the life out of her, but he realised he should check the extent of his injuries first.

Things weren't as bad as they might have been. The blow from the stick had broken the skin on his cheek and he knew from experience that a bit of blood always made injuries appear worse than they really were. He found a piece of rag to staunch the flow, which wasn't that serious in any case and soon the bleeding stopped altogether. His head still pounded with pain from the blow, but the dizziness was gradually subsiding and anyway he knew his skull was too hard to be cracked open by a skinny teenage girl. Mostly he was concerned about his eyesight after her surprise attack with the scalding tea. But his reflexes were good and he must have blinked as the liquid flew towards his face, for though his eyelids still smarted from the contact with the hot tea, when he forced them open he saw well enough. His vision was blurred for the moment, but it would soon settle back to normal. So his eyes weren't damaged. His face was going to look a mess for several weeks though, but as he wasn't planning to attend any social functions, that prospect didn't bother him too much.

He was mad as a bull at the girl for what she'd done — and at himself for allowing her the chance to do it. He'd been careless. If he caught up with her again, by the Gods of the Wall, he swore he'd have her — scar or no scar — and then he'd have her life. But there was no point in dwelling on that now. He looked around the little camp area, to check what she'd taken. Not a lot, he thought. He still had enough food and most of his weapons. In her haste to escape with the kid, she'd left him with all he needed to survive here on his own if he had to. He'd have to do everything for himself now, with no slaves to fetch and carry for him. But he'd lived this way before and it would be no great hardship to have to do so again. And he had the key. He felt and checked that it was still tucked safely inside his tunic. Then shakily he got up and had a good look around him.

He saw now, when he peered into the murkiness of the undergrowth, that there were large buildings all around him, though obscured by the vegetation. He hadn't realised before just how far he'd come inside the old town. He knew if he could find a vantage point he ought to be able to get a better view of the place. So he hacked through to the nearest of the structures and smashed away what remained of a ground floor window, through which he easily gained entry. But he found an interior clogged with vegetation that offered no safe way to the upper floors. So he went back outside and grabbed a clump of clinging ivy.

In his battered condition it was hard going, but he needed only to ascend three levels to see over an adjacent rooftop into what looked like a large clearing. In the centre of this stood a building that the forest hadn't touched, somehow protected from the creeping jungle. From where he clung, his still smarting eyes made out several box-like structures on its flat roof, similar to the metal pillars supporting the dragon rails beside the cleared forest track. On top of these were larger versions of the shiny black tiles from which he supposed the dragons drew their power to move and make fire. He saw no dragon there, though, and figured it must be lurking behind one of the boxes. Eagerly, then, he descended, dropping the final two strides to the ground and impatiently slashed his way across the adjoining overgrown streets until in no time at all he emerged into the clearing.

He saw now that the single storey building stood in the centre of a large square, virtually perfect and unblemished, while every other surrounding edifice was eroded with age and smothered by invasive greenery. Neither a door nor any windows were in evidence on this side, which he took to be the rear of the structure. A stone stairway with a rusty-looking handrail ran up from the left-hand side to the centre of the roofline. Around the edge of the roof was the now familiar low metal rail supported by the pillars he'd seen earlier, but with a gap where the staircase joined the roof. When he looked down, he saw that the ground here was covered with moss and ash, just like the cleared pathway in the forest. Thinking there must be a dragon somewhere on the roof, he instinctively drew and primed his crossbow — though by now he guessed this would be of little use against one of the metal beasts. Cautiously, he made his way round to the front, where his eyes immediately fixed on the main door of the building.

It was made of solid metal and was about two strides in width, taller than a man and devoid of handle, bar, hinge or lock. He approached and tapped it, then gave it a sharp blow with his stick, but it didn't give. How he could possibly open it was beyond him. Then he stood back and noticed that on the outside of the building around the door was an arrangement of fifty or more decorative tiles, each of which bore a different pattern of a type that looked vaguely familiar. Just behind him on either side of the door, set into the solid pavement that lay unblemished beneath the ash, stood knee-high pillars topped with more of the black, shiny squares. Red's smarting eyes struggled to take all this in and were now drawn upwards from the doorway to see what sat on the roof just above it. The dragon rested motionless on its rail at the mid-point of the roofline, its one eye focused directly upon him and flashing to acknowledge his presence. Just like the housemaid dragons in the forest, it had a fire-breathing orifice in place of a mouth, but this one was broader than the others, giving its face a

234

peculiar and unnerving expression that could be interpreted in only one way.

The dragon was grinning at him.

* * * * *

After a while, the welcome of the grinning dragon wore a bit thin for Red, because no matter how he tried, he couldn't get into the building. And to cap it all, he lost the key.

Or rather, he didn't lose it, in as much as he knew where it was. He'd noticed a slot to the right-hand side of the door, just wide enough to accept the key if presented edgewise. When he did this, something drew the key through the slot and into the wall of the building. He'd expected this to cause the door to open, but it didn't. Nor was the key returned to him and there seemed to be no way of retrieving it. There was a metal button beneath the slot that he found he could press, which he did — several times. But still nothing happened. Frustrated and angry, he swore and kicked at the wall.

Why should it be so complicated? He'd inserted the blasted key, after all. But clearly that wasn't enough — there must be more to it.

While the light faded he studied the array of tiles around the doorway again. One or two of their designs looked familiar. Then he remembered the four motifs depicted on the front of the key. He hadn't paid much attention to them, but recalled that one of them had been a circle with a point in the centre. His sore eyes ran along the tiles and yes, there at about knee height on the left-hand side of the door was a tile bearing that symbol. He walked up and placed his hand on it and found that it too could be depressed, just like the button. He tried all the tiles, every one of which yielded when pushed. All the tile designs, though individually unique, were so similar that any of them might have been one of those etched on the key. But he couldn't remember exactly what the other three looked like. And he had no way of checking now, because the key was stuck fast inside that damned slot. If only he'd paid closer attention to the key, he might have been able to recall those other three patterns. But he hadn't and he couldn't.

Frustration gave way to desperation. He ran from one side of the door to the other, randomly pushing on tiles, then pressing the button, but still to no avail. Then he tried pressing them all, one by one, first from left to right, then from right to left. Nothing happened. He repeated the exercise, this time two tiles at a time, but the door remained firmly shut. He carried on like this for ages, trying random combinations and permutations, until the daylight faded. Just about exhausted after one more chaotic attack with both hands — and feet — on the wretched tiles, he fell in a disgruntled heap on the stone floor in front of the unyielding doorway. He knew he was defeated. And when he looked up, that bloody dragon was still grinning at him!

"Right!" he said, standing and raising himself to his full height to bring his angry face closer to the head of the smiling dragon. "I'm going to wipe that blasted smile off your smarmy face!"

With that, he picked up the blackthorn stick and marched round to the rear of the building, mounted the stone stairway to the roof and gritted his teeth, resolved to get satisfaction in the only way left open to him.

CHAPTER THIRTY
A SWEET REUNION

Pain. Excruciating pain.

Like a kick from a wild horse, it thrust into Red's lower ribs, snatching him from his deep sleep and sending a searing message to his brain that he was under attack. His eyes still hurt like hell, so much that they were hard to open. And his head throbbed from Sylvia's beating. But that was yesterday. This was something else. Something new. And he was cold — must have let the fire go out. He needed to find out what was happening. Damn his swollen eyelids! He brought up his fingers to force them apart. A piercing slit of light opened up, enough to reveal the source of the burning pain in his side.

Boots. There were four of them and they were planted right next to him where he lay. Fighting the agony, his stinging eyes looked upwards to see whom they belonged to. The image was blurred and he found it hard to identify the two people who, crossbows drawn, now looked down upon him.

"What have you done with them, you heartless bastard?"

Cold as he was, a stinging chill ran through his bones. He must still be dreaming. Then the voice spoke again.

"Give him another kick, Rajeev."

In spite of the pain, he sat bolt upright and rubbed his eyes hard, at once confirming his worst fears.

"Bradley!" he gasped. "But you're... They told me they'd..." Then, in the plain realisation that the fishermen had tricked him, he merely said, "You've been following all this time."

Bradley only repeated his question. "What have you done with Sylvia and the boy?"

Red felt for his knife, then saw his armoury piled up behind the two lawmen and realised he was done for. But the initial shock to his system was now at last receding. He searched frantically inside his mind for something, anything he might have with which to bargain for his freedom. He wouldn't be too eager to tell them everything they wanted to know.

"I'll tell you. First though, what plans have you got for me?"

Shah said, "I can tell you that, you dog. First, we thought we'd cut out your tongue, lop off your ears, nose and any other appendages and then..."

"Don't, Rajeev," Bradley said with a scowl of mock disgust. "I haven't had my breakfast yet."

If this was their idea of humour, Red didn't find it at all funny. He felt some of the colour drain away from his usually ruddy complexion. But he was nothing if not hard and he spat back, "Have your fun, lawmen, but if you want to see your friends again you'll answer my question."

"We'll decide what to do with you later," Bradley said. "One way or another, you've a lot to answer for. Assuming Sylvia and the boy are alive and well — and they'd better be — your most heinous crimes concern the villagers of Nearbank. As far as I'm concerned your trial and punishment should be conducted under their jurisdiction. They've been cut off from the rest of Fenwold for years, so their system of justice mightn't be as enlightened as back in Crowtree. And you've already had your one crack at the Wall — you're not entitled to a second one."

"Yeah, that's right," Shah added. "Some of the older settlements had some really cruel punishments. I remember..."

Bradley interrupted him. "Not now, Rajeev. We have to find Sylvia and Toby, before they wander too far away."

"All right," the outlaw said with a shrug. Behind his morose, dark eyes his now fully alert mind was still racing, his criminal brain coldly weighing up his chances. "I'll point you in their direction. But nothing comes for free. First tell me what you know about that door."

"Why should we?" the deputy said.

But Bradley said grudgingly, "The sooner we tell him, the sooner we'll get Sylvia and Toby back."

"All right," Shah said. "Shall I tell him?" Bradley nodded.

"We went into the clearing early this morning to take a look at the building. Your footprints were all over the place. We followed your trail back here with no trouble — and if we hadn't we'd have found you just from your snoring. You couldn't work out how to open the door, could you?"

Red sneered. "Oh and I suppose you're going to tell me you do know how to get in?"

The Marshal said, "As a matter of fact, we do. We studied that doorway pretty closely and it seems there are six elements to gaining entry. First, there's the key, which you're about to hand over to us. Second, there's the button. And third, fourth, fifth and sixth are the four tiles."

Red forgot about his predicament momentarily. "I worked that out, but..."

"But you couldn't press all four tiles at the same time. Or didn't you even get that far because you were too dim to match the tiles with the designs etched on the key?"

Red bristled. "I knew that," he lied. "Like you said, there were too many for me to press them all at once, so when the light failed I decided to wait till morning and figure out how to do it. I would've done too, if that snivelling, lying coward of a fisherman hadn't let you two live."

Shah laughed. "Ah! Thanks for that admission of guilt for incitement to murder. That'll save time when it comes to your trial. But putting that to one side — for now — you know, you never would have been able to open that door."

"What makes you so sure?" Red growled.

"None of us could have known without a proper examination," Bradley admitted. "But after looking it over this morning, we're certain that one person couldn't do it on their own."

"Ah," Red sneered. "So I couldn't do it, but you two can?"

"No, not even the two of us. If I'm right, we're going to need five people working together to open that door. The tiles that match the designs on the key are too far from one another."

Red's lips moved as he did some mental arithmetic and said, "Five people? You mean, one on each tile and..."

"And one on the button," Shah concluded.

"So, let me see if I've got this right," Red mused. "Because the four tiles and the button have to be pressed all at once and they're spaced so far apart, you're going to need three other people to help you open the door?"

"Looks like it," Bradley said.

"Hmm. So where does this leave me?"

Bradley looked him squarely in the eye. "As much as I'm eager to get into that building, my first intention is to find Toby and Sylvia. Then we're going to take you back to Nearbank for trial and return with enough trustworthy people to do what's necessary."

"After we've seen you executed," Shah added.

Red looked coldly at the deputy.

Bradley's impatience was manifest. "So where are they?" he demanded.

Red decided it was time to exhibit the minimum of cooperation.

"They took off yesterday. That bitch of a girlfriend of yours chucked boiling water in my face and nearly stove my head in and hoofed it with the runt."

Shah nodded. "That explains the state of your face — fresh scar, bloody cheek that looks like a freshly skinned chicken. You know, you really should pay more attention to your appearance."

Red scowled, but Bradley smiled at Shah's dark humour. "Good girl, Sylvia," he said. "Now, which way did they go?"

"They ran off into the undergrowth not far from here. I can show you. Probably holed up for the night, then planned to head back towards the river, I suppose."

"Right then," the Marshal said. "Let's go and get them." But the outlaw didn't budge.

Bradley jabbed his bow towards him and said tersely, "Come on then — if it's not too much trouble."

Red said, "All right, Bradley. But there's just one small thing."

"And what might that be?"

"Well," the outlaw drawled, "You don't expect me to hand over that key and get nothing in return, do you?"

Shah rounded on him. "Look, you murdering bastard. Don't go thinking you've got any bargaining power in this. We know you have the key and if you won't hand it over, we'll just have to take it from you. And that's something you're in no position to prevent."

Saying this, he fell to one knee and prodded his primed crossbow into the outlaw's chest.

But Red didn't flinch. He only smiled and said, "All right then. Go ahead and take the blasted key."

So while Bradley stood over him, Shah searched his clothing, his filthy bedding and assorted baggage that was strewn around the camp area. All the time, the outlaw smiled cynically.

After the fruitless search he said, "Can't find it? Well now, maybe I do have something to bargain with after all."

Angrily, Shah drew his knife. "Let me loosen his tongue, Marshal! He'll tell us — eventually!"

Bradley's face betrayed his natural reluctance at resorting to torture, but Red realised he'd still have to talk them out of it. "Do you really think I'll give in to that? I'm not afraid of pain. Go ahead and have your fun. But don't think you'll ever get that key." Then he added, smiling, "Nor your scar-faced girlfriend!"

Bradley said, "Stow the knife, Rajeev. You know he's right. He'll never talk. I can't risk losing Sylvia."

Grumbling, Shah did as he was told.

Bradley looked at Red. "Go on — tell us what it is you want."

"Simple. I show you where they went, deliver the key and in return I get my freedom. I also get a half share of the treasure!"

The deputy uttered, "You bastard! You don't honestly expect..." But Bradley signalled to him to be silent. The outlaw smirked, but didn't speak.

"Anything else?" Bradley asked gloomily.

"Well, I've been thinking. Once I've helped you find the witch and the kid, we'll be five, won't we? You won't be taking me back for trial and anyway we don't need anyone else. So I reckon we should waste no time, get back to the clearing and open that door together — today."

Bradley didn't answer.

"It's like this. No deal, no key. It's up to you."

"All right," he sighed. "You'll get what you ask, in return for helping us locate Sylvia and Toby — safe and sound — then supplying the key and helping us get into that building. But we'll not be returning your weapons to you, nor will we release you, until we've won through to the far side of the Wall. That's the best deal I can give you — and it's better than you deserve."

Red smiled and said, "Thanks, Marshal. I accept your generous offer."

Then he held out his right hand across the burned out campfire and Bradley, gritting his teeth, took it in his own, shaking it once to seal their bargain, while Rajeev Shah looked on in undisguised disbelief.

* * * * *

Sylvia and Toby spent an uncomfortable night huddled on the leeward side of one of the old buildings. She hoped the beating she'd given Red would delay his following them for a while and felt their best chance lay away from the trail that he'd cleared earlier. She daren't risk lighting a fire, so they snuggled together under the two good blankets she'd grabbed on her hurried departure. Still, by morning she and the boy were shivering with cold and on rising she rubbed his freezing body vigorously to improve his circulation, while telling him of her plans for the day.

"We'll head down the trail and get you back home after we've had something to eat. I don't think he'll be bothered about us now. Don't worry, Toby. You'll be back with your Mum and Dad in two or three days."

They ate some stale bread that she'd grabbed, then gathered up their few possessions and started off down the track.

They hadn't gone far before she had the feeling they were being followed. It was a sensation familiar to anyone brought up in the woods. The forest somehow sounded different, her senses grew keener and she felt that eyes were watching her. She cursed the outlaw for his perseverance.

And she fancied she heard her name being called through the forest. Worse still, though far off, she fancied the voice that called it belonged to one whom she knew to be dead. Either her mind was playing tricks, or Red was somehow skilled in callously mimicking the voices of those he'd ordered murdered. After all she'd been through, losing her good friends, being abducted and dragged through this hostile country, there was no wonder her thoughts were confused. She was certain now that the outlaw was tracking them and taunting her. All she could think was: what would Dominic do? The answer came to her swiftly. He would take the initiative. That was what she must do now.

She worked quickly, putting to use the skills he'd taught her, using the branches and vines that abounded in this forest. The outlaw was about to get a surprise he hadn't bargained for. When she'd finished, she and Toby hid in the undergrowth and waited.

From where they were hidden, she saw only a pair of filthy leggings as their owner strode boldly along the track towards her. He called out her name again. Oh, how she detested him for his callousness! The voice had the ring of her beloved Dominic and as she listened to his cruel mockery the hot tears stung her eyes. She steeled herself, promising that he'd pay dearly for tormenting her so.

At once he was alongside and stepped on the appointed spot. Without hesitation, she cut the retaining vine to release the pent-up willow branch, which then sprang up, closing the concealed loop around one leg of her victim. Toby, terrified and confused, remained kneeling, rooted to the spot where she'd left him. But she ran out onto the trail, snarling and shaking her fist at the protesting body that thrashed and flailed about upside down in her vine trap.

He'd dropped his crossbow while being unceremoniously hoisted and he shook his body desperately to try and free himself from her trap, causing several bolts to slide out from his upturned quiver. She loaded the bow and carefully took aim directly at his madly shaking head and said, "Prepare to die, you cold-hearted swine! You'll cause no more good people to suffer!" Even as her finger squeezed against the trigger, her vision was clouded with tears of remorse and hatred.

"Sylvia! Sylvia! Look at my hair!" the hanging figure screamed.

What? Look at his hair? Whatever did he mean? But she did as he'd pleaded and studied the scoundrel's hanging locks. His hair was black. But it should have been red. Why wasn't it red? The answer hit her almost with a tangible force. It wasn't red, because it wasn't Red.

"Oh, what am I doing?" she sobbed as she lowered the bow.

Then through her tears she saw a blurred figure kneeling where she'd tied the other end of the vine and cutting it free. "Help me, Sylvia," Rajeev's voice was saying to her.

She tried to take her captive's weight, but at the last moment his body tumbled to the ground and the black-haired vision said to her, "By the Gods, Sylvia! You weren't going to shoot me, were you?"

She put her hand to her mouth and murmured, "Dominic? Is it you? Oh, Dominic!" Then she fell to her knees beside him, her mind even more confused, took his head in both her hands and without thinking put her lips to his, wetting his face with her tears.

Then Shah said, "Sylvia, I should let him get up if I were you."

She straightened and rose to her feet, then they each gave Bradley a hand and helped him up too. They said nothing then, but the three friends stood enclosed in a triple hug while time stood still. After a while, Shah withdrew and went to coax Toby from the undergrowth.

But Sylvia and the Marshal remained a while locked together in a silent embrace.

Chapter Thirty-One
Unlock And Enter

"Get her away from me! Don't let her near me! At least untie me, man!"

It amused Bradley that Red must have been dreading this moment, when Sylvia returned with them to find him conveniently tethered to a tree. After he'd given them directions, despite his protests they'd decided to leave him tied up while they went off to find the hostages. Bradley had insisted they'd free him only when their objective was achieved with his full cooperation. He'd been in no position to argue. They'd bound his wrists with a short rope fastened to a nearby oak, quipping as they left that he should "watch out for wolves" while they were gone. They left him plenty of time to reflect on the potential dangers of this place — and on his treatment of the child and the girl. By the time the jubilant party returned, his fear of what Sylvia might do to him was plain for all to see.

As soon as she caught sight of him, hatred flared up in her eyes and she quickened her step to attack him. He was defenceless against the vengeful female who without doubt was prepared to do him substantial physical damage.

"Untie me, for the sake of the Gods!" he pleaded again, holding out his hands.

But Bradley only shrugged and did nothing to prevent her rushing towards the cowering figure shouting, "You bastard!" while aiming her claws at his defenceless face. The outlaw tried to step out of the way, but her aim was good. Her nails cut deep wounds into both his cheeks and dark streaks of blood ran down into his scruffy beard, while his screams of agony sent flights of startled birds aloft from their roosts in the near-by trees. His

245

bound hands went straight up to his face then and as they did, Sylvia placed a well-aimed kick between his legs, dropping him to his knees in a defeated, groaning heap.

When she grabbed a stick to continue the assault, Bradley moved forwards and gently restrained her. Then Shah loosened the outlaw's rope from the tree and with what little strength he had left, Red held out his hands for his wrist bonds to be untied as well. But they ignored him and he protested no further but slunk quietly into a corner to lick his wounds, away from any further taste of Sylvia's venom.

Sylvia sat down on the ground and wiped the blood from her hands with a piece of rag, her appetite for revenge apparently satisfied for the time being. But she nodded in the outlaw's direction.

"You're not going to leave his legs untied, are you?"

"He's got nowhere to run," Bradley assured her. "Besides, there are some things we need him to do. And remember, although he's a thoroughly nasty man, we don't know that he's guilty of any murder. Not since his first trial, anyway."

Red shook his head and gruffly reminded them, "Where I was duly sentenced. It just so happens that I survived my punishment."

"All right," she drawled sulkily. "But don't even consider giving him a weapon." Then she addressed him directly. "You — stay away from me and the boy. And remember, I'm armed — and you know I'm dangerous."

He only glared in her direction. Then tugging at the bonds around his wrists, he said to Bradley, "Can't you loosen these ropes? They're nearly cutting through my veins."

Shah went over to where Bradley was now sitting, while Sylvia knelt to sort out some food for Toby. Keeping his voice low, the deputy said, "You know, we're going to have to untie his hands if he's to be of any use to us in opening that door. And there's still the small matter of getting him to retrieve the key, wherever he's hidden it."

Overhearing him Sylvia suggested, "The swine dragged Toby along by a noose round his neck — why not give him some of the same treatment?"

So a length of rope was selected and a noose fashioned, which the deputy took over to the outlaw.

"Wear this around your neck and we'll loosen the wristbands from time to time." He fastened the end of the noose to a near-by stump and slackened off the wrist bindings.

Red rubbed his chafed wrists and said grudgingly, "At least I'll get some circulation back in my hands, I suppose." Then he sat down, appearing resigned to the arrangement.

While Rajeev and Sylvia prepared a meal, Bradley wondered what was going through Red's mind. Was he telling the truth when he said he'd hidden the key? If he didn't come up with it, they'd have to return him to Nearbank for trial and abandon the quest. With no key, there was no way of getting into that building, short of smashing their way in with a force of men. But he hoped that wouldn't be necessary. If Red produced the key as agreed, he could go on and complete his mission — unless this was all some heartless jest on the part of the Ancient Ones. That was a thought that had recently haunted his dreams. But surely nobody would go to so much trouble for the sake of a cruel joke? Sylvia had spoken about destiny and he felt strongly that they were meant to be here, that something momentous was about to happen. It grieved him that he'd had to bargain away half the treasures to an outlaw in order to reach this point. But he'd given his word and he would honour that pledge and face the consequences when he stood once more before Fenwold's High Council. He wasn't much looking forward to that day.

When the food was ready he took some over to the outlaw. Red accepted it with grudging thanks, but tucked into it voraciously. Bradley collected his own meal and sat down next to him, saying nothing until they'd both finished. Then the Marshal spoke.

"Now, about the key. Where is it?"

"I'll produce it when the time comes."

"Come on, man. Let's not play games. You know only too well that that key is crucial to my mission. I've been patient with you and said I would free you when this is over, so now it's your turn to deliver what you promised. So let's have it — and no more excuses."

"It's not here. I hid it."

"Fair enough. Just tell me where."

"Somewhere safe, close to the clearing."

"So tell me. I want to see it."

"When we go to the clearing to open the door, I'll get it for you then. What's wrong with that?"

Bradley looked at his mess of a face, knowing the outlaw was the last person in Fenwold he should trust. But what choice had he? Quickly he got to his feet, pulling him up beside him, saying, "All right. I think we're all finished here and we've put this off for long enough. Come on everyone, our friend here is going to show us where he's hidden the key. It's time to go and find out what awaits us behind that door."

* * * * *

Bradley felt exhilarated to stand before the door mentioned in the old woman's rhyme. All the elements of the riddle had neatly unravelled to bring them to this place. He and Shah had gone to the tower at the eastern extremity of the river that flowed into the Great Sea and there located the unusual key that had hung for centuries undetected inside the metal tubing of the stairway handrail. The design on the reverse of that key had guided them to this old town in the northern part of Fenwold and now here they stood in front of the door, above which — as the rhyme had predicted — rested the form of one of the caretaker dragons, in repose bearing an expression that closely resembled a toothless grin.

All that remained was for Red to disclose the whereabouts of the key he'd hidden, for it to be offered into the slot at the side of the door and then for the button beneath it, together with the four tiles, bearing the symbols depicted on the front of the key, to be pressed simultaneously. Then the door would be opened and, after that — what? Certainly not immediate access to the land on the far side of the Wall, for that was still many leagues away to the west. But perhaps some revelation of the Gods' intentions and also, he hoped, further instructions as to how they might achieve their final goal.

If the Gods of the Wall — or humans of centuries past, as he now believed them to have been — could have looked down upon that clearing and the culmination of the plans they'd laid so long ago, they might well have been surprised or even amused at the motley bunch of human flotsam now gathered here to learn the secrets so long held in safekeeping.

In fairness, given the remoteness of this place, any travellers would surely arrive exhausted and dishevelled from their punishing journey. Truly all five looked and felt far from their best. Sylvia and Toby, each badly fatigued and emotionally pummelled following their ordeal, then so suddenly uplifted by their recent rescue, stood holding hands in a confused state of dread and expectation. Rajeev Shah, ever mindful of his duty, though dirty and ragged from his arduous days on the trail, gathered what strength he could summon to stand to attention, in a display of unswerving loyalty to his mentor and friend, Marshal Dominic Bradley. Equally scruffy and trail-weary, Bradley now felt the responsibility of leadership more than ever and tried his best to exude confidence, fortitude and calm as an example to the rest of the group. And finally the outlaw Red, the filthiest of them all and sullenly submissive, hands loosely bound and led humiliated into the clearing by the noose around his neck, felt his senses racing to balance his ambition for material gain against the desire to save his wretched skin.

But despite their differing degrees of discomfort, status, ambition and expectation, there was yet one realisation that each held in common with the others. It was the knowledge that here, this day, something was about to happen that would have far-reaching consequences for all the inhabitants of Fenwold. And the fact that each of them was a part of what was about to happen rendered them — for this brief moment, at least — apprehensive yet submissive to whatever it was that the fates now held in store.

When the five of them were standing more or less in line in front of the building, Bradley gave Red's rope a tug and said, "Right, you! Let's have that key now and no tricks!"

The outlaw snapped, "All right, all right! It's over here — I hid it in the undergrowth."

Bradley gave out some of the rope to allow Red to move towards the edge of the clearing. Here the raider knelt and rummaged with his loosely bound hands in the scorched scrub that lay along the clearing's perimeter. Soon he got to his feet and, keeping his hands out of view from the rest of the group, assured them, "Here it is — I have it."

Then he hurried back towards the slot, pulling so hard on the rope that Bradley was taken by surprise and had to trot to keep up with him. After a short, awkward act of mime, Red announced, "Right, it's in!" And though Bradley was suspicious of his clumsy theatrical antics, he had no choice but to be satisfied with the raider's declaration.

Following this minor commotion, the five stood in silence for a few moments in front of the big door, sensing an air of reverence about the occasion, each of them feeling even more that something special was about to happen. Still holding on to Red's rope, Bradley broke the silence and set about directing the proceedings.

"Now, let's see. Sylvia, you take the tile with the circle — it's over there on the left, see? Not yet though — wait until we're all in position. And Rajeev, you can press on the triangle — same side, slightly further up. See it? Good. I'll take the square with the diagonal, high up on the right here. And you, Red — no, your bonds aren't too tight — swivel your right hand and place your palm on that six-pointed star, low down on the right there. And finally, Toby, be ready to press the button."

He made another swift visual check and drew a deep breath.

"Right, now, is everyone ready? Toby, I think you should have the honour of counting us in. Would you like that?"

The boy nodded enthusiastically. "Can I do it in our old language? When I say *pip*?" Bradley smiled and nodded, so he began, "Yan — chan — tether — mether — pip!"

On the word *pip* each one pressed his or her allotted tile or button, held it pressed in and waited.

Nothing happened.

Bradley thought for a moment and then said quietly, "All let go."

As they did so, a loud *click* emitted from the door, followed by a *hiss* as a narrow crack appeared exactly down its middle. Then the gap widened as the two halves drew swiftly apart.

There were gasps from the other four, though out of a sense of leadership Bradley alone tried hard to curb any outward exhibition of the excitement he was feeling. In truth there'd been lurking at the back of his mind just a tiny grain of doubt that anything would happen at all — for this to be the futile culmination of a wasted journey. So it was with just a hint of relief that he looked around at the rest of the group and said "Well? What are we waiting for? Let's go in and see why the Gods of the Wall have brought us here."

CHAPTER THIRTY-TWO
AN AUSPICIOUS AUDIENCE

Bradley raised a hand to stop them before they crossed the threshold and pushed his head forward for a quick look inside. There wasn't much to see — only a small, bare anteroom with solid closed double doors at the far end. To the right of these, high up in the corner, suspended from the ceiling, was a glowing object, like an eye of one of the dragons they'd met on the forest trail, so he assumed their presence was being observed by someone — or something. Apart from this harmless monitoring he perceived no obvious threat, so he beckoned to the others to follow him through the doorway and into the room.

The outlaw Red was the last to step over the threshold, following a tug on his noose by Bradley. Once all five were inside the outer doors drew together with a further *hiss* followed by a *clunk* that had an unnerving air of finality about it. Instinctively everyone turned to look back to see their exit now barred. But before any real sense of dread could deflate their expectant mood, the far doors drew apart with a *swish* to reveal the main inner chamber. Bradley took a deep breath and led them in.

There were five black circles on the perfectly flat, smooth floor in front of them, on which Bradley assumed they were expected to stand, so he motioned to the others to step forward and do so — Sylvia taking Toby's hand to guide him carefully onto his own marker. She must have been worried that the little lad might be fearful of these strange surroundings. But instead the long absent sparkle returned to his eyes, showing that he was thoroughly enjoying the excitement and newness of the situation, as only a child could do. This must be a welcome contrast to the days of

251

terror spent at the mercy of the outlaw. He looked up to Sylvia and smiled, but still kept a firm hold of her hand.

Directly before the group was a horizontal rail, at about waist height, which separated them from the other part of the room and would also provide a handy support if needed. It wasn't made out of the silver metal, like the rails used by the dragons, but of a hard, white, smooth material that felt warm to the touch. Everything inside the room was formed either of this material, or of another resembling glass. Inquisitive, all five touched the unfamiliar surfaces around them — the rail, the floor and several box-like structures along the walls on either side of them. Bradley wondered if there was any danger in this, but supposed such technology as was evident here wouldn't allow itself or its guests to come to harm. Also, there was no sense of menace about this place. He'd felt only a warm, welcoming atmosphere within the room from the moment they'd stepped inside.

Beyond the rail stood three white boxes arranged in a triangular formation, each of which had its own "dragon's eye" that emitted a soft, white light. The boxes' combined luminescence now appeared to grow brighter, but then he realised that it was the main chamber that was getting darker. As this happened the floor beneath the boxes moved slowly downwards, until they were no longer clearly discernible in the ambient gloom. Almost mesmerised, the travellers' attentions were drawn to the area directly ahead of them, where the beams from the three eyes came together to form a vertical column of almost solid light — or that was how it appeared to Bradley.

The light flickered and then re-formed into shapes, quickly and astonishingly settling into that of something that was instantly recognisable to them. It was the form of a pretty young fair-skinned woman with fine, golden hair. Her tresses cascaded over a long, shimmering white robe, covering her entire body save her arms. She possessed a brightness and purity so compelling that Bradley found he couldn't take his eyes off her.

Without ceremony, the vision spoke to them.

"Welcome, children," it said.

Her dialect was strange — much like that of the Nearbank villagers when Bradley, Shah and Sylvia had first met them. But the woman had a clear, steady voice and the meaning of her words was straightforward and unambiguous. Its warmth was such that it exuded trust and love and at first Bradley couldn't place its familiarity. Then little Toby gasped, "She sounds like my

Mummy!" And the hair on Bradley's neck bristled not unpleasantly as he realised the voice must be meant to appeal to each of them in tones reminiscent of their own mothers. Sylvia squeezed Toby's hand to help calm and comfort him.

The voice continued, "You've been invited to enter this building by a wheel set in motion forty generations ago. We who called you here are no more — our time has passed. We perished in a plague that swept away the world that we knew. It threatened to end our entire civilisation. But there was time to establish a colony of our kind that was free from plague — this place you call Fenwold. To keep you from straying back into danger, we enclosed you within the confines of the Wall. But now the time has come when it's safe for you to return and populate the wider world that we knew. On the other side of the Wall we've left you the best of our science and knowledge. It's yours to use as you wish.

"It's our wish that you enter your new world in a spirit of cooperation, in the same way that you gained entry to this building. Some of you may not see eye to eye and may even bear hostile intentions towards one another, but you'll make progress only if you put aside your differences and work together. Your palm images and other genetic information have been retained and will have to be used again, so you must continue to cooperate.

"Listen carefully. Go together to the place where the Wall crosses the river. Take the key and look for the symbols there as you've done here, but remember that it will take the cooperation of all of you for you to travel to the other side.

"We appreciate that you'll have questions. At this point I'm programmed to provide answers, so far as I'm able. You may put your questions to me now."

There was silence at first. Everyone was held in thrall by what they'd seen and heard so far and stood, each grasping the rail, almost in a state of shock. Bradley's reaction was one of marvel tinged with disbelief. For a brief moment he thought he must have been dreaming. He'd thought himself the most enlightened of them all, yet even he found it hard to rationalise what he'd witnessed and was tempted to write it off as magic. Yes, he accepted that the Ancient Ones would have had the means of leaving a record of their achievements, even a kind of picture (though one whose form and composition was far beyond his understanding). But how could this depiction of an ancient woman now leap forward in time and offer to answer their questions? That was something that defied any logic — the future conversing with the past. He told himself it had to be impossible, no matter how badly he wanted to believe in it.

He realised the others were expecting him to put the first question. One reason for his hesitation was that he wanted to be respectful, but didn't how to address this woman's image. So he merely asked, "What should we call you, lady?"

There was the slightest flicker as if the image were somehow being renewed. Then he was taken aback when she responded, "I am merely an image, designed to look pleasing to you. I was never a real person. But if you wish to call me something, let it be *Cara*."

"Cara," he repeated, "we're pleased and privileged to meet you as the representative of the Ancient Ones. My first question concerns the force that drives these wonders we're witnessing. What conjures the light that forms your image, for example?"

Shah added, "And by what means do the dragons travel upon their rails?"

He might have been mistaken, but Bradley fancied that Cara was smiling at Shah's eagerness. She responded, "You've seen the black cells upon the pillars that support the rails in the woodland tunnel. They collect the heat of the sun and store it in those pillars. The heat is converted into an energy that conducts the dragons along the rail. The dragons themselves can make use of the same energy to create their fire. As to your first question, there are larger cells on the roof of this building. The energy that they collect is stored in boxes — we call them batteries — that can release that energy when required. The image you see is powered by that energy."

Then Sylvia plucked up the courage to ask, "The dragons breathed fire on the wolves when they threatened us, yet fell asleep when we approached them. How do you explain that?"

Cara responded, "The dragons — as I'm sure you know — are merely machines, but with sufficient artificial intelligence to distinguish humans from wild animals. They go to sleep when you approach so as not to provoke you to attack or damage them. They were put there for your protection, as well as to keep the forest trail clear for your journey to the town."

Shah followed up on this. "Why isn't the trail clear all the way from the bridge right up to the door of this building? And why did you go to the trouble to build such a magnificent bridge, only to make it impassable by removing the roadway and weakening its metalwork?"

"It was important that the trail — and this building — be discovered only at the appointed time and by those who were actively seeking the door, prompted by the riddle and the key from the old lighthouse. The bridge existed for centuries before the great plague came. To leave it intact would have brought people here too soon. This building and its power system are of strong construction, but there's always been the risk of damage if stumbled upon by accident. You found the trail only because you were seeking this place."

Bradley reflected on the wisdom behind these words. Sylvia took advantage of the momentary silence and asked, "Did the people of your time all dress as you are dressed now?"

Bradley thought this a trivial question under these circumstances and turned to her ready to remonstrate. But before he could open his mouth Cara responded enthusiastically, without the slightest sign of disdain or condescension, "My appearance has been designed to please you. We had many fashions in clothing. We've records of them all and I'm sure you'll enjoy seeing them — though some you may find shocking."

Now Toby must be feeling bolder, because he asked, almost in a whisper, "Did you ride horses, like the ones that Sylvia showed us at Nearbank?"

Bradley was concerned that the young lad's question was riddled with too many irrelevant references, but thought it would be interesting to hear how Cara would deal with it. She surprised him by ignoring these and going straight to the nub of Toby's query.

"Yes, we had horses — and many of us enjoyed riding them, though mainly as a form of amusement rather than as a means of transport."

Red had said nothing so far, but from his tone his patience was clearly running out. "This is all small talk!" he said tetchily. "Tell us of the treasures that are stored yon side of the Wall!"

Cara paused for a moment, then said, "I sense a misconception in your use of the word 'treasures.' We had things that were considered treasures by many, yet had no real value. We also had treasures that we failed to recognise as such and either destroyed or neglected. What you'll find on the far side of the Wall may or may not appear as treasures to you. We hope you'll find them useful and put them to good use for the benefit of all. But we can't direct you in this. You must make your own choices."

Red looked exasperated. "What kind of a stupid answer is that? It doesn't mean anything!"

"I'm sorry," Cara said. "I can only answer truthfully and I'm unable to give a definitive answer to all of your questions. By all means go to the other side and look there for your treasure."

This seemed more or less to satisfy the outlaw for the time being. Then he asked another question that must have been bothering him ever since he'd fallen into the murky waters of the swirling river. "How does the river pass through the Wall?"

Immediately the image flickered and changed, transformed into a depiction of the Wall itself, at the point where the river flowed through from the other side. Cara's voice continued however and the angle of view altered to illustrate what she was saying.

"We've prepared these images because this is an important question that we expected you to ask. The river flows through a series of culverts from the far side of the Wall on its journey towards the Great Sea. Like the metal mesh barriers that prevent your fishermen from sailing too far out and risking contact with the infection outside, so each culvert has a similar mesh barrier at its far end. Thus the water flows through, but the barriers prevent access to the far side. Fortunately the plague wasn't water-borne, so the river was always a safe source of water for the people of Fenwold."

Bradley pressed her further. "What happens when the flotsam coming downriver clogs up the barriers? How is it cleared away? Do you have dragons to do this on the other side?"

"No," she replied. "There is a mechanism..."

Then without warning Cara's demeanour altered. Her image flickered wildly and she announced in a stilted tone, "Attention! The power source is unstable. You must leave now."

Without further warning the image faded, then disappeared altogether.

Red was the only member of the group not to be completely astonished at this announcement. "Come on," he said, "we're wasting time here. We know all we need to know. Let's get going."

Now the room brightened again — though with nothing like the intensity seen earlier — and the other part of the floor slowly rose up and returned the three light-emitting boxes to their original positions.

Bradley said, "It looks like we've no choice in the matter. We'd better leave while we can."

The five stepped hurriedly then off the black circles and assembled in the outer chamber. The inner doors *swished* shut and the large outer door *clunked* open, allowing them to emerge, dazed, into a light snow shower that threatened to settle over the clearing. So they hurried off to find some shelter, but not before Bradley had deftly collected the key — which had now been thrust out of its slot — and shoved it safely inside his tunic, as Red looked across at him sullenly.

Brushing snowflakes from off his clothing, Bradley turned to Shah and said, "Something went wrong in there, Rajeev. I wonder what she meant about the power source being unstable?"

"Something to do with this snow, do you think?"

"Hmm. It might. But I got the impression those batteries Cara referred to were designed to store up power to last some considerable time. How come the power gave out before she finished her audience with us? Our meeting must have figured crucially in the Ancient Ones' plans — they'd have taken every precaution to ensure something as basic as power supply wouldn't jeopardise things. I think that when this shower stops, you and I had better go back to the building and have a closer look at those batteries on the roof."

"And there's something else I didn't understand," Shah said. "What did she mean by *genetic* something or other? What was all that about?"

"It wasn't a word I recognised. She also said something about our *palm images*. Hold out your hand, Rajeev — palm upwards."

Shah did so and Bradley stretched out his own upturned palm next to it.

"Look at the lines on our palms. See how different they are? Let's see yours, Toby and Sylvia. Yours too, Red."

The five palms were held out for examination and comparison.

"Toby's is smaller naturally, but the shapes of the lines have many differences. No two are exactly alike. This might be true for all people. If so, then maybe the Ancient Ones knew how to use these differences to record and check a person's identity."

"That's amazing!" Sylvia gasped. "Maybe that's what Cara meant by *genetic information.* I wonder what else she was referring to?"

"Well, we all sweat, don't we? What if our sweat is as unique to us as the lines on our palms?"

"So their machinery not only remembers the lines on our hands, but also the smell of our sweat?"

"I don't know. I suppose it's possible. As long as that machinery's still able to function, that is. Come on, Rajeev. The snow isn't so bad now. Let's go and have a look at those batteries."

Then Red declared grimly, "I can save you the trouble, Bradley. I took my stick to the power cells on the roof yesterday — I'll be surprised if they work again after the thrashing I gave 'em."

Shah moved quickly then, angrily wresting the restraining rope from Bradley's grasp and pulling it hard, until the outlaw's eyes bulged and his face flushed. His loosely bound hands shot up to grab the noose in a vain attempt to slacken it, while Shah yelled, "Why in the name of the Gods did you do that, you idiot? Didn't you realise you might have ruined everything?"

Bradley pushed him away from Red and regained the rope, slackening it as the outlaw rubbed his smarting neck, his eyes still swollen. Bradley's remonstrating words, though, were directed at the raider rather than at Shah.

"Answer the question, you! And it had better be good, or else I'm tempted to let him have this rope back!"

"All right, all right!" the outlaw gasped. Then as he recovered his breath, he said, "I lost the bloody key in that slot — it got swallowed up and I was left with nothing for my trouble. Once I knew I was locked out, I was in no mind to leave the pickings to anyone else that might happen along. When I saw that stupid dragon grinning down at me, I went berserk. Anyhow, I'd no idea you two were following me and still planned to get into that damned place! If I'd known that, I might've let my temper cool and waited to do a deal with you."

Bradley raised a clenched hand as the outlaw cowered, awaiting a blow from his powerful fist. But this time it was Shah's turn to restrain his boss, while the outlaw spluttered, "I did it on impulse! I acted in anger — as you threaten to do now! Anyway, what harm did I do? There was still enough power in those battery things for the Gods to pass on their message! So there's no need to lose your temper, now is there?"

258

Bradley lowered his hand and looked disparagingly at the pleading outlaw, saying nothing while he waited for his rage to subside.

Shah said grudgingly, "I suppose he's right. In spite of his actions, we heard the Gods' instructions clearly enough."

Bradley looked thoughtful and nodded. "Yes, Rajeev. But with the power source destroyed, if anything goes wrong now, it's unlikely we could assemble another team to get back inside that building. This is going to be our one and only chance."

On realising the full implications of Bradley's words, the outlaw's mess of a face broke into a callous grin and gleefully he spat through his broken teeth, "You'd better curb that temper of yours, Marshal. You heard what that woman said — all five of us have to work together now. If any harm comes to me, all your precious plans won't be worth a spit. Looks like our fates are bound together after all."

Chapter Thirty-Three
A Time For Hate, A Time For Love

"For the sake of the Gods turn me loose from this contraption! It's nearly strangling me! I'll never make it all the way back to the river trussed up like this!"

Sylvia rounded on the outlaw. "It's a pity you didn't think of poor Toby when you did the self-same thing to him. Why should it be any different now the tables are turned? You're pathetic!"

Shah said, "Maybe if you stopped moaning so much and kept your head still, the noose wouldn't keep on tightening and chafing your neck. Just keep walking and stop tugging."

"I'm telling you it'd be a whole lot easier and we'd all make better progress, if you'd just release me and let me walk normally."

Bradley wasn't having any of that. "Well, let's consider your past record: brutal cheat, murdering liar. No, I don't think there's much to support your request to go free. As soon as we untied you, you'd either run off into the woods or try to jump one of us."

"Why should I run off? What would be the point? I'd probably fall foul of wolves and who knows what other wild animals. Besides, I'd have too much to lose. Especially now you've promised me my freedom and a share in the treasure. I've every reason to behave myself now, haven't I? So come on, if you've any pity. Release me from the noose and untie my hands."

"Forget it. And don't keep reminding me of the deal we made. I've given you my word so there's no need to repeat it over and over. Anyway, as I recall, part of the agreement was that you were to be kept constrained and without weapons."

"I don't intend letting you forget your promise. And I never said I wanted any weapons. I just can't go much further with this thing round my throat. I can hardly breathe!"

"Well, that's tough," said Shah. "You'll just have to live with it. We'll be there by tomorrow. Why don't you ask little Toby how he managed to keep going with a dog chain round his neck for the outward journey? Maybe he and Sylvia could teach you something about coping with discomfort."

Bradley said, "Here, Rajeev. Let me take the rope for a while. Your arms must be tired."

The outlaw looked sidewise at Bradley and said, "Huh! His arms are tired — poor bugger!"

"All right," Shah said, handing him the rope. "But use your good side and watch that shoulder."

A few strides behind the men, Toby trotted by Sylvia's side with his little hand in hers. The boy whispered, "Miss Sylvia, why does that bad man get to go free when we reach the Wall? After all those awful things he did?"

She gripped his hand and looked ahead, hoping he didn't see the single tear escape her misty eyes and slide down her cheek. Quickly she wiped it away with her free hand.

"Are you all right, Miss Sylvia?"

"Yes, Toby. It's just a tiny insect that flew into my eye. And don't worry about that bad man. The Marshal won't let him do any more nasty things. But he had to make a bargain with him. You see, he had the key and without it, we'd never be able to reach the treasure."

The little boy was silent for a few moments, clearly pondering her words.

Still he wasn't satisfied. "But doesn't the Marshal have the key now?"

"Yes."

"Well then, why doesn't he tell the bad man he can't have his share and he can't go free?"

The thought had occurred to her, too. No decent person would think any the less of him if he did just that. But if he did, he wouldn't be the Dominic Bradley she knew and loved.

"Because the Marshal is an honourable man," she said, hoping Toby would understand. Whether he did or not, he let it be.

"What sort of treasure do you think there'll be on the other side of the Wall?"

"We're not sure," she said honestly. "Probably not the sort you might expect. You know, jewels and gold. But from what Cara told us, it should be things to help everyone in Fenwold have a much better life."

"What, even my Mummy and Daddy and the other people in my village?"

"Yes. People just like the good folk of Nearbank and Crowtree, too, where my own parents live."

He thought about what she'd said and gave it time to sink in. Then he demonstrated that talent, through simple inquisitiveness, that children have to cut through the clogging complexity of detail and reveal what's really important.

"Are you and the Marshal going to get married?"

Surprising herself, she blushed and checked that they were still far enough behind the others to be out of earshot. Thankfully they were.

"Why do you ask?"

"Well, when you caught him in your trap and then let him down, he kissed you for ever such a long time."

She smiled. "He'd been worried about me and was glad to see I was all right, I expect."

"Oh, yes," Toby nodded. "I expect he was."

* * * * *

The following morning saw them start out on the final day of their trek back to the estuary. Despite his chafing bonds, Red seemed buoyed by his perceived importance to the mission and grabbed every opportunity to remind Bradley of the terms of their bargain, as if afraid he might conveniently forget.

The prospect of the outlaw's impending release was by now exercising Bradley's imagination and he guessed Red would be having similar thoughts. He hoped he'd have the sense to be satisfied with his share of the treasure — whatever that might mean — and not cause further grief for those around him who wanted nothing more than to get on with their lives.

Though dishevelled and trail-weary, with a clear way ahead of them the group made easy progress back through the forest and to the riverbank, and it was late afternoon when at last the majestic lines of the old bridge loomed into view. Though the Wall and their appointment with destiny lay upriver, it was in the opposite direction — eastwards — that Bradley now turned to lead them along the coastal path. This was in order to keep his promise to reunite Toby and his parents, but as soon as he grasped what was happening the outlaw protested.

"What are you doing, lawman? By my simple reckoning the Wall lies to the west of here and it's there we've a job to do. We should waste no more time and get on with it!"

Bradley realised it might not just be impatience that rattled him. An encounter with Toby's father right now wasn't likely to be something he relished — especially when he was unable to defend himself. If that was so, his apprehension was well founded.

Before Bradley could argue with him, there came a violent rustling from the forest undergrowth and the thrashing branches parted to reveal the fishermen Sean and Luke. Without hesitation, they dashed to where the outlaw stood, open-mouthed and suddenly pathetic in his helplessness. Without warning, Toby's father leapt upon the outlaw and assailed him with a sustained and violent pummelling, releasing the rage he'd stored up these past few days while awaiting his son's return.

The lawmen might have intervened. They glanced at one another, each knowing what they should do, but neither was in much of a hurry about it. For the desperate fisherman, this was his moment for natural justice and revenge. This was his due.

So furious was the onslaught that in a matter of moments a bloody gash appeared above the raider's left eye and blow upon blow made changes to his already swollen features as a child might make to a lump of modelling clay. But when Sean's hand went for the gutting knife at his waist, Bradley knew it was time to intervene. He nodded to Shah and together they stepped forward to grab and pull away the attacker from the cowering frame of his snivelling victim.

To the fisherman's credit, he made no attempt to turn his fury against the lawmen. Instead he let them hold him, gasping while his rage subsided and looking with satisfaction on the mess he'd made of the outlaw's bruised and bloody features. Not that his face had been a pretty sight to start with — thanks to Sylvia's earlier handiwork. But the oozing wound above the eye, the broken, bleeding nose, split ears and lips and swelling bruises — all these combined to satisfy the need for vengeance that had brought the boatman to this place. Gradually his panting subsided, the blood lust dissipated, his venom spent. With his last conscious breath, the beaten outlaw groaned, retched and spat out a gobbet of bloody saliva containing two black teeth and bits of his own lip. Then he rolled over onto the grassy bank and passed out.

* * * * *

The reunion of the little lad with his parents was a joy to behold. Even before Red's punishment, Toby's mother had rushed out of the undergrowth to sweep her son up in her arms with kisses and hugs. But then she'd held him in front of her to witness the beating. He showed no emotion at this, only gripped his mother's hands tightly and kept his gaze fixed on the outlaw's face.

Afterwards the family shared comforting embraces and heartily thanked the trio from Crowtree for the boy's deliverance. The air of geniality and kinship was marred only by the ghastly, dishevelled mess of outlaw, now coming round and groaning on the riverbank beside them.

With dusk approaching, they hurried to make camp, light a fire and prepare supper. Sylvia grudgingly tended to the raider's injuries, while Sean's wife prepared hot drinks for everyone and taking his mug Bradley sat down next to Toby's father.

"You didn't wait for me to light a beacon, Sean. I suppose you got sick of waiting. It must have been hard for you all."

"It's been a torment, Marshal. You knew how badly we wanted to follow and help you, but what could we do without provoking that scum into harming Toby? As you rightly said, we're sailors, not woodsmen. So we thought the best plan for us — my wife, Luke and I — was to camp out here by the great bridge and wait. Then if that beast should somehow give you the slip, we'd be ready to do whatever was necessary. Or, if you had him prisoner, to give him the hiding he deserved. And I have to admit that I've neither regrets nor apologies for what I did. It was entirely planned — I didn't do it on impulse. It's pointless making excuses. I've been relishing the satisfaction of giving him that beating this past week and believe me I'll get pleasure from the memory of it for a long time to come. Does that make me a criminal in your eyes?"

Bradley shook his head. The sight of the beaten figure as it recovered consciousness gave them all a degree of satisfaction and if that were cause for any of them to be ashamed, then so be it. But the fact that the punishment was deserved and appropriate was irrefutable.

"You did what you were entitled to do. I'm not a father, but I do have my parents — back on the east coast. If either of them had been taken and held under similar circumstances, I don't think I'd have acted any differently."

"You did well to capture him. I'll never be able to repay you for bringing our son back to us. I thank you, with all my heart and soul."

So saying, he offered Bradley his hand. Accepting it, Bradley was almost at a loss for words. Never comfortable to receive direct praise, he merely nodded and said, "It's my job, Sean. Besides, I got my Sylvia back too."

"She's a fine girl, Marshal — kind and considerate. I'm sure she was a great comfort to Toby during their ordeal. I think you must love her very much."

Startled at this observation, he glanced across at Sylvia. She'd finished tending to the now snoring outlaw and was engrossed in a clapping game with Toby. He was glad that she was out of earshot. He realised he was blushing — though he told himself it was due to the closeness of his cheeks to the glowing campfire. But as he watched her, he felt a glow inside his breast, a feeling that he wanted to keep her with him, to care for her. He found himself nodding and saying, "Yes, Sean. I do."

Seeing the look on his face, Sean tipped his head slightly and said, "But you haven't told her this, have you?"

He shook his head almost imperceptibly, his eyes now smiling at the fisherman's insight.

Then Sean lowered his voice and suggested, "Tonight might be a good time."

When they'd all had some supper and night had fallen, the family withdrew to one side of the encampment, to quietly enjoy some time together before putting little Toby to bed. Shah was in the forest hunting rabbit, while the outlaw slept on. Luke kept an eye on him, but in any case he was well restrained.

Bradley went over to Sylvia and offered her his hand. "Coming for a walk?" he said.

Hand in hand they strolled along the shoreline. Their walk took them right under the enormous structure of the ancient bridge, beneath whose vaulted canopy they soon found a dry place to sit down. The swirling sounds of the river were amplified here beneath the towering archways. Birds settled noisily in their roosts above them, while fluttering bats swarmed out to try their luck with the flying insects of the night. The atmosphere was magical and enchanting and for a long while they were content merely to look and listen, until eventually he spoke.

"Sylvia," he said softly.

"Yes, Dominic?"

He took a deep breath and wished he'd given this more thought. "It seems the fates have thrown us together — something you hinted at some time ago, as I recall. And I suppose — being in each other's company so much — we're bound to feel a kind of — attachment. Almost like sister and brother."

"Sister and brother? What do you mean?"

"Well, don't you think of me almost — as if I might be like a brother to you?"

She gave him her funny little puzzled look. "No, I wouldn't say that. I've two brothers, as you know. And I'm sure I don't think of you at all as I would one of them."

"Oh," he said. "Only — I thought you — I mean we — I thought you might feel there was some kind of — some sort of a bond between us."

She giggled and put her hand on top of his. "Yes, there is." Then before he could ramble on any further, she turned to him and said impatiently, "Oh, for the sake of the Gods of the Wall, Dominic! Are you never going to kiss me?"

It was a long kiss, one that made up for all their petty arguments, their silly tiffs and childish disagreements and sealed once and for all that bond of which he'd spoken. The kiss had the taste of fire, of life and of blood, sweetened with the smoky breath of autumn. It was warm and glowing and kindled a dormant flame that now leapt to life from deep inside his breast. He forced himself to pause for a moment to consider her feelings.

"Are you sure you want this, Sylvia?" he said.

Her bright eyes glowed as she rolled onto her back and pulled him on top of her. "Oh, yes, Dominic. Yes, I do!"

Rational thought was suspended then, and they were swept onwards like mingling river currents towards that sweet, inevitable confluence of longing. Their spirits became as one with the surging waters of the river as it flowed to the sea in its endless cycle of renewal and creation.

And by this simple act of love, accompanied only by the utterance of each other's names, they made silent, solemn promises of devotion that would bind them together for the rest of their lives.

* * * * *

A crisp morning broke across the estuary. A dry, bitterly cold wind drove a low bank of grey-black cloud in across the Great Sea from the northeast, promising foul weather before mid-day. Sean and his family wasted no time in preparing to leave, skipping any attempt at a normal breakfast but approaching the others with some scraps of food left over from the night before. They accepted these gratefully and as they ate, Sean brought his son over to Bradley to talk.

"Marshal, I can add nothing to the thanks we've already expressed for the safe return of our son. You can understand that these last few days have been almost unbearable for us, but having Toby back is like a new beginning. The sky threatens stormy weather and we must start back to Nearbank before the storm breaks. If you're ready, we've room in our boats for you, but we must take our leave without further delay."

Bradley cursed not having found the opportunity midst the previous night's euphoria to explain what must now be done. And he was doubly frustrated that he'd now have to explain his intentions in as few words as possible.

Placing a brotherly hand on Sean's arm, he said, "Fisherman, the Gods wove our paths together — we'd no choice in the matter — and in spite of what you've gone through on my account, I hope we can count on one another as friends."

Sean nodded, his eyes betraying a canny suspicion that bad news was coming.

"Your son's a brave lad — he's endured much hardship this last week with little complaining and great fortitude. His courage has been such that, on his return to your village, I intend to bestow on him the rank of Honorary Deputy Marshal."

The little boy's eyes lit up at this news and he tugged hard on his father's tunic sleeve for acknowledgement. Sean, though, was clearly more interested in what else Bradley had to say.

"Yes, you can be rightly proud of Toby — he's already played an important part in our mission and I now need him to stay with me for a few days longer, to help us complete our quest to conquer the Wall."

Sean pursed his lips and scowled in disbelief. His wife was close by and had overheard Bradley's declaration. "No, Marshal!" she pleaded. "He's only a little boy! And he's been through enough! We can't let him go with you! He's just a child — how can you be so cruel?"

Then Bradley explained, as briefly as he could, all that had happened in the ancient town and about Cara's instructions.

"We must go to the place where the Wall crosses the river — all five of us, including Toby. There can be no substitutes."

Sean said, "Why not wait and take a fresh party of five adults back to the town to start the process again?"

Bradley pursed his lips and nodded towards the still sleeping outlaw. "Because he smashed up the mechanism that powered the building. This is our only chance, Sean. Believe me, I wouldn't ask this of you if that weren't true."

The woman sobbed, "But I want my son home! Please don't take him away again!"

Then Toby went over to his mother and took hold of her shawl. Holding her hand in his, he looked up into her tearful face and pleaded, "Let me go, Mummy! The Marshal and Sylvia will take good care of me — I know they will. And when we get back, I'll be an Onnery Deppiddy Marshal!"

She drew her son to her bosom and sobbed, "Oh, Sean! What are we to do?"

Stony faced, the boatman stood up and said, "There's no time to lose — the weather gets worse every moment. Luke, make ready one of the boats and take my wife back to Nearbank. I'm not sure how long we'll be — a few days, the Marshal said — so watch for our beacon and come and meet us. Toby, are you ready? Good. Very well then, Marshal — collect your things together and let's get going."

Then he pulled his son from the arms of his distraught wife, kissed her farewell, shook hands with his cousin and set off with the boy alongside Bradley and the others on the final leg of their journey towards the Wall.

* * * * *

269

Barring mishaps, it should take them only a day and a half to reach the Wall. Toby and his father walked ahead of the party, Sean clearly impatient to get this unwelcome trek over and done with as quickly as possible. Obviously he'd prefer to be with his son back at Nearbank in the bosom of the family home and Bradley sensed no small resentment on his part at having to make this unscheduled trip. Toby however seemed more than happy to extend the adventure, especially as the outlaw was no longer a threat and anyway had suffered punishment at the hands of his father.

Red was subdued. No doubt harbouring dark thoughts of his own, he chose to walk in absolute silence, still with his hands bound and the noose around his neck. Shah, holding the other end of the rope, kept a close watch on him. The outlaw's mood was hard to read because his mangled face was by now incapable of any kind of meaningful expression.

Bradley and Sylvia took up the rear and exchanged frequent loving, longing glances. Then about mid-morning they stopped for a short rest and Sean came back to speak to the Marshal.

"I understand from what you told us this morning that the five of you — including Toby and the outlaw — must together operate the mechanism to open up the passage through the Wall."

"That's right."

"I've been thinking about that. And there's something that puzzles me."

"What's that, Sean?"

"How did you persuade that raider to cooperate with you? After all, he's nothing to gain from it, has he?"

Bradley's silence spoke volumes. He guessed that Sean had already worked out the answer to his own question. It was clear that this simple fisherman had far more intelligence than he'd given him credit for. He was dreading the next question.

"What have you offered him?"

How could he lie? He'd already declared a state of friendship and trust between himself and this man of the sea. He owed him nothing less than the complete truth.

So he said, "This is the bargain: he plays his part in our gaining access to the far side of the Wall and in return he wins his freedom and a share in whatever treasures we find there."

Sean's face reddened and he yelled, "Freedom? Treasures? Are you mad, man? After everything that villain's done — the cruelty to my parents, my son and his orders to have you and your deputy slaughtered like pigs? What were you thinking when you made such a bargain? Tell me this isn't true! Tell me!"

Bradley put his hand on the fisherman's shoulder and spoke softly. "Sean, I wish I could say so, believe me. But I had no choice. He had the key concealed and he knew where Toby and Sylvia were. He used that to make the bargain. Without it, we wouldn't have come this far. And we might never have found Toby."

His face set and uncompromising in his emotion, Sean shrugged away Bradley's hand and growled, "Marshal, until this moment, I held you in high esteem and with the greatest respect. As the Council's representative, you were sent out to create order and to dispense justice. But don't you see what you've done? You've placed your desire to conquer the Wall above your primary duty. In your eagerness to win a greater reward, you've turned your back on justice! It grieves me to say as much, but I can no longer respect you for this."

The sky above threatened rough weather as Bradley, for once confused and riddled with self-doubt, lowered himself disconsolately onto a nearby grassy bank. Sylvia came over and settled beside him.

"Did you hear all that?" he whispered.

She only nodded and took his hand. He closed his other hand over hers then and looked at the devotion in her eyes, finding strength and comfort there.

After a while, Sean strode over to them and said, in a tone that suggested rehearsal and calculation, "I think I can understand your predicament. You chose to make a bargain with the outlaw, because you recognised conquering the Wall as a higher goal than the simple dispensation of justice. In that case, you'll forgive me if I put to you my own terms for allowing my son to render the same assistance as that outlaw. For without doubt, Toby's contribution must be at least equal to whatever that bastard can do."

Bradley paused to take in the logic of the fisherman's argument.

"All right," he shrugged. "What is it you want?"

"I want nothing for myself. But for Toby and our village I claim one third of the treasures that are supposed to lie beyond the Wall.

271

There'll be one-third for you, one-third for the outlaw and one-third for Nearbank. Is that agreed?"

Bradley looked at the fisherman and nodded.

"Yes," he said sadly. "It's agreed."

Chapter Thirty-Four
Digging For Treasure

For the rest of that day and all the next morning, they trudged through a series of squally showers and an uneasy truce hung over the little group.

Bradley glanced across at Sean and was glad he avoided eye contact. The venom with which the fisherman had vented his anger that Red wasn't to stand trial still stung the Marshal's conscience. But the fisherman soon slid into a sullen acceptance of the situation, ostensibly consoled by the bargain he'd struck for the benefit of his village. If indeed there were untold wonders awaiting them on the far side of the Wall, then access to a full one-third of that wealth ought to more than compensate his people for the justice they'd been denied. He now made no attempt to address, or even to acknowledge the outlaw, but seemed content that Red was bound and posed no immediate threat. But he was alert and ready in case the brute should show any sign of aggression. That was evident from the pair of sharp gutting knives that he kept in full view, secured in leather scabbards at his belt.

For his part the outlaw, while maintaining a show of sullen ferocity, appeared to be paying no mind to any of them, but mostly kept his smarting eyes fixed on the ground in front of him. Bradley reckoned revenge for a deserved thrashing probably wasn't the item foremost in his thoughts right now. Red must have received — and given — many such a beating during his criminal career and long ago accepted such as an occupational hazard. In any case, though he looked a mess, the boatman can't have been a habitual fighter, because he'd inflicted no lasting damage to the raider that Bradley could see. No, Bradley knew there was only one person in Red's mind deserving of his wrath and revenge and that was the man who'd dogged him for the better part of this year — Bradley himself. On the rare occasions that their eyes met he imagined all of Red's mental energy was now focussed on how to thwart his ambitions. And just how the outlaw might be planning to wreak his revenge occupied Bradley's thoughts until the moment the group stood at the foot of the Wall at noon on the following day.

Shah broke the brittle silence. "I've often been this close before, but it's always an amazing sight. How wide do you think the river is here, Marshal?"

"Only a couple of furlongs, I'd say. A lot narrower than at the bridge, anyway."

He swung around to slowly survey the area. From the shore where they stood a marshy flood plain extended north another furlong from the shoreline before the tree cover established its domination for as far as the eye could see. Looking across to the south bank, he guessed the same was true on that side, for there in the distance the all-pervading woodland seemed to go on forever. He wondered if this were also the case on the other side of the Wall. The very thought thrilled him because he knew — if all went as planned today — he'd soon be able to see the answer with his own eyes.

He said, "Even given what Cara told us, it's still hard to imagine how mortal men could have built such a structure. Like you, Rajeev, I've been this close to it several times before. But I've never been able to see so much of it at once. Mostly the forest grows fairly close up to it, so you can't see far along it to the right and left. With the clear expanse of the river here much more of it's visible and it looks all the more fantastic for that. Look out along the surface. Can you see the culverts that Cara told us about?"

"Yes," Shah said, concentrating. "Fifteen of them, if I've counted right, all evenly spaced across the breadth of the river."

Each semi-circular opening was roughly four strides wide and about half that in height above the surface. The culverts had been visible from some distance off, but until now they'd not revealed any sense of the Wall's thickness. Now Bradley strained to peer into the nearest of the dark tunnels. Then he heard a mighty *whoosh* as a mass of debris spewed from the mouth of the culvert, to be sped downriver by the accompanying pent-up mountain of water, which shoved the flotsam along in a frenzied torrent on its way to the sea, several leagues away to the east. The whole spectacle was both amazing and frightening and made him feel tiny and vulnerable. From their reactions, the others were equally overawed. He'd certainly experienced nothing like it. The nearest had been the combined senses of fear and exhilaration he'd felt when he'd climbed that rickety ladder months before and being almost overwhelmed by the view of the Wall in its unbroken domination of the skyline as it extended league after league towards the far horizon. Oddly, though now with his feet firmly on the ground, looking up to the top far above him created a feeling of vertigo similar to when standing on the uppermost rung of that ladder at Crowtree, where his quest had begun. Now the time had come to complete that quest and to realise the tantalising promise of the ancient rhyme.

"Right, everyone!" He drew the group around him. "We're looking for something like the door we found in the town, or an arrangement of tiles with the patterns we can see on the key here."

Saying this, he passed around the key to remind them of the motifs they should look for. This was hardly necessary, because by now each recalled well the distinct design on the tile that they'd pressed in their united action to open that door a few days before. In Toby's case, it was a button that he needed to find and Sylvia had already explained to him that it should be close to a slot that would accept the key.

Shah asked, "What do you suppose will happen when we press the tiles this time, Marshal?"

He shrugged. "I can't be sure. There might be another door, I suppose. But, seeing these culverts in operation suggests the grids at the far end open periodically to let the debris through. My guess is that one or more of those culverts will open and stay open so we can pass through."

"That sounds logical. But first, we have to use the key and press the tiles to unlock the mechanism that raises the barrier and keeps it raised."

"That's right, but we can't do anything until we find those tiles."

Red then broke his stony silence of two days. "Well, come on then," he said impatiently. "What are we waiting for? Let's get started!"

* * * * *

They searched painstakingly for those tiles for the rest of the day, but to no avail. They weren't helped much by the continuing foul weather, now cold and squally. Muffled in furs, first they searched close to the shore, casting their eyes carefully over the rain-spattered surface of the Wall as it towered above them. They concentrated on the part within a couple of strides of ground level for, Bradley reasoned, the Ancient Ones surely wouldn't have placed the tiles tantalisingly out of reach. But they'd no idea how far from the riverbank the entry mechanism might be — perhaps far enough away to avoid damage by flooding? So the group searched the Wall's lower surface for more than a furlong's distance from the shore — but without success.

Eventually Bradley said, "I can't understand it. I would have staked my life we'd have found the tiles by now."

Sean asked, "You said the Wall's been here eight hundred years?"

"According to my teachers — and confirmed by Cara."

The boatman looked out across the water. "This is a powerful and often furious river. We see it scour masses of mud and sandbanks, carry them many furlongs and drop them elsewhere seemingly at will and all within the space of a few days. It makes you wonder what changes it could bring about over forty generations."

Bradley said, "I see. So it's possible..."

"That the ground level has shifted over time. Maybe we should re-locate our search higher up the Wall."

"Oh, that's great!" Red complained. "And supposing we do find your precious tiles half way up the bloody Wall? How are we going to reach them?"

Bradley refused to lose his temper — just yet. So he said calmly, "I don't know. Perhaps we'll make some ladders. You're good at climbing, aren't you?" He smiled sarcastically at the outlaw, who nevertheless remained stony-faced. Then Bradley added more seriously, "We'll work it out when we find the tiles. Let's keep looking, shall we?"

So they continued their search, now peering further up the Wall's smooth, damp surface and working back towards the river, while what little daylight there had been grew ever dimmer.

Later, on reaching the water again, Bradley called a temporary halt to the hunt. "It's no use. We'll have to give it up until morning. Let's set up camp in the forest, get some food and a good night's rest and we'll resume at first light." Looking from face to face and sensing their disappointment, he added, "The Gods made us wait eight hundred years. One more night isn't going to defeat us, is it?"

So they all trudged towards the woodland.

After a simple supper Sylvia came over to him and whispered, "Dominic, I've been thinking. Is it possible we're looking on the wrong side of the river?"

His gut reaction to this question was to curse his own lack of intelligence momentarily — for, in truth, he hadn't even considered this possibility. Then he applied some reasoned logic to refute what was, after all, an entirely reasonable proposition.

"I don't think so. The rhyme directed us to the north bank, where the town was located. If they'd then meant us to return to the south bank, I'm sure Cara would have made the intention plain."

"Maybe. But she was cut off before she could finish telling us everything, wasn't she?"

He sighed. "Yes, well, if we find nothing here after some more searching tomorrow, we may have to trek back and signal Luke to bring us across so we can try the other bank. Meanwhile, let's turn in."

The day's toil had been punishing and for the two new lovers, passion gave way for once to sheer exhaustion. They lay silently and kissed for a while, soon falling into a deep and restful sleep, curled up like innocent babes in each other's arms. And so they remained until morning.

CHAPTER THIRTY-FIVE
AWAKENING THE GODS

A cloudy but drier night kept the frost at bay and a faint pre-dawn glimmer of sunlight promised a clear, crisp morning. Bradley was awoken early with a kiss and a mug of hot herbal tea from Sylvia and at the instant of consciousness he was hit with a revelation. Its clarity was breathtaking and reflected that of the morning star, still twinkling down on them from over the estuary.

He nearly spilled his drink as she snuggled in beside him.

"Well?" she asked. "Have you worked it out?"

"Have you been reading my mind, you little cat?"

"I used only to be a squirrel. I wonder what I've done to deserve promotion? Well, no, I can't tell what you're thinking yet, but give me time. I do recognise that self-satisfied look that's all over your face, though. So, tell me."

He finished his drink and kissed her. "Are they still asleep?" he whispered.

She nodded.

"Come here then. I'll tell you later."

* * * * *

It was all just a matter of simple logic and reasoning. If the ground level could shift over the space of forty generations, who could say in which direction that shift might be? Barring Sylvia's suggestion that they might be looking on the wrong side of the river (which he still thought unlikely), he reckoned there was only one remaining possible location of the tiles they were seeking.

279

If they existed at all, they had to be hidden below the present ground level.

After rising, he and Sylvia took their crossbows and collected two fat rabbits. On their return to the campsite Sean produced a bag of dried fish, all of which provided the makings of a feast of a breakfast, preparing them all for whatever the day ahead demanded.

The first part of the day involved a great deal of digging. Their labour began a stride away from the riverbank, where they first exposed a half stride of the buried section of the Wall. Though farmers by birth, neither Bradley nor Sylvia considered a spade a required part of hunting kit, so they were reduced to digging with knives, bits of driftwood or just their bare hands. All five of them — even Toby — found their hands perfectly adequate for the job, for although the silt-based material was muddy, it had a loose consistency and could be shifted at a swift rate by so many willing workers.

By mid-morning, between them they'd exposed about fifteen strides in length by a half stride in depth of hitherto hidden Wall surface. Bradley looked at his team of workers and grinned to see almost as much mud and silt on their hands, arms and bodies as there was on the heap of spoil behind them. Then looking down at his own limbs and torso he realised that he was just as filthy, which made him smile even more. However there was still no sign of a tile.

At this point he raised a hand to stop them digging further outwards and said, "The silt's still soft below where we've been digging. We need to dig deeper."

The going was slower though, because now they must dig further away from the Wall as well as deeper, to prevent backfill falling in and covering up the surface as quickly as they were exposing it. Then, about five strides from where they'd begun, a gleeful shout rang out from little Toby.

"There's a tile here! And another!"

They all eagerly helped to scour away more silt from where the lad had been digging and, to their joy and amazement, a whole row of tiles was soon revealed. Now everyone was euphoric and took the time to dance around on the riverbank — a strange sight indeed, all of them being caked from head to foot in muddy, black silt. Only the outlaw Red stood back and sneered at their antics, quietly anticipating the implications of Toby's discovery.

But when their joy eventually subsided, it was Sean who brought the mood back down to one of painful reality.

"You know, if these tiles we've exposed are at the top of a big door, I'm guessing we've a lot more digging to do."

This pronouncement had a sobering effect on the group. If Sean was right, the work they'd done that morning was nothing compared with the enormous task still ahead of them. But their success so far was enough to drive them on — albeit less aggressively — to face the challenge and finish what they'd started.

Bradley said, "I still reckon the culverts are where we'll pass through, rather than a door. But we still need to find the button and slot for the key."

He was right. Soon it was clear that there was no door here. After three full rows, each of ten tiles, had been excavated, the next layer revealed a single square of unfamiliar material. It was flexible and translucent and protruded from the Wall's surface. Though attached to the fabric of the Wall, it partially concealed something beneath its surface. When Bradley brushed away the excess silt, he saw what sat behind this cover.

"It's the slot and the button!" he said. Then he gripped the flexible material of the cover and, giving a few gentle tugs, found that it came away easily.

"They must have put this here to shield them for protection," he said. "We'll need to clean all the surfaces." And looking at his grimy hands, he added, "We'd better make sure that at least our palms are clean as well."

Sean and the deputy took some containers and brought water from the river. Then they all washed their hands well and helped sluice down the surfaces of the tiles.

This done, Bradley said, "Right. Each of you, find your tile. Make sure your palm rests flat on it and don't press until I say so. Is everyone in position? Good. I'm putting the key in the slot now. Toby, come here — kneel down and get ready to press the button when we all press the tiles. Ready? Now! And — release, now!"

Faintly at first — as if from several leagues away — came an unearthly rumble. Bradley realised that its source lay deep underground, from whence the sound developed rapidly into an intense throbbing far below them. Sudden shock waves welled up through their feet, shaking their bones and giving way to a regular vibration that jarred and jolted their bodies and senses and grew steadily in intensity.

He'd thought himself mentally prepared for anything that might happen at this point, yet even he was unnerved by the amount of energy unleashed by their action. The faces around him displayed a range of emotions, from astonishment to outright fear. He fought to control a grimace of his own that might betray his natural sense of dread. He tried to think of something to say to counter their distress, but for the moment he was speechless. Finally it was the outlaw Red who put everyone's feelings into words.

"By the Gods, I reckon you've done for us all, Bradley! The very ground's moving, man!"

This wasn't entirely true — although a fair interpretation of the sense of motion they were now experiencing. For now the vibrations raced to a terrifying crescendo, giving the impression that the ground and the Wall were engaged in some wild and destructive dance of chaos and mayhem.

Little Toby, white-faced yet brave as ever, pursed his lips as if resolved to ride out the ordeal, only allowing himself the comfort of Sylvia's hand, which he now gripped tightly. His father staggered to his son's other side and placed a steadying arm across the boy's shoulders. At the same time he laughed nervously and shouted above the rumbling, "Marshal, the foulest storm at sea never made me reel about like this!"

Rajeev Shah's face was aghast and he put out an arm to the Wall to steady himself — to little avail, as its once unshakeable structure felt no longer as solid and dependable as it had before. As if in shock, he quickly pulled back his arm and Bradley caught hold of it, helping to steady him, while forcing an unconvincing smile.

All at once the shuddering subsided and the rumbling settled into a deep, steady drone, by comparison almost soothing. Bradley delved into his mind to find a rational explanation for what was happening. Then he raised both his arms to the whole party and tried to reassure them with a few well-chosen words.

"It's all right! Don't worry! The earth isn't moving! Some great force is stirring beneath our feet for the first time in eight hundred years! Anything that's slumbered that long is bound to shake itself and stamp its feet on awakening!"

Then Sylvia voiced the question that each of them wanted to ask. "What do you think it is, Dominic?"

He paused and looked out across the river.

"I think we've managed — as the Ancient Ones intended — to start up some huge underground engine. Its job is to open up the culverts and hold them open so that we can pass through. Look now to where the water flows out of each opening at the foot of the Wall."

All did so and saw that each culvert simultaneously spewed forth debris and detritus into the turbulent waters. The recent storms must have caused a good deal of damage to vegetation along the banks further up-river, for a large amount of flotsam now jostled and swirled in the boiling torrent at the foot of the Wall. As if impatient to be caught by the current, great rafts of material jostled to be dragged down towards the estuary by the escaping waters. Even now, some of the flotsam from the nearest culverts washed up on the near-by shore.

Then as quickly as it had begun, the vibration ceased altogether, to the immense relief of them all.

There was no time to lose. Pointing to the beached flotsam, Bradley turned to the fisherman and asked, "Sean, is it possible to make a serviceable raft out of some of this stuff?"

"To get us through the nearest culvert? Yes — there's enough material here, if you can all help me. You have rope, don't you?"

"Plenty."

"All right then. It shouldn't take too long. It'll be some time anyway before the current flow clears away all this debris."

"Good man. You're the expert, so I'd like you to take charge of this operation. Just tell us what you want us to do."

"All right. First, we need to collect driftwood." He waded into the shallows a few strides and grabbed a passing branch. "Pieces as big as this one or bigger — lots of them. We'll have to wade out further to catch the larger ones."

Though the water was icily cold, once they got used to it, splashing about was fun as well as productive and also served to clean them up — to some extent, at least.

But collecting enough material and making and testing the raft took longer than Sean had expected. In a lifetime of making boats he'd worked with men — and women — who'd acquired their skills and crafts as second nature, having grown up in a self-sufficient fishing community. Apart from his own little son, these people here came from different backgrounds and had different skills — they knew little or nothing about boats and sailing. So he had to do most of the detailed work personally — cutting rough joints and tying the timbers together with the right sorts of knot. He daren't risk a botched job — no matter how impatient they all were to see what lay yon side of the culverts.

At one point, resenting what he saw as the fisherman's unwarranted precision, Red protested, "By the Gods man, this is a raft we're making, not a sea-going vessel!"

For once Sean looked the outlaw in the eye and said coldly, "Don't you think I want to get this job over with and take my son home as soon as possible? I know this river of old. It has fickle currents and treacherous eddies. Believe me, it's a killer. Neither lack of care in building this simple raft, nor any deficiency as a boatman on my part, is going to be the cause of failure of this mission."

So it was late in the afternoon before the makeshift craft was ready.

Sean looked at his handiwork proudly as it lay half on the bank, half on the water.

"Right. Who's going to try it first?"

Bradley stepped forward. "You and I, Sean, I think."

But Red was having none of this. Irately he thrust his way to the bank and placed one foot on the raft. "Oh no you don't! I'm not having you two sods going through without me and taking all the treasure for yourselves. We three all have a stake in this. I say we all go."

Bradley didn't argue. He merely glanced at the fisherman who gave a terse nod. So the three of them pushed off the raft and launched it out into the shallows, clambering on as best they could. Sean had fashioned a couple of sturdy oars, as well as a simple tiller to help keep the craft steady and it was due to his skill as designer, builder and steersman that the little raft carried the three of them easily up to the mouth of the nearest culvert.

Here Bradley and Red used the oars, as Sean had shown them, to mark time and hold the craft steady against the unrelenting current, so they might all get a clear view along the full length of the ancient tunnel, which was now almost clear of driftwood and debris. The distance to the far end wasn't great — Bradley judged it to be only about twenty strides — and he was relieved to see that, at several levels and at intervals of roughly half a stride, the Ancient Ones had fixed metal handles into the concrete on each side. The raft was narrow, so only those on one side were within reach and the Marshal parked his oar and grasped a handle close to him, pleased to find that it was still fixed solidly into the tunnel wall and held fast when he pulled hard on it. Working together they found they could easily pull the vessel along using these handles.

After a few strides' progress Bradley said, "This is good, Sean. You've done well. This is a fine craft. I've no doubt it'll carry us safely through. But the brightness of day fades fast now and I'd rather we arrived on the other side with a full day's sunlight to help us in our progress. Now that we know it works, let's call it a day for now and return to the others. We could all use some food and a good night's sleep, then we'll be fit and ready for this last stage in the morning."

The outlaw, impatient as ever, protested, "But that makes no sense! What are we waiting for? We're nearly there! Can't you see the other side's only a few strides away? Why put it off any longer?" He scowled. "If this is some kind of a trick, Bradley — by the Gods, you'll pay dearly for any treachery!"

Sean interjected, "Don't be stupid, man! Bradley's right. We meant only to test the vessel. We've no tools, weapons nor food with us. Why make things difficult when we can start out afresh in the morning with all the kit and provisions we need to ease our progress? I'm with the Marshal — we turn back now and rest until morning."

With a shrug Red grunted, picked up his oar and helped them steer the craft back to the other three on the shore.

But for the rest of the evening Dominic wondered what was going on behind those cold, calculating eyes.

CHAPTER THIRTY-SIX
BEYOND THE WALL OF DEATH

"I hope this isn't going to become a regular feature of our life together, Dominic."

"Huh? What do you mean?"

The bunch of unlikely companions had supped and retired early. The two young lovers were bedded down away from the others, close up to the Wall under a shelter they'd put together from driftwood and furs.

"Just a normal day's work and already we're both too tired to get passionate."

He put his arm around her. "I'm sorry, Sylvia. Are you sulking?"

"No," she laughed. "Only teasing. It's been a rough day for both of us and it'll take a month of scrubbing to get rid of this stench of river mud."

He grinned. "You mean, I've got to wait a whole month till I can make love to you again?"

She kissed his grimy face. "We'll see. But you'd best try and sleep now if you want to be awake at dawn tomorrow."

"It's not easy. I can't seem to put my thoughts to bed. Not now that we're so close to breaking through the Wall. I can hardly wait to find out what's at the far end of that culvert."

"How will you divide up the treasure?"

"I won't know the answer to that question until I see what it consists of. Cara talked about the importance of cooperation, yet here we are starting off split into not just two, but three different

287

factions. I won't be surprised if carving up the treasure three ways makes for all kinds of problems."

She raised a hand to smooth his brow. "Well, if you really can't resolve a problem because there are too many unknowns, perhaps the best thing to do is clear your mind and sleep on it."

"You sound like one of my tutors. But there are other things on my mind as well, Sylvia."

"What other things?"

"Colby, for one. Soon I'll have to return to the capital and make my report to the Fenwold High Council. My deputy's death was a careless mistake for which I'm responsible."

She squeezed his hand, "I never met your friend Colby, but if he was anything like you, I'm sure he was brave and intelligent and knew exactly what he was doing coming with you on this mission. He must have expected danger and been willing to take his chances. I'm sure the Council will understand that. Besides, the person really responsible for Colby's death is that swine snoring beside the raft over there."

"That's another matter. How am I going to explain how I bargained away two-thirds of the treasure even before we set eyes on it?"

"Don't worry," she said. "I'll speak up for you and so will Rajeev. We both know the dilemma you faced. It's all right for those old men to sit up there in judgement, but I'll bet none of them could have achieved half of what you've done."

"Bless you for that, Sylvia. It'll be a lot easier facing them with you standing beside me."

* * * * *

Sean's raft could carry three people easily, but not the six of them all at once. So it was agreed that he and Red — being the two strongest of arm and therefore most able to pilot the raft between just the two of them — should act as ferrymen, making three journeys. The first would deliver Bradley with some of their gear, the second Toby and Sylvia and the third Rajeev Shah with the rest of their weapons and provisions.

As the little craft emerged from the far end of the culvert, Bradley was eager to savour his initial view of these new lands. But his first impressions were dulled by the fact that, had he not known where he was, he might easily have been looking at

Fenwold's familiar landscape. The terrain here was level, the river and its flood plain stretching away to the west. Otherwise the dense forest dominated, spreading further inland with nothing to relieve its monotony. On the face of it there was nothing special about this place, except for the absence of men. Neither was there any immediate sign of the promised treasures. He guessed they must be hidden somewhere in the woodland, only to be revealed after much arduous felling of timber and clearing of undergrowth.

There was no ceremony involved as he made the first footfall onto the grassy riverbank on the far side of the Wall. Earlier that morning, he'd toyed with the idea of preparing a short speech, but before he could do so Sylvia had served him tea and — well, somehow the idea had flown quickly from his mind. In any case his arrival via this tiny raft onto the quiet shore lacked much in the way of any sense of occasion or drama. Also, what would have been the point of a pompous address to only two men — men, to boot, with whom he'd bargained away the greater part of Fenwold's share in the bounties of this new world?

So the landing was accomplished virtually in silence. Leaving him to sort out the gear they'd landed, the fisherman and the outlaw started back on their return journey through the culvert.

Bradley sat up on one knee and looked again at this new world on the far side of the Wall. He knew he should feel exhilarated, but for some reason he didn't — perhaps because he'd not gained entry here on his own terms. All he felt was an overwhelming sense of anti-climax. Wearily, he sighed and heaved some of the stuff they'd landed further up the bank.

* * * * *

Now with the current working in their favour, Red and Sean made the culvert with ease and reached out to grasp the metal handles, the fisherman at the front and the outlaw at the rear of the raft. At first they exchanged few words, each concentrating hard on reaching for the next handle and using all his strength to maintain the craft's stability. For it called for as much mastery to avoid being swept downstream as they'd needed in pulling against the flow to make progress on the outward leg. But for two strong men this wasn't too difficult a task and once having settled into a rhythm, Red spoke.

"You know, fisherman, I never agreed to reduce my half share of the treasure to a third just to cut you in."

Sean shot him a disdainful sideways glance. "What's agreed is agreed. Besides, I reckon my son's presence here has been as important as your own."

"Exactly," Red said. "I wasn't suggesting you shouldn't get what's rightfully yours. But if you ask me, you and I are each entitled to a full half share."

"What do you mean?"

Red's ugly features twisted into a half smile and he held fast to the next handle, forcing Sean to do likewise, momentarily bringing the craft to an unsteady halt not far from the end of the culvert.

"I couldn't say anything in Bradley's earshot, but now he's alone on the other bank I want to put a proposal to you. If we turn back now, we can overpower him. Look."

He drew aside his filthy tunic to reveal a long, sharp dagger stuffed behind the belt of his leggings.

"How did you come by that?" asked the astonished fisherman.

"I sneaked it from the gear we just landed. Well, what's your answer?"

Sean chewed on the implications of Red's proposition. The outlaw had probably expected an outright rebuttal and might win a knife fight with him, after which he was no doubt desperate enough to take his chances alone with Bradley.

"What about the girl and deputy?"

"Easy. As soon as we've done for Bradley we'll return as planned for the witch and the kid — sorry, your son, I mean. When we're back in the tunnel out of view of the deputy, we'll quietly slit the girl's throat and chuck her overboard, then go back and finish Shah. Don't worry — if you haven't the stomach to kill the girl, I'll be more than happy to do the job. These lawmen act like they own Fenwold and have our futures all mapped out for us. I reckon it's time the Council learned a lesson — that we might lack education, but we're the people and the future belongs to us!"

He ran a warty hand over his scarred face. "Well, what do you say?"

Sean thought about his proposition for a moment more. Then he looked the outlaw squarely in the eye and said, "All right. I agree. I've no more allegiance to Bradley than you have. He's already gone against his principles once for the sake of his damned quest. But your plan offers my people a bigger share in the treasure. That's all that interests me now. I have my gutting knife here. Come, let's get this over with."

"Good man."

Then the outlaw gave the fisherman's shoulder an almost brotherly grasp and turned to pull the raft back to the western end of the culvert.

* * * * *

When Red and Sean reappeared so soon and without passengers, Bradley shouted, "What's wrong? Where are Sylvia and young Toby?"

Red yelled back, "A bit of a snag, Marshal. We need to talk it over with you." Bradley's face betrayed his suspicion and he already had a hand to his bow. But the outlaw made no outward show of aggression, merely paddling his oar while Sean took the tiller and guided the craft to the shore.

"What is it?" Bradley asked, offering Red a hand as the raft landed. The outlaw stepped beside him and in turn helped Sean to the shore. Then drawing his knife, he turned swiftly towards Bradley and made a lunge at his stomach.

Bradley deftly sidestepped the blade. Instead it plunged into the folds of his tunic. But the sudden movement unbalanced him and he fell backwards onto the bank, giving Red time to retrieve his weapon and press it hard up against his throat.

Eyes blazing angrily, Bradley looked towards the fisherman.

"Sean! Stop him, man!"

But the fisherman looked helpless and did nothing.

The outlaw growled, "I was going to make it quick, but I've changed my mind. I want to watch you die slowly, the way your whining deputy did for Clamp!"

The knife scratched Bradley's neck as the outlaw turned and yelled to the fisherman. "Tie his legs and help me lift him!" Sean took a length of rope and twisted it around his ankles. Then stowing the knife in his belt, Red swiftly moved behind the lawman's head and grabbed his arms. Gripping them tightly by the wrists, he wrenched them back brutally. Then he nodded to the fisherman and together they lifted Bradley's writhing body towards the water.

"You've had things your own way for too long," the outlaw sneered. "Now it's my turn. And I've decided it's time for you to go for a swim!"

It was easy for them then, Bradley being no heavyweight. He felt helpless, his head tipped down as they carried him effortlessly through the shallows. A little further out, they slowly lowered him under the surface and into the icy cold river.

Though the water covered his eyes it was clear enough for him to make out the still sneering face of his adversary, looking down upon him with a gloating grimace of victory. His gaze remained fixed on that face as Red moved round and knelt on his chest, forcing him further under, while drawing the knife from his belt. Instinctively Bradley fought to hold his breath, until his lungs, chest and neck muscles caused him great pain and discomfort. He was vaguely aware that his left arm was now free, but it felt limp and weak. He concentrated his will to force it to reach out and grip the outlaw's wrist. He recognised the violent pounding in his head as the amplified beating of his heart and wondered if the end would be less painful if he just gave in and stopped resisting. His mind turned again to those close to him — his beloved Sylvia and his family back home. How vain had been his recent thoughts of them and of his heroic homecoming. If only he'd brought this fiend to justice when he'd had the chance! What a fool he'd been! And in trusting the fisherman, to whom the outlaw must have offered a better bargain! But now his thoughts were less defined and his mind drifted aimlessly, while his free arm still thrashed about. The pounding grew softer now and seemed to come from far, far away. He still saw — or so he fancied — the villain's face as it scowled down on him through the rippling river waters. But they weren't as clear as they'd been before. There was a tinge of colour — but he felt so weak now that he couldn't determine the hue. Was it green? No. Or blue? No, it wasn't blue. It was a colour to mock him cruelly in his final moments of life. It was the colour of his archenemy. It was red. It was as though the entire river were turning a deep, dark crimson, to remind him of the man responsible for his death here today. And that face — that scarred, ugly, vindictive, scowling, pockmarked face approached ever closer and closer. Was this to be the final vision to accompany him down through the last culvert to eternity? Yes, still it came closer and closer — surrounded by the red, swirling river.

As consciousness receded, the raider's face touched his own. And then it skimmed his cheek, to sink beneath him, and he had the sensation of being lifted and dragged into the air that now assailed his retching lungs with a thousand times more pain than that of drowning. Next thing he knew he lay on the shore, the fisherman leaning over him, calling his name and pumping his chest in a desperate attempt to make him breathe. He retched violently, spewing forth the foul waters of the river onto the bank beside him. Slowly, slowly, his senses returned, until at last he recognised a familiar taste pass across his tongue.

It was the taste of human blood.

* * * * *

"I'm sorry, Marshal. I didn't dare try to stop him with his knife at your throat."

It was mid-day and Bradley was recovering with something to eat and drink. As Shah checked their gear, Sylvia dutifully tended to her man, while Toby and his father sat across from them.

"No, don't apologise, Sean. But how did you manage to kill him?"

The fisherman looked startled. "I didn't kill him, Marshal. You did. I was ready to stick him from behind, but you managed to turn his own knife towards him while he leaned across you. Are you telling me you really didn't know that?"

Bradley shook his head. "No. I had no idea what I was doing. I thought I was done for. I must have acted instinctively."

After a pause he added, "You know, I felt bad about making that bargain with the outlaw. I had two duties, you see, and I had to choose between them. It pained me to make that decision, especially as I'd counted you as a friend."

The fisherman leaned across and placed a hand on his arm, "You may still count me as such, Dominic, even though I appeared to side with that swine. But I just couldn't face the prospect of his getting away with a share of the treasure and I knew you would never go against your word. Nor did I ever give you full credit for rescuing my son. I shouldn't have asked more than that of you.

"And Marshal, this matter of shares in the treasure — whatever it is — doesn't make a lot of sense. Now that Red's dead, as far as I'm concerned, on behalf of my village I'm happy to go along with whatever the Council wants to do. After all, they know more about such matters than me, a simple fisherman."

Bradley smiled as Sean continued, "But it occurs to me that — for the moment at least — there's only one viable route in and out of this new world."

"Through the culvert."

"Yes. And once you've made your report to the Council, I suspect that many people, with their families and goods, are going to be seeking a passage. Treasure or no treasure, there's new land to be settled and game to be had. It's clear that my simple raft isn't going to be able to cope with all that traffic. So I'm asking you to suggest to the Council that we at Nearbank be appointed the official ferrymen. My neighbours and I will design and build a dedicated craft, fit for the purpose and safely carry through all who wish to go. And perhaps even a new ferry port on the south bank, close to the Wall."

Later, cradled in Sylvia's arms on the grassy bank under the protection of the mighty Wall, Dominic turned his face towards hers and tried unsuccessfully to stifle a laugh.

She scowled. "What's so funny?"

"Nothing. I was just recalling how you looked the first time we met. You remember, that night in the forest near Crowtree, when you took me prisoner?"

"Prisoner!" she laughed. "How stupid I felt when Father chided us for not knowing you were a marshal!"

"Hmm. Well, in all fairness, you weren't to know what I was. In any event, I'm your prisoner now."

Moved by his words, she lowered her face to his and tenderly kissed his lips. Then she looked towards the dense, lowering forest that stretched far away to the west along the bank. On this uninhabited side of the Wall, eight centuries of unhindered growth had created what appeared to be an impenetrable jungle. His own eyes followed her gaze until his attention, too, was drawn into the deep, mysterious blackness. Silent now and motionless, his mind awhirl with a thousand unspoken questions, he looked on in awe and wondered about all the marvels that awaited discovery within that darkness.

What was it that Cara had promised them — the best of the Ancient Ones' science and knowledge? What had she meant by that? And where would they find it? Concealed by eight centuries of vegetation, a storehouse of wonders just waiting for them to take whatever they wanted? Well, tomorrow would provide answers to these and many more questions besides. For now, at least, all was as it should be. They were contented and ready to face the challenges of another day.

ABOUT THE AUTHOR

Chemical worker, accountant, folk singer and songwriter — Dave Evardson has been all of these. He has always enjoyed writing and, now retired, he is resolved to become a successful author. *The Fenwold Riddle* is his first published novel and he is already working on an exciting sequel.

Dave lives with his wife, Julie, in the county of Lincolnshire on the east coast of Britain. They enjoy singing, dancing, walking, travelling, their dogs — and staying young!

For more about *The Fenwold Riddle*, please visit www.DaveEvardson.com.

**For the Finest in
Nautical and Historical
Fiction and Nonfiction**

WWW.FIRESHIPPRESS.COM

Interesting • Informative • Authoritative

The Astreya Trilogy
by Seymour Hamilton

A tale of the sea, a mystery, and a love story from another time, and a different coast, where true-to-life adventures challenge believable characters.

"...a trilogy that will fascinate all those who have the sea in their blood and yearn for those days of sail. This is a sailor's yarn brilliantly told... I could not put this book down."
-- Commander David Newing, LVO, Royal Navy retired

Book I: The Voyage South
Book II: The Men of the Sea
Book III: The Wanderer's Curse

For more about Astreya's world, visit
AstreyaTrilogy.com

Available at:
Amazon.com and through leading bookstores and ebook sellers internationally. For the finest in nautical and historical fiction and non-fiction, visit:

www.Fireshippress.com

Lightning Source UK Ltd.
Milton Keynes UK
UKOW041448250712

196551UK00001B/107/P